Lifebringer

Mary Walz

RCN Media

This book is dedicated to my sort-of-publisher, Colton Nelson, because he wouldn't stop pestering me about dedicating a book to him. He was joking, of course. But it's too late now.

Also by Mary Walz

FIREBRAND SERIES
Firebrand
Stormbrewer

Author's Note

I have not felt the need in my past books to include a content warning, despite the usual fantasy violence that the stories contain. In Lifebringer, however, the issue of suicide comes up multiple times. While this is always within the context of sacrificing one's life to save another (rather than a result of mental health struggles), I am aware that this may be a sensitive topic for some readers. As such, discretion is advised.

Prologue

Three and a half years after the end of Stormbrewer

ALVIN BLACKWELL HADN'T seen the sun in more than a thousand days.

Exactly one-thousand-ninety-five days ago, they'd hauled him out of his hole in the belly of the guard station. He'd been tried before a judge, handed a life sentence, and dumped in a new cell deep within the Dundere prison, this one so tiny he could touch both ends of it when he lay down at night. For the three years that followed, he'd been served little food other than hard bread and tasteless gruel with the occasional wilted vegetable mixed in. His once-healthy frame withered from malnutrition; his beard—still patchy in some places—had grown in. At the trial, they told him that had he been a year older, his sentence would have been death.

Almost daily, Alvin wondered if he would have preferred that.

But he'd survived. He kept his head down, refrained from snapping at the guards, and never once complained about his situation. And today—*finally*—that would pay off. Today he would be moved from his tiny cell in solitary confinement to join the larger prison population, all because of his good behaviour. Alvin still wasn't sure how the others would react to him. On one hand, he was basically still a kid. On the other, he was responsible for the death of someone that a good number of them despised.

His hands and feet in heavy metal chains, he shuffled down the prison corridor after the guard. Out of the solitary wing and down another hall. The guard pointed important things out to him as they passed. The dining hall, where he'd now get to eat with the other prisoners. Warden's office. Kitchen.

Sunlight washed over his face as the guard led him outside, through a courtyard meant for exercise. He stopped short, almost surprised by the crisp scent of fresh air, the warmth of sun on his skin, and the crunch of grass underfoot. He'd nearly forgotten how the outdoors felt. The breeze was chilly—it was only a few weeks until Long Night's Eve—but it was welcome nonetheless. He squinted, and tears filled his eyes; he wasn't sure if they were from the pain of the brightness or the flood of emotions that accompanied these sensations.

A group of a dozen prisoners were engaged in a game of kickball, and they paused to stare at him. Alvin stared back.

Some wore looks of curiosity; one or two of the bigger fellows sneered at him, seeing him as nothing other than a scrawny kid, someone new to beat up.

But most of them wore looks of awe, or even fear.

Oh, yes. They knew *exactly* who he was.

"You get one hour a day here in the yard," the guard was saying as they neared the door on the other side. "Use it well."

Then they were back in the prison building, walking through a new cell block, this one much nicer than the one he'd been confined to. The cells here were larger, roomier, and each one had a proper window, two proper beds, and a writing desk. Prisoners stared as he passed. He heard whispers. Someone let out a wolf whistle.

Finally, the guard opened the door to what would be Alvin's new home. "Charles," he said to the man already inside, "this is Alvin."

The guard uncuffed him, shoved him inside, and closed the door with a clang. Alvin was left staring at his new companion.

Charles was likely a few years older than him and was everything he'd once been. Well groomed, clean shaven, clearly from the upper crust of society. And *handsome.* Alvin didn't fancy men, but even he couldn't help but notice.

Charles looked him over with a scrutinizing eye. "Straight out of solitary, I assume?"

"What gave it away?" Alvin rubbed at his patchy beard and eyed the other fellow. "Straight off the streets, I assume?"

"Second day in here." Charles wrinkled his nose, approaching Alvin. "You know, I didn't think the infamous killer of our dear former governor would be so...*skinny.*" He poked at Alvin's ribs.

Alvin snorted and swatted the other man's hand away. "Three years of prison food will do that to you. Don't worry, you won't be pretty for long."

Charles' eyes narrowed, but whatever response he might have been formulating was cut off by a guard approaching their cell, two figures in tow. "Blackwell. Your sister's here to visit."

Alvin smiled as Ashlynn walked up to the bars. His sister's regular visits—also granted thanks to his good behaviour—had been the one bright spot in the last three years. Ashlynn was the only family member who still acknowledged him, the only one who'd bothered to listen to his side of the story. The only one who'd believed him when he said that he'd expected the governor to survive the gunshot, being the healer that she was. He'd wanted to make Noelle hurt, yes. But not die.

And Ashlynn was definitely the only one who understood what he meant when he said that he *wasn't fully himself that day.*

She'd seen it happen to Aidan. And she'd warned Alvin against it too, told him not to get the earring, not to follow his brother down the same dark path he was already far too committed to.

At first, Alvin listened. But then, that one night after Ruby rejected him *again,* and Kaden informed him that she'd told everyone about his abilities, he'd been far, far too angry to care. He let Aidan pierce his ear with the Fae-gold earring and surrendered at least a part of himself to the dark.

Despite everything that followed, though, Ashlynn still cared enough to come visit when she was able. Even when she was extremely pregnant, then, soon after that, carrying an infant with her, she'd returned, a reminder that there was some good left in the world.

The child—Tristan—was two now, and he was full of energy, bright eyed and rosy cheeked, always happy to see his uncle. Today, however, he was shy, drawing back against his mother's leg as he observed Alvin's new cellmate.

"Nice place you have," Ashlynn greeted cheerfully.

Alvin raised an eyebrow and nodded. "It's practically a palace next to the old place. Look, I actually have a window!"

"I see that." Her eyes flickered to Charles. "Who's this?"

Alvin made introductions. "Cute kid you have," Charles murmured as his gaze travelled down to Tristan.

Ashlynn smiled. "Thanks, I made him myself."

"With no help whatsoever?" Charles raised an eyebrow. "That's quite the accomplishment."

She snorted. "All right, I had *some* help, but not much."

"His father isn't around anymore?"

"That's an understatement," Alvin muttered.

Ashlynn heard him and fixed him with a glare. "It's better this way." Her voice was firm and carried a clear warning not to say anything more to his cellmate. Better that Charles believe Tristan's father had simply abandoned the family.

"You're raising him alone, then?" Charles asked Ashlynn.

"We live with my parents, but once he's old enough for school, I plan to move out and get us an apartment of our own."

"How's the new job going, anyway?" Alvin asked her.

Ashlynn began filling him in on her life outside the prison, and Charles took that as his cue to return to a book he'd been reading. Alvin couldn't help but smile as Ashlynn rambled; his sister had changed for the better in the past three years. Motherhood suited her, as did her new job, it seemed. And, as much as Alvin hated to admit it, she'd been *considerably* more relaxed since Aidan died.

They didn't talk about Aidan anymore, or their parents. Ashlynn did tell him about the biweekly visits their eldest brother Arquinn had been making—always in secret, away from their family home. Alvin was glad for Tristan's sake but rather wished Arquinn would pay *him* a visit. Then again, Arquinn had been all but absent from Alvin's life since Alvin was eight. He'd run away as soon as he reached adulthood, just like Alvin had always planned to do.

When a tug on the fabric of his pants interrupted their conversation, Alvin looked down to see Tristan staring up at him. "For you, Uncle Alvin," he said, presenting a bundle.

Alvin grinned and crouched down to take the gift from his nephew—likely homemade scones, knowing Ashlynn. "Thank you, buddy," he said, reaching through the bars and giving Tristan's curls an affectionate tousle.

Tristan grabbed his hand, and Alvin let out a yelp as a strange shock travelled through him, followed by a loud ringing in one ear. Tristan giggled. Ashlynn looked down in concern. "Are you all right, Alvin?"

"I...think so." Alvin got to his feet. "The kid...shocked me somehow. Perhaps we have a future stormbrewer on our hands?"

She shook her head. "There's too much anti-magic in here for that. Must have just been static."

Right. Alvin was so accustomed to the heaviness of the anti-magic that encased the entire prison—thanks to the aro stone inlaid into the walls—that he didn't notice it anymore.

Ashlynn's eyes narrowed. "Are you sure you're alright, Alvin? Your eyes are…" She shook her head. "Never mind. It's likely my imagination." She reached through the bars and squeezed Alvin's hand. "Enjoy your fancy new cell. I'll see you next week."

As the two of them retreated, Charles let out a low whistle. "Your sister is stunning. And your nephew, well, he's going to grow up to be a handsome kid."

There was something in Charles' eyes, a certain glint and a twist to his voice when he spoke of Tristan, that made Alvin recoil. Suddenly, he had to wonder about the nature of his cellmate's crimes and was grateful that his beard hid what he knew was a still fairly boyish face. "Don't you talk about my family that way," he growled.

"You know, I'm meant to be out of here in five years," Charles went on. "Perhaps at that point I'll marry your sister, then both she and the boy will be mine." He grinned wolfishly at Alvin.

It was then that Alvin decided he wanted to kill his cellmate.

***

It was only much later, once Charles was asleep, that Alvin realized what had happened when Tristan touched him.

Hello there, Alvin, said an all-too-familiar voice in his head, *it's been a while.*

Alvin stiffened, and his hand instinctively flew up to his earring. "What are *you* doing in here?"

Hitched a ride with the kid, the voice replied. *You know the rules. Anyone in the bloodline can take me, so long as they're willing. Look in the little box he gave you.*

Alvin didn't move. Instead, his eyes narrowed. "You were *talking* to Tristan?"

Oh, little Tristan's learning my language fast. He's a smart boy. Curious, too. No surprise he stumbled upon me when his mother was looking the other way.

"And how do you intend to get back home within the required seven days?" Alvin hissed. "You're not the only prisoner here; I can't exactly return you to my father."

But you can. And that's what I want to talk about. The voice took on a devious tone. *How would you like to make a deal with me?*

"Forget it," Alvin snapped. "Last time that happened, we killed a governor, and I ended up in here."

I can get you out, though. And once I do, we can run away. Isn't that what you've always wanted, Alvin? To see the world? To have your freedom?

Alvin closed his eyes. *Of course that's what he wanted.* "What's in it for you?" he demanded.

That's simple. Before we run off, you help me exact revenge on a few folks. Some of them are people I'm sure you have grudges against. Once that's all finished, you grant me full freedom from your family name, we part ways, and you can do whatever your heart pleases.

Alvin frowned. "I'm assuming one of those people is my father. Because you're not going anywhere with me so long as he's alive. You know the rules."

Think about it, Alvin. The man beat you and humiliated you for decades. Wouldn't you like to show him who's in charge now?

Alvin tilted his head, and that slow, inky darkness that had once nearly consumed him began to swirl about in his gut. He knew very well where the feelings came from; nonetheless, he found himself nodding. He *did* rather like the idea of killing his father, he realized. "All right. So we kill Father. Then what?"

Then we head to Breoch and go after the murderous bastard who—

"Of course," Alvin interrupted. "I shouldn't have asked."

Before we kill him, though, we make him suffer.

"Which involves hurting a few more people on my own list," Alvin concluded.

You know me well, boy.

Alvin's eyebrows knitted. "Are you sure he's in Breoch?"

I'm fairly certain. And I have an idea as to how we might find him, too.

Alvin listened as the voice explained the plan. "So you want me to charm my way into King Kairus' court?"

You likely won't have to, thanks to some misfortune that's befallen the crown prince, Oliver. Interestingly enough, Oliver's betrothed, a little lady named Isabelle, is tied to some of the folks we're going after.

Alvin sighed. "All right. So once these three things are done, we part ways?"

That's right. But before any of that, we must do one thing. What do you think of that new cellmate of yours?

Alvin's stomach tightened. "He's a pervert."

A very handsome pervert, though, don't you think?

"I suppose so."

Excellent. Let's get started, then.

Chapter 1

Five Months Later

BANISHING DAY WAS a terrible holiday, but it was an excuse to visit my friends back in Sylvenburgh, as I'd done every year since the move to Kirstein.

Most of my former classmates at Sylvenburgh Academy weren't close to me anymore; they'd moved on with their lives and made new friends. They were always happy to see me when I visited but didn't seem particularly sad when I left. Silva was different. She'd been my best friend for most of my life, and a few hours' travel wasn't about to change that.

"This might be the last year I can come visit over Banishing Day," I told her that evening while we sat in her dorm. The day had been filled with games, feasting and dancing, but curfew was in effect now. Silva's roommate went home for Banishing Day most years, so I'd taken over her bunk, and Charlotte, Silva's other best friend who was quickly becoming a good friend of mine, perched on the bed next to me.

Silva cocked her head. "Really, Isabelle? You can't make it for one more year? Next year I'll be graduating."

"I know. But I'm wanted at the palace for official activities." I rolled my eyes. "Mainly just standing around holding Oliver's hand while the king drones on about the merits of the Banishing."

"Oh, the chore of being engaged to royalty!" Silva exclaimed with a smirk. "Your life sounds *so* hard!"

"I wish *my* mother had a dream about me being a queen when I was born," put in Charlotte.

"First of all, we're not *officially* engaged yet," I corrected Silva. "And second, I'm sure it wasn't *just* my mother's dreams that made Oliver's parents agree to our betrothal. My father and Kairus happen to be childhood friends."

"Still, the dreams make it seem like you two are *destined* to be together," Charlotte gushed, flopping back on the bed.

"That's what they say," I mumbled, trying not to roll my eyes at Charlotte's dramatics. "Destined."

Silva caught my tone. "How is that, anyway? Is it odd thinking about being married to a friend?"

"I mean, I've had a lot of years to think about it. I figure there are worse people to marry than Oliver."

"I'd say so. He's bloody handsome. I mean, he's a little odd, yes, but still nice to look at." Charlotte smirked.

"I *like* his oddities," I protested, crossing my arms.

"You're not worried he's going to abandon you for his collection of rocks and jewels and shiny things?" Charlotte let out a huff. "Lucky for him he's a prince who can afford to collect all that."

I couldn't help smiling. "It's...endearing. He gets so excited about the oddest things. His latest obsession is wanting to visit a circus. He's never been to one; we've had them in Kirstein, but his stepmom didn't think it was good form for a prince to attend."

Silva snorted. "That's silly."

I nodded, then let out a sigh.

"What's wrong?" Silva asked.

I gazed at my best friend for a moment, chewing on my lip. "I'm a little worried about him as of late," I confessed, lowering my voice. "Don't repeat this, but Oliver's been...unsteady on his feet lately. Tripping over things, being a little clumsy. He's never had these issues before."

Her eyes widened. "You think he's got the same illness his mother had?"

"That's what I'm scared of. He hasn't said anything about it to me, but I see the signs and..." I sighed. "I'm not sure what to do."

"What sort of illness *did* his mother have?" Charlotte probed. "I remember hearing that Princess Inari was ill, and I remember when she died, of course—we had a ceremony for her here in Sylvenburgh for those who couldn't make it to Kirstein for the funeral. But I never fully understood what was wrong with her."

"None of us did," I admitted. "My first memories of Inari are of her stumbling and occasionally dropping things. I thought she was just clumsy. But it got worse as I got older. She couldn't walk by the time I was eight; she could barely talk, and sometimes she'd drool. I was rather scared of her." I tried to ignore the pang of guilt in my chest at my admission. "Then she started having trouble breathing, and two years later, she was gone." I sighed when I recalled the months that followed: walking in the funeral procession next to Oliver as he tried to hold in his tears; Kairus' withdrawal from public life that lasted nearly a year; Oliver's obsession with creating a jewelled bust of his mother—something that he still worked on to this day.

Silva eyed me. "I think it's obvious what you need to do, Isabelle. If you're right about this, then he may be dying, and you're one of the only people who can help him."

My heart began to beat faster. Silva and Charlotte were the only two people who knew of my abilities. "You think I should *heal* the crown prince? Can you imagine the trouble I'd get into?"

Silva shrugged. "You said you've secretly alleviated pain for your grandma before."

"Alleviating pain is one thing. Healing a sickness I don't understand is another. I don't even know if I *can* do that."

"I know some folks who could likely help answer that." Silva and Charlotte exchanged a glance. "Want to join us for an extracurricular activity tomorrow?"

"What will we be doing?"

"It's a foraging lesson, focused on the plants near the edges of the Shrouded Woods," Charlotte told me.

I frowned. "And how is this meant to help me with Oliver?"

Silva leaned forward, dark eyes wide. "It's a foraging lesson," she whispered, "but it's also a magic class."

My mouth fell open. "How do we have a *magic class* at Sylvenburgh Academy?"

"We don't. We have a foraging class." She winked.

"Is it safe?" I asked. "Who runs it?"

"It's safe enough. And on paper, Mr. Jeffries' brother runs it. But he just takes the group into the Shrouded Woods. The real teachers are Woods-folk who know the plant life."

"So Mr. Jeffries knows about this class?"

Charlotte smirked. "Mr. Jeffries organized this class."

"Wait, is *he* a magic user?"

"No idea. I know he's sympathetic. If he finds out you're using magic, he basically requires you to join this class."

"I've heard that he used to help magic users escape to the Isle of Dundere, but that's not safe anymore," Silva added.

"What's unsafe about Dundere, other than those fires that have been happening?"

Silva shrugged. "Something about the attack that killed their old governor, and a bunch of people getting deported. I don't know all the details, but I know they aren't quite as welcoming of magic refugees as they once were."

"I've heard rumour that *Saray* was involved in that," Charlotte put in, "and it helped make her known as the Unbeatable One."

I rolled my eyes, and Silva threw a glance at Charlotte, who frowned. "What's your issue with Saray and Trina, anyway?" Charlotte asked.

I shrugged. "I'm sure they're perfectly fine young women. I remember Trina, and she seemed like a lovely girl. But when they ran off from the school all those years back, that was when my mother started crying all the time, and things began to fall apart between my parents. They haven't been the same since."

Charlotte frowned. "Odd that some kids fleeing a school would wreck a marriage."

"I know." I shook my head. "I still don't understand what happened. But it bothers me when people act like Saray and Trina are these legendary heroes, when all I associate them with is my family falling apart."

Silva nodded; she'd heard this story many times from me. "Back to the botany class...now that Lachlann—Mr. Jeffries' brother—can't help magic users escape to Dundere, he makes sure they're well-trained enough to be able to hide their magic."

"What have you learned?" I asked her.

"Other than the medicinal uses of yarel blooms, sagie berries, and tarsina ferns?" She shrugged. "Mainly, I've learned how to control my gift better. I'll show you tomorrow—if you come with me, of course."

"And I'll show you what I'm learning too," put in Charlotte.

I frowned and looked from Silva to Charlotte. "You two are the only people who know about my abilities. Are you sure everyone involved is a magic user themselves?"

"Well, Lachlann isn't a magic user, but his wife is. She's one of the teachers, so he's obviously not opposed to it. And the only students who are invited are ones who have magic. You'll be safe with these people."

I sighed. "If it's going to help Oliver, then I suppose it would be a good idea."

"Excellent!" Silva grinned and clapped her hands together. "Speaking of your gift, I twisted my ankle earlier during the games. Would you mind?"

"Sure." I hopped off my bed and walked over to examine Silva's ankle. I only saw a bit of swelling; nevertheless, I put my hands over her injury, closed my eyes, and began to softly sing a song whose words I knew but did not understand. As always, I felt my palms grow hot as energy surged out of them and into my friend, and I sensed the tissues of her ankle righting themselves. Silva let out a sigh of relief, and I took a deep breath as I pulled back; healing others always left me a bit winded.

"Thank you." Silva smiled and rubbed her ankle. "I'm excited for you to come to our class."

"Me too," Charlotte said, stifling a yawn. "I should get to bed; I'll see you two in the morning."

She retreated to her own room then, and I crawled into bed. *I sure hope this is a good idea.* The class sounded exciting, but revealing my abilities to a bunch of strangers felt a bit rash. *Though if it helps Oliver, I suppose it's worth the risk.*

***

The day that followed was full of the typical post-Banishing Day activities. Students slept late, exhausted from the excitement of the day before. The morning was spent hanging around in the common area with Silva's friends. I only knew two of them from my younger years at the Academy, but I'd warmed up to the group over time, and they'd welcomed me in. All of them were just as chatty and dramatic as Silva, and their theatrics made me laugh. In my family, I was the loud one, but next to these folks I came across as quiet, cautious.

I suppose I shouldn't have been surprised when the entirety of Silva's friend group piled into Mr. Jeffries' office that afternoon following the bonfire, along with a handful of younger students. I eyed Silva. "Wait, your friends are all..."

"Why do you think we stick together?" She grinned.

When Mr. Jeffries came into the room, he frowned and looked me over. Then he glanced at Silva. "Do you really think that bringing a friend to this class is a wise choice?"

"Oh, I think Isabelle will be a natural at learning the many uses of plants in the Shrouded Woods," Silva told him with a quick smile.

"Is that so?" He raised an eyebrow. "How long have you been interested in botany, Isabelle?"

"Since I was about twelve," I replied, understanding his meaning. "Though there were signs of my interest even younger than that."

"Really? Well, I suppose a lesson or two won't hurt, even if you won't be able to learn everything." He glanced around the office. "Let's head out. My brother is likely waiting for us."

Just outside the school gates, a large, very odd-looking open carriage waited for us. The fellow steering it got out when he saw us approaching and looked me over. "I see we have a newcomer."

Silva nodded. "This is my friend Isabelle. She used to go to Sylvenburgh Academy, but she lives in Kirstein now. She'll fit right in with this group."

The driver exchanged a look with Mr. Jeffries, then turned to me and smiled. "Well, in that case, welcome to our class. I'm Mr. Jeffries' brother, Lachlann."

"We call him by his first name so we don't have to deal with two Mr. Jeffrieses," Charlotte informed me. "One is enough." Several of the younger students laughed.

I looked the two brothers over, noticing the similarities in their height and facial features. They shared the same deep-set brown eyes, and Lachlann's smile was nearly identical to his brother's.

There were some differences too; Lachlann's sandy brown hair was down to his shoulders, and he wore a full beard rather than a neatly waxed mustache. Where Mr. Jeffries was greying at the temples, the grey in Lachlann's hair showed up mainly in his beard and a few streaks that contrasted starkly with the rest of his hair. He looked more of an outdoorsman than Mr. Jeffries; his skin was darker, his arms more muscular—at least, what remained of his arms. I couldn't help but stare at the left metal forearm and hand that he wore; it appeared to be moving on its own. Lachlann caught me looking and waved it at me.

I blushed. "I'm sorry, I shouldn't be staring."

"Most people stare; I'm used to it." He laughed good-naturedly and turned to the rest of the students. "Are you all ready to go?"

He was met by eager nods and a chorus of whoops.

"I've never met a group more eager to go to class on a day off school," Lachlann remarked. "All right, you know the routine. Get in, kids."

I looked the carriage over, finally realizing what was so odd about it. "Where's your horse?"

Lachlann grinned. "We don't need a horse. This is one of the new steam-powered carriages from Candesh."

My eyes widened. "I didn't know we had these in Breoch. You must have a lot of money."

"No, I have a lot of connections," he replied. "Climb aboard, and I'll show you how it works."

***

The steam carriage took several minutes to start, and it made a lot of noise, but once it got going, it moved with astonishing ease. People stared and pointed as we made our way through the streets of Sylvenburgh, toward the city gates. A few folks drew back in terror, and I heard occasional murmurs about "witchery," but no guards came after us, and we cleared the gates without trouble. Once outside the city, we picked up speed. The other students chatted amongst themselves, clearly accustomed to the experience, but I stayed silent, clinging to the seat in front of me and gaping as I watched the world whiz by. When Sylvenburgh was no longer visible behind us, Lachlann reached down and flipped a switch.

The noise and steam immediately ceased, but the carriage continued to move forward, silent except for the sound of the wheels on the dirt road. Lachlann turned back and grinned at me. "Bet you weren't expecting that."

I stared at him. "How is it still running?"

"Do you want to take a guess?"

My eyes widened further when I realized the implication of what he was saying. "So does it not actually run on steam at all?"

"No, that's just to make it look like a typical steam car. My friend Marcus created this contraption. Runs on pure magic."

"Are you using your own magic to run it?"

"Me? No, I don't use magic. In fact, I'm trained in its opposite. The car itself contains magic. It's rather brilliant, I think. Gets us to the Woods in less than an hour, which is why I had Marcus make it. Otherwise, these lessons would take the better part of a day."

"It does travel a little faster than I'm used to," I admitted.

Lachlann laughed. "And we're only going to speed up now that we're away from the city." As if on cue, the vehicle picked up speed, and I gasped and clung to the seat in front of me. The car began to jolt as it hit bumps in the road, and a few of the other students let out whoops, clearly enjoying the speed. I watched the scenery fly by, my mouth agape, holding for dear life to the seat in front of mine.

We whizzed by several farms—one of which, Lachlann informed me, was where his mother and brother lived—then the houses became more sparse, replaced by wild meadows and the occasional small pond.

When we finally reached the edge of the forest, Lachlann parked his carriage under a tall willow tree. We piled out, and my heartbeat picked up as I followed Silva into the forest. *Here we go.*

Chapter 2

ENTERING THE SHROUDED Woods—a place rumoured to be populated by criminals, wild beasts, and misfits—was more than a little terrifying for me. I gawked up at the massive trees as we walked farther in and listened to the chatter of forest animals, my senses on edge for any sort of danger. The other students did not seem nearly as concerned, and Silva shot me an amused grin. "Relax, Isabelle. I wouldn't bring you here if it was dangerous."

After about half an hour of walking, we reached a small clearing edged on two sides by a babbling stream. Charlotte turned to me. "This is where Mr. Jeffries left Saray and Trina all those years ago. And where they met Lachlann's first wife."

"The story of the Unbeatable One begins here," said a younger student, her eyes wide. I tried not to scoff at her reverence.

"That's not quite right," Lachlann cut in. "First, my brother didn't take them this far into the Woods, though you're right that this is the glade he directed them to. And second, this is where he told them to stay in order to meet Kirilee, but that's not what happened. They encountered some bandits, were forced to go find food, and ran into a little hooligan and his dog—he's the one who brought them to Kirilee. Speaking of which, good to see you, Kip."

I hadn't noticed the fellow waiting for us in the glade, but I suspected that was the point. He looked to be in his mid-twenties and was dressed in dark brown breeches and a green and brown tunic with leaf patterns stitched into it. The fabric looked rough, but the pattern was precise and intricate. He carried a quiver and bow, and his long, sandy brown hair was pulled back. Another figure emerged next to him, seemingly from nowhere: a woman who looked close in age to Lachlann, with tawny skin and long, wavy black hair that she wore loose. I gaped at her attire; she was wearing a dress that appeared to be made not of fabric, but of moss and leaves and flowers, all still very much alive. The dress fell only to her knees, leaving her calves exposed.

I noticed what appeared to be odd burn marks on both her neck and one of her legs, and she was very obviously pregnant. Lachlann crossed the grove in a few long strides, pulled her into an embrace, and kissed her, leaving little doubt as to her baby's parentage. He'd left his cloak in the car, and it struck me suddenly that Lachlann's own clothes, while darker in colour, were of a similar cut and fabric as the young man's. I frowned. "They're Woods-folk."

Silva nodded, grinning.

"Wait, how is Mr. Jeffries' brother one of the Woods-folk?"

"I'm not sure exactly. I get the impression that he's comfortable in both the Shrouded Woods and the cities, but I know he lives in the Woods, with Starla." She gestured at the pregnant woman, then at the younger man. "And Kip lives somewhere nearby."

"Do they live in a village?"

"They don't talk about their home. I just know it's somewhere in the Shrouded Woods."

The younger man—Kip—was studying me. He eyed Silva. "You brought a friend, I see?"

She nodded. "This is Isabelle. She went to Sylvenburgh Academy with me when we were children. She belongs here." Silva raised her eyebrows as she spoke, no doubt conveying to Kip that I, too, had magic.

He stepped forward and smiled at me. "I'm Kip, one of the teachers of this class. Good to meet you, Isabelle." He began to extend a hand but stopped mid-gesture as an enormous red-tailed hawk plunged out of a nearby tree and landed upon a leather pad on his shoulder. I shrieked and jumped back.

Kip grinned at my reaction. "Don't mind Persius. He's fierce looking, but he won't hurt humans unless they..." He trailed off and inclined his head suddenly. "Is that so, ai?"

"Pardon me?"

Silva laughed. "Kip claims to be able to talk to his bird. Seems unlikely to me, but Starla can talk to plants, so I suppose it's possible."

"Talk to plants?"

"Yes, and command them to do her bidding, have them grow in odd places. Sometimes I wonder if she *is* part plant." She gestured to Starla. "See her clothes? It's all plants, and they're alive. Their roots have tangled themselves up in her hair, and somehow they can survive there. Also, she can turn into a tree if she wants."

I shook my head, trying to absorb all of this information, and studied Starla. Several of the younger students had clustered around her and were chattering excitedly. Meanwhile, a few of the older boys had made their way over to Kip and were asking him for an archery lesson. He walked away from us, pulled his bow off his back and strung it, still casting the occasional glance my way.

Persius flew into the trees above once more, and Lachlann headed back to us. "You've likely gathered that this class isn't only about the botany of the Woods," he said to me. "My wife would like to know what sorts of abilities you possess so she can weave them into the lesson."

I raised my eyebrows, and Silva nodded encouragingly at me. "I can heal," I said.

Lachlann's jaw dropped. "You're a *lifebringer?*"

"A what?"

"It's what we call healers here in the Woods."

"Well, then, I suppose that, yes, I am a lifebringer. I haven't done much of it, for obvious reasons. But I've healed myself many times, Silva and Charlotte a few times, and I've also eased my grandmother's stiff joints—though I've had to be stealthy about it."

Lachlann's eyes were still wide. "You possess an incredibly rare gift, do you know that? I'll go talk to Starla and see what she can—"

He was interrupted suddenly by several things happening at once. One of the younger students let out an excited shriek, and a burst of flame suddenly shot from his hand. It engulfed Starla's shoulder for a moment, the fire catching on the leaves that draped about her arm. Starla let out a yelp of her own and began frantically patting out the flame. Then Lachlann whirled around, his hand going to a pendant he wore as he did so. An odd feeling of sluggishness shot through me, and I recoiled. The fire went out, then the young student was crying, and Starla was examining the burned foliage and reddened skin on her shoulder.

"Looks like you and I will be working on control again today, Francis," Lachlann said. The younger student nodded, his expression defeated. Lachlann exchanged a few words with Starla and pointed at me, then pulled her into an embrace.

"I'll get the lesson started for the rest of you," Kip said, making his way toward the centre of the throng of students. "Today we'll be learning how to make a sleeping tea."

I watched as the students gathered around Kip, while Lachlann stepped aside with Francis in tow. Starla, meanwhile, made her way over to me. "You must be Isabelle." She gave me a smile, but it was obviously a bit forced.

I nodded. "And you're Starla, right?"

"That's right. I hear you can heal." She gestured at the burn on her shoulder.

I nodded and placed my hand so that it just hovered above the burn. I began to visualize new skin forming as I sang, and she let out a long, shuddering sigh of relief. "Thank you," she said.

I saw unexpected tears in her eyes, and I frowned. "Are you all right?"

"Yes, just a little shaken. I'm terribly afraid of fire; I was burned quite badly several years back." She took another long breath. Then she mumbled a few words, and I watched as the ivy reformed its leaves with ease. "What made you decide to come to this class?"

I hesitated for just a moment. "I have a friend who is ill," I explained. "I know how to heal small things, but nothing substantial. Silva thought you folks could teach me how to use my gift better."

Starla frowned. "I'm sure we could find a way, though it may not be easy. Healing is a rare gift. We don't actually have any lifebringers in the Woods right now, though I know a woman who used to be one and might be able to teach you." She gave me a tense smile. "We'd best go join the lesson."

Starla went to stand beside Kip, and I perched on a fallen log next to Silva. Kip was explaining the properties of the two main ingredients for the tea—yulma berries and dragonfoot mushrooms, both of which only grew within the Shrouded Woods. "These mushrooms are everywhere," he told us, gesturing to a patch on the ground. "Though you want to make sure you're not confusing them with faefoot mushrooms, which are just as common. The way to tell is to look at the gills after picking them." He reached down and pulled a large brown mushroom from the dirt, then showed us the underside of its cap. "See how the gills are brown, ai? These ones are safe. Faefoot mushrooms have pink gills."

"Will they kill you if you eat them?" one teen asked.

Kip exchanged a glance with Starla, who shook her head and said, "Kill you, no. Make you sick to your stomach for several hours, definitely. Also, they've been known to give folks some rather terrifying visions. Combined with the yulma berries, those visions would likely take the form of nightmares." She grinned. "As always, the first rule of Shrouded Woods botany is to not eat anything unless you know exactly what it does to a person."

"Now, you might've noticed that pulling up that mushroom took me a bit of effort," Kip continued. "Can anyone think of a better way?"

"Telekinesis?" asked a boy.

"That's right. Javen, do you want to give it a try?"

Javen got up and walked over to the cluster of mushrooms. He stared down at them for a moment, then mumbled a string of words. I watched as one of the mushrooms rose from the ground into his palm.

"Very good. Now, yulma berries aren't nearly as common as dragonfoot mushrooms, so Starla grew us a tree of them just last week." He turned and gestured to a massive trunk that shot into the sky behind him, and we all gazed upward. The lowest branches were a good twenty feet in the air. "If you're a skilled climber, you can scale one of these trees, but there are easier ways to reach the berries. What do you s'pose they are?"

"Well, I'd think you'd want to find someone who can fly, but I don't know anyone with that gift," Silva said.

"That's one option. Another is teleportation." Kip turned to one of the younger girls. "Becksa? Do you want to try?"

Becksa stared up at the tree, eyes wide. "I've...never teleported that high up before. What if I miss?"

"My telekinesis is strong enough that if you fall, I should be able to catch you," Kip assured. "Once you get really good at teleporting, you can teleport straight to the ground before you hit it. But that's not a lesson for today."

She hesitated again. "Do you know how to teleport? You could go with me."

Kip raised an eyebrow. "Y'know, I've been learning. I'll go with you to the first branch at least. But you need to teleport yourself; I'm not moving you."

She nodded. "On three?"

"Sure." Kip counted down, and together they spoke the teleport spell. I watched as they vanished, reappearing on a high branch less than a second later. Becksa laughed, then floundered for a moment. Kip caught her arm and directed her to the next branch.

"This is brilliant," I whispered to Silva. "It *is* a class on Shrouded Woods botany, but it's also so much more than that."

Kip and Becksa were back soon, holding branches laden with large purple berries. Starla took over, explaining the drying process and calling on a student to change the weather so that sunlight shone into the grove, which would aid the drying. She then produced already-dried samples of both the mushrooms and the berries and had Silva come forward to create water for brewing the tea. I watched as my friend drew water from the atmosphere—at least, that's how she explained it—and used it to fill a small metal tankard. Starla dropped the ingredients for the tea into it, then called over to Lachlann. "Is Francis doing well enough with control to create our fire for heating the tea?"

Lachlann nodded. "I think so. If not, Kip can always step in."

"Kip can make fire and teleport *and* use telekinesis?" I whispered to Silva.

Kip overheard my comment and smiled. "I'm only just learning to teleport, and I've only been able to control fire since I got married. I got the talent from my wife."

"How does that work?"

"It's complicated," he said as Francis approached. Kip turned to him. "Speaking of my wife, she was just like you once. Powerful, gifted with fire, and unable to control it. She burned me fairly badly one time, y'know. But now she's one of the best firebrands out there."

"You should bring her to one of our lessons," Becksa said.

Kip shook his head. "It wouldn't be safe for her to attend." He took the metal tankard from Starla, who backed away as Francis produced a small, steady flame. Lachlann stood nearby, ready to intervene if Francis lost control.

"Now, perhaps you're wondering how I can hold on to this tankard while Francis heats it up and not burn myself," Kip said to us. "What I'm doing is using a cooling spell on a very small portion of the handle so the part I'm holding doesn't heat up. Another way to boil the water would be to use a heat spell, but there's little point in me teaching you those, as you can't learn them 'til you're eighteen." He eyed me. "We don't allow folks to learn spells other than their innate talent 'til they're adults."

Francis allowed his fire to grow ever so slightly, and soon the water was boiling. "Perfect," Kip said as he added the ingredients. "Now we let it steep for about ten minutes, then you can drink it. Makes it much easier to go to sleep."

"That concludes our lesson for today," Starla said. "Though we still have about twenty minutes until you folks need to head back to the school, so if anyone wants to work on something, now is your time."

I watched as students began to practice their own gifts. Francis went back to working on fire control with Lachlann. Becksa and one of the younger boys began playing tag; it became clear very quickly that he had the ability to make himself invisible.

Silva grinned at me. "Let me show you what Starla can do."

We joined Starla, and Silva asked her something in a hushed tone. Starla grinned and nodded, then leaned back against a nearby tree. I watched with wide eyes as her skin turned to bark, and she slowly seemed to disappear into the trunk. "That's incredible," I whispered.

"After Lachlann's first wife died, her soul lived on in a tree," Silva told me. "When he discovered this, he was able to speak to her, and she told him that he couldn't just stay married to a tree, he needed to move on. But he says that half the time he wonders if he's just married to a different tree now."

"Perhaps he has a type," I mused.

Silva laughed and scanned the grove. Then she pointed. "Over there!"

I followed her gaze, and my eyes widened as Starla began to materialize from a different tree, right next to where Lachlann was teaching. Still half encased in the bark, she reached out and grabbed him from behind, causing him to yelp before he realized what was happening. Francis and the other students dissolved into laughter. "She can...teleport between trees?"

"Something like that."

Silva began working on her waterweaving abilities, causing a quivering globe of liquid to appear in her hand. She moved it about, dispersing it into fine drops, then returned it to its previous form. "Watch this," she said.

She closed her eyes then, concentrating, and I watched as fine crystals began to form on her ball of water. They took it over, rendering it cool and opaque, and a minute or so later I was staring at a perfectly formed snowball. "Amazing," I breathed.

She opened her eyes and nodded, then a wicked grin spread across her face. She whirled around and lobbed the snowball at Kip.

Kip nearly jumped out of his skin when it hit him. He stared down at his clothes for a moment, then at the now-melting snowball on the ground. His eyes met Silva's. "You...did it."

"I've been practicing," she replied smugly and turned to me. "Kip was the one who told me I could learn to create snow."

"That'll be a handy talent during the summer. Perhaps you can—"

Kip was interrupted by Lachlann clearing his throat. "All right, folks, wrap it up. Time to head back to school."

"We'll have a snowball fight another day," Silva said to Kip.

He grinned. "You're on."

***

The group was in high spirits as we headed back out of the Woods. Some of the younger students were singing a song that sounded to be a parody of a Banishing Day melody, and Silva chattered merrily away to me about the process of making a snowball. I grinned, realizing suddenly why they were all so happy. *This is the only place where they can be themselves.* I supposed it was true of me, as well.

We made our way out into the meadow and skirted the edge of the Woods. When we reached the grove where the carriage was parked, Lachlann stopped short.

Four men stood between us and our vehicle. Two were wearing the deep red uniforms of the palace guardsmen. The other two were Breoch Guard.

Chapter 3

IN THE SECONDS that followed, several things happened. The chatter immediately died down. Francis let out a yelp as fire sprang unbidden from his hands. And Lachlann whirled around, his own hand flying to grip his pendant.

The fire went out, but not before everyone had seen it. Francis cowered, eyes wide.

The two Breoch Guards eyed the firebrand, but neither moved to apprehend him. Instead, they turned to Lachlann. "Are you Lachlann Jeffries?" one demanded.

"Yes, I am. What do you want with me?"

"We've heard you're running some sort of covert magic school for these kids." He jerked his head toward Francis. "Seems like those rumours are true."

Lachlann's eyes narrowed. "This is a class on the botany of the Shrouded Woods, sir. Today the children learned how to make a sleeping tea. One child in my care using magic in a moment of fear is hardly evidence of an entire underground school."

The guard sneered. "So you admit that the boy used magic, hmm? Seemed like that fire of his went out mighty fast. Tell me, did you have anything to do with that? Used some magic of your own, did you?"

Lachlann snorted. "I can assure you, sir, that I do not have a magical bone in my body."

"But you have anti-magic." The guard pointed at Lachlann's pendant. "We've been asked to bring you to the palace because of *that*. You're under arrest, my good man. And after that boy's little outburst, we have to assume that all these kids have magic, too. We'll be taking all of you."

There was a wave of gasps and cries of protest. Becksa began to sob, and Francis tried to hide behind one of the taller boys. Silva reached for my hand, and I gripped it tightly in return. I felt my stomach churn—I wasn't sure if it was from fear or anger. *How dare they treat us like this?*

"Absolutely not." Lachlann glared at the guards. "Take me if you must, but the children go back to school." His hand went to the pommel of his blade as he spoke.

"Oh, look, he has a sword!" The Guard sneered and pulled a small pistol from his hip. "A bit useless against one of these, don't you think?"

"You won't shoot me. You just said I'm wanted for my anti-magic."

"You're right. The children, though, I have no issue with shooting. Now get in line, or I'll—"

"Enough." I found myself stepping forward, propelled by my indignation.

The younger Guard snickered. "And who are you, little miss?"

"Ask *them*." I pointed to the two palace guards who stood just beyond.

One of the guards' eyes widened. "Lady Isabelle?"

The younger Breoch Guard frowned. *"Lady?"*

I gave him a well-practiced look of disdain. "My name is Isabelle Charmaine Lillian McAllister, and I am the betrothed of Oliver, crown prince of Breoch. And as your future queen, I demand that you let us return to the school without further interruption."

Several moments of silence passed as everyone present gawked at me. Finally, the younger Breoch Guard turned to the palace guards. "Is she telling the truth?"

"I'm afraid so, sir."

"Can she...do this?"

The palace guard frowned. "Well, our order to seize Lachlann comes from the king himself, so she can do nothing about that."

I frowned. *What does Kairus want with Lachlann?*

"As for the children, take them into custody, but don't harm them until we can speak to authorities about the matter." The palace guard turned to me. "You'd best come with us, my lady. I'm certain your parents wouldn't approve of you keeping this company."

Lachlann eyed me for a long moment, then turned to the palace guard. "Will you inform the school about their students' detainment?"

"Absolutely."

He let out a sigh of resignation and raised his hands. "You'd best go with them, kids. My brother will make sure no harm comes to you."

The students huddled together, whispering. Lachlann had lifted his anti-magic, and fire danced on Francis' hands again, condemning him. I gave the Breoch Guard one last glare, then turned back to Silva. Her eyes were wide and brimming with tears. "I'm sorry," I whispered. "I tried."

"You were incredible." She gave me a weak smile. "I hope you don't get in too much trouble at home."

"Don't worry about me, all right? I'll make sure you get out, I promise." I leaned forward to embrace her, and she clung to me, her thin arms pressing into my ribs. When she released me, there were tears soaking the shoulder of my dress. "Stay strong," I whispered and turned to follow the palace guards toward their carriage.

***

They herded the students into the back of one of the small, barred carriages that the Breoch Guard always drove, and Lachlann was led to a similar carriage attached to the rear of a much nicer palace coach. Guilt stabbed at my insides as I climbed into the same coach and lowered myself onto one of the plush seats. I imagined Silva and all the others crammed into that tiny cage, limbs entangled, trying to comfort one another, while I was led away in the lap of luxury. Their carriage departed before ours, heading back toward Sylvenburgh, while we took a different road that would lead us directly to the coastline.

The two palace guards were clearly not expecting to be escorting a lady home, and they hovered nearby, asking whether I was comfortable or if I needed anything. I refused to acknowledge either of them outside of what was necessary, mainly because I feared that if I began to speak I would end up breaking down in tears. When we stopped for dinner, they bickered about whether they should feed me the rations they'd brought for Lachlann or try to find an establishment that served food fit for someone of my station. They ended up giving me Lachlann's rations.

I ate half the package of dried meat, cheese, hard bread and fruit, and drank half the water, then said I wasn't hungry for the rest and that I would give it to Lachlann.

"I'll take it to him, my lady," the older guard said.

I shook my head. "I insist." Then I rose and walked around to the back of the carriage before they could protest further.

I peeked through the small barred window; Lachlann was barely visible in the darkened corner. "I brought you something," I whispered.

He sat up. "Isabelle?"

I nodded. "They tried to give me your dinner. I only ate half of it."

Lachlann maneuvered himself so he was closer to the window. "You sure you don't want it?"

"I'm not really hungry." I meant it, too; the afternoon's events had taken away my appetite.

"Me neither. But thank you." He eyed me as I squeezed the bundle through the bars. "Are you really betrothed to the prince?"

"I am."

"Huh. The royal family line is about to have some magic in it. Powerful magic, too."

"I hope my presence hasn't endangered any of you."

He shook his head. "By the sounds of it, those folks were coming for me, not you. I've no idea who tipped them off about my anti-magic, or the class for that matter." He closed his eyes for a moment. "If you do in fact have any power over the prince, or his father, please do what you can to see the kids released."

"Of course. And you as well."

He nodded. "Yes, me as well. Though I've been thinking that perhaps this'll be a good opportunity. The whole reason I chose to train in anti-magic was that I wished to show it to the Breoch authorities one day. I never thought I'd have the chance to speak to the king, but if I'm being given that opportunity, I'm certainly going to take it."

"Why do you want to show it to the authorities?"

"Because arming city guards with anti-magic is a far better solution to the problems magic presents than what Breoch is currently doing. Maiming and enslaving magic users is cruel. And some forms of magic can be quite helpful to society as a whole. Your gift is just one example."

I nodded. "Did the guards hurt you when they threw you in there? Perhaps I can heal you."

"No. And even if they had, magic doesn't work on me. Besides, I wouldn't ask you to reveal yourself with those two stooges likely keeping an eye on you."

I glanced back at the two guards, who were indeed eyeing me while they finished up their meals.

"You'd best get back to the coach," Lachlann said. He drained the water skin and returned it to me. "Don't worry too much about me, Isabelle. I've endured worse than a few hours in a cage."

"I'll do what I can regardless," I said. Then I headed back to the waiting guards and seated myself in the coach once more.

***

There was only one bed in the coach; the guards, naturally, insisted that I take it, so I crawled in and pulled the covers over myself.

I couldn't relax, though. My head spun with worries about what had happened to the other children—I imagined them huddled against each other in some jail cell in Sylvenburgh. *And where to from there?* I recalled learning once that all teenage krossemages were sentenced to work on a prison farm off Sylvenburgh, but nearly four years ago there'd been a bizarre incident in which a handful of Dunderi magic users infiltrated the camp and freed its entire population. I remembered the shock waves that rippled through Breoch; it was the first time since the Banishing that any sort of mass defiance against the system had succeeded.

Oliver's grandfather, King Edwin, was furious. What happened to the escaped krossemages was still a bit murky; I'd heard rumours about a battle in Dundere that was an attempt to recapture them, but also that the entire group of them had disappeared once again.

Thankfully, Oliver's father wasn't nearly so bothered by any of this. Kairus was never entirely comfortable with the krossemage system, Oliver had once confided in me. He agreed that magic couldn't be made legal but figured there was a less cruel way to enforce the law. *Perhaps Lachlann's right,* I mused as sleep began to overtake me. Maybe today's events, terrifying as they were, would result in some changes for the better.

***

I awoke to the sound of hooves on cobblestones and sat up, rubbing my eyes. *We must be in Kirstein already.* I stood and poked my head out the window; sure enough, the woodlands had given way to city streets. We wound through the multistoried buildings of downtown, past shopkeepers just putting out the first of their wares, lamplighters dousing last night's flames, and folks on the way to their jobs. The scent of sea salt permeated the air—though, as always, it was shot through with the less pleasant aromas of life in a crowded city.

Eventually, the road turned north, and we entered the twisting, tree-lined streets of the Upper City. This was, of course, where all the rich folk lived. My parents' home was not the biggest estate in the area, but it was certainly grand compared to our old place in Sylvenburgh. The coach made its way up the winding driveway to our sprawling brick mansion. The guard whose turn it was to sleep shifted in his seat when the carriage came to a stop.

The other guard dismounted and opened the door for me a moment later. "Come, my lady." My heartbeat picked up as we approached the front doors. *I'm going to be in so much trouble.*

The guard knocked, and several minutes later my mother answered. She was still in her robe, her greying blonde curls a tousled mess. She stared at me, then the guard.

"Isabelle?" She looked me over. "What happened to you? What are you *wearing?*" I glanced down; only now did I realize I was still in the simple cotton dress lent to me by Silva. The clothes I'd brought with me weren't suitable for the Woods, she'd said.

"Apologies for showing up so early, my lady," the guard said, giving her a stiff bow. "There was some trouble."

"I see that." She looked me over again. "Isabelle, why don't you go upstairs and change your dress while I speak to this fellow?"

***

Ten minutes later, I sat in the morning room wearing clean clothes, my hair properly braided again. The cook had brought me tea and fresh fruit with buttery pastries, and I ate them slowly. Mother sat across from me, frowning. I'm not sure what the guard told her, but she seemed nearly at a loss for words.

Finally, she sighed. "Isabelle. What in the king's name made you think it was a good idea to run off to the Shrouded Woods to practice magic?"

"Is that what the guard said we were doing?" I shook my head and took a bite of my pastry. "It wasn't a magic class, Mother. It was a class about the botany of the Shrouded Woods."

"You expect me to believe that? I'm not stupid, Isabelle." She sighed. "Look, I know that folks who are born with magic can't help it. If *you* have magic, I don't judge you, either." She met my gaze, and my stomach twisted as I wondered for the hundredth time if Mother knew my secret. "But intentionally *practicing* it is dangerous. Both you and your friends should know that much."

"But sometimes practicing it is *necessary* to get it under control," I argued. "And some types of magic can be very useful. There are folks who can change the weather and lift heavy things with only their minds, and make plants grow more quickly. And there are people who can heal, who probably could have saved Oliver's mother." I closed my eyes, remembering the look on Oliver's face when he told me his mother had passed away, her mysterious illness finally consuming her. "They could even possibly save..." I trailed off, unwilling to admit out loud what we both suspected.

Mother winced and nodded. "I know about healers," she said, "and I'm sure Oliver does too. But the law is the law. Doing any of those things, even healing, could have your friends put in a camp without your hand or tongue. Do you really want that for them? For Silva especially?

"They wouldn't be able to prove that Silva has magic, or that any of the others do either." I crossed my arms. "One child in the class cast in front of the Breoch Guard. I can't see how he'll be spared. But the others did nothing wrong, nor did Lachlann."

"Is that the fellow with the anti-magic?"

I frowned. "You know about him?"

"Yes, the king wishes to meet him. Or rather, Simon convinced the king that he should."

"And why would Simon want that?"

"No idea. Of all the supposed distant relatives of the king who've shown up over the past month, he's the one whose designs I understand the least."

"But why do the other students need to be kept under watch?" The panic that had accompanied yesterday's capture rose again in my chest. "I need to help Silva, Mother. Maybe I should ask for an audience with the king. If he's the one who requested Lachlann's presence, then perhaps he can grant the students their freedom."

"That may well help. We have been invited to dinner this evening, along with most of the king's advisors. You may have the chance to speak with him then. I don't doubt he'll wish to have a word with you; news of your involvement in this escapade has undoubtedly reached the palace by now." She arched an eyebrow. "I hope Oliver doesn't disapprove."

I laughed. "Oliver will likely be jealous that I got to visit the infamous Shrouded Woods."

"Yes, I suppose he would be." Mother glanced toward the kitchen, then leaned in. "So what *were* the infamous Shrouded Woods like?"

I spent the next half hour telling her about what I'd seen of the Woods and how we learned to make a sleeping tea, all while omitting the parts about the magic aspects of the class. By the time I headed upstairs to get ready for school, my mood had lightened just a bit. Kairus was a reasonable man; surely he would understand that Silva and her classmates had done nothing wrong.

And I couldn't wait to tell Oliver about the Shrouded Woods.

Chapter 4

THE PALACE DINING room was alive with laughter, conversation, and the aromas of cooking food when we arrived that evening. Most of the court was already present, along with the horde of supposed relatives that had shown up over the last six months, ever since the rumours began. Oliver's father, King Kairus, noticed us right away and came over, greeting my parents like the old friends they were. "Caspa, Lillian, I'm so glad you could join us tonight," he said, shaking Father's hand and leaning down to kiss Mother's. Then he glanced at me. "And you as well, Isabelle."

"Thank you," I said, returning his smile. Kairus had known us long enough that he'd long ago instructed our family to address him by name. Despite this, I still found him a slight bit intimidating, and not just because of his station.

Kairus was a tall, muscular man, with high cheekbones and deep-set eyes. Like all men of the royal family, he shaved his head once becoming king—a tradition which Oliver confessed to me was in place because the men of his family tended to lose their hair a little early. My parents, in their fine clothes and expensive jewelry, looked frumpy next to him; granted, both my parents were a few years his senior. But it was Kairus' bearing, not his age, that set him apart from others. He was regal in how he stood and talked, a skill that I didn't doubt was learned. He clapped my father on the back. "You must come meet our guests of honour!"

We followed him across the massive hall adorned in maroon velvet curtains and imposing chandeliers, to a table where a group of dignitaries clustered. Two strangers were present as well: an older man with long grey hair pulled back into a ponytail, whose rough clothing stood in stark contrast to the nobles'; and a middle-aged woman with dark skin and hair done up in a series of braids, who wore a robe that, while spun of rough material, was richly decorated with ornaments made of shells. Kairus introduced each of them to my parents before hurrying off to greet another guest. I hung back, wondering if a teenage girl would be welcome in their conversation. I was just about to join them when a pair of hands clamped down on my shoulders.

"There you are."

I nearly jumped out of my skin at Oliver's voice. I whirled around to find him laughing, his green eyes glinting, and I shook my head. "Are you ever going to stop sneaking up on me?"

"Never. It makes life more entertaining. Sneaking is my specialty." He gave me a lopsided grin that did not look at all princely. "Perhaps I can sneak you out of this meeting later."

"To do what?"

"So you can tell me all about your time in the Shrouded Woods, of course. And we can do daring and scandalous things, like cuddle."

I gave an exaggerated gasp and felt my cheeks heat up ever so slightly as I spoke. "Your father would be mortified."

Oliver was blushing too, but he ignored his flaming cheeks in favour of offering me his arm. "We'd best go mingle. Come with me? Please?"

"Of course." I smiled as I slid my arm through his. I was better at making small talk than Oliver was; if left to his own devices, he would often end up rambling about circuses or his collection of jewels or whatever else his current obsession was, until he realized he was boring the other person and would then hastily retreat. Princely upbringing or not, he could still be more than a little awkward.

We made our way through the guests, stopping to chat with various members of the court. Oliver avoided the relatives, for obvious reasons, and after a while we ended up talking to the woman in the fancy robe, who we learned was named Indira.

"I think the king's new policies are excellent," she was saying to another guest when we joined the conversation. "This will certainly make life easier for my people. And it will ensure that you city-dwellers eat a little better." She grinned, then looked us over. "Ah, the future king and queen." She gave us a small bow. "In the words of my people, may the seas of your life be neither too rough nor too dull."

"An interesting saying, my lady," Oliver replied, returning her bow. "Most folks only wish us long life and no adversity."

"Ah, but what good is a life with no adventure?" The woman's eyes sparkled. Then she turned to me. "I have a gift for you, my lady." From out of the folds of her robe, she pulled a comb and presented it to me. "Carved of whale bone and decorated with the finest of ayua and pyrie shells. And pearls of course."

I took the comb in my hands and gazed at it. The shells sparkled when they caught the light, the ayua an opalescent blue-green and the pyrie a deep purple. "This is beautiful," I murmured. "Thank you."

"May I?" Oliver held out a hand.

"Yes, but don't get any ideas about keeping it." I grinned as I passed it to him. He stared at my hair for a moment before sliding the comb gently into my updo. I didn't miss how his hand trembled ever so slightly. Then he stood back to admire his work. "The ayua shells match your eyes," he said. "Beautiful."

"The comb or my eyes?"

"Both." He gave me a grin, and I saw a faint blush creep into his cheeks yet again.

I felt my own face flush, and we stared at each other for a long, awkward moment. "Thank you," I finally said.

We'd been holding hands for the last year or so, and as a formality I'd been accepting his arm when he offered it since I was thirteen. But I was still getting used to how my own heart fluttered on occasion when he put an arm around my shoulders or smiled at me. Oliver wasn't handsome in the same way as his father—he lacked the muscular stature and imposing presence—but he was still attractive in a boyish way. He had dimples when he smiled, his dark curls always looked a little mussed, and his green eyes turned blue when the light hit them a certain way. He was only an inch taller than me, but I imagined that it would be easier to kiss someone my height.

"I hear rumour that you also enjoy treasures, Your Highness." Indira smiled at Oliver and held out a small box.

Oliver took the gift from her, and my eyes widened when he opened it; Indira had given him a set of cufflinks made from the same shells that graced my comb. "So you're not tempted to steal your lady's jewelry," Indira said, amusement crinkling her eyes.

"These are amazing," breathed Oliver. "Thank you so much, I'll—"

"Well, isn't this a pleasure?" He was interrupted by Simon joining our small circle. Simon gave Indira a bow and flashed a grin at me. He and Oliver ignored one another, as seemed to be standard protocol between the two of them. Most of the recently arrived relatives did little to try to get to know Oliver, and he had no desire to engage them beyond polite, cursory nods, for reasons that were obvious enough to me.

Of all the relatives, Simon was an oddity. He was younger than most of the other arrivals—I doubted him to be past his mid-twenties. He was admittedly more handsome than the rest of them, too. His dark hair hung nearly to his waist, and he wore it loose, flowing down his back save for a single thin braid that he liked to toy with. He had a quick but slightly wry smile that matched his sense of humour, and warm brown eyes that looked nearly golden when the light hit them at a certain angle. His clothes, while luxurious, lacked some of the ostentatiousness of those worn by the rest of the court, and he spoke with an accent that I couldn't place.

"And who might you be?" Indira asked him.

"Simon of the house Rothwell, at your service." He grinned. "I'm the king's cousin."

"Ah." Indira's eyes flickered to Oliver for a moment, and she frowned. My heart sank a little. *So she's heard the rumours as well.* It was easier to convince myself that nothing was wrong until half a dozen men and women showed up at the palace, all claiming to be related to the king in one way or another, each of them with their eyes clearly set on one thing.

Oliver nodded at Indira, and his hand slipped into mine. "Come on," he whispered, then he was pulling me through the crowd, away from Simon. He stumbled when we were near the edge of the room and caught himself on the wall. "Sorry about that," he mumbled, cheeks burning again.

"Are you all right?"

"Of course." He straightened up and gave me a smile that was obviously forced. "Just tired is all." He looked beyond me to the dining table, and I followed his gaze; only now did I see that the cooking staff was bringing in dishes of steaming food. "We'd best seat ourselves."

***

Dinner at the palace was always sumptuous, and tonight I sampled roast boar, wild-caught pheasant, baked soft cheese served with blackberries, and an array of breads and salted meats and pickled vegetables. Between courses, Kairus and his second wife, Queen Calendra, introduced Indira and Corden, the older man in the plain clothes. "These two are the newly appointed governors of the Eastwilds and the Caron Islands, our two new Special Territories," Kairus said. "Our agreement with them will supply the nation with shalite and aro stone, gold, pearls, ayua and pyrie shells, and kimli seaweed, which can be baked into bread to keep folks from getting scurvy."

Everyone at the table nodded. Neither community used coin, and Kairus' decision to allow these regions to pay their taxes in goods instead of money, as well as to exempt them from certain laws around fishing and mining—the two major industries in these communities—had been a controversial one. Most of the more progressive folk approved of it; the rest of the country saw it as unfair.

"We have another matter to discuss tonight, especially with the abundance of aro stone we are about to acquire," Kairus went on. "We have recently detained a fellow with extraordinary abilities, and Simon here has convinced me that they may be of use to Breoch." He nodded at a pair of guards then. "Bring him in."

Bringing prisoners to court dinners for interrogation—usually to intimidate them—was a common tactic of Kairus' father Edwin. My eyes widened when I saw who the guards were escorting into the room.

Lachlann looked tired; his eyes were shadowed by dark circles and his forehead creased with obvious worry. Nonetheless, he bowed when he saw Kairus. "Your Majesty."

Kairus looked him over. "What is your name?"

Lachlann lifted his head and said it aloud.

"All right, Lachlann, do you know why you've been brought here?"

"I was arrested while leading a group of young folks out of the Woods the other day. I took them to the outskirts for a lesson in the plant life of the Woods, at the request of my brother. The children and I were taken into custody on suspicion of them being magic users."

"Suspicion?" Kairus scoffed. "My guards informed me this morning that the Breoch Guard *caught* them using magic."

"The Guard caught *one* of them using magic, Your Majesty," Lachlann replied. "With all due respect, how does one child losing control of their magic in a moment of fear implicate the whole group?"

"Perhaps this group is not actually learning about plant life, hmmm? Perhaps they are actually a group of magic users that you are taking into the Woods for training? What need do city children have to learn the botany of the Shrouded Woods?"

"There are plenty of reasons, Your Majesty. The plant life of the Shrouded Woods has many medicinal uses. I know folks who brew teas that can treat a cold, help a person sleep, and help with wound healing."

Kairus frowned. "Fascinating. To be honest with you, though, it's not what the children can or cannot do that's brought you here. Tell me, Lachlann, what did *you* do when that child used magic?"

"I used anti-magic to stop him from casting, Your Majesty."

"Because you didn't want us to catch him, hmmm?"

"I have no desire for any child under my care to be mutilated and enslaved. I believe there are better ways to deal with magic, and one of them was the very ability I utilized."

"Anti-magic?" Kairus' eyes narrowed. "You know that there are some folks who view anti-magic as its own form of magic, right?"

"I'm aware, Your Majesty. But they're wrong. Anti-magic was not something I was born with, it was something I chose. And cutting parts off of me won't hinder my ability." He paused and took a deep breath. "May I speak freely, Your Majesty?"

Kairus frowned but nodded. "Go ahead."

"I learned anti-magic in part so that one day I could show the authorities in Breoch how useful it could be. I'd rather hoped for an audience with a person in power so I could explain all this. Of course, I didn't expect it to be with the king himself." He smiled. "I've spent some time in Dundere, Your Majesty, and I've seen how they use anti-magic to control their mages. Magic is legal in Dundere, and it's well utilized, from what I've seen. But it's not a free-for-all; magic users aren't allowed to use their gifts however they want. There are training protocols and a licensing system, and their police force is equipped with anti-magic so that mages who are breaking the law can be dealt with. It's a brilliant system, Your Majesty; in my opinion, it's much better than what we do to magic users here in Breoch." He squared his shoulders. "I believe my skills could benefit this kingdom, Your Majesty."

Kairus frowned, and I watched him turn to Simon and speak quietly. Then he turned back to Lachlann. "All right. Tell us how you became an anti-mage."

I listened as Lachlann explained the potency of the aro stone and how some anti-mages would allow it to bind itself to their bodies in order to become more powerful in their craft. When he was done, Kairus looked him over. "Show us what you can do, Lachlann."

Lachlann frowned. "In order to properly demonstrate, I'd need someone to cast a spell, Your Majesty."

"Yes, I'm aware. Pieter?"

I felt Oliver stiffen next to me as an aging fellow with round spectacles and grey hair pulled into a ponytail stood up. "My name is Pieter, and I'm the court mage," he informed Lachlann. "I will cast a spell."

Lachlann's eyes narrowed, and he looked back at Kairus. "You have a *court mage*, Your Majesty?"

"He's the only legal mage in the country," Kairus said, nodding. "We need to have someone in the court with knowledge of magic if we are to keep it at bay."

Pieter approached Lachlann and mumbled a phrase. When a small ball of fire appeared in his palm, he nodded at Lachlann.

Lachlann reached up and touched the piece of stone, and I flinched as the strange sensation I'd felt yesterday swept over me. My senses suddenly felt muted, my limbs heavy. Pieter recoiled, and his fire extinguished. "Try casting again," Lachlann said to him.

Pieter mumbled a phrase, then tried another spell. Nothing worked. "Fascinating."

"Useful for controlling the misuse of magic, don't you think?" Lachlann said, smiling. He touched the pendant again as he spoke, and the strange feeling disappeared.

"Indeed," Pieter agreed, looking to Kairus. "This could certainly be of use, Your Majesty."

"It absolutely could," Simon put in, twirling his braid around his finger as he spoke. "You see why I requested you bring him here."

Lachlann eyed Simon. "Do we know each other?"

"Our paths crossed once before. I was impressed by your talent."

"It *is* impressive," Kairus said and turned back to Lachlann. "All right, we'll give your anti-magic a chance. But you'll be staying with us for a little while so we can better learn about your skills."

"What you're saying, Your Majesty, is that I'm to remain your prisoner, is that right?" Lachlann said.

Kairus raised an eyebrow. "Indeed."

"What about the children? The ones who were with me when we were captured."

"Well, I'm going to need to keep them in custody until we can determine whether they are all magic users," the king replied. "Don't you worry about them, Lachlann. They'll be cared for."

Lachlann opened his mouth as if to protest, but then nodded. As the guards led Lachlann away, Kairus turned to Simon. "What do you think? Is he what you wanted?"

"He is exactly what I wanted," Simon said.

"Do you think his idea of using anti-magic instead of the krossemage system is of any value?"

Simon shrugged. "It seems to have worked in some places, sire. I do have an idea as to how his anti-magic could be used to our advantage. But Lachlann's not going to like it."

Kairus frowned. "You'll have to tell me about that a little later. Right now, I have another matter I must deal with." He stood, and his eyes met mine. "Isabelle. I need to speak with you privately."

My eyes widened. "Me?"

"Yes, come along, my dear. We'll speak out on the balcony." He gestured toward the double doors that led outside.

I exchanged a questioning glance with Oliver, then stood and followed Kairus.

It was warmer outside than I expected, and a silver moon hung above us. I could see most of Kirstein from up here, the neat rows of city blocks punctuated by dots of lamplight, the establishments of downtown lit up for nighttime revelry, and the sea sparkling in the distance. Kairus reached up and removed the heavy, jeweled crown he'd been wearing for the entirety of the evening and set it on a nearby table. "Isabelle, I wish to speak to you not as king, but as a friend of your parents', and as your future father-in-law." He smiled. "I've known you for your whole life, and it's been a pleasure watching you grow. You're intelligent, compassionate, and curious."

I frowned, wondering where he was going with this.

"But intelligence and curiosity can cause trouble when they're utilized incorrectly," he went on. "I'm not sure what you were doing out in the Woods yesterday afternoon, but I suspect it might have been something you could get in deep trouble for." He sighed. "It's not wrong to have magic in your blood, and you needn't feel shame if you do. A good quarter of Breochi citizens have it, you know. But utilizing that magic puts everyone in danger. That's why the Banishing happened, why the laws exist."

I stared at Kairus for a moment, wondering if he somehow knew my secret. "What makes you think that yesterday's adventures were about magic?" I finally managed to ask.

He smiled and shook his head. "Botany of the Shrouded Woods? Why would anyone want to learn that? We know there was at least some magic present in that group." He sighed then. "I don't want you putting yourself in situations where the Guard might take you, Isabelle. You're incredibly lucky that the palace guards were there yesterday, otherwise you might be with the other students now."

I took a deep breath as I saw the opportunity I'd been hoping for. "Do you know where they are, Your Majesty?"

He waved a hand. "Oh, stop with the honourifics. And I don't know their exact location at this moment, no. I could find out easily enough."

"What's going to happen to them? You can't prove they were all using magic."

"You're right, I can't. But they are still under suspicion, and Simon thinks it's best to hold them until certain things have been cleared up."

"Since when do you take orders from Simon?" The words came out harsher than I meant them.

Kairus gave me an odd look. "Isabelle, I am king. I take orders from no one. But I'm not about to ignore the advice of someone as intelligent as him, either."

"You know exactly why he's come here, what he's after." I shook my head. "What they're all after."

"Yes, well, I still have some hope that none of them will ever be able to have it." He eyed me before changing the subject. "Why do you care so much about the fate of those students?"

"My best friend, Silva, is among them." I blinked back tears as I spoke.

"Ahhh."

"Please, Kairus. She's done nothing wrong. None of them have."

"Well, if you're telling the truth, then you needn't worry. No harm will come to them so long as they haven't broken the law."

I frowned. "You mean you won't make them into krossemages?"

"Well, I'm not so sure about the little firebrand, but none of the others will be harmed unless it can be proven that they were using magic. You have my word on that much."

I relaxed slightly. "Thank you."

"Don't worry yourself too much, Isabelle. Your friends will be fine." Kairus smiled at me. "Now, let's head back inside, shall we? I'm sure Oliver would enjoy a dance."

I sighed but nodded and followed him back into the ballroom.

Chapter 5

WHEN MOTHER SUGGESTED the following morning that I take one more day off school to recover from my adventures, I was relieved. I knew full well that the rumours—that I'd snuck into the Shrouded Woods, that I, the betrothed of the crown prince, was a witch—would be circulating like mad. I had enough trouble making friends at my school thanks to my connections to the royal family; this, of course, would not help matters.

When I was thirteen and news broke of my betrothal to Oliver, the other children had either avoided me, treated me like a celebrity, or heaped disdain upon me. However, the novelty of my status faded after a year or so, and the only kids who treated me like a celebrity nowadays were the younger children. Most boys ignored me completely, as did a chunk of the girls.

The girls who did not ignore me saw me as competition, and any weakness I showed—whether it was a bad grade on a math test or a day when I was feeling downcast and moody—was a point against me.

They would have a field day with these new rumours.

I spent the morning puttering about the house. As a lady in training, I'd taken up many of the usual hobbies of the aristocracy—reading poetry, embroidery, gardening, painting, horsemanship—but none of these things felt even remotely appealing today, so I ended up pacing the property for a good portion of the morning, uncertain what to do with myself and almost wishing I'd gone to school. So when Father told me at lunch that he was heading over to the palace for the afternoon, I asked if I could join him.

We seated ourselves in the carriage, and I looked my father over. My face was similar to my mother's, but I got my colouring from Father. Both parents were blue eyed, but my mother was pale and blonde and wispy, while Father was rosy-cheeked and robust like me, and his hair, though grey and thinning now, had once been the same chestnut-brown as mine. "I hear you had yourself an adventure while visiting Silva?" I didn't miss the disapproval in his tone.

I nodded. "That's what I wanted to talk to you about. Silva was one of the students who was taken by the Breoch Guard."

He nodded. "I'm aware. I got word from her father this afternoon."

"I'm sure he must be worried sick about her."

"He is. I'm a little concerned myself. Silva was like a second daughter to me when you were young."

"Surely you feel terrible for him."

Father cocked his head. "What are you getting at, Isabelle?"

I sighed. "I'm trying to figure out where she and the other kids were taken. Would you be willing to help me search for her?"

"Search for her? Isabelle, if the Breoch Guard wants her in custody, there's little you or I can do about it. You have to trust that the king knows best."

I shook my head. "I used to. But Kairus has changed as of late. He's letting some of the cousins sway him in ways he wouldn't have gone before."

Father stared at me for a long moment, then shook his head. "Do you really think Kairus would harm a bunch of children?"

"Perhaps not personally, but he hasn't closed down the krossemage camps, and teens are still being sent there."

"For their own good. Can you imagine what would happen if we had a bunch of teenagers running around without control of their magic? If they can't control it enough to keep it hidden, then they shouldn't have access to it, period."

I huffed. It was an argument I'd heard Father use before. Only those able to keep their magic under wraps should be allowed access to it. The krossemage system was to weed out those with little control. This would mean that only magic users with good control would be allowed to fully participate in society, and would hopefully in time produce a generation of magic users fully in command of their abilities—then, Father reasoned, we could reassess the necessity of the Banishing.

We were pulling up to the palace now, and Father gave me a small smile. "We'll discuss this more later. I have a meeting with the court."

***

An hour later, I sat on the cobblestones with Oliver, our backs up against the old bell tower that sat toward the rear of the palace grounds. The tower was an eyesore, its moss-covered walls beginning to crumble in some places, its roof sagging, and the bell itself covered in rust; but as children it had been our hideout. We would climb the narrow spiral staircase that led from the base of the tower to a drafty room immediately below the bell level, full of broken furniture and home to a family of bats, likely an office at one point. The furniture could be arranged to make forts and hideouts, and the bats didn't seem to mind us as long as we kept our distance. A small staircase led from there to the top level, the bell room itself, which was somewhat open to the elements. It had been our favourite place to tell stories and play make-believe in the summer months.

It was also the site of our very first, very forbidden kiss, when Oliver was ten and I was eight.

The tower was deemed unsafe less than a month later—the staircase had begun to crumble, and we were prohibited from climbing it ever again, but we still enjoyed sitting at its base, reminiscing about days gone by. It was one of our two favourite hangouts; the other, much to my parents' chagrin, was the porch swing at my house. My parents were relatively easy going around Oliver when we were at the palace. Whenever he visited us, though, they fussed and fretted, scolding the house staff if the meal wasn't perfect or the parlour wasn't clean, as if they thought Oliver would judge us for living in a home that was not a palace like his. Oliver tried to convince them it was fine; in fact, he liked getting away from the palace and pretending he was a normal teenager, but they didn't seem to understand.

Oliver's coming to my house wasn't just an escape from palace life, I'd realized a year or so back. It revealed something else about him, namely that underneath all the princely charm, he was lonely.

As was I.

Oliver was an only child, and I was the youngest of my siblings, though my two older brothers were more than a decade older than me, both long ago moved out and married. And Oliver had the same troubles making friends with other teens that I had, only more so. His father's decision to have him privately tutored likely didn't help that issue, but I imagine that if he'd attended King's Academy with me, he too would be ignored or despised by the other students, either for his title or his odd obsessions.

"What did Father want with you last night?" Oliver asked me, poking at a cobblestone with his boot.

"He was worried that my time in the Woods was spent using magic."

"Well, was it?"

"Of course not," I lied. "We were learning about the plant life of the Shrouded Woods. I learned how to make a sleeping tea using mushrooms and berries."

"What were the Woods like? I never got a chance to ask you yesterday."

"Woody," I replied, and he laughed. "The trees are taller than anything you see on the coast. Lots of wildlife, very peaceful. I also got to meet a few of the folks who live there; they were the ones to teach us about the plant life."

His eyes widened. "What were *they* like?"

I shrugged. "They were kind enough. Their clothes were odd, and one of them had a bit of a strange accent."

"Do you know where in the Woods they live?"

"The Woods is a massive place, Oliver. How would I know that?"

"Just wondering. There's a rumour about a whole village in the Woods somewhere, full of criminals and magic users." He smirked. "I want to visit it one day."

"Why, so you can arrest them all?"

"Of course not. They don't need to know that I'm a prince; I can disguise myself. I just think it would be fascinating."

I nodded. "It probably would be."

"Perhaps I'll make visiting the village my next goal, after seeing a live circus."

I laughed. "I think the circus is a more attainable goal than that. If there's a village in the Woods, I doubt its people want to be found. Especially not by Breochi royalty." I stifled a yawn.

"Tired?" Oliver asked.

I nodded. "I slept in a carriage the night before last, and I didn't sleep well last night either. I'm worried about Silva."

"Did you talk to Father about her?"

"He told me that none of the students will be harmed. But he's insistent on holding them for a little longer. Apparently, Simon thinks it's a good idea." I rolled my eyes. "I'm not sure why your father likes him so much."

Oliver nodded, and his face fell slightly. I reached out to take his hand. "I'm sorry. I shouldn't have brought him up."

"It's fine. Don't worry about them." He gave me a quick smile. "Tell me more about these Woods-folk."

"As you wish." I sat back and regaled him with stories about Starla and Kip until Father came to fetch me.

***

At home, I headed upstairs to get ready for bed. The moment I closed my door, I knew something was wrong. I could hear voices, as if someone was in my room, though I couldn't place them.

"Are you sure this is the right house?" A woman's voice, relatively young by the sound of it.

"Absolutely. Persius directed me here, and he doesn't make mistakes." This was a familiar male voice. *That accent...*

"So what now?" the woman asked. "Do we just knock on the balcony doors and hope she answers?"

The balcony. The curtains were drawn, so I couldn't see anyone out there, but I crossed the floor in several long strides and threw the doors open, hoping to catch the intruders off guard.

It worked.

I took a step back, my eyes widening. A young man and woman—at least, I thought the shorter one was a woman, it was hard to tell—stared back at me. Both were clad in waistcoats and breeches. The shorter one had mahogany skin and curly black hair, cut shorter than was common for a woman, but the waistcoat was fitted to accommodate a bust.

The taller figure had long brown hair pulled back into a ponytail, and, gazing up at him, I realized that I'd placed the accent correctly. *This was the fellow who was helping with the botany class.* He returned my gaze and gave me a cautious smile. "Isabelle, right?"

I nodded. "Kip?"

"My apologies for showing up on your balcony like this," he said. "We must've given you quite a fright. But we were hoping to get your help."

I stared at him for a long moment, then crossed my arms. "First of all, how did you get up here?"

"Ah. That was Kaden." He gestured at the shorter figure. "She has the ability to fly; she's the one who brought me here." Kaden flashed me a wide grin.

"How did you know where I live?"

"Persius told me." He gestured behind him to where I saw the familiar hawk sitting placidly on the edge of my balcony. "He's been watching your house for quite some time now, y'know. But never mind that. We need your help, and we're hoping to negotiate an exchange of services."

"Exchange of...how?"

"Starla told me that you're a healer. She said that you were hoping to learn how to better use your gift so you could heal a friend without them knowing."

I nodded.

"Well, Starla herself is in need of your skills immediately," he explained. "She went into labour early, likely from the shock of being told her husband was captured. The baby's very small and weak, and she'll die without help."

"And you want me to heal the baby?"

"I want you to try," he said. "In exchange, we'll give you the teaching you need to heal your friend."

"But wouldn't I have to learn that from a fellow healer? I thought Starla said there were none in the Woods."

"You're right. But we do have a woman who *was* one long ago. She's willing to train you."

I frowned, recalling Starla saying something similar. "How long will my training take?"

"A while. Likely a couple of months. You can go back and forth from her place, though—we'll sneak you out at night. Healing the baby should only take an hour or so."

"We know this is abrupt," put in Kaden, "but you're our only hope. And you'll be around folks who understand you, and who accept you for who you are. You won't need to hide your magic where we're going."

Her words made me think of Silva. "I'll come with you so long as I can add one more thing to our agreement."

"What's that?"

"My best friend was among the teens who were taken," I said. "I want your help tracking her and the others down. In return, I can tell you a bit about where your friend Lachlann is. I have some idea what's happened to him."

Kip's eyes narrowed. "Is that so?"

I nodded. "My parents...work in the palace, and I sometimes go with them. I overheard a few things."

Kip exchanged a glance with Kaden. "Sounds like we need to bring her to Marcus."

"Who's Marcus?"

"My father-in-law," said Kip. "He's the one who...runs things where we're going."

"And where is that?"

"You'll see." Kaden extended a hand. "Are you willing to come with us, then?"

I sighed. "If it means healing my boyfriend, then fine." I took her hand.

"Wonderful." She grinned. "Kip, get us out of here."

"I thought you were the one who could fly."

"I am. But we're not flying for this first part."

As she spoke, Kip moved so he stood behind us. Then he put a hand on each of our shoulders. "Ready?"

Kaden nodded, and Kip tightened his grip. *"Arius Ravenous Momentous,"* he in-toned.

Chapter 6

AN ODD RUSHING sound filled my ears, and only a moment later we were standing not on my balcony, but in a moonlit meadow far from the city. I gaped at Kip. "Right! You can teleport, can't you?"

He nodded. "I'm not good enough to get us all the way home, so this is where Kaden takes over."

"Where are we exactly?"

"A little way out of Kirstein. Far enough that we can get high up without anyone seeing us."

Kaden was still holding my hand, and now she squeezed it. "Ready for the fun part?"

I nodded. "I...suppose so."

She grabbed Kip's hand on her other side. "*Incantus Momentus Gravita,*" she whispered, then pushed off with her toes.

Our feet left the ground, and we began to slowly rise upward. My breath caught in my throat, and I gripped Kaden's hand tighter as the earth fell away beneath us. For a moment I floundered, kicking frantically, and she laughed. "Easy. You're under a flying spell right now; even if I let go of you, you wouldn't fall."

"It's true, see?" On her other side, Kip released Kaden's hand and shot up into the sky ahead of us, executing a midair flip before coming to a hovering stop perhaps a hundred feet above.

"Show-off," Kaden called up to him. She kicked her feet to increase our speed; we caught up to Kip quickly enough then levelled out. Then we began to move forward, aided by a light breeze at our backs. I stared down at the trees a little ways below us, trying not to panic. "You can let go if you want," Kaden said.

"Absolutely not."

She grinned, then spread her arms wide. "Try this. It's exactly how people imagine you'd position yourself when flying, and it is the most comfortable way."

I copied her, relaxing muscles that I didn't even realize were clenched as I slowly spread my arms wide. "Like this?"

"Exactly. Now breathe deep," she encouraged. "Try not to worry about falling. Pay attention to how free you feel."

I closed my eyes and inhaled slowly, deliberately, fighting the urge to panic and latch onto Kaden. Then I exhaled.

I repeated the breaths a few times and kicked my feet as if I were swimming. Kaden chuckled. The air currents butted up against my arms and toyed with my hair.

"Are you enjoying yourself yet?" she asked.

"I...I think so."

"Good. Are you ready to open your eyes?"

I squeezed them shut for one final moment before letting them flutter open, then I gazed out over the trees below, at the small moonlit puffs of cloud that dotted the sky around me, and shook my head in disbelief.

I was *flying,* of all things. How was this even possible?

I let out a small whoop of elation, and Kaden chuckled. A moment later, I was pulled out of my reverie by the wind catching my dress, causing the skirt to puff out like a balloon. I gasped as it pulled me back suddenly, and Kaden burst out laughing. "This is why I wear trousers as much as possible when I fly." She changed direction ever so slightly, so the wind wasn't blowing directly up my skirt.

The forest had grown dense below us; now we were forced to weave our way around the occasional tree that stretched far above the rest of the forest canopy. A raven perched on a branch let out a throaty croak as we passed.

Up ahead, I noticed a massive river that cut through the forest, the quickly fading daylight glinting off its surface. "We follow the river," Kaden told me.

"How much longer?" I asked.

"A while," she admitted. "This isn't an easy flight. I'm not used to flying this many people so far, especially on a round trip."

"Once we get past the fork in the river, I should be able to teleport us the rest of the way in," Kip said from Kaden's other side.

"Are you sure you have enough magic to do that after our last jump?"

"Not entirely. But we can try." Then he frowned. "Actually, wait. I have a better idea." He pulled what appeared to be a small wooden whistle out of his shirt.

Kaden chuckled. "Now you're thinking."

Kip blew the whistle before I could ask what was going to happen, and I frowned. "Why can't I hear it?"

"Because the thing we're summoning can hear higher pitches than humans," Kip told me.

"What sort of *thing* did you just summon?"

"Wait and see." Kip's smile was nearly as mischievous as Kaden's.

We flew onward for several minutes more, impatience and anxiety growing in my gut as I waited for whatever was going to happen. I was about to demand much more firmly that Kaden and Kip tell me exactly what was going on when I heard a voice from behind us. "What's the matter, Kaden, you running out of magic?"

I turned my head and let out a shriek.

Trailing us was a massive dragon with emerald scales and membranous, gossamer green wings. Atop the dragon sat a young man with reddish-brown hair and a big smile who looked about the same age as Kip. Kaden let out a laugh at my reaction. I recoiled as the dragon pulled up alongside us.

"Kaden, you're terrible! You should have let the poor girl know we were coming!" The scolding came from the young woman who sat behind the fellow. She had something attached to her back, and my eyes widened even further when I realized it was a leather pouch of sorts holding a toddler. The woman shook her thick mane of dark hair and gave Kaden a disapproving glare. Then she looked me over with her big blue eyes. "Who is your friend anyway?"

"This is Isabelle," Kip said. "She's a lifebringer, believe it or not."

The young man whistled. *"A lifebringer?"*

"My thoughts exactly. We're headed to see Starla—not sure if you'd heard yet, but she gave birth early, and the baby is quite sick."

"We heard," the fellow replied. "Well, hop aboard, folks. We'll get you to Ankrossi in no time."

"Ankrossi?" I repeated.

"The village we're headed to," he replied. "I'm Ambrose, by the way. This is my wife Daisy and our daughter Raelle. And *this,*" he patted the dragon's scales, "is Spark. She won't harm you, don't worry."

The saddle that Spark wore had room for two additional folks, and Kip landed easily. "Come on," he said to me, patting the seat behind him. "It's like riding a horse, you'll get the hang of it."

I frowned, debating the trustworthiness of this massive beast. Kaden pulled me toward the saddle and deposited me behind Kip. Hovering in midair, she showed me how to tie myself in using leather straps. "You won't fall out now," she assured, "but you may want to hang onto Kip regardless."

I nodded and adjusted my dress, then leaned forward, wrapping my arms around Kip's waist. I could feel the dragon's scales, smooth and nearly metallic, against my legs. Kaden perched behind me, sitting on the very edge of the saddle and gripping Spark's haunches with her feet. I glanced back at her. "Won't you fall off?"

"If I do, I can catch myself," she assured me.

"Here we go," called out Ambrose, and we lurched forward. Below us, Spark's massive wings flapped, sending gusts of wind into our faces. I hung onto Kip for dear life as we banked right. I heard a giggle from in front of me and peeked over Kip's shoulder to see Raelle grinning. Clearly, she was accustomed to this.

The flight was much faster now that we were atop a dragon; we surged forward, following the river with ease. The wind blew at our faces, and Daisy's long hair flew back, nearly hitting Kip in the face. Spark descended slightly so that we were closer to the trees, while keeping us directly above the water, and the wind eased somewhat. I gazed down at the moonlight glinting off the river's surface.

When we rounded a bend some time later, I caught a few flickers of light coming from within the forest, and I leaned forward to catch my first glimpse of our destination.

Ankrossi was nestled in a sprawling meadow surrounded by towering trees on three sides, and butted up against the river on its last. Candles burned in the windows of homes and what appeared to be shops, dwarfed only by the pale pink luminescence that seemed to come off a massive tree in the centre of it all whose twisting limbs spiralled up into the sky. *Or was it two trees?* It was hard to tell from this vantage point.

The tree gave off enough light that I could make out the shapes of people below, most of whom seemed largely unconcerned with the dragon looking for a place to touch down.

Ambrose chose the riverbank as our landing spot, and as soon as Spark's feet met land, Kip turned to me. "Untie yourself," he said. "We need to move."

I undid the ties and was about to climb off the dragon when Kip grabbed my wrist and mumbled the same phrase I'd heard him use earlier. A second later, I found us standing in what appeared to be a large bedroom.

The interior of the room was lit by a series of lamps that I guessed to be magical; colourful lights glowed inside intricately crafted metal lanterns. Foliage snaked around the walls, flowers blooming here and there. A large bed took up most of the room, and Starla sat up in it, clutching a bundle to her chest. The playful demeanour that I'd seen during the lesson was gone; her face was pale from exhaustion, her hair matted, and her forehead creased with worry. Two younger women hovered near her, both dressed in the clothes of the Woods-folk. One had the same tawny skin as Starla, though her black hair was streaked with vibrant ribbons of bright purple. The other was pale and freckled, with fiery red hair pulled into a braid. Another woman sat in a nearby chair, this one very old. She was hunched over, her dark skin weathered and her white hair a frizzy halo around her head. Starla met my eyes and gave me a weak smile. "Isabelle. Thank the Fae."

The girl with the purple in her hair stood up and walked over to me. "I'm so glad you're here," she whispered, grasping my hand. "I've heard all about you from Mother." She gestured at Starla. "We haven't had a lifebringer in the Woods for many years now, and, well, I don't know if little Aria will survive without some help. Have you filled her in on what's happened, Kip?"

He nodded. "She knows. I'll leave you ladies to it."

"Thank you for bringing her." The girl smiled at Kip before he disappeared down the hall, then turned to me. "I'm Trina, by the way. And this is Saray, my adopted sister." She gestured at the redhead. "Claudi will help you with the healing." Here she pointed at the elderly woman.

"Pleasure to meet you all." I nodded at each of them, then my head snapped up. "Wait. You two are *Trina* and *Saray?*"

Saray let out a laugh. "I see our reputation precedes us."

I gaped at her for a moment; she looked like any ordinary young woman, not the legend I'd heard so many rumours about. "I used to go to Sylvenburgh Academy," I finally managed to explain. "I remember when you two ran away. I was pretty young, but it was a big deal. There are all sorts of stories about you in the cities."

They exchanged a glance. "We know," Trina said.

I looked her over. "I remember you fairly well, actually. Didn't you used to be blind?"

She nodded.

"What happened?"

"You're not the only lifebringer out there," she told me. "I was healed by...someone who I cared about deeply."

She and Saray exchanged another look, then Saray cleared her throat. "Speaking of lifebringers, we'd best get the little one healed."

"I agree," Starla said. "We'll need Claudi for this part as well."

"Right." Saray looked Claudi over. "Ready?"

"Ready when you are," Claudi replied, and I gaped as the old woman rose into the air and settled on the bed. She grinned at my expression. "Don't mess with Saray."

"You did that?" My gaze shifted to Saray. "I thought you were a firebrand."

"I am, but I've taken on some of my husband's powers as well, thanks to a magical bond we forged at our wedding."

I cocked my head. "You're married to Kip."

"That she is," Starla said. She patted the space on the bed between her and Claudi. "Come, sit."

I hitched up my skirt and crawled rather awkwardly onto the bed. Once I was settled, Starla pulled the infant from inside her clothes. "This is Aria."

I stared down at the baby. She was tiny, smaller than the length of Starla's forearm. Her skin was bluish, her eyes squeezed shut against the light. I could see her heart pounding beneath her ribcage. She did not cry, and her breath came out in small gasps. "She came nearly two months early," Starla told me. "I went into labour quite suddenly after I found out that Lachlann had been taken. Must have been the shock of it." Her voice wavered as she spoke, and Trina reached out and squeezed her hand.

I touched Aria's shoulder. Her skin was nearly translucent, and it felt fragile, almost papery under my fingertips. "I...have no idea how to do this," I admitted. "I've only ever healed myself, and the occasional cold or twisted ankle for people I'm very close to. I don't even know where to begin with this little one."

"That's why I'm here." Claudi's voice was authoritative.

I turned to her. "What can you do?"

"I was a lifebringer myself at one time," she explained. "I lost my healing powers decades ago, but I still have the ability to see what caused a wound or an illness and what's needed to cure it."

"How did you lose your healing powers?"

"That's a long story, and not one that I'm going to tell tonight. Right now, we have little Aria to deal with. I'll show you what I do to determine what she needs." Claudi reached out and let her hands hover just above Aria's body. She closed her eyes and began to sing a slow, haunting tune that sounded slightly like the healing song I was familiar with, but more mournful. "I'll teach you the song another day," she told me when she was finished. "What I can tell you right now, though, is that Aria's lungs aren't well developed, and that her mouth and digestive system will need strengthening if she is going to be able to nurse. If these things aren't fixed, she won't survive."

"How do I fix them?"

"Put your hand on her chest, and sing your healing song. The magic should tell you what to do." Claudi's last word came out with a gasp, and she sagged against the pillows, clearly exhausted from exerting the effort.

I did as I was instructed, marvelling at the fact that my hand covered Aria's entire trunk—her heart thrummed beneath my palm. I closed my eyes and let the song come, allowing the energy to flow down my arm and into her body. I found myself suddenly envisioning a pair of tiny lungs strengthening, the passageways within them widening ever so slightly to bring life-giving oxygen to the heart, and then the muscle that allowed them to inflate and deflate growing stronger. I concentrated on that image. As my song ended, Aria coughed, then suddenly took a deep breath in, her skin flushing a tawny pink. Then she began to cry.

Trina's eyes were wide. "You did it!" she exclaimed, clapping her hands.

"I did part of it, at least," I said, passing Aria back to Starla. "I don't feel like I was able to figure out what to do about feeding."

Starla nodded as she tucked Aria back into her clothing. "Her mouth might be too small to latch on to me."

Saray cocked her head. "Perhaps that's not about healing, but rather about ingenuity," she mused. "When a mother is nursing, she can, uh, milk herself, right?"

Starla nodded.

"Well, my father has these little glass tubes that he uses when he's experimenting with alchemy. What if you were to put your milk into a glass and use one of those tubes to drop it into Aria's mouth?"

"So long as it's a tube that hasn't had dangerous chemicals in it, that might well work," Starla said.

"I'll go ask him about it." Saray left the room, and Starla looked to Claudi. "Is there anything else Aria will need?"

"I can look, though I may need some help from the rest of you. Using magic is quite exhausting."

"Of course. Though I'm not sure how useful I'll be, I'm fairly exhausted myself." Starla closed her eyes. "Giving birth will do that to you."

"Isabelle and I can do it; I just learned recently how to join my magic to other people's," Trina said.

"What do you mean?" I asked.

"Watch. Mother, you're going to need to get closer to Claudi; Saray isn't here to move her."

I crawled out of the space between the two women so Starla could move nearer to Claudi. The older woman reached out and touched Aria's head, and Trina took my hand. "Put one hand on Claudi's shoulder," she instructed me.

I did as she said, and Trina followed suit. Then she mumbled a phrase, and my eyes widened. I could suddenly hear birdsong in my mind, and I was aware of a taste in my mouth, a tangy sort of fruit that I'd only had a few times. "Pineapple," I mumbled.

"Ah, yes, you're sensing our magic." Trina smiled. "It's an odd sensation when you're not used to it. You're free to cast now, Claudi."

Claudi began to sing, and I felt my magic surging through my arm once again, this time directed into her. When she opened her eyes, she was frowning.

"Is everything all right?" Starla asked.

"Aria will need significantly more care," Claudi told her. "What I'm seeing is that it would be best to have someone create a little box with heat magic in it, as well as a little water magic to keep it humid, and a sort of darkened glass shield to keep out bright light. Aria should live in that little box for the next month, at least. It will act like a second womb, to help her grow."

Starla's eyes widened. "Does this mean I can't hold her?"

"Of course not. But when you're not holding her, she should be in the box."

"Well, it's a good thing Marcus is on his way," Starla said. "If anyone can create a box like that, it's..." She trailed off as her eyes flickered to the door. "Ah, I see we have more visitors."

I looked over to the doorway. Kaden was back, her arm around a girl who was a few inches shorter than her, with loose, wavy blonde hair and wide brown eyes. She looked me over and gave me a smile. Standing next to them was a fellow who looked about

Kip's age. He was a couple inches taller than Kaden, with a mop of blond curls, a beard, and skin darkened from obvious exposure to the sun.

"Jasper!" Trina leapt up from the bed and crossed the floor in a few strides, flinging her arms around the man. "I didn't know if you were going to make it!"

Jasper laughed and returned her embrace. "Of course I made it." He pulled away from her. "It's good to see you, Trina. We miss you on the ship." He looked beyond Trina to Starla, then at me. "Who's this?"

"This is Isabelle. She's a lifebringer. Kip and Kaden brought her in so she could heal Aria."

His eyes went wide. "A lifebringer? Really?"

"Told you Kaden was bringing in a special delivery," the blonde girl said, punching Jasper in the arm. She walked over to me and extended a hand. "I'm Ruby. Kaden's girlfriend and Jasper's sister, just so you know how we're all connected."

"Isabelle." I shook her hand.

"We're thrilled to have you here, Isabelle." Ruby perched on the bed. "Is she fully healed then?"

"Her lungs are in better shape than they were," Starla answered. "But Claudi says she'll need some special care over the next while."

"I can imagine. She's so tiny." Jasper grinned and put a hand on Starla's shoulder, then reached down and stroked Aria's head.

"Do you want to hold her?" Starla asked.

"May I?"

"Of course you may, silly," Trina said. "Everyone else here has. Just be gentle."

Jasper took Aria from Starla and nestled her in the crook of his arm. "Hey there, little lady," he said, smiling at her.

"You're a natural." Starla gave him a grin. "Half the men I've met have no idea what to do when someone passes them a baby. A good number of the women as well."

"I remember the look on Kip's face when he held her yesterday. I think he was scared he was going to drop her." Trina laughed, then glanced at the door. "Speaking of Kip, look who's here."

I felt something in the room shift as I turned to the doorway. Kip and Saray were both back, accompanied by an older fellow, a tall man with a full head of hair that was completely white and bright blue eyes that looked almost mischievous. Saray's eyes widened as she looked the scene over, and Kip frowned. "What are *you* doing here?"

"Don't start, Kip." Trina's voice was firm. "Jasper's here because I invited him."

"I came to meet the newest citizen of Ankrossi." Jasper's jaw tightened as he handed Aria back to Starla. "Is that a problem?"

"Of course not," the older fellow said, raising an eyebrow at Kip before he walked into the room. He looked me over. "You must be Isabelle, the infamous healer. I'm Marcus."

"Saray's father," Ruby added.

I shook my head. "Is everyone in this town related?"

Marcus chuckled. "Not quite everyone." He held a slender glass tube out to Starla. "I hear you need one of these to feed the wee one. This is fresh from the glassblower, never been used."

"Thank you." Starla smiled. "We might need you for something else as well; Claudi here has an idea for a box that Aria can be kept in while she grows."

The older adults conversed amongst themselves about the box. Kaden, meanwhile, lay back on the bed with Ruby and began playing with her hair. Saray shook her head at her husband, seeming to disapprove of his behaviour, then crossed the room to where Jasper and Trina were talking to join their conversation. Kip frowned at them for a moment, then his eyes flickered to me. His expression changed, and he gave me a smile. "So what do you think of Ankrossi so far?"

"It's, uh, lovely," I told him. "Though I haven't seen much of it yet."

"You'll see more next time you come to train with Claudi," he promised me. "I s'pose we'd best be getting you back home soon." His gaze shifted. "Don't you think, Kaden?"

Kaden let out an exaggerated sigh. "Oh, come on, Kip, give me a few minutes. I just lay down."

"I want to speak to Starla about something before I leave," I told him. "Though I doubt I'll get a private moment with her."

Kip's mouth opened, and I suspected he was about to ask what I needed from Starla, but Marcus cut him off. "Kaden, Jasper, why don't you two come help me design this box," he said.

Kaden groaned in protest, but she stood up.

"And the rest of you, shoo," Trina put in. "We don't need everyone in here watching my mother express milk."

"Well, I s'pose we'll be waiting 'til Kaden's done helping Marcus," Kip said, eying me.

I was about to follow him out of the room when Claudi called my name. "You stay, Isabelle."

"Me?"

Claudi nodded. "I need to speak with you."

I hung back, watching the others as they filed out into the hall. Once they were gone, Claudi turned to me. "Isabelle, my dear, we're going to need you to stay here for at least a month."

My eyes went wide at her words. "A *month?* I thought I was just here for the evening."

"That was the plan, but Aria here needs you around."

"But I've done what I can for Aria. And Marcus is going to make her that little box so she can grow properly."

"Even with all of that, her health will be very fragile for the next little while. If we're going to ensure her survival, we'll need you nearby. I'll train you while you're here, of course."

"We can't force you to stay," Starla put in. "But it would certainly be appreciated."

"My parents will have no idea where I've gone! And my...my boyfriend too."

Trina frowned. "You could write a letter and have Persius deliver it to your house. He knows where you live."

"But what would I say? I can't tell my parents that I've gone off to a secret city in the Shrouded Woods to use healing magic to save a baby..." I paused, remembering my earlier train of thought. "Actually, Starla, I wanted to speak with you about something. I suppose this is as close to privacy as we're going to get."

Starla turned to face me, pulling her clothing back over her chest as she did. "What is it?"

"I can help you. In fact, I can help your entire community." I took a deep breath and met her eyes. "I know why they took Lachlann, and I have a rough idea of where he's being kept."

Her eyebrows lifted. "Is that so? What can you tell me?"

"If I tell you, I want something in return from you folks. When they took Lachlann, they also took a bunch of kids from Sylvenburgh Academy. They're being held somewhere on suspicion of magic use, even though there's no proof. My best friend Silva is among them."

"Ah. So you want help locating your friends in exchange for giving us information about Lachlann?"

I nodded.

Starla cocked her head for a moment. "Trina, take Isabelle to Marcus, and have her repeat to him everything she just said. He may need to call a council meeting. Kip will have to stand in for me."

My heart sank a little; I'd hoped that by going directly to Lachlann's family I could avoid bureaucracy. But I followed Trina out of the bedroom.

Kip and Saray were lying on the couch in the main room, Kip's arms wrapped around Saray's form. I blushed slightly when he met my eyes; it felt like I'd intruded on a private moment. "Are you ready to go, then?"

Trina shook her head. "Isabelle's stay is being extended," she said. "Where is Marcus?"

"He and the others are planning out the box in the kitchen."

Trina nodded and led me down a hallway. "Don't mind them," she whispered. "Kip and Saray are always all over each other. They're worse than Ruby and Kaden, and that's saying something." She shook her head, but I detected a note of jealousy in her voice.

In the kitchen, Marcus, Jasper and Kaden were hunched around a large sheet of paper laid out on the countertop. Ruby stood behind Kaden, a hand on her shoulder, watching them. She gave me a smile. "What is it?"

"Isabelle needs to speak with Marcus," Trina said.

Marcus lifted his head and looked at me. "In private?"

"That might be best," I replied.

"All right, I'll be back." He rose and gestured that I should follow him into a spare bedroom. Alone, he turned to me. "What can I do for you, Isabelle?"

I repeated to him what I'd said to Starla, and his eyes narrowed as I spoke. "So you wish to gamble with Lachlann's life in order to ensure your friends are found, is that it?" I didn't miss the accusatory note in his voice.

"From what I understand, his life isn't in danger," I assured. "As for my friends, well, I'm not certain what will happen to them. I imagine there's a risk they'll be made into krossemages."

Something in Marcus' expression softened, and he nodded. "I see why you're concerned. I'll have to call a council meeting to address this."

"Are you in charge, then?"

"In a manner of speaking, yes. Though perhaps not in the way you're used to." He gestured at the door. "We'll call a meeting in the morning. You'll have to stay the night."

"According to Claudi, I'll need to stay more than just the night," I told him.

Back in the kitchen, Marcus informed Ruby that there would be a meeting in the morning. "Isabelle will need a place to stay, and I don't want to ask Starla to host right now," he told her. "Do you have room at your place? I'm assuming Jasper is also staying with you?"

She nodded. "Isabelle can stay in Alisa and Shawnie's old room."

Kip and Saray appeared in the doorway. "So we're not taking you home tonight?" Kip asked me.

I shrugged. "Apparently not."

"I s'pose Saray and I will head home then." Saray nodded and gave us a wave, then they went to say goodbye to Starla.

I watched Marcus, Kaden and Jasper continue their work on designing the box, my mind only half present. *How am I going to explain this to my parents?* I didn't want to worry them, not after everything that had happened lately. *But Aria needs my help. And so does Silva.* I couldn't just abandon them.

"I think we've got it!" Marcus exclaimed finally, sitting back. "I'll start working on crafting this in the morning. You kids had best get to sleep, it's nearly midnight."

Ruby nodded. "I need to get home anyway. There's a storm coming in."

Chapter 7

I FOLLOWED KADEN, Ruby and Jasper out of the treehouse. We made our way over a bridge fashioned from branches and vines, then climbed down a series of roots and headed toward a second bridge. I gaped when I realized it was part of the massive tree-structure in the centre of the village. The bridge was mostly made from a sturdy reddish tree, but it was interspersed with the delicate white branches of the other tree whose flowers glowed. Jasper paused at the bridge's edge, leaning down and touching one of the blooms. "Good to see you again, Kirilee," he murmured.

"Kirilee?" I repeated.

He gave me a grin. "You haven't heard of our matriarch whose spirit lives in the Mothertree?"

"I, uh, think I heard the name once," I said. "She lives in the tree?"

He nodded. "Long story. We'll fill you in at some point. Come on." He gestured at Ruby and Kaden, who were far ahead of us now, scampering over the bridge with practiced ease.

I took a step onto the structure and inhaled sharply. This bridge didn't feel as sturdy as the first one I'd crossed; it swayed beneath my feet, branches shifting ever so slightly as I traversed them. Jasper seemed largely unconcerned as he made his way across the bridge ahead of me. I took another step, gingerly, then let out a cry as my toe caught between two branches. Jasper turned around. "You all right?"

I nodded and cringed. "This is terrifying. I don't understand how you all make it look so easy."

"Well, Ruby and Kaden are used to it, and I'm used to walking across yards and climbing shrouds in the midst of massive waves." He turned and started toward the bridge's edge. "Falling off this thing is harder than you'd expect, though, it's—" He tripped as he spoke and pitched forward.

"Jasper!" I shrieked as he disappeared off the side. Without thinking, I rushed toward the edge, my heart pounding.

Only to find Jasper grinning up at me from a white viletta branch that cradled him like a child. "See? Can't fall off."

I gaped. "You nearly scared me to death!"

He smirked, and I watched as the branch extended, lifting him up to allow him to clamber back onto the bridge. "Figured it was best that you see Kirilee's magic in action."

"Kirilee's...magic?" I repeated, trying to calm my breathing as I spoke.

"Remember how I said Kirilee's spirit lives in one of the trees? Well, she's learned to manipulate it to her own liking, and for the good of the village. The Mothertree won't *let* you fall." He gestured at the drop. "Want to try it yourself?"

"I'm...good." I replied, then took a deep breath, wanting to change the subject slightly. "So Kirilee's tree is called the Mothertree?"

"This entire structure is called that. Part of it is Kirilee's tree, part is the oadek that was grown to honour Marcus' late wife, and there's quite the assortment of other plants and vines that have added themselves to it." Jasper resumed walking as he spoke, and I followed him, less cautiously now, daring to look around as I did.

It was still hard to see much of the village, but the structure below me glowed, lighting up my feet and hinting at interesting things between the branches. I saw a few hammocks hanging among them, as well as what looked to be several private rooms closed off by woven vines. A set of swings dangled from a branch, while one of the larger limbs was made into a slide that seemed to travel from the bridge to the ground far below. Several night-creatures scurried from bough to bough. I then heard a rumble above me and looked up to see dark clouds gathering.

We cleared the other side of the bridge, and Ruby and Kaden disappeared into one of the treehouses. Jasper and I followed them inside. I could tell immediately that this particular house wasn't a massive, sprawling thing like Starla's place. The interior was mostly one room, lit by several colourful lamps whose lights looked to be powered by magic. Most of the furniture was part of the tree itself; a few thick branches flattened out into surfaces that formed an eating table and benches, as well as the bases for a couple of couches, which were covered with brightly coloured cushions. The kitchen counters were constructed similarly. A curtain of vines cordoned off one room, while a ladder made of rope strung between two branches led up to another. A hammock hung in a far corner of the main living area; underneath it were a few bags and what looked to be a fiddle case. Jasper walked over to the hammock and plopped down in it. "This is where I live when I'm here," he informed me.

I nodded, studying the furniture. "This is a really creative use of the tree. Or was the furniture grown magically?"

"Definitely the latter," Kaden said from the kitchen. "Most of the houses in this village were grown by Starla and a woman named Carmine. We have a few more plantspeakers now, but those two are the best trained." She held up a kettle. "Tea?"

"Please," I said. Kaden nodded and put her hand on the side of the kettle, mumbling an unfamiliar string of words. I watched as the water came to boil within seconds. She caught me staring and grinned.

"Show-off," Jasper said from his hammock.

"You're one to talk, pretty boy," she shot back as she scooped tea into a large glass teapot and poured the water in. "You have your ways of impressing the ladies, and I have mine."

"Kaden, stop flirting with the newcomers," Ruby reprimanded from the room beyond the vine curtain.

"What are you doing in there?" I called out.

"Trying to calm down the storm that's coming in," she replied. "We need the rain, but not the lightning."

"She'll be a while," Kaden said. "I'll be up another hour or so waiting for her. You can go to bed if you're tired, though." She jerked her head in the direction of the rope ladder as she brought two mugs into the main room, one for me and one for Jasper. Then she headed into what I assumed was her and Ruby's bedroom with a third mug.

I glanced at Jasper. "I hope I'm not taking away your room."

He shook his head. "On the ship, I sleep in a hammock like this in a room with a dozen other fellows. Sleeping in a normal bed feels a little odd now."

I nodded. "So you live on a ship but come back and visit occasionally? How'd you get here? I assume we're not near any ports."

"Ruby and I have teleportation stones," he said, seeming to expect me to know what those were. "Though she's more likely to visit me than I am to come here."

"I gathered that. Kip seemed a little surprised to see you."

Kaden snickered as she joined us once more and settled on the couch with her tea. "That's one way of putting it."

"What's his problem with you?" I asked Jasper.

"That, my dear, is a very long and complex story. Though the short version is that Ruby's and my father is a high-ranking Breoch Guard. We were raised believing magic was evil, and my older brother and I were expected to join the Guard right out of school. In my Breoch Guard days, I had an encounter with Kip, as well as a few of the others you've met. I may have shot him."

"Oh." I frowned. "I, uh, assume you don't believe those things anymore?"

"If I did, I'm fairly certain I wouldn't be allowed in Ankrossi."

"That must have been hard for Ruby, growing up in a home like that."

Jasper nodded solemnly.

"So you shot Kip, and then what? I assume a lifebringer healed him?"

"Something like that. I could tell you the story, but we'd be up fairly late."

"Another time then." I took a sip of the tea, noting its fruity taste. "I'm sleeping upstairs?"

"Yes," said Kaden. "It's a cozy little room, I hope you like it. Probably nothing like what you're used to, though, judging from your house."

"You're probably right." I sighed as my thoughts returned to my parents, who would likely be frantic with worry once they discovered me missing in the morning. "I wish I could go back and tell my mother that I'm safe."

Kaden frowned. "I could probably arrange for that tomorrow, if you really want."

"How? Would you fly me back?"

She shook her head. "I need to attend the council meeting in the morning, and Ruby and I have plans in the afternoon. But I could see if Ambrose would take you along with Chester."

"Who's Chester?"

"Friend of ours. He's the best vanisher in all of Ankrossi. He can make himself, you, Ambrose, and Spark all invisible for the entirety of the journey and back. He may need to borrow a little magic from you and Ambrose, but it's not hard. The person we could really use for the endeavour is Willem, but he's in Dundere right now. He's a master teleporter, among many other things." She frowned. "We'll figure that out tomorrow. You should head to bed, you look exhausted. I can lend you some nightclothes if you need them."

"Please," I said.

Kaden ducked into the bedroom and returned a moment later with a folded-up garment. "We'll get you some clothes for the Woods at the market tomorrow."

I thanked her, bid her and Jasper goodnight, and climbed the rope ladder. The room at the top was small and cozy, lit by more of the colourful lanterns. The bedframe was part of the tree, of course, but the quilt on top was soft, and the bed itself decently made, I decided as I crawled into it. The thick weave of branches and vines that made up the walls was enough to keep out most of the rain, but I could hear it drumming against the trees in a peaceful, steady rhythm. I let the sound lull me to sleep, trying not to think too hard about what tomorrow would bring.

***

The next morning, I awoke to birdsong and sunshine peeking through the cracks in the treehouse. I blinked, unsure for a moment where I was, then sat up suddenly as I recalled all that had happened the night before. I fought a pang of guilt as I rose and dressed, imagining just how terrified my parents would be when they went to my room and discovered it empty.

Downstairs, I found the rest of the house awake, eating a breakfast of fruit and what looked like scones. "Morning," Ruby greeted me, patting the bench next to her. "Dig in. We've got a council meeting to attend."

Right. I sat down beside her, then picked up a scone and spread some preserves onto it. "Mmm!" I exclaimed after taking a bite. "These are good!"

"Ankrossi food is infinitely better than ship food," said Jasper, his mouth half full of scone.

"What will you do while we're at the meeting?" I asked him. "I'm assuming you're not on the council if you don't live here permanently."

"I'm not," he replied. "I figure I'll go check on Starla and Aria, and possibly bother her other daughter while I'm over there." He grinned, then finished off his food, taking his plate over to the sink. "In fact, I think I'll do that right now."

"It's a little early for surprise visits," remarked Kaden.

Jasper snorted. "Have you ever met a baby? They have very little respect for their mother's desire to sleep in. Starla's likely been up for hours. And Trina's rather adorable when she's barely awake." He smirked, but I couldn't help noticing a certain fondness in his expression. He set his plate in the drying rack, retrieved his fiddle case from the hammock, then strode out the door whistling.

I stared after him for a moment. "Do they fancy each other?" I asked, turning back to Ruby and Kaden. "Jasper and Trina, that is."

Both of them rolled their eyes. "Yes," Kaden said, "but neither of them is doing anything about it."

"Why not?"

"Well, Trina's clearly had a crush on him since she got back from the ship," Ruby said. "Though I'm fairly certain she's had something resembling feelings for him since she first properly saw him four years ago. But there's an age gap...wouldn't have been appropriate back then. It's not so much of an issue now, but I think she assumes he wouldn't be interested in her because of it."

"How old are they?"

"Jasper's twenty-seven, and Trina's twenty-one, a year older than me," Ruby said.

I nodded. "And why doesn't he pursue her?"

"Because Jasper has it in his head that Trina deserves someone better than him. There's a long, complex history between him and her family."

I frowned. "Do *you* think Trina deserves better than him?"

"I think they could make each other happy, regardless of the past," Ruby replied. "But it's not my call to make. Hopefully, one day one of them will do something about their situation." She sighed. "Let's clean this up and head out. Don't want to keep the council waiting."

***

Ankrossi in the daylight was fascinating, I decided as I followed Ruby and Kaden across the tree-bridge once more. The village was flanked by the river on one side, its centre dominated by a grassy meadow peppered with wildflowers. The tents in the middle of the meadow, surrounding the perimeter of the Mothertree, looked like the only man-made structures in the village. The houses and bridges that surrounded the meadow were so much a part of the forest themselves that a casual onlooker might have missed them. The river was dammed in one spot to direct a stream toward a patch of plant life that looked especially verdant. "What's that?" I asked, pointing.

"That's where most of our crops are grown," Ruby said.

I frowned. "Doesn't look like any farm I've seen."

"It's not a farm, it's a food forest. We grow the crops in a way that benefits them, the ground, and us. Apparently, the plants like it better that way, or so Starla says."

"We tried to have traditional farmers' fields at first," Kaden put in. "But it didn't work well in this soil, and some of the Woods-folk from other parts told us that this is a better way to grow food here."

"Do you farm animals?"

"We do now, much to Trina's disdain," Ruby said. "We let them wander a fair bit, though. We don't keep them cooped up." She pointed at a cow contentedly grazing in the central meadow. "Case in point."

I nodded. "What about those tents down there?"

"Mainly shops and services. Doctors, blacksmiths, tailors, and such. You'll see a lot more of that tonight, when the market opens up." Kaden paused and pointed at the slide that I'd noticed last night. "This is the quickest way down to the council chamber. Wanna go for a ride?"

I eyed the slide, then my skirt. "I...suppose so."

"Good. See you at the bottom." She grinned, plopped down on the slide, and promptly disappeared.

"It's not as terrifying as it looks," Ruby assured me before taking off after her girlfriend, leaving me staring dubiously at the decline.

I settled gingerly on the smooth wooden surface, then glanced down at the slide's twisting path and snorted. *I rode a dragon yesterday, and I'm scared of this?* With that thought, I pushed myself off.

The ride down was fast and incredibly scenic. I passed through thick canopies of leaves, spirals of white branches, and large bunches of pink and purple flowers. When I reached the bottom, Ruby and Kaden were waiting for me.

Ruby offered me a hand up, and I gazed around. The space we were in wasn't exactly a room, but more of an entrance into whatever the inside of the Mothertree held. Behind us, one viletta root poked out of the ground and looped above our heads, forming a sort of archway that led deeper into the structure. "Where to now?" I asked.

"Well, we're going to head to the council chamber to discuss what you've brought to us," Ruby said. "Marcus will come fetch you when we're ready. In the meantime, take a seat." She gestured at a hammock slung off another looping viletta root. "I believe Alexander will be along soon; he has someone with him who will keep you company."

She and Kaden disappeared into the Mothertree before I could ask who Alexander was, and I sighed, sitting gingerly on the hammock. I had a better view of the meadow from this vantage point, and I watched as the citizens of Ankrossi started their day. The savoury aroma of roasting meat soon wafted from a tent, and the definitive noise of a blacksmith's hammer came from somewhere in the distance. Two young women walked by carrying a tray of baked goods, and an older woman called out to them, then used her hand to sign something. They both nodded and laughed. I frowned when I realized that the signing woman was missing a hand. *Is she a krossemage?*

Nearby, several teens congregated, chattering loudly. I stared at them, taking in their attire. Teens here wore their hair in all sorts of ways, some in more traditional styles, others in odd, angular cuts or extravagant braids or dramatic updos. A few of them had bright colours in their hair, and nearly all wore equally vibrant clothing. The dresses were simple, most not falling past the knee, and several girls sported bare shoulders or even trousers. A short, slightly stocky girl shot a curious look in my direction. She had her hair—which was brown but streaked with ribbons of bright blue—in two braids, and she wore an extravagantly patterned coat. She said something to the person beside her, and the two of them sauntered over. "You must be Isabelle."

I stared up at the girl. "How did you know that?"

"Everyone's heard there's a healer in town who fixed Aria up. You're famous, you know." She grinned and extended a hand. "I'm Sophie. And this is my friend Chester."

I shook her hand, then studied Chester. His black hair was styled into sweeping waves, and he wore a simple shirt and trousers over his thin frame. He looked back at me with a pair of large, curious eyes. "Pleasure to meet you," he said. Something about him registered as unusual, but I had trouble pinpointing exactly what it was.

I was about to respond when a chirping noise drew my gaze downward. "Mischief!" Sophie squealed. She scooped up what I now saw was a large red fox. "What are you doing here?"

"Coming to a council meeting, obviously," came a voice from behind her. I looked up to see a tall, striking man with long, curly black hair and a waxed mustache and goatee. He wore a coat similar to Sophie's. "How's my young protege?" he asked, clapping her on the shoulder.

"Busy as ever," replied Sophie, wrinkling her nose. "Willem left us all loads of homework before he headed to Dundere."

The man's eyes crinkled. "Sounds about right."

"Where's Ember?" asked Chester.

"Someone had to watch the shop. They'll be at the market tonight, though." The man stepped forward and bowed to me. "You must be the one we're having this meeting about. I'm Alexander. And I see you've met my fox, Mischief. Don't worry, she won't hurt you."

"I'm Isabelle," I told him, dipping my head.

He nodded. "Well, I'll leave Mischief with you. Sophie, Chester, you'd better get to school. Don't want to keep Shawnie waiting."

"Shawnie's in the meeting," Chester said. "He told us to practice magic in the meadow 'til it's done."

"Right. Well, then, you'd best get to it. Isabelle, I'm sure I'll see you soon enough."

Alexander disappeared into the Mothertree, and Sophie and Chester gave Mischief a few more pets before returning to their friends. I carefully arranged myself in the hammock, then lay back and gasped when Mischief hopped up on me. "Hey, careful there," I reprimanded, "you're going to ruin my dress."

Mischief made another chirping noise and sniffed at my face. I ran a tentative hand through her fur. I was used to interacting with some animals—horses, of course, and occasionally the barn cats at home or dogs belonging to schoolmates—but I'd never been near a fox before. Satisfied with her observation of me, Mischief curled into a ball on my chest and promptly fell asleep. I stroked her as I turned to watch the teens practice their magic.

I must have drifted off, because next thing I knew, Marcus was shaking my shoulder. "Get up, sleepyhead. It's time for you to join us." I blinked up at him for a few groggy seconds, then sat up slowly. Mischief hopped off me as I rose, and I followed Marcus through the viletta archway into whatever lay beyond.

Chapter 8

WHEN WE REACHED the main room—if you could call it that—my eyes widened. The massive chamber was fashioned from the twisting limbs of the two trees. Viletta blossoms glowed overhead, giving the area an ethereal feel. Seated on the benches—which were formed from living tree roots—were what must have been the members of the Ankrossi council, including Kip, Saray, Ruby, Kaden, Ambrose and Daisy. Sitting next to Kaden was another couple—a big fellow with bouncy black curls and skin similar in colour to Trina's, and a girl whose brown hair fell in soft waves around her face, who was very obviously pregnant. They didn't look any older than the others.

Next to the pregnant girl was a fellow who was her spitting image, only younger, and a boy with white-blond hair and porcelain skin. Alexander was present as well, of course, and I was surprised to see Mr. Jeffries sitting next to him.

Marcus introduced the council members to me; the younger couple who were expecting were Shawnie and Alisa, the fellow next to Alisa was her younger brother Jessen, and the blond boy was Jessen's boyfriend Kylar. "Your council is young," I said to Marcus.

He grinned. "A lot of the folks here are apprentices. Our Minister of Nature just had a baby, our Minister of Magic is currently in Dundere, and our Minister of Security—well, we're hoping you can tell us more about what's happened to him."

I lifted my chin. "So you've agreed to help find the students, then?"

Mr. Jeffries let out a laugh. "My dear, you came into this thinking that finding those children was not already one of our top priorities. Of course we're looking for them. We've already sent scouts to the Sylvenburgh Breoch Guard garrison, and we plan to send another group to Kirstein tomorrow." He raised an eyebrow. "That said, you are more than welcome to aid us in our search. Now, what can you tell us about Lachlann?"

Heat rose in my cheeks. *Of course they're looking for the children already.* "Lachlann is being kept somewhere in the palace, though I'm not sure exactly where," I told him. "The court has a use for him."

"And how do you know this?" Saray asked.

"My parents work in the palace. I was there when he was brought before the king."

I explained to the council how Kairus had questioned Lachlann about his anti-magic, and how Pieter had used magic to test its validity. Several of them began to mutter amongst themselves when I mentioned that Kairus employed a court mage. "Simon, one of the king's relatives, wants to utilize Lachlann's anti-magic somehow, and he's talked

Pieter into working with him," I said. "I don't know for what exactly, but Simon said that Lachlann probably won't like it."

"So it's just a matter of sneaking into the palace and locating him, then," Kip concluded.

I frowned. "Technically, though sneaking in isn't as easy as you'd think. The palace is very well guarded."

"It's easy enough if you're a vanisher," Mr. Jeffries said.

"A vanisher who knows how to climb," put in Kip. "Likely, being able to both vanish and teleport would be the best way in."

"So we set Tomlin up with a potion of teleportation," Alexander said. "Or we give a teleporter a potion of vanishing. I can make up a batch of either of those."

"Why not just teleport Isabelle in?" Kaden suggested and glanced at Alexander. "Do you, uh, think that's a good idea? She's the only one here who knows the palace."

Alexander nodded. "It would be fine, yes."

"I wouldn't have to teleport. The palace guard knows me; I could just walk in easily enough," I said. "But I've been told I need to stay here in Ankrossi for the next little while, to keep an eye on Aria."

Marcus nodded. "We'd need more time to come up with a plan for this anyway. But at least we have a head start on locating the children." He sighed. "I rather wish I knew where they're sending young krossemages nowadays, but I suppose the fact that we don't know is no one's fault but our own."

"If you want someone to pose as a Breoch Guard to try and find out that information, you could talk to Jasper," Ruby suggested.

Kip snorted. "Please don't bring Jasper into these operations."

"And why not? He managed to get me to you folks by going to Tomlin and acting as a Breoch Guard."

"That's true, but the moment someone recognized him, they'd likely bring your father or oldest brother into it," Saray pointed out. "And there's bound to be folks in both the Kirstein and Sylvenburgh contingents of the Guard who would know Jasper by sight."

"I could likely sneak into one of their bases," Mr. Jeffries volunteered. "The palace might be hard for a vanisher to infiltrate, but I'm fairly certain I can handle a Guard station."

My eyes widened. *Mr. Jeffries is a vanisher?*

"Sounds like a good place to start." Marcus looked me over. "Does this satisfy your request, Isabelle?"

"As much as it can, I suppose."

"And you're willing to train with Claudi while also keeping an eye on Aria?"

I nodded. "I'm willing, but I do want to let my parents know I'm safe. I understand they can't know about this place, but I don't want them worrying about me needlessly. Ruby and Kaden suggested that Ambrose could fly me home this afternoon."

Marcus nodded. "As a parent, I can appreciate that gesture. Though I imagine they'll worry about you regardless."

"Do you think it's safe for her to go back home?" Kip's brow furrowed. "What if her parents try to force her to stay? Or talk her into it, or make her feel guilty for leaving?"

He glanced at me. "No offense, but we don't know your parents, and I'm not sure how persuasive they are."

"The trick is to send someone more persuasive along, then," Alexander said. "Sophie can accompany them."

"What can she do?" I asked.

He grinned. "You'll see."

"Is that everything?" Shawnie piped up. "I have students outside waiting for me—they may have destroyed the meadow by now with their magic antics."

"I highly doubt that," said Marcus. "But, yes, we can adjourn."

As people began to file out, Ambrose approached me. "Meet me in the meadow after lunch. I'll run ahead and let Sophie and Chester know they'll be needed."

He disappeared into the retreating council members, and I was left staring after him, wondering exactly what I'd gotten myself into.

***

A little while later, I sat atop Spark again, looking out over the Shrouded Woods. The trees spread out below me in every direction, their green only interrupted by the sliver-blue veins of the river and a line of mountains that rose up to the west. The sky was vibrant today, dotted with a few puffy clouds. Behind me, Sophie and Chester chattered eagerly about the happenings at their school. Their favourite topic of discussion was drama between two students who'd dated and broken up the year before, and who each had new partners. "I need Trina to chat with them," Sophie concluded. "She deals with having Ambrose around just fine."

"Trina and Ambrose dated?" I asked.

Sophie nodded. "They were together for a good year shortly after we moved to Ankrossi. We all thought they were going to get married, but then they broke up, and Trina ran off to sail on the Lady Liara for a year. Partway through, she came back with Daisy and was actually the one who introduced her to Ambrose." She shook her head then and laughed. "This is why I've got no desire to have a relationship."

"Oh! I thought you two were..." I eyed her and Chester and blushed.

"We get that a lot." Chester grinned. "Sophie and I are best friends. But she doesn't have any desire to get married or do any of the things that come with it."

"Kissing is gross," Sophie put in. "Why would I want to stick my face right on someone else's?"

My mind went back to the one kiss Oliver and I shared all those years back. "It is pretty weird," I admitted. "Though I've only been kissed once, and I was eight. I would probably like it more now."

"Wait, don't you have a boyfriend?" Chester asked. "You've never kissed him?"

"He was the one I kissed, so yes. But nothing since then. His parents are...strict."

"Ah." Sophie exchanged a glance with Chester. "We know about those."

"Your parents are strict?"

"Well, my mother died when I was a baby, but my dad is...anxious. When I was a kid, he was very overprotective. It's a bit of a story."

The forest below us was thinning out, giving way to a meadow. I could see farmers' fields in the distance. "Time to go invisible," Chester said. "You may want to hold on to the saddle; this can get strange."

I nodded and gripped the handhold in front of me. I heard Chester mumbling a few words, and my mouth fell open as Spark and all her riders dissolved. I looked down at where my hands and legs should have been, only to find nothing between me and the ground. *Where is my body?!*

I flailed, my breath coming in gasps and my heart beginning to hammer in my chest. An involuntary, panicked screech escaped my lips, and Spark flinched. Immediately, a warm, reassuring hand landed on my arm. "Easy," Chester said. "You're safe." His hand trailed down my arm and slipped into mine. I noticed that it wasn't much bigger than my own, which was odd. Oliver was only an inch taller than me, a couple inches shorter than Chester, but his hands were considerably bigger than mine.

Kirstein came into view quicker than I expected, and I peered down at the rooftops, trying to place my home amongst them. "You'll need to give me directions, Isabelle," Ambrose's disembodied voice said.

I frowned. "Fly toward the castle. I can probably figure it out from there."

Soon, I was able to direct Ambrose toward the rooftop of my home. "We'll land in the backyard," he told me, "and you and Sophie can go inside to talk to your mother."

"The invisibility spell will lift once you get far enough away from Spark," Chester added. We were descending now, and I fought to control my panic as the ground got closer and closer.

Our landing was softer than I expected. Sophie and I disembarked, and I cast a glance backward as we began our walk to the house. Spark's presence was still obvious enough to me—I could hear her raspy breathing, and her smell, while not unpleasant, was definitely still that of an animal. But the only visual indicator of her presence was four odd divots in the grass where her feet sat. "Amazing," I whispered.

Sophie chuckled. "It is, isn't it? Come on, let's find your mother."

***

A few minutes later, Sophie and I were seated in the parlour, Sophie's eyes roaming over the room's fine furniture and soaring ceilings. We'd run into Magda, the cook, as soon as we'd come in, and she began to scold me, but Sophie convinced her with surprising ease to seat us and fetch Mother. I turned to Sophie, about to ask how she'd managed such a feat, when I heard footsteps approaching. I sat up straight and watched the door.

Sure enough, Mother appeared. Her eyes went round, and she practically ran toward me. Sophie and I stood just in time for Mother to crush me in an embrace. "Where *were* you?" she demanded, pulling back from me. "We were so worried!"

"Your daughter was in good hands, ma'am," Sophie said.

Mother turned to her. "Who are you?"

"My name's Sophie. I'm a friend of Isabelle's." She executed a perfect curtsy, then met Mother's eyes. "Some friends of mine called for her last night; we had a need for Isabelle's talents. We meant to have her back before sunrise, but things got complicated."

She twirled her braid as she spoke, and my eyes narrowed. Something about the way her hands moved seemed familiar to me, though I couldn't place where I'd seen it before.

"What do you mean, Isabelle's tal—" Mother's eyes widened. "Wait, are you talking about her *healing magic?*" She whispered the last two words.

My mouth fell open. "You...*know?*"

Mother turned to me, and I saw that her eyes were slightly glazed. "When you have a child who never gets ill, and who recovered from a badly sprained ankle in less than a day, you quickly realize something is afoot. Your father and I have likely known longer than you have, my dear." She frowned. "How long *have* you known?"

My heart pounded in my ears; there was no denying things now. "Since I was twelve," I squeaked.

"Same age I was when I discovered my talents." She smiled wryly at my astonishment. "Oh, come now. You know these things are inherited, don't you?" She turned back to Sophie before I could respond to her confession. "Now, what do you need my daughter's gift for?

"There was a baby in our community who was born premature and would likely die without intervention," Sophie explained. "Your daughter saved her life. Unfortunately, though, we'll need Isabelle to stay with us for a little longer to ensure the child lives." Sophie's fingers were working her braid again. "She'll be safe with us. We'll return her as soon as the child is healthy enough to live on her own."

Mother's head tilted. "What should I tell her father? Let alone Oliver, or the king for that matter?"

Sophie frowned. "Why do you need to bring the king into this?"

"My parents work in the palace, remember?" I cut in, not wanting Mother to explain this part for me.

"Right. What do you think she should tell them, Isabelle?"

"Tell Father that I ran off to try and find help locating Silva, that I've found some folks who are willing to aid me, and that I'm safe," I decided. "As for the others, they don't need to know that I visited." I winced at my own words, worrying about how my absence might affect Oliver, but I figured it was better not to bring the royal family into this.

"That's probably for the best," Sophie assured her.

"I...suppose so." Mother's eyes took on the glazed look once more. "You'll come back soon?"

"As soon as I can," I assured, trying to keep the shock from my voice. *How is my mother agreeing to this?*

"You take care of yourself, dear. I'll miss you."

I nodded and hugged her again, holding her tight against myself. "I'll be fine. I'll see you soon."

Mother embraced me for a few long moments, then pulled back and looked me over. "Well, I suppose you'd better get back to the child you're tending to. Be safe, Isabelle. You too, Sophie."

"We will," Sophie said. I gave Mother's hand one last squeeze, then followed Sophie to the back of the house.

***

Within minutes, we were airborne again, and I gawked at the spot where I knew Sophie was sitting. "How did you *do* that?"

"Do what?" Her disembodied voice was smug.

"Get my mother to agree to everything, obviously. She didn't even ask where we were going."

"That's my magical ability." Sophie laughed. "I suppose you've never heard of charmers?"

"They can use magic to persuade people," Chester put in. "Sophie doesn't use her magic quite that blatantly very often, but it's useful from time to time."

I frowned. "How do I know you aren't going to charm me into doing things in the future? Did you charm me to stay and take care of Aria? You could be charming me right now."

Sophie snorted. "First of all, it's hard to charm someone if they can't see you. Second, you didn't meet me until after you'd agreed to care for Aria. And third, now that you know I'm a charmer, my gift will have less power over you. I can still try to charm you, but you might pick up on it."

"Ah. Well, your ability certainly worked on Mother." I shook my head. "I can't believe she's known about my gifts all this time."

"She made a good point. If your kid never gets sick, you're likely to suspect something's a little different about them."

"I wonder why she never brought it up?"

"Likely because she hoped you wouldn't figure it out yourself," Chester suggested.

"Perhaps."

Silence reigned for a few moments after. I was still processing the afternoon's events, and the others seemed preoccupied as well. I only spoke again once we'd cleared the city gates and were flying back over the farmers' fields. "So now what? Back to Ankrossi?"

"That's right." Sophie's voice took on an eager edge then. "It's market night, and I'm excited to show you everything our little village has to offer."

Chapter 9

A FEW HOURS later, the central field of Ankrossi was crammed with vendors selling their wares in tents. Or rather, *not* selling them, I learned.

"We began working off the barter system," Sophie explained as she led me through the market. "But we realized it didn't really work with a community this big. Different folks have different needs, and sometimes they don't match what is being bartered. If I have a large family and I need food, but the only person who shows up to my stall to barter makes fancy clocks, no one gets fed. So we began using what we like to call Gareth's principle."

"Who's Gareth?"

"A sea captain who a lot of us are connected to. He's the one Jasper sails with. Gareth's way of running his ship is that anyone can sail for free so long as they're willing to do their share of the work. Now we run the community like that. Everyone has a job, and those with magic have further responsibilities. But everyone's needs are taken care of."

"Don't some folks take more than they need?"

"We've had that happen, but it's not as common as you might think. We have ways of preventing it. Here's my stall." Sophie paused in front of one of the more colourful tents. A large sign hung in front of it proclaiming it the Emporium of Wonder. Inside, the air was thick with incense, and a large assortment of colourful clothing was displayed on stands and tables. I saw coats that were similar to the one I'd noticed Saray wearing, gaudy dresses without sleeves, large chunky necklaces and bright, silky scarves. At the rear of the tent was a shelf of glass bottles with stoppers, each one labelled, as well as a display of pendants that glistened with a light that seemed otherworldly. Between those displays sat Alexander, along with a person with hair that was sculpted into flames and coloured different shades of red, orange, and yellow. They—I couldn't immediately tell if they were male or female—wore a pair of breeches and one of the fancy embroidered coats, this one emblazoned with the image of a fire-breathing dragon. "This is Ember; they're Alexander's spouse," Sophie told me. "Ember, this is Isabelle."

"The lifebringer, right?" Ember gave me a smile. "I've heard about you. It's a pleasure to meet you."

I returned Ember's greeting, noting the way Sophie referred to them. "This is a lovely shop," I said. "What do you sell?"

"Plenty of things. Clothing, jewelry, knickknacks of all sorts, and—our specialty—magical potions and charms." Ember gestured at the bottles and pendants. "Would you like to try on some of our clothing? You'd find these Woods easier to navigate in something lighter than that." They eyed my ensemble. "It's beautiful, but not very practical."

I looked over the dresses and frowned. "Those are all very...extravagant."

"Ahhh. Not accustomed to the fashions of the Shrouded Woods, I see. Perhaps you'd be best to visit Tasia's tent, then. Her clothes are made for the Woods but are a little more subtle. She's three tents over to the right, not hard to find."

"If you don't like our clothing, perhaps I can interest you in one of these." Alexander plucked a potion off a shelf and placed it in my hands. "Fairy magic. It'll allow you to use your gift in a situation where anti-magic is present."

I frowned. "Why do I need this?"

"I don't know yet. But it called to me, so I knew to give it to you." Alexander turned. "Sophie, my dear, would you mind watching the shop while Ember and I go get our groceries?"

Sophie nodded, and Ember smiled at me. "Tasia's shop is on our way to the food stalls. Come along."

***

Half an hour later, I was dressed in new clothes and had three more outfits in a bag stashed in Alexander and Ember's stall. I couldn't help but feel self-conscious in my new dress. It was made from a soft, muted green fabric and fell to only just below my knees. The sturdy boots and stockings that Tasia had picked out for me covered my calves, but I was aware that everyone could see the shape of my legs, something that was frowned upon in most Breochi cities. Even more scandalous was the dress' sleeves—or lack thereof. This dress left my shoulders bare, and I was extremely aware of the wind tickling my skin.

There were plenty of other folks here wearing far less than me—some women wore dresses that were backless or had plunging necklines, and a few men wore nothing on top but open animal-skin vests—but I couldn't help feeling like everyone was looking at me. My other two dresses were no less scandalous—one was cut very much like the first but was deep brown and made of a warmer material, and the third was bright blue with sleeves down to the elbows and a scooped neckline that made me more than a little nervous. Ember insisted that I also take a pair of breeches, saying they might be necessary for life here in the Woods. I wore them long enough to determine they fit me, then took them immediately off. The pale pink blouse I chose to go with them was nice enough, but I doubted I'd wear it much.

Alexander also armed me with the fairy magic potion, a wooden whistle that could be used to call for Spark if she was in the area, and a small knife that he told me was enchanted. Throw the knife at an attacker, he said, and it would always strike exactly where I wanted it to.

Now I wandered the market alone, taking in the sights. There were all sorts of stalls here, many providing the same sorts of things that one would find in a normal market: fruits, eggs, and bread, seeds and plants for gardening, and coats, breeches, and boots of all kinds. But there were also stalls that offered vibrant art and handmade jewelry and glass pieces blown using magical fire.

I found Trina in a stall normally manned by her mother which contained wooden furniture crafted from branches that Starla had grown into particular shapes; several of the chairs had wooden backs formed into flowers and butterflies and hearts. Kip occupied a rather large stall that sold smoked meat he'd hunted and a large variety of teas, most of which helped with different ailments. I smirked when I saw this. "Now that I'm here, you might have trouble selling those. I'm likely to put you out of business."

Kip snorted. "You forget that we don't use money in these exchanges, so I'm not worried about that. Also, you might be able to cure colds and headaches, but sleeping tea will still be popular. And I doubt you can do much to compete with my most popular tea." He held up a small tin. "This one prevents pregnancy."

My eyes widened. "A tea can do that?"

"With a particular combination of mushrooms and herbs, absolutely."

I frowned. "So folks just walk in here and ask for it? Isn't that awkward?"

"It usually is for new couples, or younger folk who don't want their parents to know that they've paid me a visit. But I never tell who my clients are."

"And some of us simply have no need for the tea." I turned at the familiar voice to see Kaden grinning at me. She eyed Kip. "Showing off your wares, I see?"

"Isabelle here claimed she could put me out of business. I had to tell her otherwise."

"Ah." Kaden inspected Kip's selection of smoked meat, then began putting a few items into her basket.

"You and Ruby are running low already?" he asked.

"Not yet. But we have two more mouths to feed now, so I figured I'd best stock up on groceries."

"Right." Kip shifted, clearly ill at ease. "How long is he staying this time?"

"Who, Jasper?" She shrugged. "He told me this afternoon that he's not needed here like he thought he was, but that the Lady Liara is in port in Kirstein getting some repairs, so he can stay a couple more weeks."

Kip frowned. "Why would he be *needed* here?"

"Not my business. Talk to him yourself if you have such an issue with it." I didn't miss the edge to her voice, but then she turned to me and smiled, her uneasiness vanishing. "Come with me?"

I nodded and bid Kip farewell, then trailed after Kaden, following her around for an hour or so while she purchased various food staples. Once we were finished, we stopped at a bakery stall and sampled buttery, flaky pastries crammed with a fruit I didn't recognize.

Next to the bakery stall was the tavern, a permanent fixture which boasted large windows, a cheery fireplace, and live music. I did a double take when I realized that the fellow playing the fiddle was Jasper. I also noticed several folks who communicated with hand signals as we walked; a closer look showed them to be what I assumed were krossemages. "Do they need to be healed?" I asked Kaden.

She shook her head. "There were a good number of folks from Yarel Island who chose not to get healed. Don't bother asking them; if they want healing, they'll come to you."

"But how do they communicate with the rest of you?"

She shrugged. "Sign is practically a second language here. Nearly everyone knows it. If you want to speak to them, you'll likely need to go through one of us."

After some time, a good number of the vendors began to close down, and Kaden and I returned to Alexander and Ember's stall, where Chester was deep in conversation with Sophie. We retrieved my bag of clothing and made our way onto the overhead bridge. I'd been quiet for most of the night, taking it all in, but now I turned to Kaden. "I have so many questions."

"Such as?"

"Well, first of all, how did this place come to be? I knew there were folks living in the Woods, but I never imagined a whole village of them. And how exactly is the village run? You folks all just barter? And why does Kip dislike Jasper so much? I want to hear that story." I frowned. "Also, why are clothes so different from home, and why do some women wear men's clothes? There are some folks who...I can't quite tell if they are male or female."

"You're thinking of Ember?" Kaden guessed.

"Ember and Chester. I know Chester says he's a boy, but he looks sort of like a girl to me."

Kaden nodded knowingly. "Well, your questions about how this place is governed would be best directed to Ruby; she's training to be Marcus' successor. As for how Ankrossi came to be and the story about Jasper and Kip, you'll want to talk to Ruby, Jasper, Trina, and possibly Saray. But I can explain folks like Ember and Chester."

I nodded. "I don't think I've met anyone like them before."

"You probably have, but they were just hiding it," replied Kaden. "It's not as uncommon as you might think for folks to not feel at home in their own skin. I spent a lot of my childhood wanting to be a boy."

"Do you still want that?"

Kaden shrugged. "It's not that I want a body like a boy's. It's that I want to do the things that boys got to do in the world we grew up in. Climb trees, work outside, learn the sword." She grinned. "My parents tried to force me into pretty dresses and good manners, and it didn't work so well. I did learn some good things from those years—I learned to dance, which I'm happy about, and to play piano, which I'm grateful for because it's how I met Ruby. But I'm happier now that I don't have to act like a proper young lady.

"Ember and Chester both had experiences that were a bit more intense than mine, and both of them are quite open about their stories. I don't think they'll mind me telling you." She walked over to the edge of the bridge and sat down, her legs dangling off the side. Then she patted the space next to her, and I perched there, still a bit nervous about being this high up.

"Ember grew up in the far reaches of the Cherinese empire," Kaden began. "They grew up in a culture where it was accepted that some folks are not exactly male or female, or have the characteristics of both, depending on how you look at it. Those people were called *arkaves*, in Ember's first language, and it was rather like a third gender. Ember began to see themself as one of these folks pretty early on." Kaden smiled, a wistful look coming to her eyes. "In that culture, children undergo a ceremony when they are fifteen, and after that ceremony they are considered an adult man, woman, or arkave. Arkaves, at that point, get to choose a new name for themselves, and begin to refer to themselves as 'they.' They also have particular duties in the community. Ember was never looked upon poorly while they lived at home. It was only once they went to sea that they encountered prejudice."

"Why did they leave home, then?"

"Why do any of us leave home? They wanted to explore, to see the world. The folks on the Lady Liara were always quite accepting, but sometimes in ports Ember would get odd looks and unkind remarks."

"I heard they have a shop in Flavalan; do the people in the cities treat them and Alexander badly?"

"From what I've been told, they're looked upon as a bit of an oddity, but a rather endearing one. The folks from Flavalan tend to enjoy eccentric artist types. That, and their craft is very desired in the city. They've been mostly fortunate, living here." Kaden sighed, her face falling. "Now, Chester has a more difficult story. Chester comes from Amberline, a small northern farming town that's a lot less diverse than Flavalan. He's a boy but, like Ember, was born into what most of us would consider to be a girl's body. He had a lot of the same experiences as me, being forced into dresses and typical girls' activities, but for him, it didn't just feel uncomfortable, it felt *wrong* in a way that I don't fully understand. When he was little, he used to insist he was a boy, and his parents would ignore him. Kids at school were cruel to him for not fitting in. So when he realized that he was a vanisher, he spent a lot of time using his gift. He told me once that he would rather be invisible than see himself in dresses and jewelry."

I nodded, wincing. "Poor kid."

"Eventually, he reached a point when he was about thirteen where he began to insist he was a boy and refused to dress otherwise. His parents threatened to kick him out of the house. He'd become friends with Jessen and his boyfriend Kylar by that point, and the three of them spent a lot of time at Alisa's parents' house. Both Kylar and Chester ended up moving in there, just to escape the hostility of their own homes."

"I'm glad Alisa's parents were more accepting."

"Alisa's parents are wonderful. After we all came to Ankrossi from Dundere, Alisa decided to go home for a time. She knew it wasn't safe for her to live in Amberline, but she wanted to see her family. She was reunited with Jessen and got to learn about who he was becoming as he grew up. And it was while she was visiting that Chester was taken by the Breoch Guard."

My eyes widened. "Really? He was a krossemage?"

"No. He managed to get away from the Guard before they got that far, thanks to his invisibility. But it scarred him in other ways; he's absolutely terrified of running into them again." Kaden sighed. "He managed to get back to Alisa's family, and that was when she suggested that Chester join her in Ankrossi. Jessen and Kylar wanted to come as well; they were both getting bullied at school for their relationship. That eventually turned into Alisa's parents selling their farm and moving out here themselves, along with Alisa's six younger siblings. Jessen and Kylar are both non-magical, so Lachlann's taken them on as his apprentices, and all the younger kids are in various stages of learning magic. The Callahan family is quite the brood." Kaden grinned. "And Alisa's parents are thrilled to become grandparents soon."

"Does Chester feel more at home here?"

"Oh, absolutely. He can use his magic freely, and dress and act how he wishes. And Alexander has given him some potions that will change his body to be more to his liking.

Those are actually Alexander's specialty; he's famous among the Breochi elites for his work—although, of course, it's all very underground."

"Potions that make you more like a boy or a girl?"

"No. Potions that alter your appearance in various ways. They can cause a person to grow taller, gain or lose fat or muscle or hair, grow bigger breasts, or deepen their voice. They can also make bones grow in particular ways, like changing facial structure. These potions are normally very expensive, but Alexander keeps some around for folks like Chester and will sell them very cheap or barter for them. Chester's used the ones for height and muscle and voice deepening, and a little of the one that changes facial structure, though Alexander has suggested he wait 'til he's an adult before making too many modifications there. Ember also sells charms that can allow a person to completely alter their appearance, but those take a lot of energy to use for more than a few hours, so if Chester wants to look completely like a typical male for a short time, he can. He tends to save that for special occasions, though."

"It's...really kind that Alexander and Ember are willing to help him that way."

Kaden nodded. "The one unfortunate thing about the potions is that there are certain things they cannot undo. They can't make a person shorter, or get rid of, um, certain body parts." She glanced down at her chest as she spoke and smirked. "Although, when this came up in conversation, I jokingly suggested that I could ask Kip to have someone put a sleep spell on Chester and remove said body parts with his hunting knife, since he's used to cutting through flesh and apparently was involved in amputating Lachlann's arm. Chester seriously looked like he'd take me up on the suggestion." Kaden cocked her head. "Now that we have a lifebringer present, we might actually be able to do that."

"Wouldn't it be better to find an actual surgeon?" I suggested. "No offense to Kip, but I imagine that's a complicated process."

"Perhaps. It's a thought, anyway." Kaden eyed me. "But does that answer your question as to why there are folks here who don't seem like typical men and women?'

"I suppose so."

"Here in Ankrossi, we make a point of letting people be who they are. That includes guests." She eyed me. "I know you've grown up in high society, but while you're here, you're free to be yourself. If you want to wear breeches, or colour your hair green, or climb trees or fall in love with a woman, it's safe."

I tilted my head, unsure what to make of her offer. "I'll...consider that."

"I'll make sure we tell you more about how Ankrossi came to be another night," she promised as we arrived at the treehouse. "You'd best get some sleep; you'll be travelling by portal to a school halfway across the Woods tomorrow."

"Really?" I gaped.

"It's not as terrifying as it sounds, don't worry."

Kaden bid me goodnight, and I found myself thinking over our conversation as I got into bed. I had plenty more questions, but staying in a place where folks were free to be themselves seemed like a good thing. *What might I change about how I come across, if given the chance?* I found myself pondering as I drifted off to sleep.

Chapter 10

TRAVELLING THROUGH A portal the next morning was one of the more odd experiences I'd had over the last few days. We soon found ourselves in the foyer of the underground structure that served as both the school of magic and the home of Willem and Claudi, who I now learned was Willem's mother. The other students followed Shawnie down the hall to their class, while I was led into a cozy yet elegant parlour. I was more than a little surprised to find Marcus there waiting for me. "What are you doing here?" I asked him.

"I'm helping with your first lesson," he replied with a grin. "Take a seat."

I did so and looked from Claudi to Marcus expectantly. Claudi looked me over and gave me a smile. "So. Healing magic. Where to start?"

"You tell us," Marcus replied.

"From what I saw the other day, it's clear enough that you have some knowledge of your

magic already," Claudi said to me. "What you don't have is the ability to see into wounds and illnesses. This is a complex process, often harder than the healing itself. In order to properly heal a wound, you need to *understand* it."

I frowned. "I healed my friend's twisted ankle recently without any trouble. And I've been making my grandmother's aching joints feel better for years."

"You've been able to soothe them, yes, but not fully heal them," Claudi countered. "If you knew how to see into wounds, you might be able to make your grandmother's joints stop aching altogether. Though healing things that are simply a result of old age can be difficult." She smiled. "As for a twisted ankle, that's easy to heal because the source of the injury is clear. Sometimes it's not that simple, though. For our first lesson in this, we have the perfect volunteer right here." She gestured to Marcus.

I looked him over. "You're injured?"

He gave me a wry grin. "You didn't notice my hand, I see."

My gaze travelled down to his right hand, which I only now realized was bent in on itself, claw-like and useless. "No, I didn't," I admitted.

"Not surprising. As a former krossemage, I spent a good twenty years without that hand—losing the use of it wasn't hard to adjust to."

"What happened?"

"That's what you're going to determine," Claudi informed me. "Or rather, you're going to determine the injury's source location. I won't be teaching you to fully see into wounds quite yet. I will tell you, though, that it wasn't an injury to Marcus' hand that caused this."

I frowned, not fully understanding. "What do I do?"

"First, I'm going to teach you the beginning of a new song to help you see into this. When you sing it, you should feel yourself drawn toward the source of the injury. It goes like this." Claudi closed her eyes and began to sing softly in another language. I bit my lip, trying to memorize both the languid, mournful tune and the unfamiliar words. When she finished, I cocked my head. "That was shorter than I expected."

"It's only the beginning of the song. The rest of it will help you see more about the wound. Once you know the whole thing, you can weave it seamlessly into your original healing song, and it will sound like one continuous melody. Now, sing the song back to me."

My voice was halting when I attempted the tune, and I stumbled over a few words, but when I was finished, she smiled. "That's good. You have the melody, you just need to work on the pronunciation." She repeated the song to me.

"Can I write the words down?" I asked. "Just so I don't forget?"

Claudi nodded and gestured to a nearby pen and paper. She led me through the words a third time, and I wrote them down as they sounded. Then I sang them back to her once more.

"Excellent," she said when I was finished. "Now, let's try the spell on Marcus."

Claudi instructed me to hold his injured hand in both of mine, close my eyes, and sing the spell slowly. I took his hand and immediately noticed the atrophied muscles in his fingers. "Will I have to heal his hand itself, or just the injury site?"

"You'll need to heal both, but we'll begin at the source. Now, close your eyes and sing."

I did as Claudi said, taking a deep breath before I began. I focused on the words as I sang, putting as much of my energy as I knew how into the spell.

At first, I felt nothing. Then there was a sort of tingling under my hands, a current that seemed to extend up Marcus' arm. I frowned and stopped singing.

"Finish the song," I heard Claudi say. "Follow the path of the wound with your fingers, but keep singing."

I resumed the tune, allowing my hands to make their way up Marcus' arm as I did so. The odd tingle was getting stronger, and when I reached his shoulder, it had increased to a near-burning sensation. I touched the spot on the back of his shoulder that seemed to be the source, and I was surprised when I felt a hard knot through his shirt. "This is it." I frowned. "What am I feeling?"

"Scar tissue," Claudi told me. "Well done."

"What happened here?"

"Sing the song again, but with your hand on the wound, and see how much you can determine," Claudi suggested. Marcus was wearing a lace-up shirt; as she spoke, he undid the lace with his good hand and opened the neckline, shrugging his shoulder out of it.

I stared at his large, pinkish scar for a moment, then tentatively placed my hand on top of it. "Does it hurt?"

"Not anymore," Marcus assured me. "Go ahead, do what Claudi suggested."

I nodded, closed my eyes, and began to sing again. The scar tingled under my hand, and I gasped slightly as an image appeared in my mind's eye. It was as if I was seeing into Marcus' shoulder; the entire thing had gone translucent, other than the wad of scar tissue and a few other features. The scar extended deep into his shoulder, eating into what I assumed was muscle and a fragment of what looked to be bone. The thing that stood out most clearly, though, was a long thread of something that wove through his shoulder and down his arm. The scar tissue cut through that thread entirely, breaking it in two.

When my song was finished, I opened my eyes. "The scar tissue goes deep into his shoulder, which means something must have punctured it," I guessed. "I would think a blade, but that doesn't seem quite right. An arrow, perhaps? And the arrow, or whatever it was, cut through a..." I closed my eyes, thinking. "A nerve?"

"Impressive." Marcus glanced back at me, eyebrows raised. "I didn't know they taught the workings of the body in high schools."

I shrugged. "I learned a bit in school, but I learned more from my boyfriend. He went through a phase where he used to pore over anatomy books."

"You may have an advantage then; learning anatomy is one of the first lessons of a lifebringer," Claudi said.

"You didn't quite get the background of the damage, but you certainly managed to discern the problem itself," Marcus told me. "The nerve was severed, which makes my hand relatively useless. In order for my hand to work again, the nerve must first be repaired."

"What caused the damage then?" I asked.

Marcus winced slightly. "Something that you, as a young lady of society, are probably unfamiliar with. How much do you know about guns?"

I tilted my head, thinking about the weapons that the palace guard had recently started carrying. How they worked was still a bit of a mystery to me, but they looked deadly. "You were shot," I surmised. "With...a bullet?"

Marcus nodded.

"What happened?"

He let out a long sigh. "If you knew how to see into wounds, I'd let you look into it yourself so I don't have to explain."

"I can tell her," Claudi interjected. "Or, even better, can you join my magic to hers? Then if I see into your wound, she'll be able to as well."

"Ah. Good idea."

Claudi took my hand in her small, weathered one, and Marcus turned around, put his hand on top of both ours, and mumbled a spell. I noticed the taste of pineapple in my mouth again as our magic connected, and Claudi smiled. "Now I will look into Marcus' wound, and you can observe what I see." Keeping my hand in hers, Claudi gestured for Marcus to turn back around and laid her palm on his scar. She began to sing what seemed like an extension of the song she'd taught me. I closed my eyes, and images began to dance in front of them again, but these ones were vivid, colourful...

...A group of people clustered around a slab in a large, airy atrium of a building. Blood. And Ruby, lying prone on the slab, screaming in pain as a woman with long black hair sang what sounded like a healing song...

...Marcus next to the woman, using his own magic to aid her. Kaden holding down Ruby's feet, Jasper pinning her shoulders. A bloodied crossbow bolt falling to the floor.

In the background, Lachlann facing away from me, arguing with Trina, Kip and Saray about something...

...Ruby letting out a gasp of relief. Marcus putting his arm around the dark-haired woman, obvious love and pride in his eyes. Then, a gunshot...

...The woman keeling over and crying out in pain. Lachlann whirling around in shock. Jasper pulling a startled Ruby from the slab and hiding behind it. Marcus scooping the woman up and putting her onto the slab, reassuring her that they would get the bullet out...

...Then another shot, this one piercing the back of Marcus' shoulder. Marcus letting out a cry of pain but refusing to go down, determined to help the woman save herself...

...A third shot narrowly missing the top of Ruby's head...

...A signed conversation between Lachlann and the injured woman. Lachlann's face falling in defeat before reaching up to grip his anti-magic pendant...

...A wave of anti-magic blasting through the room, revealing a young redheaded fellow holding a gun, a sneer on his face and an odd golden sheen to his eyes...

When Claudi finished her song and my eyes opened, I realized they were wet with tears. She eyed me sympathetically. "What did you see?"

I relayed my vision to her, and she nodded. "You saw correctly, then. The bullet that Alvin fired severed the nerve in Marcus' shoulder. Hence, his injury."

"So Lachlann used his anti-magic to locate the fellow with the gun, but that prevented the lifebringer from healing both herself and Marcus?"

Marcus nodded and turned to face me again, his own eyes shining with tears. "By the time it was safe for Lachlann to drop his anti-magic, Noelle was too weak to heal herself, let alone anyone else." He let out a long sigh.

"Noelle. Was she your wife?"

"For almost twenty years. One of the most incredible women I've known."

I nodded solemnly. Then my eyes widened. "Wait. Your wife was named Noelle...and she was a lifebringer who was shot? This isn't Noelle *Westwood* we're talking about, is it?"

"It most certainly is." There was a note of pride in Marcus' voice, and he gave me a small smile.

"So you're the husband of the former governor of Dundere. And you're living out here in the Shrouded Woods. *Why?*"

"Because these are my people." There was a defensiveness in Marcus' voice. "I'm well aware I could've stayed in Dundere. But I knew my daughters would be safer here, and the people needed someone to lead them. Or they did at first. They can run this place fine on their own now, but I'm happy here." He looked away for a moment, wiping at his eyes, but when he turned back to me, he was all smiles. "Back to your lesson. You've learned why I cannot move my hand and what caused the wound. Now is the fun part where you get to heal it. Isn't that right, Claudi?"

She chuckled. "Yes, though this will need to be done in stages. First we'll repair the nerve, then the damage inside your shoulder. Then we'll do a bit of work on your hand itself." She nodded at me. "Let's get to it, Isabelle. Put your hand on Marcus' shoulder and focus on that severed nerve while you sing. Healing that will be easy."

It *was* easy. It only took a few seconds of singing to restore the nerve itself. Healing the scar tissue that cut through the muscle, however, was another story.

I concentrated as hard as I could, willing the tissues to become flexible again. I felt Marcus' shoulders drop as I worked; undoubtedly, I was releasing tension that had been built up in them for years. Finally, I felt the skin under my fingertips smooth out, the puckered surface replaced by normal skin. When I stopped singing, my head spun, and black spots swam in my vision. Claudi looked me over and pointed to a chair. "Sit. Now."

"But...are we done?" I gasped.

"We've done enough for one day. We can finish it tomorrow." Marcus' voice was authoritative. "Sit. Breathe deep."

I sat down and put my head in my hands for a moment, gulping in air until the lightheadedness subsided.

"Healing can take a lot of energy," Claudi told me. "This is a pretty normal reaction at the beginning."

"But...I didn't feel like this when I healed Aria," I protested weakly.

"That's because you were borrowing the magic of others nearby to do it."

I looked up, eyeing Marcus' hand, which still appeared withered. "Did it work?"

"Well, my shoulder feels better than it has in four years," he replied. "As for my hand..." He extended his arm, and I could see that, despite their atrophied appearance, his fingers were opening and closing ever so slightly. "It's very weak; I won't be able to move it fully until you finish the healing. But it *can* move." He grinned. "Thank you."

"I think you've learned enough from me for one day—you can join the other students after lunch for regular lessons," Claudi said to me. "Truth be told, I'm quite tired myself. Teaching at this age is exhausting."

"Is there anything I can do to help?" I asked her. "I know I can't heal old age, but is there anything specific that's in pain?"

"Alexander's been supplying me with potions to keep the pain away, so that's not the problem," she said, smiling. "The problem is that I'm *tired*. And I don't think you can fix that. I appreciate the offer, though." She glanced at the clock at the far end of the parlour. "It's nearly lunchtime. Head over to the school, I'm sure the others will be happy to see you."

***

Not long after, I sat with Sophie and her friends, eating sandwiches and fresh fruit. In the time I had before the students broke for lunch, I'd wandered the halls of the school and discovered a whole row of unused dorm rooms, several deserted classrooms, a large empty room whose walls were lined with a pearlescent white material, and a massive library. I questioned Sophie about my findings as we ate, and she smiled. "We don't use the dorms anymore. We used to when the school opened, but since we built the portal we think it's best that the students stay in Ankrossi where they can be part of the larger community. Also, there's not many of us students left right now, so dorms aren't really needed."

"Why aren't there many of you left?"

"Because most of our class is made up of the youngest of the krossemages that were rescued off Yarel Island," answered a tall mahogany-skinned fellow. "We were all twelve when the rescue happened. There are a few kids in the village who are younger than us— mainly Jessen's siblings—but other than them, there's not many."

"I thought I saw a few toddlers in a class," I replied.

"Ah, yes. That's the next generation—the kids that folks had after they got here. They're all under four, though."

"There were a *lot* of babies born that first year," Chester said, grinning. "Kip had his pregnancy-preventing tea, but a lot of folks had no desire to use it."

"Are he and Saray going to have kids?" I asked.

Sophie let out a cackle. "You're certainly not the first person to wonder about that. Last I heard, they're not interested in having kids at this point. Also, Willem was a bit concerned about what might happen magically if they did."

"What do you mean?"

"Well, Kip and Saray aren't related by blood in any way, but Kip got his magic from Saray's grandmother. Willem's a bit worried that if they had a kid, the kid's magic could be...wrong in some way, like how if siblings or cousins have kids together, the kids sometimes have disabilities. The child's magic might be destructive, or possibly too powerful, especially with Saray being a mental caster and Kip being a Bearer."

"What's a Bearer? And how did Kip get his magic from Saray's grandmother?"

Sophie laughed. "That's a bit of a story. You'd best ask Saray about that, or Trina. And Claudi is the best person to ask about the Bearers, as she is one herself."

The conversation soon turned to other things, and I studied the group. There were nine of them in total, not including Jessen and Kylar, who didn't attend magic school but showed up after lunch for regular lessons. I'd gotten the names of the students earlier but was having trouble remembering them amidst all the others I'd recently learned. The couple who'd recently broken up were sitting on opposite corners of the table, both studiously avoiding the other. One girl was loud and dramatic and talked with her hands, while two others hung on her every word. Both of these girls wore bold colours in their hair; one's was a rainbow of vibrant hues, while the other's was a simple, bright green. The green-haired girl dressed more like a boy, but her hair hung nearly down to her waist, and her eyes were ringed in dark makeup. I thought back to last night's conversation with Kaden and wondered how I'd look with green hair, then laughed aloud at the thought.

Everyone stared at me. "What?" asked the green-haired girl, her voice holding a tinge of accusation.

Cheeks flushing, I shook my head. "Nothing. I'm just watching you all, and, uh, admiring your styles." I eyed her. "I like your hair. Yours too." I nodded at her friend.

The rainbow-haired girl laughed. "We should get Ember to put some magical dye in your hair. What shade would you like? Or do you want multiple colours, like me?"

"I...uh...I appreciate the thought, but it's likely not a good idea."

"What, fancy people don't like their children to have brightly coloured hair?" Sophie teased.

"Not really," I admitted. "I think my father would faint if I came home like that."

"If you *could* have your hair any colour, what would you choose?" asked Chester.

I frowned. "Maybe pink? Just a few small streaks."

He grinned. "You'd look lovely with pink hair. We'll make it happen someday."

I chuckled and returned to my lunch. I highly doubted that Prince Oliver's betrothed would ever get away with having pink hair. But it was a nice thought, at least.

Chapter 11

THAT EVENING, KADEN informed me that we would not be eating dinner at home. Instead, we were going to visit the tavern, where Jasper was finishing up his shift. Once he was done, he, Ruby, Trina and Kaden were going to tell me the story of how Ankrossi came to be—which apparently was tied to the stories of how Jasper shot Kip, and how Kip inherited Saray's grandmother's magic.

The tavern was alive with music and the bustle of patrons and servers. Kaden, Ruby and I seated ourselves at a long wooden table. Jasper was not playing his fiddle today; instead, he was serving food while a trio of women in their twenties sang, accompanied only by a large drum.

Jasper noticed us and walked over, grinning. "Good evening ladies, and welcome to Persius' Perch. Can I get you started with some drinks?" His voice oozed with practiced charm; it was clear enough that he was playing up his role. Ruby rolled her eyes at him.

I frowned, realizing I hadn't noticed the tavern's name on the sign outside. "Wait, is this place named after Kip's bird?"

"Absolutely. It's not just a name either; Persius likes to sleep in the rafters here. We've been calling it that since—"

Jasper was cut off by Trina practically running into the bar, clearly out of breath. "Sorry I'm late," she gasped, sliding onto one of the benches. "One of the baby goats escaped its pen, and I had to run after it. It wouldn't listen to me, silly thing."

"You're not late at all," Jasper assured her. "I was just filling Isabelle in on the name of this place. Now, would you care for a drink?"

Trina, Kaden and Ruby all gave Jasper their orders, then he turned to me. "I can't serve you any liquor—we don't give it to folks under eighteen here—but our barkeep can make a non-liquored version of most drinks. What do you fancy?"

Kaden looked over the menu with me and helped me pick a sweet, fruity drink that she figured I'd like. Once Jasper left, Ruby asked me about my day, and I filled her in on partially healing Marcus' hand and the afternoon classes that closely resembled my lessons back home. Soon enough, Jasper arrived with our drinks and took our food orders. When he returned next, he was no longer wearing his server's apron, and he carried an extra tray of food for himself. "So," he said, taking a seat next to Trina, "I understand Isabelle wants to hear the story of how all this came to be?"

I nodded eagerly.

"It's quite the tale. And I'm the bad guy in part of it." Jasper's smile faltered when he said this, but only slightly.

I raised an eyebrow and leaned in. "Do tell."

Trina began to relay the story of how she and Saray were forced to flee Sylvenburgh Academy for Dundere after Saray's gift was revealed, and how they ended up travelling with Kip, Lachlann, and Kirilee to Willem's place so Saray could train. "Lachlann and Kip had to go run an errand while Saray was training," Trina explained, sipping on her drink. "While they were away, though, Lachlann was shot with a cursed arrow, and Kip dragged him back to us, barely alive."

"What's a cursed arrow?" I asked.

"I don't quite understand it myself, but there's a sort of decay magic that some folks know how to use. If it's made into a potion, you can dip arrows into it, and if they hit a person or animal, they'll kill that person unless the poison is stopped. If it pierces a limb, you can usually survive if the limb is amputated."

"Ah." I nodded. "That's why Lachlann has a metal hand."

"Exactly," Trina said. "So then we had to wait around for Lachlann to heal up enough to travel. It was during that time that Lachlann and Kirilee finally admitted they were in love. They'd both had feelings for a while, but Kirilee was convinced they couldn't work out because of the curse she was under."

"What sort of curse?" I asked.

"The short version is that Kirilee was much older than she looked, and she was unable to age or die until she fulfilled a set of conditions. But once we decided Lachlann was ready for travel, we teleported to Gareth's ship, and Gareth married Lachlann and Kirilee. The wedding was crashed by Breoch Guard, led by *their* father." She smirked and pointed to Jasper and Ruby.

I dug into my meal and listened as Trina recounted Jasper's arrival on the ship the next day, the days that came after, and their reaching port in Dundere, which was quickly followed by Jasper's betrayal. "You should probably tell the next part of the story, since I wasn't there," Trina said to him.

Jasper frowned. "Here's the part where I become the bad guy." He explained how he held Kip hostage to force Saray's cooperation and took both of them back to a Breoch Guard ship, only to be instructed to kill Kip. "The minute or so after that is a bit of a blur. I remember Father telling me I had to do it, and Kip going all tense when the captain gave the order. I remember trying to rationalize the decision. And then I remember squeezing my eyes shut as I pulled the trigger, hoping the gun would fail."

"I'm guessing it did?"

Jasper shook his head.

"But...he's alive."

"We're getting there," Trina assured me. "For a little while, Kip was very much *not* alive."

Jasper recounted what happened on the Breoch Guard ship following Saray's capture, how the Lady Liara had given chase, and how his second attempt to make sure she would make it back to Breoch in chains was thwarted by Saray herself. I frowned when he finished. "I know the story of Saray's escape from the ship, but the version I heard had her setting the ship on fire and teleporting off, only to let the entire ship go down in flames and everyone on it die."

Trina snorted. "Half the stories that circulate in Breoch about Saray and me are exaggerations. Saray did set the ship on fire, but she didn't raze it."

Trina took over telling the story from there, explaining how she, Lachlann and Kirilee had made it to the governor's place, where Kirilee was surprised to learn that the governor was married to her son, Marcus. Following the rescue, Gareth brought Saray to them, along with Kip's body. "By that point, I'd heard some stories of ways to bring people back from the dead," Trina said. "There's soul magic, which is something that was used on Kirilee many years ago but resulted in her curse, and there's also something called a life transfer, which takes the life of one person and uses it to resurrect another. Noelle wasn't willing to do either. I got pretty upset at that point, and Noelle suggested that she heal my blindness."

I nodded. "And that worked, I assume?"

"It did. I remember opening my eyes and seeing Saray. It was surreal. It took me a bit of time to adjust to having vision, even though I'd had it in my early childhood."

After that, Trina told me, they'd learned through a series of events that Marcus was Saray's father. And the following day, he and Noelle offered to adopt Saray and Trina, only to have Kirilee's curse suddenly break as the final condition of the spell was met. Kirilee, knowing she only had hours left to live, offered herself as the subject of a life transfer to bring Kip back, who was then endowed with Kirilee's magic. "I remember looking at Kip several times in the month that followed, hardly believing he was alive," Trina recalled. "I think he struggled to believe it himself."

"That must've been awful for Lachlann," I said. "Though at least Kirilee was still in that tree."

"True, but we didn't know that 'til several years later. It was a hard time for Lachlann." Trina explained how he and Kip departed for the Woods soon after, Kip eventually returning to Dundere and Lachlann beginning to bring young magikai from Breoch to Dundere for safety.

Then Trina polished off the rest of her food as Jasper took his turn storytelling. He spoke of the dark place he'd fallen into after the shooting, how he tried to numb his pain with drinking and teakflower and women. "Then something happened with Ruby that forced me to snap out of it," he concluded. "Perhaps I'll let her tell—"

"Hey, play us a song, darling!" a rather drunk woman cut in, her gaze on Jasper. Looking at the stage, I noticed that tonight's entertainers were packing up.

He gave the woman a wry grin. "Right now we're busy telling a story," he told her. "But you're welcome to join if you want to hear. Isabelle doesn't know the tale of how this place came to be."

"Ah! That's a good one!" She came over, trailed by a few others, and soon nearly a dozen folks were packed around our table.

Jasper looked over at Ruby. "As I was saying, I believe this is where you come in."

Ruby nodded. "While my brother was in his bottle-sucking skirt-chaser phase," she began, earning a raised eyebrow from Jasper and a giggle from Trina and Kaden, "he was also beginning to question everything he'd been taught about magic. Our eldest brother Jade, on the other hand, was being lured in the opposite direction, thanks to his relationship with our neighbour Gabby, who came from a family of Witch Slayers." A few of the new members of the audience let out jeers at the mention of the slightly familiar name.

I frowned. "Witch Slayers. They're the ones who believe all magic users should be killed, right?"

"Not just that. Many of them feel it's their right to torture magic users and treat them like animals," Jasper said.

I shuddered. "And your brother's girlfriend was one of these?"

"His wife, eventually," Jasper corrected. "And she began to drag Jade down the same path. Unfortunately, I was too lost in my own world of pain to see how bad he was getting."

Ruby nodded, closed her eyes briefly, and began to tell me the story of how she'd diverted a storm while sailing and likely saved the lives of Jade, Gabby, and herself, only to have them turn her in to the Breoch Guard upon reaching harbour. "The prison farm was where I met Kaden, and we bonded over playing piano together. We had a plan to escape the farm, too. But then my brother showed up and hauled me off, and I couldn't communicate that I wanted to bring Kaden along."

Ruby and Jasper walked me through the story of Jasper's rescue, how they had convinced a rather begrudging Lachlann to take them to Dundere, and how they'd ended up on the Lady Liara, where Jasper fell back into drinking and flirting. Our new friends tittered, and one of them punched Jasper in the arm at the mention of Jasper's exploits, then the crowd erupted into a chorus of boos when he ended his monologue with, "And this is where we meet the Blackwell family."

"Who are they?" I asked.

"An influential Dunderi family. There are four Blackwell children—well, three now. Arquinn is the eldest. Then there's the twins, Ashlynn and Aidan—though he's dead. And Alvin is Trina's age. Ashlynn and Aidan were on the ship with Ruby and me, going home from university, and Aidan took an instant dislike to me because I was popular with the ladies. I was able to just ignore them for the most part, but then I got involved with Violet, a girl who Aidan had eyes for." He told me how Ashlynn had walked in on him and Violet in the girls' dorm and immediately told Aidan. "Aidan cornered me and punched me in the face the next day, then threatened me with fire—though, in honesty, I hardly remember that part, because I'd been drinking."

"*I* certainly remember it," Ruby put in. "I tried to defend you. Then Ashlynn of all people came along and told her brother to back off."

"Oooooh, tell us more about Violet!" exclaimed one of the hecklers.

"I'd...rather not." Blushing slightly, Jasper turned to his sister to change the subject. "So, what happened after that? Magical pirates?"

"Magical *what?*" I repeated, my eyes widening.

"You heard him." Ruby grinned and filled me in on the rest of their adventures at sea, how she and Harvey, the first mate, had used mist from the ocean to escape pirates with magic, and how they'd finally reached Dundere. "Then we went to see your family," she said, looking over at Trina.

She nodded. "Marcus and Noelle warned us that you two were coming. Saray acted like she didn't care, but I could tell she was scared. I was more curious than anything." She glanced at Jasper. "I remembered you from our time on the Lady Liara, but of course I couldn't see you at that point."

"Then you finally did see me and couldn't stop gawking," Jasper teased.

"You...remember that?" Trina's cheeks went pink.

"There were a lot of things that happened that day, but I do remember Noelle scolding you for staring, then realizing it was me you were looking at." He frowned. "Why *were* you staring?"

Her blush deepened. "I...uh...thought you were handsome," she admitted.

The newcomers whooped at her admission. "Damn right he's handsome!" exclaimed the woman who'd asked him to play a song.

Jasper laughed and turned back to Trina, smirking. "You *thought* I was handsome? But you don't anymore?"

"Jasper!" Ruby exclaimed.

"No...I mean, yes, of course you are, it's just that I'm not shocked by it anymore." Trina looked like she wanted to disappear. "All those years, Kip and Saray had talked about you like you were a monster. But then I meet you, and I find out you're good looking, and nice too, and..." She trailed off.

"All right, I get the point," I cut in. "Jasper is handsome and charming, and Trina saw him for the first time and was caught off guard by this. What happened after that?"

Trina grinned, the blush fading from her cheeks. "Then Kip showed up and punched Jasper in the face."

One of the men in the group nearly spit out his ale. "Of course he did! Good for Kip—you probably deserved it, boy!"

"Yeah, that one I did deserve." Jasper rubbed his jaw absentmindedly. "I had no clue he was alive. Lachlann decided not to tell me, because he, and I quote, *wanted to see the look on my face when I saw him.*" He snorted. "Bastard."

"I thought we might have a full-on fight on our hands, but thankfully Noelle intervened and healed me," Ruby put in. She began to fill me in on the events that followed: the decision to have Ruby stay at the mansion while she trained in magic, her attempts to find a way back to rescue Kaden, and the trip into the Woods with Kip that culminated in a visit to Willem—only to find out that the things needed for the rescue would take far longer than she'd hoped. "I was beyond frustrated," she told me. "So I was happy when my magic classes started up, because I needed a distraction."

"And, boy, did you ever get one," Jasper said. "In the form of Alvin Blackwell." The name, again, was followed by a chorus of jeers.

Ruby explained how she and the others learned about the cull planned for Yarel Island and began to stage a large rescue; meanwhile, her friendship with Alvin quickly turned into a romance. She told me the story of how Aidan walked in on her and Alvin making out in his bedroom and responded by going to the pub and viciously attacking Jasper, which led her to decide the Blackwells were dangerous and break up with Alvin. "A few days later," she concluded, "Willem showed up and said we were ready to invade Yarel Island."

My eyes widened. "Wait...that story about a bunch of krossemages disappearing off an island—that was *you* folks?" I frowned. "I'd heard Saray was involved in that part of the story, but I didn't know if it was just another rumour."

"Saray was definitely there," Kaden said. "Thank the Fae everyone showed up when they did—things were getting unbearable on the island." Several of the audience members nodded in agreement, and I realized they'd been imprisoned krossemages too at one point.

I listened as all four of them told the story of the rescue, how Trina was shocked to discover her mother was a krossemage there, and how they had to use magic to fight off a small contingent of guards but ultimately got everyone off the island unscathed.

They told me about the months that followed, the krossemages getting healed and learning how to use their magic, how Ruby got back together with Alvin while Kaden slowly developed a crush on Ruby, and how, through a series of events, the two of them learned that Alvin was a charmer. Kaden told me about how she followed Ruby on one last date with Alvin, after Ruby decided to give him a chance, and how she had to intervene when the two of them got into a heated argument after Ruby revealed that she knew Alvin's secret. "The following day, Ruby officially broke things off with him again," she concluded. "And we hoped that he'd leave her alone and things would get better."

"But, of course, that wasn't what happened," put in one of our new friends.

"Things were fine for a few weeks," Ruby said. "Then, after Saray's birthday party, Alvin cornered me in my room. Thankfully, Marcus and Noelle overheard our confrontation and intervened. Meanwhile, Aidan had launched an attack on Jasper again."

Jasper told me the story of how Aidan, ramped up on some sort of fairy strength potion, attacked him in Lachlann's apartment, and how he nearly succeeded in making Jasper unconscious, only to have Lachlann arrive home, intervene, and ultimately end up killing Aidan. "The next morning, the police showed up at the Blackwells' place to inform Aidan's parents of his death, and they learned that Alvin ran away in the middle of the night," he concluded.

"The next part is where we don't know everything," Ruby said. "We know that Alvin used the portal connecting Dundere to the Shrouded Woods, got to one of the major cities, informed the Breoch Guard of the escaped krossemages' location, and promised them that Saray would also be there for the taking."

One of the newcomers frowned. "I still don't get how that kid convinced so many Breoch Guard to march through the Shrouded Woods to a portal."

Trina raised an eyebrow. "He's a charmer. And it wasn't just Breoch Guard who attacked, it was also Witch Slayers."

They then told me how the Breoch Guard set fire to the school of magic, trapping the former krossemages inside, and how the Dundere guardsmen, aided by a bunch of magic users under Lachlann's command, fought them off. Ruby explained how she, Kaden, Jasper and Saray helped save the mages who were trapped in the school, earning nods of approval from our audience. "I thought things were going to get better after that," she said, "but then I got shot with a crossbow." She recounted how Jade's wife shot her out of the sky, only to be killed by Kip. "Then Kip picked me up and ran me to Noelle. She and Marcus worked together to get the bolt out of me and heal me. Then…" She sighed, and I felt the collective mood among the listeners darken. "Then Alvin showed up invisible, with a gun, and started shooting people. He got Noelle first, Marcus second, then Noelle ordered Lachlann to use his anti-magic to find the shooter. Lachlann did, and Alvin appeared right next to Saray, grabbed her, and put a gun to her head."

"Right. I saw part of that when Claudi and I were healing Marcus' shoulder earlier."

Ruby and Jasper walked me through the particulars of the attack—how Ruby had tried to distract Alvin so that Jasper could shoot him, and when that plan failed, how Sophie had revealed herself as a charmer and intervened, leading to Alvin's surrender and arrest. "Then we lost Noelle," Ruby concluded sadly. "We managed to win the battle, but we lost the island's governor and only lifebringer." Our audience, notably less rowdy now, nodded in agreement, and a few of them swiped at their eyes. "After that, the Candeshis showed up and decided they didn't want us Breochi refugees in Dundere anymore," Ruby concluded. "So a team of us came here and turned this grove into a village, and a few months later Willem opened up a portal so folks could immigrate here. That's how Ankrossi was born."

"And you've all lived here ever since?" I asked.

"Well, Kaden and I have. Jasper spent most of his time at sea, and Trina joined him for about a year after she and Ambrose broke up."

"So how did Daisy and Ambrose get together?" I asked.

"Daisy was part of the group of girls who sailed on the Lady Liara with Ruby and me on our way to Dundere. She was discovered as a magikai in her hometown about a year after I went back to sea, and she managed to escape before the Guard caught her," Jasper said. "She came aboard the Lady Liara, we reconnected, she told me she was unsure where to go next, and Trina suggested that we take her back to Ankrossi. Trina learned that Daisy has the same gift as both she and Ambrose—they can all speak to animals—and the two were instant best friends." He grinned. "It was kind of adorable."

"I got to know Daisy and what she wanted out of life, and I found myself realizing she'd be perfect for Ambrose," Trina admitted. "So I asked her if it would be weird if I introduced her to my ex. And, well, it worked."

"So they got married, Saray and Kip got married, Lachlann and Starla got married, and two of the three couples got pregnant pretty quickly," Kaden concluded. "And here we are."

"Are you two going to get married?" I asked, eyeing her and Ruby.

"Oooooh, do tell!" exclaimed a young woman in our group, taking a swig of her drink.

They exchanged a glance. "Probably one day," Ruby said. "We've talked about it, we just haven't decided on a date."

"So that's all that's happened since you showed up here? A bunch of weddings and some babies?"

"That, and building an entire society from the ground up," Ruby said. "It's taken a lot of work." She eyed me then. "Now we've told you our story; I think it's time you tell us yours. You're here because you want to heal your boyfriend and rescue your friend Silva, is that right?"

I nodded and closed my eyes, thinking how best to explain everything to them without fully divulging my identity. "Silva and I met in primary school," I began. "I don't remember what drew us together, but we spent most of our time there paired up. My family moved from Sylvenburgh to Kirstein when I was nine, the summer after you and Saray ran away." I nodded at Trina. "Silva and I were crushed about being separated. We promised to keep in touch, and we did. We wrote letters back and forth for years, and every Banishing Day I'd make the trip back to Sylvenburgh and spend the holiday with her. There were a few years where we seemed to be drifting apart; she had her new friends, and I had mine, but that all changed when we were thirteen. That was the year we both discovered we were magic users and ended up confiding in each other.

And some...things happened in my life that made me lose a lot of friends, so I wanted to make sure I didn't lose Silva too."

Kaden sat back, crossing an ankle over a knee. "Do tell."

I sighed. Our audience had begun to disperse after the others finished their tale; clearly they were more interested in that story than mine. I figured everyone remaining at the table was trustworthy. "I'm betrothed. I refer to Ollie as my boyfriend, but really, he and I were arranged to be wed by our parents." I hadn't called him Ollie in years, but I hoped that the nickname would keep my new friends from figuring out his identity.

Ruby nodded. "My mother used to talk about setting one of those up for me. It's not uncommon in wealthy families."

"Do you like the fellow you're betrothed to?" Kaden asked.

"Of course! I wouldn't be learning how to heal him if I didn't." I rested my chin on my hand. "Ollie and I have known each other for as long as Silva and me. Our parents are friends. We both come from very wealthy, influential families."

Kaden snorted. "You most certainly do. I saw your house."

I nodded. "Ollie's family is far richer than mine, though. And being betrothed to him...it means that I don't have as many choices as you folks do when it comes to my future. There will be expectations."

"You're expected to be the supportive wife and bear him children?" Ruby guessed.

"That's some of it, yes."

"And is that what you *want?*"

"No one's...ever asked me that before." I bit my lip. "You know how it is. Most wealthy women have those expectations put on them. Perhaps their marriages aren't arranged, but they're expected to play a part. We don't get to decide what we want to be when we grow up."

Ruby and Jasper both nodded. "I know women who have gone to drastic measures to avoid that fate," Jasper said.

"If I wasn't marrying Ollie, well, I'm not sure what I'd do with my life," I admitted. "I knew I didn't have a choice, so I haven't given it much thought."

Jasper raised an eyebrow. "I hear that lifebringers are paid handsomely in countries where magic is legal. You could always run away."

I frowned; the thought hadn't occurred to me.

"Or you could stay here with us," Trina added.

"I could. But then Ollie wouldn't get healed." I sighed. "It's complicated. I do care about him. A lot. I want him to get better. But perhaps having my life decided for me isn't fair."

"Do you want to *marry* him, though?" Ruby asked.

"I do now. We've been getting closer as of late, and I'm starting to fall for him. There was a time in my younger years when I was angry about it, though. All the other girls at school were starting to date, but I was left out of those conversations. Which brings me back to Silva." I frowned. "I told one friend at King's Academy about my betrothal when I was thirteen, and she told everyone. And since Ollie's family is rather prestigious, the other students started to act differently around me. The girls saw me as competition, like I thought I was better than them—which I *don't*—and the boys stopped interacting with me completely. The students back at Sylvenburgh didn't know about the betrothal, though, so they were nice enough to me, and Silva didn't treat me any differently, even though she'd known about Ollie for years." I sighed. "So that's why I want to rescue her, if that makes any sense."

Kaden smirked. "Are you sure you don't actually have a crush on *Silva,* and that's what's making you want to rescue her?" She elbowed Ruby as she spoke.

I laughed. "I'm pretty sure I prefer men over women, and so does she. Though it is amusing how similar that part of our—"

I was interrupted by a screech, and all eyes turned upward as Persius flew into the bar and settled among the rafters. Jasper sighed. "That's our cue. When Persius comes in for the night, it means it's time for the tavern to close down," he explained to me.

My eyes narrowed; I was under the impression that taverns stayed open later than this.

"Anyone who wishes to keep socializing usually retreats to the Mothertree's central chamber," Trina said. "We can go there, if you'd like. I'm still quite awake."

I stifled a yawn. "You folks are welcome to. I'm tired, and I have school tomorrow."

Ruby and Kaden exchanged a glance. "We'd best head to bed as well."

Trina's face fell slightly. "Jasper?"

He smiled. "I'll come along with you, sure." She lit up. I didn't miss the sly grins that Ruby and Kaden exchanged.

I couldn't help but notice the feeling of contentment that settled in my stomach as I followed Ruby and Kaden home. There were so many things still left unknown. Oliver was sick, Silva was missing, and I could only imagine the amount of trouble I'd likely be in when I got back to Kirstein. But I was making friends and beginning to feel at home in this strange little village, and I was thankful for that much.

Chapter 12

THE FOLLOWING MORNING was spent attending to the rest of Marcus' healing. I used my magic to strengthen his wrist, hand and finger muscles, and I watched him curl and uncurl his hand, pick up items of various weights, then finally declare our experiment a success. After Marcus left, Claudi turned to me. "Do you think you have enough strength left for another healing?"

"Possibly, for whom?"

"Me. I realized I was foolish to turn you down yesterday. Old age has made walking hard for me; I can't get around anymore without those." She gestured to a pair of canes that sat against the side of the couch.

We spent the remainder of the morning strengthening her legs, and by lunchtime I was exhausted, but Claudi was able to walk without her canes. She was still hunched over, though, and she told me that perhaps her back would be the next thing to heal.

After my other classes, I made my way back through the portal to Ankrossi and across the meadow to my home, Sophie in tow. Halfway through my journey, I heard someone shout my name and turned to see a woman I didn't know running toward me, clutching a baby to her chest. "You're the healer, right?" she asked.

I nodded.

"I'm Darya, and this is my son, Corbin. He's caught a nasty cough, and I'm worried about him..." Her voice broke, a few tears trickling down her cheeks. "Can you help him?"

Sophie put an arm around Darya, and I took Corbin carefully. "I'll see what I can do," I said. "Let's sit somewhere."

We found a fallen log near the edge of the meadow where I closed my eyes, trying to see Corbin's illness, but it was hard for me to determine exactly what I needed to do. "May I take him to Claudi?" I asked Darya. "She can likely tell me how to help him."

"Please do," Darya said, her voice trembling. "Anything you or Claudi can do to help him would be incredibly appreciated."

"We'll wait here," Sophie said.

I made my way across the meadow again, clutching Corbin to my chest, his weak cries punctuated by coughs. "It's all right," I whispered to him.

The portal, thankfully, had not yet been closed—other students were still trickling through. I slipped back in and headed into Willem's home, where I found Claudi napping on her living room couch. I paused for a moment, unsure whether to wake her, but then Corbin let out a cry and Claudi's eyes opened. "Isabelle? What are you doing?"

I explained the situation as she slowly sat up, and Claudi smiled. "Corbin is in luck. It's likely just a bug, and those are the easiest things to heal. Let me take a look."

I passed the baby to her, and she sang softly to him, closing her eyes. Then she nodded. "Yes. Wee little thing just has a cold."

She walked me through how to heal him, and I put my hand on his chest and willed his lungs to strengthen and his body to fight off the bug. When I was done, he was breathing evenly. My head was spinning, though, and I keeled forward, nearly taking the baby with me.

"Careful." Claudi's metal hand shot out to keep me from falling off the couch. "Lie back, close your eyes."

I did as she asked, and I felt her take Corbin from me. "You're getting a reputation in Ankrossi."

"Makes sense if I'm the only healer to have been around in years."

"I agree. Perhaps this week we can set up a tent for you at the market and recruit a few other magikai who don't mind lending you some of their magic for the night. I can help you with seeing into people's problems, and you can heal."

"That sounds exhausting," I admitted. "I already feel like I can barely walk."

"You've healed three things in one day. That's impressive, for someone as inexperienced as you. But if you have the magic of others to lean on, you won't tire out this quickly."

"Right." I nodded. "I'll talk to Kaden and Ruby about it, see if they can get me a tent."

"Good idea. Now, can you stand?"

I got to my feet slowly, and Claudi put Corbin in my arms. "You'd best get this little fellow back to his mother. And after that, go home and rest. You've had a long day."

***

The next few days progressed much like the ones before. In the mornings, I worked with Claudi, learning to pinpoint the sources of various injuries and practicing my healing, mostly on her. She also began to teach me anatomy, and I learned the various names of bones and how muscles, tendons and ligaments all worked together to enable movement. I learned about the functions of organs I didn't know well, like the liver and the kidneys, how the nervous system worked, and how the heart and lungs collaborated to keep the body alive.

Afternoons were spent on regular lessons, and every day after school I'd drop by Starla's to check on Aria. Sometimes I would need to give her lungs or digestive system a small healing boost, but she was doing better now that Starla had figured out how to feed her using Marcus' glass pipe. After that, I would head back to Ruby and Kaden's for supper and usually spend the evening in the meadow somewhere, either with them or Sophie, Chester and the other teens. It wasn't uncommon for folks to approach me with healing needs in the evenings. Most were easy enough to deal with, but I asked a few of the more difficult cases to return to me on Thursday night, when I'd have a market stall, access to Claudi's wisdom, and borrowed magic at my disposal.

On Thursday evening, Kip went to Willem's home to fetch Claudi and teleported her into the tent I would be using. I got called away to help Sophie right after they arrived, and when I returned they were deep in discussion. I paused outside, listening, when I heard my name.

"...we need to find a way to convince Isabelle to stay," Kip was saying to Claudi.

"You can't make her stay, Kip." Claudi's voice was firm. "She has a family and a boyfriend back home, and I'm sure they are all getting worried."

"I know that. I'm just trying to think of a way..."

"We've survived four years without a lifebringer in our village. Perhaps we can give her a summoning stone and call her back for emergencies, but we can't force her to live here."

Kip sighed. "It's not just that having her here would be advantageous, y'know. Don't you see, Claudi? She's the next Bearer of the Sea Stone."

"How do you know that? Did your stone tell you?"

"No, but...who else would it be, ai? I don't see any other healers around here."

"Sorry, what are you two saying about me?" I demanded, entering the tent.

Claudi looked away, and Kip flushed. "How much did you hear?" he asked.

"I heard that Kip thinks I'm a Bearer, whatever that is, and that you want me to stay here." I crossed my arms. "Which is not going to happen. I like it here, but I have obligations back home that you don't know about, ones that are more important than whatever you have planned for me."

Kip let out a long sigh. "You weren't meant to hear any of that. But is there no chance that your boyfriend can come here? That's how Saray and I solved our issues."

"Absolutely not. What is a Bearer, anyway?"

Kip was just about to answer when a young man with a limp made his way into my tent. "Hi, uh, can you help me out?"

It was a steady stream of people seeking healing from that point on. Saray joined us soon after, and she and Kip allowed me to rely on their magic to help with the healing, while Claudi helped me determine the sources of the different ailments and injuries. Some of the sources were easy enough for me to diagnose, but a few were much more complex. Mostly, I healed colds and joint injuries and vision that was beginning to fade with old age, a type of healing that required precision and that even the most experienced healers often didn't get right. One or two people came to me with fractures that had healed wrong, and Kip had to cast a pain reduction spell on them before re-breaking their bones so I could set them properly. All of these ailments and injuries were easier to heal than I'd expected; it seemed that the healings almost happened more quickly here in the meadow than at Willem and Claudi's place.

It wasn't all easy, though; one woman had a painful joint disease that took a good half hour to heal. My last client of the night was a krossemage who had initially chosen not to be healed by Noelle, but who now felt like he'd made the wrong decision. I let Claudi walk me through the tedious process of regrowing a hand and tongue, and by the end of it, Kip, Saray and I were all tired. "I think we're done for the night," Kip said when the man left the tent to find Marcus, who would help him learn to use his newly reformed body parts. "Claudi can explain what a Bearer is to you tomorrow. I'm exhausted."

"Me too," I admitted. "Though in some ways it was easier than I expected."

Saray nodded. "That's likely because you're right by the Mothertree. Magic is…different when you're in her proximity."

"It's easier to cast, you mean?"

"Very much so. In fact, sometimes folks who don't possess an innate magical gift are able to cast minor spells. We're not sure why the magic is stronger here, we just know that it is. Not even Kirilee seems to know why; though she did tell Lachlann that she'd been drawn to this particular spot ever since she discovered it, which is part of why she suggested it as an ideal place to build Ankrossi."

"The magic here is more similar to what it was like before the Shift," put in Claudi. "But that's something I can explain tomorrow. We'd all best get some sleep."

We closed down shop, and Kip took Claudi home, moving much slower this time than he had before. I headed back to Ruby and Kaden's, wondering what the next morning's conversation would bring.

***

"So who are the Bearers exactly," I asked Claudi the following day, seated on the couch next to her, "and why does Kip want me to be one? And what is that shift you were talking about?"

"The Bearers are people who help balance out and temper certain aspects of the magic of the Shrouded Woods," Claudi explained. "Though I suppose I should explain the Shift before the Bearers, as it happened first. I'm likely the only person in Ankrossi old enough to remember the Shift well.

"At one time, magic in Breoch was accessible by all people," she explained. "Not everyone was born with an innate talent, but with enough practice, anyone could learn to cast at least minor spells. But then, about a year after Breoch gained its independence, something shifted. The magic became weaker and more difficult to cast."

"Does anyone know why?"

"No, though there is a theory that Breoch's magic was tied to Cherin, and when Breoch gained its independence from the empire, it severed that connection. What we do know is that it became nearly impossible for folks without an innate talent to learn magic at all. And that's a large part of why the Banishing happened."

"I thought the Banishing was related to magic being dangerous."

"It was, but that wasn't the only reason," Claudi replied. "There were concerns that the shift in the magic created two classes of people, magikai and non-magic users, and that the magic users could easily overpower their peers. The Banishing was partly to prevent that."

I tilted my head. "Odd that I didn't know that. I've learned a lot about the history of the Banishing in school, and that was never mentioned."

Claudi caught my skepticism. "Has it occurred to you that perhaps those in power don't want everyone knowing their motivations?"

I bit my lip, nodding. *Does Kairus know any of this?* I wondered. *Does Oliver?*

"Even after the Banishing, though, folks were afraid," Claudi went on. "Particularly, there was an apprehension about the fairies. There was speculation that the fairies might be able to inhabit human bodies, which would give them an immense advantage over us."

I raised an eyebrow. "Has that ever happened?"

"It's rumoured to have happened at least once before," Claudi replied. "And it was this fear that led the Witch Slayers to invade the Woods a decade or so after the Banishing, in an attempt to burn the forest down and rid Breoch of fairies.

"When they did that, though, the magic within the Woods changed yet again." She frowned. "It took on a life of its own, and sometimes it acted in ways that didn't make sense. People would lose their abilities at random, or there'd be certain concentrations of magic within the Woods where folks who gathered in that area would find themselves under the effect of a spell." She chuckled. "That's actually the origin of the Moon Dance, you know. That particular grove tended to have large concentrations of Charm magic under a full moon, so people would show up there and get high off it."

"What's a Moon Dance?"

"You haven't heard about those? Ask Ruby or Kaden to explain to you—I think there's one happening tomorrow, actually." She chuckled. "Anyway, this fluctuation of magic wasn't very convenient in an overall sense, so four of us were chosen to serve as anchors for the different magic types. The original four were my husband Ashlar, Kirilee, Hilda and me. When Ashlar died, he passed the mantle to our son, and Kirilee passed hers to Kip through the life transfer." She smiled. "The Bearers themselves are no more gifted than most magikai, but when the four of them use their powers together, they are a force to be reckoned with. Their combined magic is about the only thing in these Woods stronger than the magic of the Fae, which is the only reason we let Alexander and Ember peddle their fairy magic potions and charms in Ankrossi. If there was nothing that could stand against them, allowing folks to purchase fairy magic could be very dangerous indeed."

"What different sorts of magic are there?" I asked.

"*Different sorts* may not be the most accurate way of explaining this," Claudi admitted. "It would be better to say that in order for magic to be wielded by a person, four things must be in alignment, and there is magic in each of these sources.

"The first source is the earth itself. We aren't sure how magic got here, but we know that it's present within all of the Verdant Isles, and that in some places, like the Shrouded Woods, it's especially strong. If you sail away from the Isles, to Cherin or Candesh or any of the lands beyond, it grows weaker. This source is symbolized by the Earth Stone, whose Bearer is Kip.

"The second source is the fairies, who also exist all throughout the Verdant Isles. We aren't certain if the fairies' arrival here enchanted the land, or if the fairies were drawn here because the land was already enchanted, but the two are interdependent on one another. The Bearer of the Air Stone will always have a special connection to the fairies, as Hilda most certainly does.

"The other two stones are related not to the world around the magikai, but to each magikai themselves. The third element necessary for magic to work is a degree of willpower and intelligence in the caster. They have to *want* to cast, to be able to learn how to utilize and focus their power, and have the willpower to see the spell through. If this isn't developed, a person's magic will lie mostly dormant, or will perhaps flare up on occasion but won't be of much use. This is symbolized by the Fire Stone, which Willem bears.

"The last stone, the Sea Stone, is mine. It's important for a person to have the will and intellect to cast, but they must also have the physical capability within their bodies to cast with words or motions. At this point in time, having an innate talent is also necessary. All of this is represented by the Sea Stone, as we humans are born from water and contain a great deal of it. And because this element involves matters of the physical body, its Bearer must always be a lifebringer." She raised her eyebrows at me.

"Ah." I nodded. "So that's why Kip thinks I'm the next Bearer. If he's right, would that mean I'd need to stay here in the Woods?"

"Not necessarily. The Bearers of the Air and Earth stones tend to be more tied to locations than Fire and Water. I actually lived a good twenty years outside of the Woods, in Flavalan. I was close enough to the Woods to help keep the magic in balance, but I was also close to the sea, which is something that Sea Stone bearers tend to crave."

"But I'm from Kirstein, that's nowhere near the Woods."

Claudi frowned. "Yes, that might be a bit too far away. If you're meant to be the Bearer, though, I'm sure it will work out. For all I know, the stone might not choose you at all."

"The stone gets to choose?"

"Sort of. A Bearer will usually select their successor, but sometimes the power transfer doesn't work, which means that the stone itself knows it isn't the right person. Usually the Bearer will sense that, so this sort of thing is rare."

"Do you sense that I'm the right person to be the Bearer of the Sea Stone?"

Claudi cocked her head and paused. "You're the only lifebringer I've seen in these parts in over a decade. So you must be." She shrugged. "But Bearer or not, you have a rare and important gift, and I'll work with you to develop it. Now, let's get to today's lesson."

Chapter 13

THAT EVENING AT dinner, I asked about the following night's Moon Dance, and Ruby smiled. "Right, that's tomorrow, isn't it? I'd nearly forgotten."

"How could you forget something like that?" Trina, who'd joined us for dinner, looked almost offended.

"I haven't been to one," Jasper put in. "I've never been here quite at the right time."

Trina grinned. "Well, here's your chance."

"I'm meant to head back to sea tomorrow, though."

"Stay one more night," she urged him. "You can head home after it's over."

Kaden smirked. "Our celebrations are definitely your sort of fun. Lots of dancing, a bit of drinking and food, plenty of pretty women." She winked.

"Ah, so a typical night on the Lady Liara," Jasper shot back.

"Yes, but even better. There are more people, a lot more room to dance, and the whole thing has a very magical feel to it. The fairies have finally begun showing up, which is half the reason the ritual exists."

"The *whole* reason," Trina argued.

"Why does it exist?" I asked.

She turned to me. "There was an incident many years ago where a bunch of Witch Slayers came through the Woods hunting fairies. They also tried to burn the Woods down."

"Claudi mentioned that to me earlier."

Trina nodded. "When that happened, several of the Woods-folk, including Kirilee and Hilda, helped hide the fairies. Afterward, Hilda created a sort of sanctuary for them in a secret cottage deep in the Woods. The fairies all congregate there and only come out into the rest of the Woods on rare occasions."

"How do the Moon Dances tie into that?" I asked.

"There's this group called the Seekers; some folks see us as a religion, but we're really more of a social movement. We believe that the Woods are at their most magical when the fairies are allowed to run free there, and that the fairies will be happier that way as well. So we try to make the Woods a safer and more enticing place for them. We create little gifts and leave offerings, and hold Moon Dances every full moon in hopes of drawing the fairies out of hiding. Hilda is our leader, and there are several members here in Ankrossi. My mother, Lachlann, and I are all involved."

"I've never seen a fairy. This all sounds fascinating."

"It *is* fascinating." Kaden smiled at me. "I think you'll enjoy it."

***

The next night, I found myself soaring over the Woods yet again. The grove where the Moon Dances were held was a several hours' walk, so most attendees travelled by flight, dragon, or teleportation. Today, Ruby and Trina lent some of their power to Kaden so she could give us all the ability to fly.

In front of us, the sky turned several shades of pink and orange. I noticed a few clouds sweeping across with unnatural speed, and when they settled, the sunset was even more gorgeous. I glanced over at Ruby. "Did you do that?"

"Of course." She smiled. "The sky is my canvas." Then, with a backwards glance, she said, "Look."

I followed her gaze to where the moon sat, large and yellow and low on the horizon. It was partially obscured by a few hazy clouds, so she slid them out of the way but left them close enough to light up their edges with a silver sheen.

We touched down in a large clearing whose centre was already illuminated by a massive bonfire. Several folks who I did not recognize were clustered around it, making music on pipes and drums, and a good dozen more were already engaged in a frenetic dance. Not all of Ankrossi attended these events, Ruby had told me earlier, and there were a good number of Woods-folk who were from other parts of the forest. They were easy to pick out, I realized; most of them looked even more wild than the people of Ankrossi. There were musicians decked out in clothing made mostly of fur, and dancers whose attire only covered the most necessary parts of their bodies. A mother sat on a log holding a small child, both of them with hair worked into knotty ropes. I noticed dozens of tiny, colourful balls of light flitting about the grove, and it was only when several of them landed on Trina that I realized they were fairies. I held my hand up tentatively, and a small pink fairy landed on it. I stared at the creature in wonder.

My reverie was soon interrupted by Jasper. "Are any of you ladies up for a dance?" He extended an arm.

There was a pause, then Kaden punched Trina in the shoulder. "Go for it. You know you want to." Several of the fairies that had landed on Trina floated over to Jasper, as if agreeing with Kaden's sentiment.

Trina shot Kaden a glare but took Jasper's arm, and they walked toward the other dancers, several fairies trailing after them. Ruby turned to Kaden. "Well, what do you say? Shall we—"

She trailed off as Kip came stalking across the glade. Saray followed, her eyebrows knitted in frustration. "Kip, stop," she demanded, tugging on the sleeve of his coat. "Just leave it alone!"

Kip responded by snatching his arm away and tossing her a glare. When he reached us, he scowled down at Ruby. "I thought your brother was meant to leave today."

Ruby crossed her arms and returned his stare. "Trina invited him to stay for one more day so he could attend a Moon Dance. Is that a problem?"

He huffed. "Moon Dances are sacred gatherings to honour the fairies, y'know."

"And everyone is welcome at them," Ruby shot back. "Just because *you* don't like Jasper doesn't mean he's not allowed to attend, or to spend time in Ankrossi for that matter. I'm getting tired of this, Kip."

"She's right," Saray put in. "Remember the first time we attended a Moon Dance, and the people there were unsure about Trina and me because we were city kids? Kirilee stood up for us and said that all are welcome."

Kip turned to Saray. "Maybe so, but have you considered how much information about the Woods Alvin likely gleaned when Ruby here brought him to one of these dances? We have to be cautious."

"Don't you dare compare my brother to Alvin!" Ruby fumed.

"Why not? They both shot innocent people! I—"

"Innocent? *You* betrayed me!" retorted Saray.

"You're bringing that up *now?* Eight years later?"

"*You're* bringing up what Jasper did at the exact same time!"

Kip huffed. "I can't believe this. You're my *wife*, and you're siding with *him?*"

"I'm siding with the rational people!" Saray glanced at Trina and Jasper, who were clearly unaware of our conversation. "This isn't about the safety of the Moon Dance, this is about *them.* You can't stand the way they look at each other."

Kip snorted. "What, and you think they'd be a good match? I just don't want Trina to get hurt!"

"Trina's an adult, Kip. She's the same age you were when we got married. She can dance with whoever she likes." She crossed her arms. "And you know what? So can I! In fact..." The song was ending as she spoke, and I noticed Trina and Jasper making their way towards us. Saray turned to them and extended a hand. "Jasper, would you care for a dance?"

Jasper stared at her incredulously. "You want to dance with *me?*"

"I do." She grinned. "I promise I won't set you on fire."

Jasper looked from Saray to Kip, no doubt catching Kip's furious expression, and a wry smile formed on his face. "Well, I suppose we could have one dance, for old times' sake." I didn't miss Saray's slight flinch when Jasper took her hand, but she walked with him to join the dancing couples, tossing Kip a disdainful glance as she did.

Trina stared after them. "What was *that* about? What's going on, Kip?"

He responded by letting out an aggravated grunt and storming off into the Woods.

"He didn't approve of your dance partner," Kaden informed her.

"Ah." Trina nodded knowingly. "And Saray decided to antagonize him."

Ruby nodded, smirking. "Serves him right."

"Ruby! You're not normally this hostile!"

"Yeah, this is weird. For once, I'm the peacemaker." Kaden raised an eyebrow.

Ruby sighed. "I'm just tired of the way Kip acts whenever Jasper comes around. I get it, they don't like each other, and that's fine. But who does Kip think he is, acting like it's up to *him* whether Jasper comes to the Moon Dance or stays in Ankrossi?"

Trina sighed. "Kip's gotten a lot better in the time I've known him. He's overcome his fears, learned to trust people, and forgiven a good number of folks. He's relaxed a lot. But Jasper just...sets him on edge. And Kip's very protective of me. I can see why Jasper dancing with me would..." She sighed.

"Why's he so protective of you?" I asked.

She turned to me. "Do you remember the story I told you about how Kip's mother was the one who attacked me and made me go blind? He was there when it happened. He was ten years old, and he wanted to step in and stop her from hurting me, but he was too scared. So he took his brother and dog and fled. He spent the next seven years thinking I was dead because he didn't protect me."

"So he's bent on looking after you now so that he doesn't have to feel like he failed you again."

She nodded. "He was pretty averse to me being on the Lady Liara, too."

Kaden sighed. "Kip's in the wrong, but he and I understand each other. I'll see if I can track him down." She disappeared into the Woods without further comment.

"I'm sorry you had to see all that during your first Moon Dance," Trina said to me.

I shrugged. "I've seen married people fight; I know how it is. My parents are worse than that sometimes, and they're in their fifties."

She frowned. "I'm...sorry to hear that. Anyway, I suppose we'd best find you a partner." She steered me toward a group of students from the school of magic, and soon enough I was dancing with the mahogany-skinned boy from my class, whose name I'd learned was Dane. The music was like nothing I'd ever heard before, wild and capricious, and Dane seemed to know how to move to it perfectly. I'd been dancing for years, but this was nothing like the formal dances I'd learned; there were no steps, for one thing. At first I floundered, trying to understand exactly how to move, but it didn't take long for me to figure it out.

The song ended, and Dane passed me on to a new partner, a kid who looked to not be from Ankrossi and whose name I instantly forgot. I felt myself relaxing as I moved, letting go of the propriety I'd always associated with dancing. I tossed my head back and laughed, earning both a confused look and a chuckle from my partner.

The dancing progressed, and I was passed from partner to partner, laughing and whirling in time to the beat. Kaden had returned, and she and Ruby were locked in an embrace, seeming to forget the earlier conflict; meanwhile, Jasper and Trina had abandoned dancing in favour of joining the musicians. Saray moved among the students, chatting with people she knew, and I noticed that, while Ambrose and Spark were absent, Daisy had shown up with Raelle. I was so enthralled with the dancing that I almost didn't notice the new arrival. It was only once my newest partner—Chester—stopped moving that I became aware of the fellow who had appeared in the grove without warning. "Willem's here!" Chester exclaimed, letting go of me.

Willem. I turned my attention toward the man who'd materialized in the middle of our party. Looking at him, I could easily see his resemblance to Claudi. Their skin was the same colour, and their hair possessed the same curl—though Willem's was more grey than white, with sparse patches of black scattered throughout—and I thought I saw a hint of Claudi's mischief in his face when he smiled. He greeted several friends and spent a few minutes watching as some of Alisa's younger siblings demonstrated talents they'd been working on. When Marcus reached him, the two men embraced, then spoke in hushed tones for a few minutes. Then Marcus cleared his throat. "Willem brings news from Dundere," he announced. "Any who wish to return to dancing may do so, and any who wish to hear the news may congregate over there." He pointed to a cluster of felled logs.

Chester headed over to the logs, clearly eager to hear Willem's news, and I noticed that most folks from Ankrossi were trickling over as well. I followed curiously.

Willem lowered himself onto a stump, looked around the assembled, then began to speak. "There are some very odd things occurring in Dundere right now. I was sent over to investigate the fires that have been happening near the edges of town. Neither natural nor magical means have been able to put them out, which tells me that we're likely dealing with the Fae."

Trina's eyes narrowed. "Why would the Fae be starting fires? I thought they generally liked humans, so long as we weren't unkind to them."

"The fairies of the Shrouded Woods are accustomed to humans," Willem said. "They are, in a sense, tame. That's not always the case in other places, though."

"That still doesn't answer why they'd act like this," Saray said,

"I know there have been uprisings among the Fae before," Marcus put in. "This could be something similar."

Willem added, "There are some who theorize that the Fae were involved in Noelle's death."

Marcus' eyes narrowed. "How so?"

"The Blackwells were known to have connections to the Fae. Some folks wonder if Alvin was being influenced by one when he shot her. Speaking of which, that's another odd piece of news I have for you folks." Willem frowned. "From what I heard, Alvin behaved well enough that he was moved into the general prison population a couple of months ago and given a cellmate. That same night, he was found dead in his cell, and his roommate vanished from the prison."

Marcus let out a long breath, and Trina and Saray exchanged a glance. "Perhaps that's for the best," Saray said, her voice trembling slightly. "Now Alvin can't hurt anyone."

"That's not where the deaths ended, though. Only a few days after that, Alvin's parents and sister were found murdered in the family home."

"Wait." Daisy gaped at Marcus. "Ashlynn's dead?"

"That's what I've been told, yes," he replied. "I'm sorry."

"I...I just...we weren't exactly close, but..." Unable to finish the thought, Daisy put her head in her hands.

"It was...just Ashlynn and her parents who were killed?" Jasper asked. Looking at him, I noticed that he, too, had gone pale.

"Them and a couple of servants. No one other than that, though, to my knowledge."

Jasper nodded slowly, eyes narrowing.

Willem sighed. "There's speculation that the Fae were involved in that string of deaths as well. We're not sure what to make of it all. And the Dunderi folk are very nervous."

"Unsurprisingly," Marcus commented.

"There've been rumours of people going out into the wilds to hunt the fairies down, much like what happened here in the Woods. If a war between the Fae and the humans begins in Dundere, I'm not sure how it'll turn out."

Marcus frowned. "Has anyone considered asking the Fae what they want?"

"Do you think they're after something in particular?"

"From what I know of the Dunderi Fae, I would think so. Fae are tricky and can be hard to understand, but they don't usually attack without reason."

"What if their reason is that they want the island to themselves?" countered Ruby.

"There's certainly a chance of that. But no one will know unless they are asked directly. Though that does raise another issue—not many people in Dundere, if any, know how to speak to the Fae. If we were going to negotiate with them, we'd need a translator. Perhaps Hilda can help."

"Hilda might be able to help for a short period," Willem said. "Though keep in mind that she's responsible for the fairies of the Shrouded Woods. I'm not sure if she could help for any length of..." He trailed off, and his eyes went wide. We all turned and followed his gaze.

Standing at the edge of our celebration was a squadron of soldiers. Four of them wore the flat white caps and red sashes of the Breoch Guard; the other six were dressed in bright red uniforms trimmed with gold. I gasped when I recognized their regalia. *Those are palace guards from Kirstein.*

There was a collective murmur, and several of the Woods-folk drew weapons. Shawnie morphed into his cougar form, not seeming to care about ruining his clothes; Saray let fire dance on her hands, and several wild animals came to gather around Trina. Willem seemed to conjure a pair of swords from nowhere, and they glowed with magic, lightning crackling along their steel blades. I heard a gasp and turned just in time to see Chester fall in a dead faint. Jessen, who was standing next to him, barely managed to catch him before his head hit the ground.

Another man, this one dressed in typical nobleman's clothes, stepped forward through the ranks of palace guards, and my heart dropped into my stomach. *Father?*

Marcus took a few steps toward the soldiers, positioning himself between them and the rest of the party. "What do you want with us?"

"Relax, witch," one of the younger Breoch Guard said, approaching the fire. "We're not here to hurt anyone today. We're looking for a runaway."

"I'm here." Heart hammering, I stepped forward with my hands raised.

"Isabelle!" Father exclaimed.

"Please, nobody hurt anyone," I begged, glancing between my friends and the guards as I walked toward them. "I'll come with you willing—"

Before I could finish my sentence, Father had cleared the space between us and engulfed me in a hug. My eyes widened; he wasn't typically given to public displays of affection. "We were so worried about you," he whispered.

"I...I'm sorry," I mumbled, returning his embrace. "I had to help them, and I..."

I was interrupted by a derisive laugh and pulled away from Father to see the young Breoch Guard staring across the circle. "Oh, hello, you two. Should've known I'd find you out here with this sort of scum."

I followed his gaze to Ruby and Jasper, who were both staring back at him. "Jade," Ruby said. "I, uh, hope you're well."

"Like you care, witch." Jade snorted. "It's too bad I'm not allowed to take prisoners, otherwise I'd..." He paused, his eyes scanning the gathering again. Then he turned to one of the palace guards. "You know, I imagine they might make an exception to that order for *her.*" He pointed to Saray.

I felt the mood of the group shift. Willem stepped in front of Saray, glowing swords at the ready. Shawnie emitted a growl, and Ruby let lightning dance and crackle on her hands.

"Leave it, Jade," my father said. "We've got what we came for."

"But, sir, this is Saray McAllister, one of the most wanted witches in all of Breoch," Jade argued.

My eyes narrowed. *McAllister?*

Father let out an odd gasp, and I stared at him as he looked Saray over. Then his jaw clenched, and he snorted. "You know what? You're right. Bring her along; she shouldn't exist anyway."

I gaped at him. *What are you doing?*

Jade advanced, and Marcus let two of his daggers fly from his belt, where they hovered in mid-air. "Touch my daughter, and I will send these through your eyes, boy."

Jade snickered. Then he reached up and pulled a pendant from his shirt, closing his hand around it. A strange, shuddering jolt swept across the field, eliciting a chorus of cries from the magikai, and suddenly my senses felt muted, as if I were moving through a thick fog. Marcus' blades dropped to the ground, then Willem's swords disappeared completely, and Saray's fire fizzled out. Shawnie morphed back into his human form and scrambled to gather the remnants of his tattered pants around him. The rest of the Breoch Guard clutched similar pendants, I saw. My eyes widened. *Anti-magic.*

"Wait, how are you—" Willem protested but was cut off by my father.

"Your *daughter?* Oh, this is rich. Finding Saray here is one thing, but *you...*" He stalked toward Marcus like a cat hunting its prey.

Marcus frowned, then his eyes widened with recognition. "Caspa?"

"I didn't recognize you either." My father's voice was silky with malice. "It's odd seeing you with both hands. And a voice. And freedom, for that matter." He snorted. "I should have you arrested along with Saray."

"For what?" Marcus spat. "Simply *existing* as a magic user? You notice that the krossemage thing didn't work out so well."

"You've done a lot more than just *exist*, and you know it. But no, I don't think I'll have you arrested. I think I'll leave you here with the knowledge that your bastard daughter will pay for her crimes, and there's little you can do about it." He eyed Jade. "Take her away."

Jade's gun had been trained on Saray, but now he moved to aim it at Daisy. "I suggest you come with us without a fuss, Saray, otherwise I'll be shooting that baby." Daisy's eyes widened, and she turned away from Jade, shielding Raelle with her body.

"That's enough." I turned as Jasper stepped forward, his own gun drawn. He stood between Jade and Daisy. "You came here to bring Isabelle home. Take her and be on your way. Stop with this bravado—you wouldn't actually shoot a baby."

"Is that so?" Jade's voice turned menacing, and he drew another pace closer to Jasper. "You think you know me well enough to dictate what I would and wouldn't do?"

"I know you well enough to know that you're full of empty threats," Jasper countered. "You may be on the wrong side, but you're not a monster."

"No, I'm not. Saray and all these other witches, they're the monsters. And *I'm* the one making empty threats?" Jade eyed Jasper's gun and smirked. "You say I wouldn't shoot a baby. I say that you wouldn't shoot your own brother."

"I don't want to," Jasper said through clenched teeth.

"And you won't. You're too soft for that. Though I'd invite you to try." Jade lifted his chin. "Shoot me, Jasper. Do your worst. Because if you do, the others will open fire on you and all of your friends, and it'll be more than just one baby who dies." I watched in horror as both the remaining Breoch Guard and the palace guards drew their own weapons.

"Jade!" Ruby came to stand next to Jasper, her voice indignant. "Who are you turning into? You never used to be this cruel!"

"Yes, well, having my *wife* murdered by your friends may have changed me a little," Jade sneered. He flicked his gun ever so slightly, and Ruby shrieked when he fired. A second later, Daisy cried out in pain and collapsed as the bullet embedded itself in her leg.

"Stop. All of you." Saray raised her hands. "I'll come with you."

"Saray, no!" Marcus gasped.

"I can't let them hurt the people I love just to get to me," she said, her voice wavering. She looked from Marcus to my father, then to me. "This is your father?" she asked me, tilting her head.

I nodded.

"What's your mother's name?"

I blinked, baffled as to why she was asking me this. "Lillian. Why?"

Saray's lips parted, and she exchanged a glance with Marcus. "Are your parents still together?" she asked me.

"Enough," Father cut in. "Jade, take her away."

Jade smirked as he advanced on Saray, his gaze almost predatory. Then he turned back to the rest of the Woods-folk, removing his anti-magic pendant and holding it high. "You can thank your friend Lachlann for this, by the way." He dropped the pendant over Saray's head, eliciting a gasp of pain as it made contact with her skin. Then he grabbed her arm and led her over to the remainder of the Breoch Guard.

"Isabelle, come with us." Father's voice was clipped, devoid of its earlier affection.

Walking toward him, I felt my stomach sinking as a realization settled into my mind. *This is my doing.* The guards came here looking for me, because I was the one who ran off. I watched, horrified, as the Breoch Guard surrounded Saray and put her in chains.

Saray, the Unbeatable One, had finally been beaten. And it was all my fault.

Chapter 14

THE JOURNEY OUT of the Shrouded Woods was silent, save for the footsteps of our party and eventually the horses. The Breoch Guard kept Saray several paces behind me and the palace guard. When we reached the meadow beyond the Shrouded Woods, I found a sight eerily similar to the one that had awaited me after the fateful botany lesson: a coach and a prison carriage. The Breoch Guard locked Saray into the prison carriage, and Father and I were led to the coach.

I began talking the moment Father and I were alone, well aware that he was likely going to lay into me about my disappearance. "What happened back there?" I demanded. "With Saray, with Marcus?"

Father frowned. "Saray is a very wanted criminal. We apprehended her."

"But the original orders were to come just for me. And you weren't going to allow her arrest until you heard her name." I shook my head. "Who is Saray to you? Who is *Marcus* to you?"

"They're nothing to me."

"If you don't tell me, I'm going to ask Mother."

He let out a long sigh. "Very well. If you must know, Saray is the product of a tryst between your mother and Marcus."

"*What?*" I felt my jaw go slack.

"You can see why I'm not too fond of him, or of her for that matter."

I blinked, trying to wrap my mind around the implications of this new information. "So that means that Saray is my..."

"Your half-sister. And a very dangerous and very wanted magic user."

"So now you're going to let them kill her, just to punish Marcus?" My voice was getting louder. "That's not fair! Saray can't help where she came from! How can you—"

"Enough! Saray is wanted for all kinds of misdeeds, and she'll be punished for them as the king sees fit. You have no right to lecture *me* after what you did, young lady." Father shook his head, his gaze turning icy. I felt my stomach lurch; as a child, that look was usually followed by a beating. "Do you have any idea how much worry you've caused your mother and me? Not to mention Oliver, and the king himself! What possessed you to run off into the Woods and join a group of rebel witches? Do you understand how much danger you may have put yourself in?"

I kept my chin high, my eyes on his. "Mother said it was all right for me to go with them."

"Your mother was out of her mind when she said that! Trust me, I wasn't too happy with her either." Father pinched the bridge of his nose. "Isabelle, *why?* Why did you run off? Your mother said something about the people in the Woods needing your help?"

I nodded slowly, trying to figure out how best to explain myself. Father might be angry at me, but I couldn't see him turning me in to the Breoch Guard over my actions. "If I tell you," I finally said, "do you promise to keep it to yourself? Mother can know, but no one else. I could get in real trouble for this."

"You're already in trouble," he replied. "But yes, I won't tell the authorities, if that's—" He stopped, and his face went white. "You were healing people."

I averted my eyes and nodded. "I've only ever used my magic to heal myself before this." That wasn't entirely true, of course, but it was close enough to the truth. "My abilities came up during the botany class. The Woods-folk were curious if I had any magic, and I told them the truth."

"So they kidnapped you from your home to be their healer?"

"No! Why do you assume the worst? I went with them willingly." I let out a long sigh. "After Lachlann was taken, his wife went into labour unexpectedly from the shock of it all, and her baby was born very, very premature. She was going to die. So the Woods-folk found me and asked if I'd be willing to come back with them to heal her. It was meant to only be for a few hours, but it turned out the baby needed more than just a quick heal. So they asked me to stay, in exchange for help learning how to use my gift."

"You shouldn't be *learning* any of it." Father's tone was laced with disappointment. "Listen, I understand that you can't help healing yourself. But you know well enough that using your magic on anyone else could get you turned into a krossemage."

"Of course I know that!" I shot back. "It makes no sense, though. I understand why fire magic and moving things with your mind and stormbrewing can be dangerous. But healing? I could do so much good with my magic, Father! I know you sometimes complain about your bad knee; I could fix that. And Grandmother's back pain...and...and Oliver..." I trailed off, tears springing to my eyes.

"You'd best not be trying any of that on the crown prince, my dear." Father's voice softened slightly. "Listen, I can only imagine how tempting it must be to use your magic. But the law is the law. If we allow one kind of magic, then it's only a matter of time before other witches demand to be able to use theirs, and soon enough, we're back to the conditions that existed before the Banishing. A free-for-all where folks are allowed to use their abilities however they want."

"It doesn't have to be a free-for-all. Did you not hear Lachlann's suggestions? They manage to have legal magic in Dundere without any of those issues."

"And yet it was that fellow with his charm magic who managed to manipulate a bunch of our guards to attack Dundere, who killed off the governor, and who could have easily started a war between our two nations. Clearly, their magic is *not* perfectly under control." Father shook his head. "If you have an issue with this, you should be talking to Kairus, not me. Speaking of which, I will have to discuss your running away with him."

I drew in a breath. "Please don't tell him about the magic."

"What do you want me to tell him, then?"

"Tell him I ran off because I was looking for people to help me find Silva and the other students. That's somewhat true."

Father nodded slowly. "I'll do that. But I don't know what this will do for your prospects, Isabelle. I don't know if the king will want his son marrying someone who has a penchant for running off and getting herself into trouble."

I nodded; I'd already thought about this.

"You'll be staying at home for the next little while unless escorted, I will tell you that much right now. You also have schoolwork to catch up on."

"Of course." The carriage was slowing down; I looked out the window to see that we were in Sylvenburgh now.

"We have rooms rented here for the night," Father told me, answering my unspoken question. "We'll head home in the morning."

Our rooms were in the Sylvenburgh Grand Hotel, and Father had rented a lavish two-bedroom suite for himself and I. Only once we were safely in our room did Father seem to notice the changes in my appearance. "What are you *wearing?*"

I shrugged, glancing down at myself. I was in the blue dress and a pink waistcoat from Alexander and Ember's shop today, and Trina had put pink and yellow makeup around my eyes before the dance. "These were the clothes they gave me; they're easier to navigate the forest in."

"They're highly inappropriate. I should have thought to bring a change of clothes for you." He let out a long sigh and put his fingertips to his temples. "Go to bed, Isabelle."

I retreated to my room, peeled off my dress and crawled into bed completely nude, as I had no nightclothes with me. Alone, I found myself shaking in the dark. My head spun, and I wanted to cry, but I could not. The accusatory thoughts from earlier began to spin about in my head, taunting me, and I lay back and stared at the ceiling, wondering if I would sleep at all tonight.

Somehow I doubted it.

***

The drive from Sylvenburgh to Kirstein the next morning was silent, save for occasional sighs from my father. The knot of dread in my stomach grew tighter as we neared the city, and by the time we reached home, I was nearly ready to lose my breakfast.

I should have known that Mother would respond to me a little better than Father had—at least, I suppose it was better. She all but pulled me out of the carriage and into her arms, sobbing. "I should never have let you go," she blubbered. "Never again..."

"Mother, you're hurting me," I protested, trying to wriggle free of her grasp.

She clung to me for a minute longer, then pulled back, tears still streaming down her face. "It's all right, Mother," I said, trying to sound reassuring. "I'm here. I'm safe. I was safe all along."

She shook her head. "I don't know what got into me, letting you go with that girl." Her voice was riddled with guilt. "I swear I must have been out of my—"

"Isabelle?" a familiar voice cut in, and my head snapped up.

I had not expected Oliver to be there awaiting my arrival, but here he was, staring at me with his luminescent green eyes, his curls slightly askew. I gaped at him for a moment, then forced a smile. "Hi, Oliver."

He cleared the space between us—limping slightly, I noticed—then opened his arms tentatively. I stepped away from Mother and embraced him. "I've missed you," he murmured as he wrapped his arms around me.

"I've missed you too. A lot." I meant the words as I said them.

"Lillian," my father said, "perhaps we could give these two a moment alone? There's something I need to tell you, and you're not going to be happy about it."

I watched my parents retreat into the house, then turned to Oliver. "So, did I miss anything exciting while I was gone?" I tried to keep my voice chipper.

"Yes. A lot, actually, but I don't want to talk about it now." He smiled. "I want to know about your adventures. Will you tell me? Is there actually a secret village in the Woods?"

I hesitated for a moment. "I suppose I can, a little later perhaps, but...aren't you mad at me for running away?"

Oliver shrugged. "Not mad. I was worried, of course, but I can't be angry at you for doing something I'd likely do myself if I had the chance."

"You...want to run away?"

"Maybe not forever. But for a few weeks, like you did. It'd be nice not to have to be a—" He was cut off by the sound of a door slamming inside the house, and a moment later my mother let out an anguished wail. Oliver frowned. "Do you want to go check on her?"

I was about to respond when Renee, the head of the staff, joined us in the front yard. She bowed to Oliver. "You'd best head home, Your Highness. Your father is expecting Isabelle's family for a visit, and she needs to get cleaned up."

"Of course." Oliver squeezed my hand. "See you in a few hours," he said to me before making his way to his carriage.

"All right, my lady, time to get all that Woods-nonsense cleaned off you." Renee's voice was firm.

I shook my head. "I should go see Mother."

"Leave her. Your mother has just received some devastating news, and she's asked for some space. Now come."

I sighed and followed her into the house, trying to ignore the sound of my mother's quiet, desperate sobs.

***

A few hours later, I sat in the royal family's private living quarters. Renee had successfully managed to tame my "Woods-nonsense"; I was now dressed in an elegant floral-patterned dress, ankle length and sleeved, my makeup was gone, and my hair was pulled back into a braided updo.

Mother had pulled herself together for this meeting, but I couldn't help noticing her puffy eyes and the way she refused to look at my father. She huddled near Calendra, making soft small talk, trying to appear as if her only cause of distress was my behaviour.

The first thing I'd noticed upon my arrival at the castle was the heavy presence that I knew to be anti-magic. The entire palace was draped in it. I couldn't identify the source, but I had no doubt it had something to do with Lachlann. I'd been surprised to see

Simon talking with my father and Kairus when Mother and I arrived. As soon as Oliver showed up, though, Simon ducked out of the room, clearly not wanting to be present for whatever happened next.

Now Kairus turned away from his conversation with my father and looked me over. Something had changed in his face since I'd last seen him—he looked older, more tired, somewhat devoid of his usual *presence*. Eyebrows pinched with worry, he let out a long sigh when he met my gaze. "Glad to see you're safe, Isabelle." Mother and Calendra ceased their conversation, and all eyes were on me.

I nodded and dipped my head, not quite sure how to respond.

"I see you and Oliver have already reunited." A smile tugged at his lips.

"He came over to see me earlier." My shoulders hunched. "Where's Saray? What's going to happen to her?"

"There will be a hearing tomorrow, don't you worry." He shook his head slightly. "But Saray should be the least of your concerns right now, young lady, after you ran off the way you did. Do you know how much heartache you caused your parents? Oliver? Me?"

I sighed. "I...I'm sorry, sir. I did tell Mother that I was safe; I hoped she'd be able to pass that on to the rest of you."

"All that did was make us wonder about your poor mother's sanity." Kairus shook his head. "Well, we won't have to worry about you running off again, after what your father, Simon and I decided."

A hollow feeling formed in my stomach. Then I glanced at Oliver, who had gone rigid and refused to meet my eyes. "Are you breaking us up?" The words came out as a whisper.

"No, absolutely not. On the contrary, we're bringing you closer together." Kairus eyed me. "The two of you have been betrothed for many years now, and we've decided it's time to take the next step toward your union. This afternoon, messengers were sent to all corners of Breoch to announce Prince Oliver's official engagement to Lady Isabelle McAllister. The two of you will be married in the fall, when Oliver turns eighteen."

The words hit me like a punch in the gut. I gaped at Kairus. "Married?" I repeated. "But...I'm not even seventeen! I haven't finished school yet."

"You can finish your lessons from the palace easily enough, my dear." Kairus dismissed my concerns with a wave of his hand. "It's for the best, Isabelle. You've had your fun consorting with the Woods-folk. It's time for you to grow up now."

My gaze shifted to Oliver, who eyed me, smiling in a way that seemed almost shy. "You...you knew about this."

"Father talked to me about it, yes."

"And you're not opposed to getting married so young?"

He shrugged. "I mean, we were going to be wed eventually. Why not sooner rather than later?"

I blinked, struggling to find the right words to answer his question. "I suppose it's just that I thought I had a few more years of...freedom."

"Freedom?" Oliver's face fell. "You think being married to me would be like imprisonment?"

"No, I didn't mean that, it's just…" I sighed. "Your father did make it sound like a punishment." I glanced at Kairus. "We're being married soon to keep me from running off again."

"There's more to it than that, my dear," Kairus said, but I barely heard him. My eyes were on Oliver's face, on the crushed expression I'd caused.

"You know what? You're right." Oliver's voice was soft, defeated. "Marrying me would be a punishment at this point."

"Oliver!" I protested. "I didn't mean it like that! It's just that being a princess will have a lot of obligations, and I'm not sure if I'm ready."

He shook his head. "You don't understand, Isabelle." His voice was hollow. Without another word, he turned and limped out of the room.

I was left staring at Kairus and my father. "I…I wasn't trying to hurt him."

"Of course not. Some things have happened while you were away, and he's a little sensitive right now." Kairus sighed, the sad, worried expression crossing his face once more. He turned to my father. "You three had best head home. Tomorrow will be busy with the hearing, and I need to speak to my son and get some rest."

Chapter 15

THE FOLLOWING MORNING, I was back at the palace, though this time in the throne room. Growing up, it was Kairus' father Edwin who sat on the throne, and so it was always a little odd to me seeing Kairus perched there. The crown he wore for legal proceedings wasn't the massive jewelled thing he'd worn at his coronation, but it was enough to remind us all who was in charge. I sat next to my mother, waiting for the hearing to begin. Oliver was seated close to his father; he'd met my eyes earlier and offered me a thin smile but hadn't yet spoken to me.

The doors at the far side of the room opened, and we all turned to watch as Saray was led into the chamber, in chains. She looked very much like she had yesterday, only her hair was more mussed, her eyes puffy with either a lack of sleep or crying. *Likely both,* I decided. She held her head high, though, only dipping it to bow to Kairus when she was an appropriate distance from the throne.

"Saray," Kairus said to her, "it's a pleasure to finally meet you."

Saray dipped her head again, clearly a little unsure what to say in response.

"I was quite surprised when they brought you here," he went on. "I sent my men into the Woods to find a missing girl, and they came back with one of the most wanted witches in all of Breoch? We had no idea you were even on the island. Though, I imagine that was the point, wasn't it?"

When Saray didn't respond, Kairus shook his head. "Ah, well. I didn't bring you here to interrogate you, girl. I wanted to explain my plans for you."

"Plans, Your Majesty?" Saray's eyes narrowed.

"Of course. What did you think I was going to do, let you rot away in a cell?"

"I was told once by a Breoch Guard that I was to be executed publicly, as a warning to all other magic users."

"Ah, yes, that was my father's plan if he ever caught you. And it's still an option, if need be. But I think it'd be a shame to waste your talents."

"My...talents?" she repeated. "Your Majesty, aren't my *talents* what got me arrested in the first place?"

"Yes. But even so, they could be of use. Pieter, please stand."

I watched Pieter climb to his feet and bow to Saray. "Saray, my dear, Pieter here is my court mage."

Pieter nodded, and I couldn't help but notice the way his nose scrunched up when he looked at the firebrand, as if she smelled bad or was in some other way unpleasant.

"I would demonstrate my talents for you, but your friend Lachlann is doing a mighty good job of keeping all the magic at bay. Talented fellow, he is."

Saray glared at him. "Don't try to fool me, sir. I don't believe for a moment that Lachlann is helping you willingly."

"Oh, he seemed quite willing once the proper pressure was applied," Pieter responded, the disdain in his voice more obvious now.

Saray's face paled. "You tortured him."

"*I* didn't personally. And it wasn't the torture that broke him. We have someone here who knows your friend's weakness, and Lachlann's been quite cooperative ever since we used it against him—he's been lending us his anti-magic, even gave us the location of your celebration."

"We're getting off topic," Kairus cut in. "As you can see, Saray, Pieter here is getting a little older, and he will soon be looking for a replacement. I would like to have you train under him and become my next court mage."

Saray stared at Kairus for a moment, her eyes wide. "Your Majesty, may I ask what exactly a court mage is meant to do in a land where magic is illegal?"

Kairus nodded at Pieter, who faced Saray. "In order to keep magic under control, it must be well understood. The court mage is meant to study magical theory, then act as a resource to the council as needed. On the rare occasion, I'm asked to utilize my magic, but I'm mostly just an advisor. For example, several years back a revolt began on a prison farm. The witches there happened upon some knowledge that could have allowed them to overthrow their captors. I was the one who knew enough to see the true danger of the situation, and thus advise a cull of the entire island."

Saray's face went white, and she turned back to Kairus. "Your Majesty, do I understand correctly that the court mage is often asked to work against their fellow magic users, in order to better contain them?"

"Very much so," Pieter answered before Kairus could respond. Kairus shot him a glare but nodded in agreement.

"Then I will refuse your offer, Your Majesty."

"Is that so?" Kairus frowned. "You do realize that I am trying to save you, Saray. My hope was not to follow through with my father's plan. But if you refuse my offer, your only other choice is death."

Saray's chin lifted. "Then I choose death."

My heart dropped into my stomach.

A murmur rippled through the room, and I noticed a satisfied smirk on Pieter's face. Kairus closed his eyes briefly, then squared his shoulders. "So be it. Guards, take the prisoner away. We'll arrange for a hanging at noon three days from now in the palace courtyard; we don't want any magic in the vicinity."

"No," I heard a strangled voice beside me whisper. I glanced over to see Mother gaping at Saray, her face pale.

The guards took Saray away, and the court began to disperse. I stayed rooted where I was, shaking, hardly noticing that Oliver came to sit next to me. "Are you all right?" he asked.

I turned to him. His hurt from the day before was no longer evident on his face; all I saw was concern. "What do you think?"

He put a hand on my shoulder. "I'm sorry. Father tried to save her."

"By convincing her to work against the people she cares about?" I huffed. "I'm not surprised she turned him down."

"It was your mother's idea, you know." Oliver frowned. "She seems very determined to save Saray."

I nodded slowly. "That...makes sense." Speaking of Mother, she seemed to have vanished from the room. "I should go find her."

"Do you want company?"

"Not right now. But perhaps later?"

Oliver nodded, a vague smile tugging at his lips. "I'd like that. I've...missed you, you know. And as I said yesterday, I want to hear more about the Woods."

I attempted a smile in return. Telling Oliver about the Woods would provide me a distraction at the very least. "All right. We can talk after dinner."

I left the throne room and began to walk down the long, winding hall toward Mother's chambers. My head spun, and I was hardly aware of someone falling into step next to me. It was only when I accidentally bumped into him that I noticed and stopped. "Simon? What is it?"

"Isabelle." He gave me a sympathetic smile. "I imagine that today must have been hard for you."

I nodded, uncertain how else to respond.

"Would you take a walk with me?" he asked.

"I, uh...I'm looking for Mother."

"Perhaps she needs some privacy." Simon twirled his braid in his fingers slowly as he spoke. "Come on. I need to speak with you."

I followed him nearly without thinking, and he led me out into one of the palace's winding gardens. He was quiet until we were far from the noise of the castle. Then he turned and looked down at me. "I imagine this has been a difficult few days for you."

I snorted; I could hardly help myself. "And what would give you that idea?"

He studied me with his dark eyes. They turned almost golden when the light hit them a certain way, I noticed. "You've gotten close to Saray, I imagine? And to...whoever else you met while you were off in the Woods?" He began to twirl the end of his braid again as he spoke.

I found his gaze to be oddly disarming, and I sank down onto a nearby bench before replying. "I wasn't particularly close to Saray, but I still care about what happens to her. There were others who I got to know a little better than her."

"Others?" He smiled at me. "We've all heard the rumours about a village in the middle of the Woods. Tell me, are they true?"

His eyes bored into mine, and when I said, "Yes, it's true," it felt like a release.

"Please, tell me more. I'd love to visit someday." Though his fingers still worried the end of his braid, his face was alight with wonder.

Almost without my consent, I found myself telling him everything that had happened during my time in Ankrossi, about the market and the strange fashions, the odd governmental structure, and the way magic was incorporated into everyday life. When I was finished, he nodded slowly. "Saray was a big part of that place, wasn't she?"

I bobbed my head. "Everyone thought she was invincible. It's going to kill them, losing her."

"I can only imagine. Losing both her and Lachlann would be difficult." His eyes narrowed. "I assume Lachlann was a part of the village as well?"

"Of course. He's greatly missed."

"By many, I imagine. I mean, I assume he has family there?"

I nodded. "His wife lives in Ankrossi, and their newborn baby. She's the reason I was brought to the village, actually—they wanted me to use my healing magic on the child." My eyes widened as soon as I spoke. *Why did I just tell him I have magic?*

However, Simon seemed to all but ignore my confession, tilting his head to one side before changing the subject entirely. "Isabelle, if I wanted to visit Ankrossi, how would I get there?"

I laughed. "That's a good question. I'm fairly sure there are roads in and out of it, but when I went there it was via flight and teleportation and dragons. I know there's a river close by, but I don't know how to get there."

"A shame." He shook his head. "I suppose I'll have to go find a dragon to take me."

"They're more common than you likely think." Staring up at Simon, I found myself remembering what I'd heard courtiers say about him having Kairus wrapped around his finger. "Simon? You seem to be good at getting the king to listen to you—do you think you could persuade him not to kill Saray?"

Simon frowned. "And what would you have him do with her instead? Life in prison is no better a sentence, believe me."

"Maybe he could just let her go. She hasn't caused trouble with her magic in many years, and she was safe and happy in Ankrossi." I frowned. "With your desire to visit there, I imagine you're a little more amenable to magic than some."

Simon laughed lightly. "You may be right about that, but I'm not certain that even I can persuade the king to just let Saray go. I'll talk to him, though, all right?"

I smiled, the knot in my stomach releasing ever so slightly. "That would be very much appreciated. Thank you."

He stood. "I'd best get back to work. Thank you for walking with me, Isabelle, you've given me plenty to think about."

Leaving me alone with the flowers, Simon strolled off, and I sat for a long moment wondering what exactly had prompted our conversation before exiting the garden myself.

***

Later that evening, Oliver and I sat in the palace courtyard, our backs pressed against the bell tower while I told him some very select stories about Ankrossi. "I knew it." He grinned. "Father always suspected that there was a village in the Woods somewhere."

"You're not going to tell him any of this, though, right?"

"Of course not. Your secrets are safe with me."

I sighed. "I'm worried about the people back there. Losing Saray is going to be incredibly hard for them."

Oliver slipped an arm around my shoulders, and I leaned into him. "Is there anything I can do to make you feel better?"

I frowned. "Do you think you could get me into the dungeons, so I could visit her?"

"Probably. I could try, at least."

"That would likely help. I'm sure she'd like to see a friendly face." I sighed. "For now, though, this feels nice. Just...being with you like this."

"It doesn't feel like a *punishment?*"

"Not at all. I'm sorry my words came out like that. This whole thing was...just a bit of a shock for me."

"I imagine so." His arm around me tightened, and I relaxed into him. Our relationship had always been so dictated by decorum, by what was considered appropriate for a prince to engage in, and I'd never really allowed myself to lean into him, to press my body into his like this. I rested my head on his collarbone, and he buried his face in my hair for a brief moment. Then he sat up straighter. "So, given that we're, uh, engaged and all now, I believe I'm *officially* allowed to kiss you. If you want, that is."

I looked up at him. A smile played on his lips, and he twirled a piece of my hair in his fingers. "Do you think it'll be better now than it was when we were young?"

He laughed. "I almost forgot about that. I would hope so. I suppose we'd better get used to kissing, given that if we're to be married soon they'll expect..." He looked away and blushed.

I felt heat rise in my own cheeks. I was well aware that many of my classmates had begun sleeping with one another years ago; I heard the stories whispered in the halls and bathrooms. With us, that was clearly never an option. Kissing, though, seemed far less intimidating. "We could try kissing," I said.

"Are you sure? I don't want to push you, especially with how you're feeling right now."

"No, it's fine. I think it might be a nice distraction."

"If you say so." Oliver smiled down at me for a moment. "This might be easier standing."

"Right." I got to my feet, and he followed suit. I noticed that he swayed slightly as he stood, and I frowned. "Are you all right?"

"I'm fine," he assured me, adjusting his stance. "Come here."

I moved in, and Oliver put his arms around me carefully. I was suddenly very aware of my hands, unsure where to put them. I settled for placing one on his bicep, as if we were dancing. We stared at one another for a few long moments, our faces only inches apart. My heart was pounding; I could feel his breath on my skin. Then he leaned in and brushed his lips against mine, his movement hesitant. I gently wove my fingers into his curls and nudged his head just a bit closer to mine. The next time our lips met, there was more decisiveness.

A hunger that I hardly knew I had begun to rise inside of me, and I kissed him back, hard. I heard his breath catch in his throat—clearly, he did not expect this ferocity from me, and he pressed his lips against mine more fervently. I felt the tip of his tongue flick curiously against my teeth, and I responded in kind. One of his hands made its way into my hair, his other staying firmly pressed against my back; he seemed to have no intention of letting it wander any lower, but I felt his body beginning to relax. He pulled away for a moment, gasping for breath. "Well," he panted, "I'd say that was better than when we were kids."

"Me too," I agreed, then pulled him toward me once again.

Our kissing turned ferocious, and I was barely aware of the world around me. His lips on mine, his body pressed against me, were everything. He pulled away for a moment to shift slightly, then leaned down and pressed his lips to me once more.

And promptly lost his balance.

He plummeted forward, knocking me back and sending us both sprawling. I let out a yelp as my elbow met the cobblestones. Oliver landed on top of me, gasping, and immediately scrambled off. "I'm so sorry, Isabelle," he said, his cheeks turning red. "Are you all right?"

"I'm fine," I said, ignoring the pain in my elbow that I knew would resolve in a matter of minutes. "Are you?"

"Yes, I'm...well, actually, no." Oliver got to his feet unsteadily and offered me a hand. "I should explain."

I accepted gingerly, suddenly unsure if helping me up would set him off balance again. We settled back against the bell tower, Oliver refusing to meet my eyes. "I shouldn't have kissed you, Isabelle," he said. "None of this is fair to you."

"You mean our being rushed into marriage?"

"No, it's more than that. There's something else you need to know."

I frowned, all my recent fears coming to mind. "You're sick, aren't you? With the same disease your mother had?"

He averted his gaze and slowly nodded. "I didn't know for certain until last week. The doctor says I likely won't live past twenty-five, Isabelle." His voice broke as he said the words, and a tear trickled down his cheek.

The truth hit me like a punch to the gut. The world spun around me, and I felt tears welling in my own eyes. I blinked them away, forcing myself to look at Oliver, whose shoulders were shaking as he wept silently into his hands. I suspected that he hadn't let himself break down and cry about all this until now.

I moved so I was kneeling in front of him, then pulled him toward me and wrapped my arms around his shuddering frame. "I'm so sorry, Oliver," I whispered. I wanted to say more, to speak some form of comfort to him, but I was utterly at a loss for words.

He pulled away from me after a minute or so, swiping at his eyes. "No, *I'm* sorry," he said, his voice shaking as he took my hands in his. "You shouldn't have to marry me when I'm in this condition. You saw how my mother was. You shouldn't have to endure that."

"But..." I shook my head. "But I *care* about you. I don't want you to die alone. It would be all right. We would have a few years together at least, and then I could remarry. I..."

"No. It's more complex than that." He closed his eyes briefly. "The reason they're pressuring us to marry so quickly isn't to keep you from running off again. That may have been your father's motivation, but it's not my father's."

"Then what is it?"

"My father wants an heir. If I die without having a child, then when Father passes, the throne will go to one of the cousins who've been lurking around, trying to win his favour. If we marry and have a child, you'll still be the mother of the future king or queen after I'm gone. You'll have to stay around the palace and raise the child, alone. I don't know if you'll be given the chance to remarry." He sighed. "As I said, this entire situation is unfair to you. If you want to run back to the Woods, I understand. It's about the only way I can see for you to escape this."

I stared at him for a moment, slowly digesting his words. "Your father is willing to trap me like that so his bloodline can keep the throne? That doesn't sound like him."

Oliver frowned. "I think it's more that he doesn't trust any of the alternatives. Well, other than Simon. But this whole thing was Simon's idea."

"Why would Simon want us to produce an heir if he has his eyes on the throne?"

"I've wondered that too. My guess is that he's hoping Father would name him regent after my death, so that if our child inherits the throne before he's of age, Simon can influence them to rule how he pleases."

I stared at Oliver for a long moment, my thoughts racing, then took a deep breath. "I know another way to solve this. But I'm not sure if you'd be willing to go through with it."

His eyes narrowed. "What's that?"

"You know that many of the folks in the Woods have magic," I said, choosing my words carefully. "Well, I know of a young woman who has healing magic. She could likely cure you."

He eyed me. "You're suggesting that I allow someone to use *magic* on me?"

"I know it's illegal. But it's literally a matter of life and death for you."

"But word has gotten out about my illness. If it suddenly disappears, folks would be suspicious. Father would know, at the very least, and I'm not sure what he'd do if he found out I let it happen."

"You don't think he'd be happy you get to live a long and full life?"

"I'm sure he would. But he'd have to deal with pressure from the council—not to mention the cousins—to punish me in some way."

"I imagine that any punishment he'd dole out would be worth not dying like this, Oliver."

"Maybe." He sighed. "I'll think about it, all right?"

I settled back into sitting next to him, my body leaning into his, and we were both quiet for a few minutes. "Do you want to go see Saray tomorrow?" he finally asked me.

I nodded. "That would be wonderful."

"All right. Come back here with your parents in the morning, and I'll see about getting us into the dungeon." He stood carefully and offered me a watery smile. "You should get home. Tomorrow will be busy, and the last few days have been exhausting for both of us."

Chapter 16

I HARDLY SLEPT that night. My anxious thoughts kept me tossing and turning, unable to shut my mind off. The following morning, bleary-eyed and barely awake, I followed Oliver into the palace dungeon. We'd snuck down here a few times as kids and spent hours wandering the labyrinth of cells, gawking at the prisoners and trying to escape the notice of the guards. One time, we'd happened upon the interrogation room, and Oliver hopped onto the rack and splayed himself wide on it, letting out silent screams and stage-whispered cries. That was one of the only times our presence in the dungeons was discovered. Kairus told us both, very sternly, that if we ever tried that again, he'd let the head jailer have a few minutes with both of us in the interrogation room. I was never certain if he was serious.

Today, the guards seemed to pay us little heed as we made our way through the cold, damp cellblocks. I kept my eye out for Lachlann but didn't see him.

We found Saray at the far end of the dungeon, in a cell whose bars were thicker than most. The muted feel of anti-magic was stronger here than in the rest of the prison, and I saw several of what looked like anti-magic pendants fastened to the bars.

Saray still seemed very much like herself. Her eyes were bright, and her red hair had come loose from its braid, tumbling every direction in a mass of curls. They hadn't taken away her Woods-clothes; she still wore her vibrant blue and gold coat, pulled tight for warmth in the damp prison block. But something about her did feel subdued, almost frail. Looking at her, I realized that despite her reputation, despite all the rumours about her being nearly unkillable and one of the most powerful magikai in all of Breoch, she was, still, barely an adult. She gave me a ghost of a smile as I approached. "Isabelle?"

I did my best to smile back. "Hi, Saray."

"How did you get in here?"

"I...uh...have some connections." I gestured at Oliver, who was standing back, allowing us space for our conversation.

Saray looked him over. "Is this your boyfriend?"

"Fiancé," I told her, the word feeling surreal on my tongue. "Happens to be first in line to the throne of Breoch."

Saray's mouth fell open. "You're engaged to Prince...Oliver, is it?" She eyed him, a faint blush colouring her cheeks. "I'm sorry, Your Highness, I haven't lived in the cities for a while, and I've forgotten the lineage. I only remember you as a child."

"It's all right." Oliver dipped his head. "Sometimes I forget I'm a prince myself."

Saray gave him a nervous laugh, then turned back to me. "Why didn't you tell us you were engaged to the prince?"

"Because I didn't want to scare you all, or make you think that I was untrustworthy. Though it seems that my connections did manage to hurt you." I sighed, blinking back tears. "This is all my fault. If the guards hadn't come into the Woods looking for me, they wouldn't have found you."

Saray shook her head. "These things are never one person's fault, Isabelle. They were bound to catch up with me eventually. I just hope that the folks back in the Woods are..." She trailed off, her voice wavering, then took a deep, shuddering breath. "This could break them. For so long, they've looked to me as someone who couldn't be beaten, as proof that they also might be invincible. Without that, I worry about the morale of Ankrossi. And I'm scared of what this'll do to Father and Trina...to Kip..." A few tears trailed down her cheeks. I reached through the bars to offer her my hand, and she squeezed it. "He'll blame himself, you know."

"Kip?"

"Yes. Remember our fight at the Moon Dance? He'll get it in his head that if he'd been there, he could've saved me. Which isn't true, but he'll still think it." She swiped at her eyes. "Are you...considering going back? To Ankrossi?"

I frowned. "I don't know. I miss Ankrossi already—I love the people there, but do you think they'd welcome me back after this?"

"I'm not sure. And it's not up to me to decide whether you should return. But if you do, can you pass some messages on for me?"

"What are they?"

"Well, first of all, make sure my family knows how much I care about them. Especially Kip. I don't want him to think that I died angry." Her voice wavered, and she paused and took a deep breath. "And I also want them to know the truth about Lachlann, or what I know of it anyway."

"Which is what?"

"Well, Ruby and Jasper's brother said that Lachlann was the reason the guards were able to use anti-magic the way that they were. And I'm guessing he's the reason the entire palace is shrouded in the stuff." She shuddered. "But what the court mage said about how he's cooperating now that they figured out how to break him..." She shook her head. "I'm not sure what they've done to him. Knowing they tortured him breaks my heart. But at least we know he hasn't turned on us willingly. Lachlann's been a leader to the people of Ankrossi ever since our village was founded, and I don't want them thinking he's a traitor."

I nodded. "If I do go back, I'll tell them all of that. I'm not sure I can leave without risking another search party, though. I suppose this time I could just tell my parents that I'm going."

"Right. Your parents. We need to talk about them." She frowned. "Isabelle, what I'm about to tell you might seem...outlandish. I promise you, though, I'm not making things—"

"I already know," I cut in.

"You...do?"

"Father told me that my mother—*our* mother—had an affair with Marcus, and that you're the result of that."

Saray's eyes widened. "I'm surprised he'd tell you."

"I demanded to know what the theatrics at the Moon Dance were about. I told him that if he didn't tell me, I'd ask Mother."

"Did he tell you *how* my parents knew each other?"

I shook my head.

"Well, back when my father was a krossemage, he was enslaved by your father's parents, then your parents themselves."

I frowned. "I don't recall my parents ever owning slaves."

"This was before you were born. Your father inherited Marcus from his parents, and they only kept him as a slave for a couple of years before things went...wrong."

"Do you know how the affair began?"

"I know they fell in love. Rather madly, from what Father's told me. Your parents had been growing apart for years, with her caring for your brothers and him busy at work, so it had been a while since they were together. When our mother found out she was with child, she knew it wasn't Caspa's. She signed papers officially releasing Father and told him to flee. From what Father has told me, he found his way to Dundere from there and met Noelle. Then Mother gave birth to me and deposited me at Sylvenburgh Academy, and, well, I think you know the story from there."

I nodded as I digested everything. "You know, I remember when word got out that you'd run away from Sylvenburgh Academy. Suddenly, my parents began fighting all the time. They'd been sort of happy for a while, but my mother changed after that. She became sad and withdrawn. I never understood why until a couple of days ago."

Saray eyed me. "Are they still together?"

"They are, but they're not happy. Father had another mistress last year, and everyone knows about her. I imagine my parents are only staying together because of what it might do to their reputations if they split."

Saray nodded. "I always hoped I'd get a chance to meet my mother."

"Do you...want me to see if she'd like to meet you?"

"Well, we don't have much time, but if you can get her here safely, then absolutely."

I turned to Oliver, who watched us with solemn eyes. "Do you think we could make that happen?"

He nodded. "We can try, at least."

"We'll do what we can," I promised Saray.

She nodded and squeezed my hands again. "Thank you."

Oliver and I were both silent as we left the dungeon. My head began to swim when we reached the finer parts of the palace, and I had to pause in a doorway, trying to breathe deeply. Tears swam in my eyes. Oliver cast a concerned glance at me. "You don't look well."

I couldn't find words. My vision blurred as I looked at him, and I felt my face crumpling.

He slipped an arm around my waist. "Let's get you up to your rooms." His voice was authoritative.

"No," I protested. "I need to find Mother...she needs to speak to Saray..." My words were lost in a sob.

"Your mother can speak to Saray a little later in the day. You need some rest before you're ready for that."

I let Oliver lead me carefully up another flight of stairs. As his betrothed, I had a small suite of rooms in the palace to myself—a bedroom, bath, and sitting room—and it was here that he took me. The moment the door was closed behind us, he pulled me into an embrace, and I burst into tears. Oliver leaned us up against the door so he could bear my weight without falling and let me cry into his shoulder. I wept for Saray, for Kip and Marcus, for my mother. For Oliver and his health, for myself. So much had happened in the span of a few days, and I could hardly handle the gravity of it all. "This is all...my...fault..." I managed to gasp.

"It's not your fault," Oliver reassured, stroking my hair.

"It is!" I pulled away, staring up at him through my tears. "Father sent the guards after me, and that's how they found Saray. Now they have an excuse to force us into marriage, and I'm no closer to finding Silva than when I left! I should've just stayed home, we'd all be better off that way..." I dissolved into tears again.

Oliver held me tightly. Only once my sobs had tapered off did he speak. "I'm not sure what to say about Saray's situation," he finally said, "but you couldn't have done anything to make me better. My being ill is hardly your fault, Isabelle. They would've found a way to force us into marriage even if you hadn't run off." He gave me a squeeze. "And I suspect the Guard would've gotten the location of your friends from Lachlann in time, even without your father looking for you." He sighed. "Come on. I think you should lie down."

"But I have to talk to Mother," I protested weakly.

"Tell you what. You nap for a bit, and come lunchtime I'll tell your mother that you're not well and would like lunch brought to your rooms. You can talk to her about Saray then. It'll give you some time to rest before you have to face everything again."

I nodded and swiped at my eyes. "I suppose that's not a bad idea. Though I doubt I'll sleep. I've barely slept since I got home."

"Well, then, I have an idea." Oliver led me over to the bed that occupied most of my chamber. He shrugged off his waistcoat, then lay down on top of the quilt in just his shirt and breeches, extending an arm. "Don't tell anyone about this. But I suspect you'll sleep better if you're being held."

I glanced down at my dress dubiously; thankfully, this one was a simple day dress and wouldn't likely be too rumpled. I lay down and gingerly let my back rest against Oliver. He enfolded me in his arms and took my hands in his own, and I found myself letting out a long sigh. "This does feel nice."

"I figured it would." Oliver planted a kiss on the side of my neck. Being held like this certainly didn't solve any of the problems I was facing, but it was good to know I wouldn't be alone in them.

***

I suppose Oliver's plan to get me to fall asleep worked, because the next time I opened my eyes I found myself peering up at Mother. Oliver was gone from the room, and I was wrapped in a blanket. "Are you all right?" Mother reached out and took my hand. "Oliver said you weren't feeling well?"

Smoothing down my hair, I sat up. "I'm not ill. I was just very upset earlier, so Oliver insisted that I lie down."

Mother nodded, and I saw something wistful in her expression. "He's good to you."

"He is." I sighed. "I need to talk to you about something. This might be a difficult conversation."

"What about?"

"Saray. Oliver took me to visit her in the dungeon. It's a bit of a story, but...I know who Saray is to you. I know she's your daughter."

Mother's eyes went wide. "Did she tell you that?"

"She told me some of it. I learned the rest from someone else." I frowned, not sure that I wanted to tell Mother how Father had been the one to order Saray's capture. "I know how she came to be, as well. And I know you must be in terrible pain right now."

I saw tears spring to Mother's eyes. "How does *she* know who I am?"

"She knows because her father is in her life now. Marcus is a lovely fellow. He's actually one of the folks in charge where they live. He's had quite an interesting life."

Mother's eyes got even wider, and she sat back. "How in the king's name did they find one another?"

I frowned. "I don't fully understand the story, but I believe it had something to do with the fairies, and a curse on Marcus' mother that meant she couldn't die until they were reunited. Oh, and also a magical hawk."

Mother shook her head. "That doesn't sound right. Marcus' mother died in child-birth."

"No, she didn't. She was executed days after he was born, but she didn't stay dead. Long story. In fact, she's not completely dead now—her soul lives in a tree." I shook my head. "I know, it sounds rather mad."

"Why are you telling me all this?"

"Because Saray wants to meet you. Oliver and I can get you into the dungeon this afternoon."

"She wants to *meet* me?" Mother's voice came out as a whisper. "After I abandoned her?"

I shrugged. "I think she knows the story well enough to understand why you did. But it's up to you whether you want us to take you to her. I know it'll probably make all of this more painful for you."

Mother shook her head. "I'd be a fool not to take her up on this. By all means, I'll see her."

***

A few hours later, Mother and I followed Oliver back into the damp prison block. The guard gave us a frown when we passed by, but he allowed us to approach Saray's cell.

She was lying on the bench when we arrived, but her eyes fluttered open. Then she sat up, staring incredulously at Mother. Her eyes flickered to me. "Is this..."

"Saray, meet our mother, Lillian," I said.

Saray and Mother stared at one another for a few tense seconds. Then Saray rose and walked over to the bars. "I thought I'd never get to meet you," she whispered.

"I thought the same." Mother extended her hands, and Saray squeezed them tightly. "My dear, can you ever forgive me?"

"For what?"

"For giving you up like I did. Abandoning you to the Academy. I..." Mother's voice broke, and a tear ran down her cheek.

Surprisingly, Saray let out a soft chuckle. "You're lucky you're meeting me now and not eight years ago. I let my father have it when I first met him. I was so angry about being abandoned. But I'm not anymore."

"You're not?"

Saray shook her head. "Growing up an orphan was difficult. I spent a lot of years wondering why I was left at the Academy. But Marcus answered a good number of my questions, and my life has been much happier since. Well, until a couple of days ago at least." She took a shaky breath. "I do still want to know a few things, though."

Mother met her eyes. "Ask me."

"Why did you give me up, exactly? Were you afraid of what your husband would do to me?"

Mother sighed. "I don't think Caspa would have harmed you. He actually seemed to like you when you were a baby."

Saray's eyes narrowed. "I always figured he just ignored me."

"He tried. But you were rather adorable. And you seemed to like him, too. He used to sing to you and toss you in the air." Mother sighed. "You were bald as a baby, and for a while, I hoped that we could keep you and just pretend you were one of ours. But then your hair started coming in, and it was bright red. It was clear enough that you didn't look at all like him. It was at that point that Caspa began to insist we give you up once you were weaned. The older you got, the more you looked like Marcus, and the more distant he became from you." She shook her head. "Caspa cares about reputation, a lot. And he knew that if folks figured out you weren't his, they'd treat him and me differently. And they'd treat you differently as well. Growing up in our home might not have gone well for you. You might have felt more secure, but I don't doubt there would have been talk about your parentage, from your schoolmates and the adults around you."

"You think there wasn't that sort of talk growing up as an orphan at the Academy?" Saray's voice held a bitter note.

"I suppose it wouldn't have been easy for you in either situation." Mother sighed. "In the end, I couldn't handle being the one to give you up. Caspa took you to the school and signed you off. You were barely two." Her voice broke. "It was the saddest day of my life."

Saray nodded and squeezed Mother's hand. Then her eyes flickered to me. "What happened after that, though? I'm assuming you and Caspa patched things up, given that..." She inclined her head in my direction.

Mother followed her gaze. "Caspa and I have an odd relationship. We didn't choose one another; our marriage was arranged. We've had times when things were good, and times when they were not. He's strayed more often than I have—in fact, nearly the whole palace knows that he and one of the ladies in waiting were romantically involved last year." I frowned; it was the first time I'd heard Mother acknowledge this. "After we gave you up, I fell into a deep sadness that I couldn't shake for several years. Caspa noticed, and he became concerned. He started trying to pull me out of it by courting me, taking me on dates and being more affectionate, and in time it worked. I feel like that was the first time we truly fell in love with one another. When Isabelle was born, I became even happier. I felt like I'd been gifted a daughter to replace the one I'd lost." She eyed her elder daughter. "I'll admit, Saray, that there was a good eight years where I didn't think of you much. I chose to believe that you were safe and happy, and I focused on my life instead, my children who were in my care and my relationship with my husband. Then we moved to Kirstein, when you were about sixteen, so Caspa and I could join the court. It was a big change, but it gave me a new purpose, and I got along well with Calendra and the other court ladies. I was excited for Isabelle's prospects too.

"Then we got word that you'd run away, and things changed somehow. I couldn't stop thinking about you, worrying about you. Things got bad between Caspa and me again; he told me to stop obsessing over things I couldn't control, and one night we had a big blowup where I called him cruel and insensitive, and I dare say things haven't been the same since."

"I...I'm sorry," Saray offered. "It sounds like I caused the rift between you two."

Mother shook her head. "Honestly, Caspa was beginning to notice other women in the court again, so I imagine it would have happened eventually, even if you hadn't run off."

"You're still with him, though?"

"I am. We both know we'd be happier apart, but Caspa is so concerned about his reputation that he refuses to divorce me."

"Well, then, why don't *you* leave?" Saray asked. "Go somewhere other than Kirstein. That way he can save his reputation and make you look like the one who ran off, and you can both be happy again."

Mother sighed. "Where would I go?"

"Go to Ankrossi. They'd accept you. You could be with my father again."

"Marcus?" Mother frowned. "Has he not married after all these years?"

"He did, but his wife was killed four years back...Noelle was a wonderful woman, I miss her terribly." A smile tugged at Saray's lips. "Though if there is a life after death, perhaps I'm going to see her very soon."

"Oh, Saray..." Mother's voice broke. "I wish I had more time with you."

"Me too. But we have the rest of the afternoon, and tomorrow as well. You can stay and visit for as long as the guards allow." Saray sat down on the floor of her cell and gestured that Mother should also sit. "Do you want to join us, Isabelle?"

I glanced at Oliver. "We should probably give you two some time alone," I said. "Enjoy your talk."

***

Mother stayed at the palace long into the evening. Oliver retired early, saying he was exhausted, and I spent the remainder of the day wandering the halls, feigning a search for him. In reality, though, I was combing the palace for Lachlann. I checked every room I was allowed into, checked offices and storage rooms and rooms used mainly for entertaining foreign dignitaries. I even returned to the dungeon, claiming to need to speak to Mother, and scoured the cells once again, to no avail.

The following day, Mother went back and sat with Saray again. Oliver came to my house and tried to distract me from the dread that sat heavy in the pit of my stomach. We took two of the horses and left the city, riding the roads that skirted Breoch's rocky coastline, and surprised the owners of a tavern in a tiny settlement a few hours east of Kirstein by dropping in for lunch. The staff made a fuss over Oliver, treating us both to a massive slice of fruit pie for dessert, and Oliver treated them back by leaving tips that were likely a month's wage for each of them. Then we rode back, arriving at my house shortly before dinner. Mother wasn't home yet, but Father talked to Oliver about his lessons and horsemanship, a passion they both shared, all while pretending that tomorrow's events and Oliver's diagnosis were non-existent.

After dinner found Oliver and me on the porch swing, engaged in another furious kissing session. It was only here, with my body pressed up against his and his hands tangled in my hair, that I was truly able to forget about what would happen tomorrow. I was brought back to reality very swiftly, though, by a heated argument coming from my parents' balcony.

"I am not putting myself through this." Mother's voice rang through the house, clear and firm. "You cannot force me to watch the execution of my own daughter."

"Lillian, you have to." Father's voice was equally firm. "Do you remember the rumours that began after Saray was born? They've started up again. I've heard a few of the palace staff commenting on your visits to her cell, the way you acted at the trial. If you don't attend, they'll know for sure, and that'll change the way we're seen." I pulled away from Oliver, stood, and tiptoed toward the house, settling into an arch that led to the garden.

Mother snorted. "You're worried that folks at the palace will see us differently because I had an affair sixteen years ago? You ought to be more worried about your own dalliances, Caspa. The entire court knows about you and Hazel."

Father scoffed. "Rumours are one thing, but Saray is physical proof that you strayed." Oliver joined me inside the archway and grabbed my hand, eyes on my parents. Father, meanwhile, sighed and put a hand on Mother's shoulder. "Just think, Lillian. You've spent all these years worrying about Saray. After tomorrow, you won't have to wonder or worry anymore. It'll all be over."

Something visceral rose up inside me. *How dare he!*

Before I knew it, I found myself storming out of my hiding spot. "Is that meant to be a comfort?" I demanded, glaring up at my father. "You should be happy your daughter is dying tomorrow because you won't have to worry about her anymore?"

"Isabelle, that's not what I meant—" Father began.

"You have *no right* to try and comfort Mother over this loss," I interrupted. "Not after you specifically had Saray arrested to hurt Marcus."

Mother clapped a hand over her mouth. "You didn't," she whispered.

"He absolutely did," I answered for him.

Tears swam in Mother's eyes, and she turned and ran back into the house.

Father glared at me. "You didn't need to tell her that." His eyes flickered briefly to Oliver, then back to me. "Are you trying to make things worse between us?"

"You did that yourself when you insisted the guards arrest Saray," I shot back. "She doesn't deserve this, and neither does Marcus."

"Are you saying that your mother having an affair with him was justified?" Father raised an eyebrow. "Because if so, I'm rather worried for your fiancé." His eyes slid to Oliver again.

"It wasn't right, but neither is what happened between you and Hazel." I sighed. "No one is innocent in this situation, except Saray."

"I already told you, Saray is wanted on several counts of assault, among other crimes." Father's voice was ice.

"You know what I meant. Saray can't help where she came from, and it's not fair to use her for revenge against Marcus, especially when you've not been faithful either."

Father let out a sigh and took a step forward, resting his hands on the balcony's edge. "Perhaps. But what's done is done. And don't forget that Saray was given a choice in all this. If she'd taken the king's offer, we wouldn't be here. Now, you should go to sleep soon, Isabelle. I don't imagine tomorrow will be easy for you."

"Are you going to force me to attend as well?"

"No. But I'd like you to. It would be best if we show up as a family. And perhaps Saray will find some solace, having a couple of friendly faces in the crowd?" His voice softened slightly as he spoke. Then he spun on his heel and disappeared inside.

Oliver turned to me. "Are you going to attend, then? I'll be there; I have little choice."

I took a deep breath. "Will you sit with me?"

"Of course." He squeezed my hand.

"Then I suppose I'll come. Father's right, it might make things easier for Saray if there are people who care for her."

Oliver nodded. "I'll see you tomorrow. I should head home."

I bid him goodnight and headed to my room, doubting I would sleep at all tonight.

***

I had been to hangings before, but never on the palace grounds. Usually, they were performed at a public square across town, where a large gallows stood permanently. The palace courtyard was packed with people—mostly curious onlookers who'd heard stories about the firebrand all those years ago. I imagined only a small percentage of them actually wanted to see Saray suffer. Most of them likely wondered if she'd manage yet another last-minute escape.

I stayed close to Mother as we seated ourselves. She was wearing a brimmed hat that would hide her face easily enough, a move that I figured was intentional. I scanned the faces in the crowd, looking for anyone I might recognize from the Woods, but saw no one. Oliver caught my eye, though, and made his way over to us. When he seated himself next to me, he gripped my hand tightly.

The noise of the crowd diminished, and I looked to see Saray being led into the courtyard. Her hands were bound in anti-magic cuffs, and she had a guard on each arm, plus two more following. I waited for the inevitable string of jeers and taunts that so often accompanied executions.

It didn't come. The people of Breoch, I realized, were rather in awe of Saray.

She kept her head high as the guards led her to the gallows. Her eyes met mine for a moment when she mounted the stairs, and I saw both fear and determination in her gaze. I gave her the hint of a smile, trying to let her know that she wasn't hated by everyone here.

Pieter stepped forward as the hangman fitted the noose around her neck. "People of Breoch, today we are here to witness the execution of Saray McAllister, a young woman who has caused our kingdom a great deal of anguish. Eight years ago, Saray fled Sylvenburgh, killed city guards who gave chase, destroyed a Breochi ship and assaulted several members of the Guard. Four years later, she aided in the destruction of a krossemage encampment and assaulted several of the prison guards, and when the Breoch Guard attempted to recapture the fugitives, she participated in a rebellion that left the governor of Dundere dead." Saray stiffened at his words, and my eyes widened.

"If Saray was an ordinary witch, we'd simply make her into a krossemage and forget about her. But this young woman is a type of witch we've never encountered before. She can cast with her mind, an ability that makes her far more dangerous than the average elfieblood. And as such, she cannot be given an average sentence." He turned to face her. "Saray McAllister, for your many crimes against Breoch and your unrestrained practice of witchery, you are hereby sentenced to be hung by the neck until dead."

Saray kept her head high, but her face was wet with tears. My heart pounded in my ears as the drumroll began. The hangman reached toward the lever.

Seemingly out of nowhere, an arrow sailed toward him and caught him in the chest.

I blinked, momentarily bewildered, as he keeled forward, but an instant later I was distracted by a massive flock of crows diving toward the stage, cawing and pecking ferociously at the guards. A cannon broke free of the battlements then and launched itself toward the gallows, landing directly before it.

The crowd panicked, and several onlookers began to make a run for the palace walls. I stayed rooted where I was, unable to move or speak. I heard Oliver demanding to know what was happening, but his voice felt distant, muted. A fork of lightning snaked into the courtyard, electrocuting one guard where he stood. Then I noticed a figure who'd been in the audience, a lithe young woman with mahogany skin, darting toward the stage with two knives drawn. *Is that Kaden?*

Kaden reached Saray, and the two began conversing quickly as Kaden put her knife to the hangman's rope, clearly intending to cut Saray free. Hope swelled in my chest.

And then Pieter, cursing and slapping at the crows that swarmed him, lunged to pull the lever himself.

Saray dropped, nearly taking Kaden down the hatch with her. A moment later, I heard the sharp *crack* of her neck snapping.

The world began to spin around me. On one side, my mother pitched forward and vomited, an odd keening sound punctuating her retching. An anguished cry sounded from the palace wall, and I made out the figures of a young man with a quiver on his back, hunched over and wailing. A young woman next to him held him close, some of the crows circling her. *Kip and Trina.* Kaden was busy fighting off a pair of guards who'd rushed her, her twin knives moving with ease and grace.

Then a dragon appeared out of the sky. It dove to take Kaden in its talons. People shrieked and began streaming from the courtyard en masse, trampling one another in their desire to escape the danger. The dragon paused atop one of the parapets long enough for Kaden, Trina and Kip to alight. Several guards fired at it, but their bullets seemed to do very little to the creature; however, I heard Kaden let out a cry.

My vision was growing dark yet again. I heard Oliver calling my name, but he sounded far away. The last thing I saw before I fainted was Saray's lifeless, twitching body swinging from the gallows, neck bent at a grotesque angle, clearly very dead.

Chapter 17

WHEN I AWOKE, I was lying on top of my bed in my palace room. My head pounded, and I realized I'd hit it when I collapsed. Oliver hovered over me, his face worried. I groaned and rubbed the goose egg on my forehead, then tried to get up.

"Don't." He pushed me gently back down. "You're injured. You need rest."

"I'll be fine." I meant it, too. Whatever I'd done to my head would right itself in the next half hour. "Where are my parents?"

"Your mother is here, recovering. Your father went home."

"What happened after I fainted?"

He shrugged. "People panicked and started fleeing the courtyard. The attackers got away. I don't think they injured anyone in the streets."

I shook my head. "They wouldn't injure civillians. They were just trying to save..." Tears sprung to my eyes, and I swiped at them.

Oliver frowned. "You knew them, then?"

I nodded slowly.

He sighed and took my hand. "Isabelle, I don't think it's safe here for you. The court is in an uproar about the attack. Some of them are telling my father that we need to clamp down on magic use even more. Others are suggesting a full-scale assault on the Shrouded Woods. If they managed to get the location of that dance from Lachlann, then I don't imagine your friends are safe in their village. And I know my father thinks you have magic. I want to believe he wouldn't hurt you, but I'm not certain anymore." He sighed. "Look, Saray told you to go back to the Woods, and I think it might be safer there for you right now."

I sat up, frowning. "You just said that the Woods are likely going to be attacked. Why would I be safer there than here?"

"Because here everyone knows exactly where you live. It would be easy enough for the Breach Guard to snatch you from your home or school, or even from the palace. At least you'd have a fighting chance in the Woods. And you could warn the others as well."

I eyed him. "Why are you siding with the Woods-folk on this?"

"Because if it'd been you standing on those gallows, I would've used every bit of power I have to keep you alive." He squeezed my hand.

A lump rose in my throat. "What about you? If I run, you'll be alone."

"That's the other reason I think you should go." Sadness crept into his eyes. "You know what will happen if you stay here. You deserve better than spending years watching me fall apart and die, then having to raise our children alone. I don't want that for you."

"But...you'll be alone," I repeated, my voice wavering as I spoke. "I don't want that for *you*."

"Me neither. But I'll be all right." Sinking down on the bed, he sighed and put an arm around me. "Sometimes loving someone means you need to let them go."

My eyes widened, and I felt my head begin to spin. "You...*love* me?"

"Of course I do. You're one of my oldest friends, and I think I'm beginning to love you in other ways as well."

I closed my eyes, trying to process his admission. "Maybe you won't have to be alone," I finally said. "I'm sure your father will find someone else for you to marry."

"Of course. He'll still want me to produce an heir. But I'll refuse." Oliver shook his head. "One of the cousins can take the throne, for all I care. Some of them might do well." He stared at me, his green eyes pleading. "Go back to the Woods, Isabelle. Stay with your friends, be free, enjoy yourself. If you stay here, your life only has one path, and it won't end in happiness. Out there, you can choose your own. Take your mother with you, like Saray suggested."

My mind went to little Aria, to Daisy and Kaden both getting shot, and Claudi and her hopes for me. To Saray asking me to tell Kip she loved him. Then I thought of Silva again and my plans to rescue her. *I won't be able to do any of that if I stay.* I sighed. "Fine. I'll leave in the morning."

He nodded and buried his face in my hair, and my stomach knotted at the thought of him deteriorating physically, dying young, without having ever known love.

"I need to have dinner with Father and a few of the officials," he told me. "Someone will bring food to you and your mother. I'll come check on you this evening."

I felt the tears begin to trickle down my face as Oliver slowly left the room, his gait halting. I flopped back down on the bed, trying to process everything. *Oliver says I should leave. If I do, I'll never see him again. And Saray is dead.*

Dead.

I let out a great heaving sob as my mind went back to her body swinging from the gallows.

I wanted to dissolve into tears again, to hug my pillow and weep for my losses, but something in the back of my mind kept me from fully surrendering to my grief. *You can mourn for Saray later. But you haven't lost Oliver yet. Focus on what you can control.* I took several deep, shuddering breaths to calm myself, wiped at my eyes, and tried to think logically about the problem at hand.

Again, I wondered if there was some way—*any way*—for me to ensure Oliver lived a long life, with or without me. *I wonder if I could heal him without him knowing.* I doubted he suspected that the young woman with healing gifts I'd described was me. *So if his condition simply disappeared, he'd have no way of knowing magic was even used—especially with Lachlann's anti-magic blanketing the palace—and therefore he couldn't be held responsible.*

But how would I do it? I recalled the potion Alexander had given me that would allow me to cast in the presence of anti-magic, and I wondered if it was for this particular purpose. But that only solved one of the logistical issues. How could I place my hands on

Oliver, sing the songs needed to determine the cause of his illness, then cast my healing spell without him knowing?

When a solution came to mind, I nearly laughed at how perfect it was. It did carry some risk, and if the wrong people found out, Oliver and I would both be in a massive amount of trouble, but it would certainly put me in the position I needed. And, I had to admit, the idea was appealing in more than one way. I slowly climbed out of bed and smoothed down my rumpled dress, intent on getting to work on my plan immediately.

A palace servant brought a coach around at my request, and soon I was home and in my room, carefully packing my Ankrossi clothing in a bag. Then I went to Father's study, where I found him reading, a glass of something strong smelling in one hand. He looked up at me, and I was surprised to see that his eyes were red, as if he, too, had been crying. "Isabelle, are you all right?" he asked, his words coming out slightly slurred.

"My head is fine, if that's what you're asking." I sighed. "Look, Mother and I are staying at the palace tonight, and we're going to Flavalan in the morning. I think we need a few days away from everything."

Father nodded, seeming unfazed.

"Can you arrange for two horses to be sent to the palace first thing tomorrow?" I asked. "We don't need a carriage; we'll travel alone."

Father looked for a moment like he was about to protest, but then he nodded again. "Is she all right?"

"What do you think?" My voice came out more hostile than I intended it to.

"I wasn't trying to hurt her, or you, for that matter." Father stood and walked toward me, his gait slightly unsteady. "You know I care about you, right?"

I nodded, uncertain how to answer him.

"Have a good time in Flavalan," he mumbled and opened his arms.

In truth, I didn't really feel like hugging him right now. But I let him wrap his arms around me anyway, knowing full well that I might not see him ever again. "Bye, Father," I said, giving him a squeeze.

Then I pulled away, nodded to each of the servants as I passed them, and walked out the door of my childhood home, possibly for good.

***

Dinner was brought to me in my room at the palace a couple of hours later, and I went over the rest of my plans while I ate. Once I was finished, I went to find Mother.

She was resting in her opulent palace rooms, just as I expected, sitting in a chair next to the window. Her hair had come loose and fell around her shoulders. I came up behind her, and she startled, lifting her bowed head when I put a hand on her shoulder. "Oh, Isabelle," she whispered, meeting my eyes, "I'm so sorry."

"*I'm* sorry," I said, leaning down to put an arm around her. "She was your daughter."

"But you knew her better than I did." She took a deep, shuddering breath. "I don't think I can go home. I don't think I can face your father."

I nodded and took her hands in mine. "That's why I came to see you. I don't want to go home either. And Oliver says I need to run—he thinks it might be safest to return to the Woods, to where Saray lived. I want you to come with me."

"Come with you?" she repeated incredulously. "Is it safe?"

"Perhaps not entirely. But you'll be in good company. And you won't have to go back to Father."

"You wouldn't judge me if I left him?"

I shook my head. "You two haven't loved each other for years. Like Saray said, if you come with me and write him a letter saying you've gone, you'd let him save face. He can claim you wronged him, and you'll never have to see him again. You can both move on and be with people you actually love."

Mother's eyes narrowed. "And who do I actually love?"

"Well, me, for one. And I'm not quite sure if you still love him, but Marcus will be where we're going."

Her eyes widened. "I suppose he would be."

"Will you come with me, then?"

She paused for a moment, closed her eyes, then nodded. "When are you leaving?"

"Early tomorrow morning," I told her.

She sighed and grasped my hands. "Fine. I'll come with you. I don't think I can handle losing you as well."

"Good." I gave her hands a squeeze. "I'll meet you in the courtyard just after dawn." She nodded, and I held onto her for a few long moments before leaving her alone.

***

Back in my room, I prepared for the second part of my plan. After a hot bath, I changed into my Ankrossi dress, studying myself in the mirror and fussing with my hair a bit, then resorted to pacing the room, heart pounding as I contemplated my next move.

It was getting dark by the time I heard a knock on the door. "Sorry that took so long," Oliver said when I answered. "The officers are a little chagrined by today's happenings. Fancy a walk?" He looked me up and down then, and his eyes narrowed. "Why are you dressed like that?"

I leaned out into the hallway, eyes darting back and forth. When I saw no one else nearby, I signalled to Oliver to come into my room.

"What is it?" he asked.

With him inside, I closed the door, then took a deep breath and gripped his hands in mine. "I'm running away tomorrow, like you said. We might never see each other again." I smiled, trying to ignore the hammering in my chest. "We might not have a lifetime together, Oliver, but we could have one night."

His eyes went round. "You're asking me to...take you to bed?"

I nodded and squeezed his hands. "It might be our only chance. It might be *your* only chance ever, if you're so determined not to let your father marry you off. I don't want you to die having never known another person like that." I felt myself blushing furiously as I spoke. "I want you to be my first."

"Isabelle, I..." Oliver nearly stumbled as he reached back for the couch and seated himself. "Aren't you worried about what it might cost you?"

"Cost me?"

"You know how men of society are. They like their wife to be untouched when they marry. Also, you could end up pregnant."

"The Woods-folk don't seem to care much about those traditions. And they have a tea that prevents pregnancy. I'll just need to find some when I get there." I sat next to him. "I've been thinking about this ever since you left for dinner. And I want this. I want *you*."

Oliver let out a shuddering sigh, and he looked me up and down again. I felt his eyes land on my curves, truly taking me in for the first time. When his eyes met mine again, there was hunger in them. "I want you too," he whispered. "But...I don't exactly know what I'm doing."

"Do you think *I* know what *I'm* doing? We can learn together."

A smile spread slowly across his face. "All right. But it may need to wait an hour or so. The palace doctor is meeting me soon to give me medicine." He got to his feet. "Why don't you come to my room with me? You can hide in the closet before the doctor shows up. I have some things I've been meaning to show you."

When we left my rooms and walked down the hall to his family's quarters, Oliver didn't speak, and I noticed that his hand was cold in mine; he was clearly nervous about our plan. He shot a hasty glance around outside his room before opening the door.

I'd visited Oliver there before, but it was always quickly to fetch one thing or another. I looked around as he closed the door behind him, surprised for a moment at how cluttered it was. It was also extravagant, of course, with intricate tapestries on the walls, a massive fireplace dominating one corner, and a huge, canopied bed topped with colourful linens. But the mahogany desk was covered in papers, the adjacent bookshelf crammed with thick tomes. An easel held an abandoned painting that looked to be a series of circus tents, and another bookshelf contained his massive collection of stones and jewels, all meticulously displayed. But it was the fireplace mantle that drew my eye, and I immediately knew what Oliver wanted to show me.

"I finished her," he told me proudly, leading me to his masterpiece, the porcelain bust of his mother that he'd spent the past five years sculpting. It was painted a delicate ivory, with a deeper blush present on the cheekbones, and inlaid with crystals and precious stones, all polished, or in some cases, hand-cut, by Oliver himself. Her eyes were inset with two cut peridots, her lips made from polished carnelian. She wore twin sapphire earrings and sported a bejewelled gold necklace that I knew once actually belonged to Inari. "She's gorgeous," I breathed. "What kind of stones are these?" I referred to the polished, round stones used to mimic his mother's curls.

"They're a mix of quartz, citrine, and jasper."

I chuckled. "I have a friend named Jasper. In fact, all the children in his family are named after precious stones; his sister is Ruby, and his brother is Jade."

"Brilliant," Oliver replied. "If we have children we should..." He trailed off and sighed, then turned back to the bust. "I'm just glad I finished this when I did. I don't think I have the coordination to paint or cut gems anymore. It's why I haven't finished these other projects." He waved at the model ship and the painting. Then his eyes darted to a shelf next to the easel. "Let me show you something I recently had made."

He took me over to the miniature rendition of a circus set on a ceramic base, its tents and trapezes and acrobats all created of wood, paper, and wire. "Watch," he said, carefully winding a handle on the base's side. A tune came out of it, and the circus began to gently spin—acrobats moved across the tightropes, a wooden clown juggled three balls, and a paper elephant peeked out of a tent.

"Amazing," I breathed.

"I want to see a circus before I die. I don't care what Calendra says." Oliver's voice was obstinate.

"I'm sure we can arrange for that."

"I'm glad you're on my side about this." He grinned, then glanced up at the large clock that sat in one corner of his room. "Dr. Matthews should be here soon. You'd best hide."

I ducked into Oliver's closet crammed with fancy clothes and shoes, and he seated himself on his couch. Only now did the reason for my visit to his room resurface. My heart began to pound again, and I felt my hands go icy. At the same time, though, I was aware of a warmth in the lower regions of my abdomen, an anticipation of what would come.

Am I ready for this? Is he?

I heard the doctor arrive and speak in low tones to Oliver. He was only present for a few minutes, and soon enough Oliver's door clicked shut again.

And we were alone once more.

"Isabelle? You can come out now."

I extracted myself from Oliver's clothes and emerged from his closet. He was sitting on the small loveseat near the fireplace, his eyes on me. I joined him, trying to control my breathing, my pounding heart. "Hi," he said, a blush colouring his cheeks.

"Hello, Your Highness." My words came out as a nervous giggle, and I gave him a tiny curtsy.

He raised his eyebrows at my use of his title, took my hand, and kissed it. "What do you want to do now, Lady Isabelle?"

"How about this?" He gasped slightly when I seated myself in his lap, straddling his legs. Then I leaned down and pressed my lips to his.

Oliver returned my kiss eagerly, his hands tangling themselves in my hair as he did. The hunger I'd felt before returned, and I let my hands trail down his jawline, then his neck, until I found the top button of his shirt. His tongue flicked against my own, and I let out an unexpected giggle, a conversation we'd had shortly before our first childhood kiss suddenly coming to mind.

"What?" he gasped, pulling away.

"Do you remember how when we were younger, we talked about how gross it was that adults use their tongues when they're kissing?"

He laughed. "What would our younger selves think about what comes...*afterward?*" he asked, caressing my neck with his lips between words.

"And what does come afterward, hmm?" I purred and continued to unbutton his shirt.

His lips grazed my collarbone. "I think we're about to find out," he whispered. Then he leaned back and began to shrug off his jacket.

I helped remove his shirt, then he leaned into me, lips grazing my neck again as he fiddled with the laces of my dress. It came off easily. Part of why I'd chosen to wear my Ankrossi clothes was the undergarments that went with them—women in Ankrossi rarely wore petticoats under their dresses, instead choosing bloomers and a light brassiere. Oliver's eyes widened when he saw me in so little. "You're beautiful," he murmured.

I sat back for a moment and looked over the smooth planes of his chest, then reached to run my fingers down the trail of fine dark hair that ran from his sternum to his bellybutton. "So are you."

He pulled me toward himself and kissed me with renewed fervour, and I savoured the feeling of his hands running over my bare back. He tore his lips from mine and let them wander lower, and I kissed his closed eyes, then buried my face in his hair. When Oliver pulled away from me next, his gaze was wild with desire. "Shall we move this over there?" he suggested, inclining his head.

I followed his gaze, then nodded and crawled off him, and together we walked over to his bed, where he leaned down and kissed me once more before reaching to remove the last of my clothing.

***

Later, I lay in Oliver's bed, my body pressed against his. He was breathing deeply, sound asleep, while I knew sleep would not come to me for a while, not after what I'd just experienced and what I needed to do next.

The last hour or so had been...intense, an odd blend of awkwardness and novelty, desire and tenderness, pleasure and pain. We'd taken our time getting to the painful part, though, and it hadn't lasted very long—which, Silva once assured me, was quite normal for a fellow if it was also his first time. Afterwards, we'd lain together, basking in the afterglow, and he'd fallen asleep relatively quickly. Now we lay on our sides, his arm slung over me. I stared in wonder at the tendons in his hand, then studied the hard muscle of his forearm. A pang went through me when I imagined that muscle withering away.

Time to get started, I suppose. I extracted myself from Oliver's embrace, crawled out of bed, and found my dress on the floor. From inside the pocket, I grabbed the small vial of fairy magic potion I'd hidden, uncapped it, then downed it. Returning to the bed, I grasped Oliver's hands in mine and began to sing, my voice barely more than a whisper.

This, I figured, was the best way to get Oliver asleep, unclothed, and in my proximity. Now, as I sang, I could feel my magic leading me up his forearms. I turned and wrapped my arms around him; he mumbled something and returned my embrace.

I had no idea if this would work. But I would try.

The magic led me around his shoulders, down the smooth planes of his back. I felt the ridge of his spine under my fingertips. *Whatever is hurting him is in his spine,* I realized. I began to sing again, this time ready to channel my healing power into him.

And met resistance.

Something was blocking me, keeping me from healing whatever was wrong inside him. I moved my hand to different places on his back but felt the same block. *I can't heal him until I know more about what's harming him,* I realized.

And this was a skill I had yet to learn. I still didn't fully know how to see into wounds, to determine their origins. I shook my head. Oliver's condition seemed to baffle doctors, so who was I to think I could determine its source without training?

Perhaps I can learn what I need to, then come back, I mused. I wouldn't be able to marry him at that point, of course. I already knew running away again would certainly disqualify me from becoming his wife. But at least he could be made whole and live a full life and hopefully have children with someone else, someone he loved. *Sometimes loving someone means you need to let them go,* he'd told me only hours earlier. I sighed, rolled back over, and settled into his embrace, relishing the feeling of his body pressed against my own. *Perhaps I need to let him go in return.*

I drifted in and out of sleep and rose when the first rays of light flooded the room. I donned my Ankrossi dress again, then stood over Oliver, watching the steady rise and fall of his chest. I leaned down and kissed him lightly on the temple. "I'll miss you," I whispered. Then I turned and left the room, swallowing the lump in my throat as I did.

I might not be able to keep Oliver, but I knew I would cherish the night spent with him.

Chapter 18

MOTHER WAS WAITING in the courtyard with the horses I'd ordered from home. I saw Josie, our stable hand, had accompanied them. Mother smiled sadly up at her and handed her an envelope. "Give this to Caspa," she told him. "Isabelle and I aren't coming home."

Josie frowned. "Ma'am?"

"We're striking out on our own. The letter will explain everything." She climbed up onto her horse and motioned that I should do the same. Then I followed her out of the palace gates, away from Josie's bewildered face.

We made our way out of the city and broke into a trot once we cleared the gates—an experience that I quickly realized would be immensely uncomfortable after last night's activities. Mother noticed the grimace on my face when we stopped to eat the biscuits I'd saved from last night's meal and asked me what was wrong. I shrugged and told her I was bleeding. It wasn't entirely a lie—I'd noticed a small amount of blood after using the privy that morning, but of course she figured I was talking about my cycle. "Can't you...make it hurt less?" she asked.

"I suppose I could." I'd been so preoccupied with the day's plans that I hadn't thought about this, and I closed my eyes to direct a small amount of healing energy toward my lower regions. The pain eased, and I sighed.

We remounted and rode through the rest of the day. It was approaching nightfall when we reached Sylvenburgh. I led Mother around the outside of the city, not bothering to use the gates, then started us on the road that I knew would lead to the Woods. We finally reached the farmhouse where Mr. Jeffries lived, and I dismounted to knock tentatively on his door.

It was answered by a petite woman with long grey hair pulled back into a braid who I guessed to be Mr. Jeffries' mother. "Can I help you, dear?" she asked.

"Is Mr. Jeff—er, Tomlin here?" I asked.

She shook her head. "He's away for a few days. Are you one of his students?"

"Not anymore, but I was at one time."

"Is there something I can help you with, then?" Her eyes darted toward Mother, and she lowered her voice. "Is this an issue involving magic?"

My eyes widened when I realized that I had a way to win this woman's favour. "Are you Tomlin and Lachlann's mother?"

She nodded. "My name is Helenne."

"I'm Isabelle, and I'm a lifebringer. You might have heard of me; I'm the one who saved your granddaughter, Aria. I'm trying to get back to her so I can make sure she stays healthy." I gestured behind me then. "And this is my mother, Lillian. She's coming with me."

It worked beautifully. "By the Fae," the woman whispered. "Yes, that makes sense. Tom mentioned that the healer who was helping Aria had been taken...Come in, then, both of you. I'll show you where to stable your horses. Do you need somewhere to stay the night?"

"Most likely," I told her. "We'll talk more inside."

***

Soon we were sitting in Helenne's living room, sipping tea by a roaring fire. I'd told her our story, and now she looked us over with grave eyes. "I'm so sorry about Saray," she said. "I never met her, but from what I heard she sounded like an incredible young woman."

Mother nodded. "And I'm sorry about the predicament your son is in. I wish we knew where to find him."

"I looked all over the palace while I was home," I said. "I know he's somewhere on the grounds, though; Saray said that she's fairly certain the anti-magic is coming from him."

"He might be in one of the guarded rooms," Mother said.

I shook my head. "I checked the prison when I went to find Saray."

"Not the prison. There are a few parts of the palace only accessible to guards and certain members of the royal family. Offices containing sensitive information and such. Lachlann could be in one of those."

I nodded; I hadn't thought of that. "I know the folks in Ankrossi are thinking of breaking into the palace to look for him; I'll mention that to them."

"Speaking of Ankrossi, I'm guessing that you two hope to travel back there," Helenne said.

"Yes. My plan was to see if we could get a ride to the edge of the Woods in the morning. Then, once we're deep enough in, I'll use this to call for Ambrose and Spark." I held up the small wooden whistle.

Helenne smiled. "I have a better idea. We can go tonight, if you wish."

My eyes narrowed. "How?"

Her smile widened, and she pulled a smooth pink pendant out of her dress. "Ever heard of a summoning stone?"

I frowned. "I think so. Ruby and Jasper have those so he can come back from the ship to visit her, right?"

Helenne nodded. "Tom had one made for me quite recently; he's in Ankrossi right now. I've been ill the last week or so, so I've been putting off joining him, but I'm feeling better now. I think it's time for me to finally go see this magical village and meet my granddaughter." Her eyes teared up a little.

"How do these stones work?" Mother asked.

"Well, there's two things you can do with them. If you rub the stone in a clockwise motion, you're asking the other person to come to you, and if you rub it in a counterclockwise motion, you're requesting to go to them. That's what we'll do tonight. Hold on to me, you two."

We each took an arm, and Helenne began to rub her stone until it started to glow a little. The room faded from view, and for a brief second we were *nowhere*; there was nothing but darkness and silence and an odd but undeniable sensation of movement. Then my senses began to return; I heard hushed voices and saw candlelight, and a moment later we found ourselves in the main room of Starla and Lachlann's house. Tomlin's eyes widened when he saw Mother and me. "Well, now," he said, "I didn't realize you'd be bringing guests...Isabelle?"

I smiled at him. "Good to see you again, Mr. Jeffries."

"You don't have to call me that out here, you know. Tomlin is just fine. Who's this?"

"This is my mother, Lillian. Mother, this is Tomlin and Starla."

Starla had stood to embrace Helenne, and now she looked Mother over. "Pleasure to meet you, Lillian. What brings you here?"

"It's a bit of a story," Mother said, nervousness evident in her tone.

"How is Aria holding up?" I asked.

"She's been stable enough, though I'm sure a visit from you would be helpful."

I nodded. "I'll come check on her a little later, once Helenne here has had a chance to visit."

"Right, of course. Come with me." Starla took Helenne by the hand, and they headed upstairs.

I turned to Tomlin. "Do you know where Marcus is?"

"Likely at home, given the hour. Do you need him for something?"

I nodded. "I imagine there will be some folks here in Ankrossi who won't be happy to see me again, after the trouble I've caused you all. I figure it's best to talk to him first."

Tomlin frowned. "You realize he might not be happy to see you himself, right? Given that he just lost his daughter?"

"I know. But I might be able to change his mind. Come on, Mother."

Mother's eyes widened as we left the house and stepped out onto one of the walkways. She stopped for a moment to take in the other houses made of twisting tree limbs, the candlelit shops, and the massive structure in the centre of everything illuminated by viletta blooms. "This is beautiful."

"Wait 'til you see it in daylight."

We continued on our way, and I led her to Marcus' home, my heartbeat picking up as we got closer. I noticed that the village was devoid of the usual nighttime revelry; people were subdued, talking in hushed tones. Mother and I earned a few wary glances as we walked, but I kept my head low, hoping that no one would recognize me.

We reached Marcus' place, and I knocked on the door. When he answered a few moments later, it was clear that he was not doing well. His hair was mussed, his eyes red, and his clothing rumpled. He blinked at me a few times. "Isabelle?"

I swallowed my nervousness and forced a smile. "Hi, Marcus."

"What are you...doing here?"

"I've come back to care for Aria and learn from Claudi. And I've brought someone with me who I think you'd like to see." I stepped aside and pulled Mother forward. "Marcus, this is my mother, Lillian. I believe you two have met before."

Marcus' eyes went round as he looked my mother over. "Lillian?" His voice came out as an awed whisper.

Mother reached to take his hands in hers. "It's good to see you, Marcus. And good to finally hear your voice."

He blinked, clearly still in shock. "I can't believe you're...I thought I'd never..." He trailed off, his voice trembling.

"Well, here I am." She gave him a sad smile. "I'm sorry we have to be reunited under such terrible circumstances. I hardly knew Saray, but Isabelle told me that you've been in her life for the last eight years. I can't imagine your pain."

Marcus nodded slowly, then his eyes widened even further when he looked to me. "So Isabelle is your daughter as well, correct? And her father is..."

"She's Caspa's," Mother said. "We had some better times a few years after you left. Things have been very...up and down with him and me."

"Are you still with him?"

"As of this morning, no. I don't think I could live with him after he forced me to attend the execution."

Marcus let out a long breath. "I'm sorry you had to see that."

"I'm just glad you didn't have to. Though I wish you'd gotten a chance to say goodbye."

"I've had a chance of sorts. There's a teleporter and a vanisher in our village who were able to steal her body after it cleared the palace gates."

I gaped at him. "Who managed that?"

"Willem and Tomlin. Both very skilled in their trades." He looked back to Mother then. "Her body is in the main chamber inside the Mothertree, under a preservation spell, so everyone can say their goodbyes before she's laid to rest. Would you like to see her?"

"Please," Mother replied, her eyes wide with shock.

"I'll take you there now."

***

A few minutes later, we entered the cavernous room, where a couple folks were huddled near a bundle at the far end. When we got closer, I realized it was Trina and Kip.

If I thought Marcus looked dishevelled, then Kip was an absolute wreck. His eyes were puffy and his face blotchy and red, his clothes were stained with dirt and sweat, and he sported a few days' stubble on his jaw. Trina didn't look a whole lot better initially, but her face lit up when she saw me. "Isabelle! You're back!"

Kip's eyes narrowed, and when he spoke his voice was hollow. "Why is *she* here?"

Marcus let out a sigh. "Isabelle's returned to take care of Aria and learn—"

"You realize that she's the reason my *wife* is dead, right?" There was acid in Kip's voice, and he stood. "And you thought it was a good idea to let her come back? The whole city's in danger with her being here!"

"Kip!" Trina protested.

"And who's this?" He whirled to face Mother. "Another one of the city folk, likely to bring more Breoch Guard our way?"

"That's enough." Marcus' voice was firm. "You will not talk to your mother-in-law that way."

Kip blinked. "My what?"

Mother stepped forward and looked Kip over. "I'm Lillian, Saray's mother. I'm also Isabelle's mother. I asked Isabelle to bring me with her when she decided to return to Ankrossi." She reached out and put a hand on his arm. "I'm incredibly sorry for your loss, son."

Kip gaped at her for a moment. Then his eyes shifted to me. His jaw was tight with anger, but I saw tears glinting in his eyes. "We'd best be having a council meeting about Isabelle's presence here in the morning," he said, his voice shaking as he spoke.

"Yes, that's the plan," Marcus replied. Then he sighed and put an arm around Kip's shoulders. "Come on, boy. We're going to take you to the bathing pools, then put you to bed. You'll feel better once you've slept and have some clean clothes on."

"Don't talk to me like I'm a child," Kip grumbled.

"You're not. You're a grieving man who's just lost his wife. This is something I understand. Let me help you, Kip."

Kip sighed but let Marcus lead him away. Trina eyed us for a moment, then stood up and came over. "I'm Trina," she said to Mother. "Marcus is my adoptive father, and his late wife Noelle was my adoptive mother. Saray was my sister and best friend." Her voice broke.

"Pleasure to meet you, Trina," Mother said. "I'm sorry for your loss as well."

"Thank you." Trina gave her a small smile, then turned to me. "I'm so glad you're back. I know someone who will want to see you—I'll be back in a moment."

She left Mother and I alone, and only then did we get a good look at Saray. She was still dressed in her fancy blue coat with fire embroidery, and her face was free of dirt and blood but still pale with death. Her head's angle, while nothing like what it had been when I saw her hanging, still didn't feel quite right. Beside me, Mother took a deep, shuddering breath. "I wish I'd gotten to know her better."

I nodded and put an arm around her.

"It's good to see Marcus, though," she went on.

"Does he look how you expected?" I asked.

She nodded. "Looks exactly how I remember, just older and with white hair. Same smile." A slight grin pulled at the corner of her mouth. "I like his voice. I'm glad he got it back."

Trina returned soon after with Kaden, who gave me a cautious smile. "I wasn't expecting to see you again. Wanna help me out?" She rolled up her sleeve to reveal a bandage. "I got shot the other day. Marcus took the bullet out, but my arm's still in bad shape."

I nodded. "I saw them shoot you."

Her eyes narrowed. "You...were there?"

"I was. I didn't want to be, but..." I sighed. "It's a long story." As I spoke, I removed the bandage to peer down at the ugly wound on her forearm. I placed my hand tentatively over it and began to sing; Mother watched in awe.

The familiar power flowed through my own arm and into Kaden's. She let out a long sigh as I completed the healing, and when I removed my hand the bullet hole was gone, replaced by fresh, if slightly bloodied, skin. "There you go. Just need to wash your arm off and you'll be good as new."

"Thank you." She studied me. "I suppose you'll be staying with us again?"

"If I may. I'm not sure where Mother will sleep, though."

"Why not with Marcus?" Kaden raised an eyebrow.

"Kaden! They haven't seen each other in over twenty years!" Trina exclaimed. "I'm sure she can stay with my mother. Though, if she does want to stay with Marcus, I won't judge her for that, either."

Mother frowned. "I thought you said your mother was dead."

"My adoptive mother is dead. My real mother, well, I think you already met her." Trina chuckled. "Don't worry, our family confuses everyone. You'll get used to us. I think you'll enjoy Ankrossi, Lillian."

"So do I." Mother's smile faltered. "If your council will let us stay, that is."

I nodded, my stomach knotting at her words. The people of Ankrossi had been more than welcoming the last time I showed up, but would they want me back now, after all that had happened?

Chapter 19

A LITTLE WHILE later, I sat in the main room of Ruby and Kaden's place. Marcus had returned to sit with Saray's body after Kaden's healing, and I'd taken that as my cue to pay Aria a visit, leaving my mother and Marcus alone to talk. Aria was doing better than I expected; she was continuing to grow strong and seemed healthy and alert. Starla told us, rather proudly, that Aria had managed to properly nurse for the first time last week, and that she had a steady stream of visitors keeping an eye on her. "Jasper's been especially attentive," Starla noted. "It's cute, seeing him interact with her." She exchanged a look with Trina that told me Trina found it rather adorable as well.

After my visit, I retreated to Kaden and Ruby's place, and Trina joined us. It was only once I had my bags safely stowed in my old room that I recalled my need for a particular tea. I brought it up to Ruby when I rejoined her, Kaden, and Trina in the main room.

"I don't imagine you and Kaden would have need for it," I said, "but do you know where I could get some of that tea to prevent pregnancy?"

Ruby's eyes widened. "Well, Kip's the main source of that stuff, but he's a little preoccupied right now. I'm sure you could get some at the market on the weekend. Do you need it right away?"

I nodded. "As soon as possible."

Kaden gave me a long look. "Do I want to know what you're up to?"

"I'll explain once I get some tea," I told her, grinning.

Ruby rolled her eyes. "I can always see if Jasper has some."

She ducked out of the hut and returned a few minutes later with Jasper in tow. "I hear you're looking for Kip's magical tea," he said, winking. He went to his hammock and rifled through his bags, producing a small package that he placed in front of me. The smile he gave me was genuine, but I noticed he didn't look a whole lot better than Kip. His hair was a tangled mess, and his eyes were bloodshot, as if he hadn't been sleeping well.

"Thank you." I opened the package and breathed in the scent of the tea; it had an earthy smell. I eyed him. "I'm surprised you're still here; I thought you were going back to your ship."

"I planned to, but then all this happened with Saray, and I figured my friends here needed more support right now than the crew on the Lady Liara." He sighed, then nodded at the package of tea. "Do you know how to use it?"

I shrugged. "Boil some water, throw the tea in, and let it steep for...?"

"Ten minutes is ideal. It'll be strong, but it works. You can add a dash of honey if you find it too bitter."

"It doesn't always work," Ruby cautioned. "As Alisa and Shawnie found out."

"True." Jasper frowned for a moment. "It works best if both people drink some every morning, but as a woman you can always drink it right before or after, and it should do the trick."

"What about the day after?" I asked as Ruby put the kettle on.

"I'm...not completely sure," Jasper admitted.

I nodded slowly; I'd been worried about that.

"When did you bleed last?" Trina asked me.

"Oh. I finished up about five days back." I glanced sideways at Jasper as I spoke, wondering if it was appropriate to talk about these matters in front of a man, but he seemed unfazed.

Trina's shoulders relaxed. "Well, you're not likely to have an issue, then. Though I've heard of it happening on rare occasions."

Ruby set a mug of boiling water in front of me, and I emptied the packet of herbs into it. "All right, tell us. Who did you sleep with last night?"

"Do you recall me wishing to heal my, uh, boyfriend?"

She nodded.

"Well, to make a long story short, some very unfortunate things happened, and I had to run. I know I might never see him again, and with his illness, I'm worried that he might not have another chance to be with a woman. So I convinced him to sleep with me. And once he was asleep, I tried to heal him."

Jasper raised an eyebrow. "Well, that's a sneaky way to heal someone."

"Only it didn't work," I added. "That's part of why I came back—I want to learn more from Claudi. Though even if my plan didn't totally work, we, uh, had fun." I felt my cheeks warm at the memory.

Trina nodded. "Did it hurt? I hope you don't mind me asking, but I've never, uh..."

"A little bit. I imagine that it'll feel better the next time. But overall...I liked it." I couldn't help the smile that played on my lips.

Ruby frowned at Trina. "So, wait, you and Ambrose never slept together?"

Trina shook her head, a faint blush rising in her cheeks. "We talked about it, and we definitely, uh, messed around a fair bit. But his parents were strict, and they didn't want him to sleep with a girl until he was married. As far as I know, he succeeded in that endeavour."

I nodded. "Sounds like my boyfriend's parents. Only he didn't succeed."

"Ambrose is an adult, though," Ruby said. "Why would he feel the need to abide by his parents' wishes?"

Trina shrugged. "His family is complicated. But I wasn't about to push him, because I was mortified at the idea of going to my cousin for the tea."

"As I said before, you should have just gone to someone else and asked if you could borrow a bit of theirs," Jasper said.

"Wait, how do you know this story and I don't?" Ruby asked.

He shrugged. "Trina and I got talking when we were on the ship. She told me a fair bit about her and Ambrose."

"How did *that* happen?" I asked.

Trina and Jasper exchanged a look, and I saw them both blush slightly. "When Trina arrived on the ship, I'd just gone through my first real breakup as well," Jasper explained. "I was dating this girl named Annabelle, and I was convinced I was going to marry her. I had plenty of other girlfriends when I was younger, but none of them were serious. Annabelle and I loved each other, but when her father found out about my past, he was determined to tear us apart. His older sister was a magic user who'd been taken by the Breoch Guard, so the fact that I was one several years back—even for a short time—was unforgivable to him. He pulled Annabelle off the ship so we couldn't be together." He sighed. "Trina came aboard about six months later, fresh from her breakup with Ambrose. We understood the heartbreak that the other one was feeling, so we bonded over complaining about our exes."

"Why didn't you and Ambrose work out?" I asked Trina.

She shrugged. "Ambrose and I began dating about a year after I moved to Ankrossi, and it was...intense. But as time went on, I began to realize what a life with Ambrose would entail. It meant living out in the wilds, far away from my family and friends. And Ambrose lives close to his parents, who, as I said, are a little old fashioned and very involved in his life. I wasn't sure what I wanted, but it wasn't that. I told Ambrose all this, and at first he tried to change my mind. Then he became frustrated because I couldn't tell him exactly what I *did* want, and he said he needed someone a little more mature, who had some idea what their goals were. The breakup was pretty awful."

I nodded, picked up my tea and took a sip; it was slightly bitter, but not in a way I disliked. "Is it hard, seeing him with Daisy?"

She snorted. "I was the one who set them up."

"Are his parents' views about sex outside of marriage...common in these parts?"

Trina picked up on my unspoken question. "If you're worried about not being able to find a new boyfriend here in the Woods because you're not a virgin, don't be."

I relaxed my shoulders a bit. "I used to hear girls at school talk like no one would want you if you'd been with someone else already, as if you were...damaged."

"That's nonsense," Jasper assured. "If you've been with a lot of people, you might have more hurt from those relationships, but you likely also know yourself a little better too, and might have a clearer idea of how to be a decent lover."

"Also, the city folk are really only particular about *women* being virgins when they marry," Kaden put in. "Which is absolutely ridiculous, in my estimation."

"It's true," Ruby said. "I remember Mother giving me a very stern talk once about how I'd best make sure I kept my bloomers on, or I'd disappoint my future husband. But according to Jasper, he and Jade never got that talk."

"No, we didn't," Jasper added. "The closest thing I ever got to a *talk* was my brother encouraging me to go charm my way under girls' skirts. Jade made it sound..." He trailed off and let out a long sigh.

Ruby put a hand on his shoulder. "I'm sorry, I shouldn't have brought him up."

"I just wish people in my family would stop hurting those I care the most about." I didn't miss the way his eyes darted to Trina when he spoke.

Trina nodded slowly. Then she cleared her throat and stood. "I should get home. I'm glad you're back Isabelle; we can talk more later." She gave me a quick smile, then turned and disappeared out the front door.

Jasper let out a long sigh once she was gone. "Something's up with her."

"What do you mean?" I asked.

"I remember what she was like after she lost Noelle. She was quiet, withdrawn, crying all the time. But with Saray, she's almost acting like nothing's wrong."

"You're right." Ruby frowned.

"Maybe she's trying to be strong, seeing that Kip is beside himself with grief and Marcus isn't doing so well either," suggested Kaden.

"Or it hasn't fully hit her that Saray is dead." Ruby's voice shook as she spoke. "It hardly feels real to me either."

"I admit, I'm feeling perhaps a bit too optimistic about it all," Jasper put in. "I know these things are complex, but when you show up at someone's house and a fellow who you shot in the head walks up and decks you, it makes it hard to take death seriously." He chuckled. "I keep waiting for someone to come up with a way to bring her back."

"You know that can't happen, though," Ruby said to him. "They weren't able to bring back Noelle, and we've had several people die in this village over the past few years. The only reason they were able to resurrect Kip was because Kirilee volunteered for the life transfer." She sighed. "The entire village feels different now, more so than when we've lost others."

I nodded. "I noticed that too. People are much quieter."

"People feel *defeated*," Jasper said. "Saray's entire reputation, all of the stories about her, were based on her being essentially unbeatable. And now, she's been beaten." He sighed.

Tears sprang to my eyes. "This is my fault. If the Breoch Guard hadn't shown up to collect me..."

"It's no one person's fault." Kaden put a hand on my shoulder.

"Kip sure didn't seem to think that," I said, bitterness evident in my voice.

"Kip is hurting terribly. Don't mind him. I should check on him tomorrow."

"You think he'd talk to you?" I asked.

"Talk to me, maybe not. Spar with me to get some of his grief and anger out, possibly." She looked at the others. "We should get some sleep. It's been a long day for all of us."

***

The following morning, I sat with Mother in the same large cavern we'd visited last night, studying the somber faces of the council members. Kip was more subdued today, but his eyes were puffy with lack of sleep, and his gaze kept darting to Saray's body at the far end of the cavern. There were a few non-members present at the meeting; Trina and Jasper had both shown up, as had Chester. A young man I'd never seen before sat next to him.

Daisy arrived walking with a cane, and I immediately healed the wound in her leg from where Jade shot her, much to her relief.

Marcus called the meeting to order, then looked me and Mother over. "People of Ankrossi," he said, "today we're gathered to decide whether it's safe to take in Isabelle and her mother, Lillian." He said my mother's name with a hint of fondness. "In order to best make that decision, we need to hear their whole story. And to help us better learn that story, we have Soren with us." My eyes narrowed. *Who's Soren?*

The young man who'd been sitting with Chester walked over to where Mother and I sat. He was clad in a long black tailcoat and carried a cane, and his dark hair was swept back, revealing keen brown eyes and a young, freckled face that looked familiar, though I couldn't place it. When he spoke, it was with an air of authority. "Isabelle, Lillian, it's a pleasure. My name is Soren, and I'll be your interrogator."

"Interrogator?" Mother repeated.

"That's right." He pulled up a chair next to me and sat unceremoniously, legs spread wide, then picked up his cane and began to twirl it. "So," he began, "tell me *everything.*"

"Where do you want us to start?" I asked.

"Let's start at the beginning. Why exactly did you come to the Woods in the first place, Isabelle? Was it really to heal your boyfriend and find your friend, or were there other motives?"

I frowned. "First of all, it wasn't my idea to come here. Kip and Kaden literally showed up on my balcony and asked me to come heal Aria. It was only after that I got the idea to have these folks help me find Silva. As for healing my boyfriend, that was the reason I went to the botany class in the first place, and it's a large part of why I'm training with Claudi right now."

"So there was no desire to bring the Breoch Guard down on us? To alert the king to our whereabouts?"

"No!" I replied indignantly. "I'm a magikai, why would I sell you out to the guard? And what makes you think I have connections to the king?" My palms began to sweat as I spoke.

Soren's eyes locked on mine, hands twirling his cane rhythmically as he spoke. "You tell me, Isabelle. What are your connections to the royal family, exactly?"

I felt an odd, calm sort of euphoria wash over me, a feeling that everything would be fine, that Soren could absolutely be trusted with the information I'd been hiding. A nagging feeling in my gut told me that this sensation was familiar, but I ignored it and met Soren's gaze. "My parents are members of King Kairus' court, and I'm betrothed to Prince Oliver. Or I was at least. I don't think we're together anymore."

I heard several gasps around me. Kaden stared with eyes as big as saucers, Trina clapped a hand over her mouth, and Kip began whispering furiously with Willem. Jasper let out a snicker. *"Ollie,"* he said softly. "I should've known."

Mother, meanwhile, was shaking her head. "Isabelle," she whispered, "why would you—"

"It's all right, ma'am," Soren interrupted, turning to her, and Mother relaxed visibly. Again, a small strand of memory tugged at my consciousness.

"All right, everyone, let's allow Soren to finish his job." Marcus' voice cut through the noise.

The crowd began to quiet down, and Soren turned back to me. "So you're engaged to the heir to the Breochi throne, and you came here to help heal him. What exactly is wrong with Oliver?"

I hesitated for just a moment, then sighed. *People are talking about this back home anyway.* "He has a mysterious illness that's likely to kill him in a few years' time. His mother had the same thing. The king and my father want us to marry soon so we can produce an heir before Oliver dies. There are a bunch of supposed cousins hanging around the palace, trying to convince the king that they should take the throne if there isn't an heir produced."

Soren frowned. "Is there not an established lineage?"

I shook my head. "King Patrick had four children, but only his eldest, Graman, stayed in Breoch. The rest left for other lands. Graman's wife was only able to have one child, Edwin. Edwin's wife bore five children, and all of them but Kairus died young. Kairus' first wife, Inari, fell ill a few years after Oliver was born. His second wife, Calendra, has not been able to have children. None of Patrick's other children thought that Breoch would last as an independent kingdom, so they didn't keep good records of their lineages. Figuring out who is second in line has been complicated."

"Huh." Soren sat back and frowned. "So were you not expecting your father to exercise every possible lead to find you, especially given that you're a rather important person to the future of the nation? And do you not think he, or the king, will do it again now that you are here?"

"Father likely won't come after us. Mother wrote him a note explaining why we've left. As for the king, well, that's partly why I came here. There are a few things I need to tell you folks." I looked around the room. "After the rescue attempt at Saray's execution, Kairus is being encouraged to send soldiers into the Woods to find you. This village might well be in danger, and not just because of me."

A collective chatter arose again at my words, and Marcus silenced it. This time he stood and walked over to me himself. "You said there's more. What are the other things you have to tell us?"

I sighed. "First of all, you need to know that Lachlann isn't willingly working against you. The anti-magic that the guards used when they invaded the Moon Dance did come from him, but he isn't cooperating with them because he wants to. I don't know the details, but I know that the guards have broken him somehow."

Marcus' eyes narrowed. "You mean torture?"

"From what I heard, yes, but it wasn't the torture that did it. It was something else." I heard Starla gasp.

Marcus closed his eyes briefly and nodded. "All right, what else do you need to tell us?"

"I spoke to Saray before the execution, and she wanted me to tell you all how much she loved you." My eyes landed on Kip. "Especially you. She felt awful that your last interaction was a fight."

Kip closed his eyes and nodded, clearly trying not to cry.

"The last thing I need to tell you is that your rescue attempt may bring a crackdown on magic users in the cities. The king suspects that I have magic. Oliver is worried I might be in danger, which is the other reason I'm here. He told me to flee."

"So you're hoping to find refuge here in Ankrossi, then?" Soren asked.

"Yes. I want to stay here where it's safe, for now at least, and as for Mother, well...I know she hopes to start a new life here." I shifted my gaze to Marcus as I spoke and gave him a small smile. "I don't think Ankrossi is in more danger with us here than it would be already. But that's not to say there's no danger at all."

"Right. We will need to make a plan for that."

"We could always send Sophie to the king, see if we can convince him not to—" I stopped mid-sentence as the pieces I hadn't yet connected fell into place. I gaped at Soren. "You're a charmer." Then I turned to Mother, my eyes wide. "And so is Simon."

Chapter 20

MOTHER AND SOREN both turned to me and spoke at once.

"What's a charmer?" asked Mother.

"Who's Simon?" asked Soren.

"A charmer is a person who can use magic to influence others to do what they want. You already met one, Mother. And Simon is one of the king's relatives who showed up vying for the throne. I did notice that he seems to be able to get Kairus to do whatever he wants. And he..." My eyes went wide, and my stomach sank. "He convinced me to tell him about Ankrossi."

"What?" Mother gasped.

"Just after Saray was sentenced. He took me into the garden and started asking me all these questions. I told him...everything. Well, everything but how to get here, because I didn't know."

"This is bad."

"Yes, it is," Soren agreed. "A charmer getting that close to a king could be devastating."

"But how is he using his abilities with the anti-magic that's present in the palace?" Mother mused.

"Probably has access to fairy magic," Soren answered. "That stuff can be potent."

"And why would he want to know about Ankrossi?" Marcus put in. "Do you think he'll tell the king?"

"I have no idea." I took a deep breath, trying to steer the conversation away from what I'd done. "Are we all forgetting the part where Soren just charmed Mother and me?"

He shrugged. "I'm literally just doing my job."

I turned to Marcus. "How does this village have *two* charmers? I thought the gift was rare."

Marcus hesitated for a moment, and Soren spoke first. "It's all right, Marcus. I'll tell them. They know I'm a charmer now, so this disguise won't work anymore."

"Disguise?" Mother repeated.

Soren nodded and pulled a pendant from his shirt. He rubbed it, and I gasped as the boyish features and body disappeared and were replaced by Sophie, now dressed in boys' clothes that were too big for her. She gave me a sheepish grin. "Surprise."

"I remember you!" Mother exclaimed. "You're the girl who convinced me to...oh." She sighed. "That makes sense."

"My apologies to both of you," Sophie said. "We needed Isabelle to stay here, which was why I charmed you initially. And this time, well, again, I was doing my job. We needed to know exactly what your agenda is."

"And now we do," Marcus said. "Isabelle and Lillian will likely both be safer here than back in Kirstein. The question we must answer now is, will their presence here make an attack on Ankrossi more likely?"

"If what Isabelle says is true, then it sounds like Ankrossi might be attacked regardless," Starla put in. "And I know Aria will be safer with them here. I say they stay."

"So do I," Willem added. "I don't generally vote in favour of things that could endanger our village, but I know that my mother is eager to start training Isabelle again, and if she's planning to stay indefinitely this time, then maybe she's actually..." He exchanged a glance with Kip.

Kip let out a long sigh. "If the village is in danger, then we need to make a plan to defend it in case the Breoch Guard shows up. Kaden, you and I should start training these folks to fight without their magic." Kaden nodded.

"But you're not opposed to them staying?" Marcus asked Kip.

Kip closed his eyes for a moment. "It's hard for me not to think that Isabelle's presence here was what brought the Guard down on us last time. But if they're likely to show up anyway, there's not much point in turning her or Lillian away."

"I...don't think I should stay in Ankrossi if the Breoch Guard are likely to return," Chester said, his eyes wide. He turned to Willem. "Can I stay at your place until we're out of danger?"

"I think it would be wise to protect *all* our younger folks from whatever might come," put in Marcus. "Perhaps we could open the dorms at the school until we deem Ankrossi safe? The teens, and anyone with small children who wishes, can stay there."

Willem nodded. "That shouldn't be too hard to facilitate."

"We can stay in dorms as well, and help with running them," volunteered Shawnie. Alisa nodded.

"I'm sure my parents would be willing to help with that as well," Jessen put in.

Marcus turned back to Chester. "Does that satisfy your concern for your safety?" He nodded.

"We'll make arrangements to open the dorms then, though it'll take a few weeks to make it happen," Willem said. "I doubt that we need to worry about an invasion quite yet. The Breoch Guard still needs to get the information from Lachlann—who knows how easy that'll be?—then figure out how to even get to Ankrossi. They also need to convince some of their ranks to venture this deep into the Woods."

"They'll likely send a bunch of Witch Slayers, like they did in Dundere," Starla said. I didn't miss the trepidation in her voice.

"True, though it'll still take some time to plan. And we don't know for certain whether they'll attack; this is all speculation. In any case, we should be able to keep the young folks safe at the school."

"I'll stay in the village," I put in. "I figure I'm needed to take care of Aria, and if there is an attack, I'll be needed in Ankrossi to heal. Also, I'd rather stay close to Mother, for now."

"You think Starla and Aria won't stay in the dorms?" Willem asked.

But Starla shook her head. "Honestly, I'd rather stay where I am. I'll be close to Trina, and I have a way to protect Aria and myself in the event of an attack."

"Even with anti-magic present?"

She nodded. "Kirilee and I have a plan. I already asked Jessen to use anti-magic on me to see if it works. Kirilee's magic is attuned to the fairies now, so it's still doable." She smiled. "I'll stay where I am for the time being."

"Well, then, it's your choice, Isabelle," Willem said. "You can stay in town and use the portal to get back and forth from the school to train with Claudi, or you can stay in dorms."

"There's no possibility of attackers breaching the portal to the school?" I asked.

Willem shook his head. "Folks can only go through it if one of a few approved people invites them. That's why Shawnie has to bring the teens through every day. Same with the portal to Hilda's place. Both of those locations are safe from invasion through Ankrossi."

"It seems like we've reached a conclusion." Marcus smiled at me. "Welcome back, Isabelle. And Lillian," he continued, his gaze softening as he turned toward Mother, "I can't wait to show you around."

People began to clear out of the chamber slowly. I turned to Mother, about to comment on the proceedings, when Sophie approached me. "I hope you're not mad at me," she said, her tone a bit sheepish.

I shrugged. "I get why you did it. I had no idea it was you in that body, by the way."

"It's pretty convincing, isn't it?" She smirked.

"Do you have any other disguises I need to worry about?"

"I do, but Ember has those pendants, and I'm only allowed to use them under special circumstances." She reached out and squeezed my hand. "I'm glad you're not mad."

Willem joined me just as Sophie left, and he smiled. "Isabelle. I don't think we've formally met, though I've heard a lot about you. Claudi is eager to start working with you again."

"Good, because I need to talk to her."

"About what?"

I took a deep breath. "Since it looks like I'll be staying here, I can take on the role she asked me to." I met Willem's eyes. "I'm willing to be the next Bearer."

***

"Are you sure about this?" Claudi asked me a few hours later, after I'd had a chance to tell her what I'd decided and recount everything I'd revealed earlier at the meeting. We were back at Willem's place, and I sat on the couch between the two of them.

I nodded. "I'm sure. You folks need a new Bearer, and it looks like I'll be staying here."

She frowned. "What about Oliver? You don't see yourself going back?"

"Not permanently, at least. I might go back to try and heal him, but even if Oliver and I want to be together, I doubt we'll be allowed, now that I've run off a second time." I felt a pang of regret as I spoke; I already missed Oliver's laugh, his quirky interests, the way his lips felt pressed against my own.

Claudi and Willem exchanged a long glance. "All right, then," Claudi said to him. "I suppose you and I can facilitate the spell, without involving Kip or Hilda?"

Willem nodded. "Given how busy Hilda's been, and how much Kip is carrying right now, that's likely best."

"What has to happen for me to take on the role?" I asked.

"It's actually very simple. I need to put this necklace on you." Claudi held up a small silver pendant shaped like a drop of water, inlaid with a single blue stone. "If the pendant accepts you, we'll see the effect of the power transfer immediately. Before we do that, though, I'd like to ask you some questions. The last time we conducted a power transfer, we did it without the consent of the person, which, looking back, was unfair."

"You mean Kip?"

Willem nodded. "Kirilee put the pendant on him because she assumed that the life transfer would also entail a power transfer. The Earth Stone did choose him, but he didn't choose the stone, and it caused some problems. So I want to make certain that you are, in fact, willing to take this on." He met my eyes, his face grave. "Isabelle McAllister, do you accept the role of Bearer of the Sea Stone, and the responsibilities that accompany it?"

I nodded. "I do."

"Do you understand that bearing this stone will tie you to the Woods, and that you'll need to remain close to them more often than not, or else risk unbalancing the magic of the Shrouded Woods?"

"I do."

"Then, together, Claudi and I name you the next Bearer of the Sea Stone."

Claudi smiled, unclasped the pendant, and leaned toward me. My heartbeat picked up as she fastened it around my neck.

And nothing happened.

Willem and Claudi exchanged a look. "Well, that's odd," Claudi said.

"That can't be right." Willem scratched his head. "Isabelle's the first lifebringer we've seen since Noelle. Why would the stone *not* choose her?"

I gazed down at the pendant, just as confused. "Maybe...it's not my destiny?" I guessed. A wild hope welled up in one corner of my mind; perhaps, I thought, this meant that Oliver and I were fated after all.

"But if not you, then who?" Claudi shook her head. "I don't know how much longer I can hold out."

"I have no idea." I closed my hand around the pendant, waiting for a surge of power, a feeling, *anything* to confirm that I was, in fact, the next Bearer. When nothing came, I undid the clasp and passed the pendant back to Claudi. "Perhaps it's not the right time yet? You might still have a few years left in you. How old are you?"

"Eighty-eight," she said.

I raised my eyebrows; that *was* quite old. "Either it's not time, or there's another lifebringer who will take this on."

Willem nodded. "Exactly. Either way, you'd best get practicing your healing." He stood. "And I'd best get over to the school. There are a lot of scared teenagers who need comfort."

***

That evening was market night, but the mood in Ankrossi was subdued. Folks visited the stalls mechanically, then retreated to their homes. Word had gotten out about the possibility of an attack on the village, and that, combined with the loss of Saray, seemed to have everyone on edge.

I hardly saw Mother; she spent the entire afternoon with Marcus, and now the two of them walked through the shop stalls, deep in conversation. I wandered aimlessly, unsure what to do with myself. Occasionally, someone would come up to me and ask for healing; I was able to manage the first few on my own but then found myself becoming exhausted. I was near Kip's stall at that point, and I wandered in, only to find Kaden manning it. "Where's Kip?"

She shrugged. "He needed the night off. He's still not doing well, unsurprisingly. Why, do you need him?"

"No, but I may have to borrow someone's magic to help me heal folks. I'm getting tired."

"Well, I'm here if you need me. And I think Trina's in the tavern. You could hang out there and steal her magic if need be."

That's a good idea, I decided. The tavern was a central location where folks could find me easily enough. I thanked Kaden and headed over to the bar, where I found Jasper on stage. His music tonight was mellow, an obvious attempt to adapt to the mood of the bar's patrons. I found Trina sitting at a table nearby, nursing a drink, and sat with her. "How are you?"

She shrugged, her unnaturally chipper mood from the night before seemingly gone. "Do you think about death much?" I noticed her voice was slurred.

"Well, I've certainly thought about it more than normal in the past week."

"Do you think there's anything beyond this life? Everyone talks about this 'next world,' but no one seems to be able to prove it exists. I asked Kip what he experienced when he was dead, and all he remembers is feeling like he was travelling somewhere, then being pulled *backward* to this world." Jasper finished his set then, and Trina glanced over at him as he packed up his fiddle.

I shrugged. "I have no idea. I suppose I always felt like I wasn't allowed to think about it, because it sounds similar to religion, and religion is similar to magic."

"Right. I suppose it's hard not to think about it now, though." She sighed. "Do you think Saray's happy where she is? Do you think she's happier than she would be if she were here?"

I was about to answer when Jasper joined us, carrying a drink of his own. He sat next to Trina and studied her. "You look...melancholy."

She nodded and dropped her head onto his shoulder. "Just thinking about death. What comes after it? Regrets and..." She sighed.

"You're grieving. What you're saying sounds pretty normal to me." Jasper slipped his arm around her, then eyed me. "How's your day been?"

I told him everything that happened at Claudi's, and how I'd barely seen my mother since the meeting with the council. "It's been a strange day," I concluded.

"Indeed." Jasper frowned, looking down at Trina, who'd all but buried her head in his chest. "I think you've had a bit too much to drink."

Trina looked up at him, and I saw tears in her eyes. "I can't stop thinking, what if I were to be taken away suddenly? I'd regret not doing some things, you know."

"Wouldn't we all?" Jasper chuckled. "Don't worry, Trina, you're not going anywhere."

"You don't know that." She raised her head to look him in the eye. "All I know is that if I go very suddenly, I'd definitely regret not doing this." My mouth fell open as Trina reached up, pulled Jasper's face toward her own, and kissed him.

For a moment, Jasper seemed to return the kiss, then abruptly pulled away. "Trina," he whispered, "what are you doing?"

She gave him a woozy grin. "Come home with me tonight," she begged. "It's clear enough that we both want each other."

Jasper stared at her for a long moment, then took a deep breath. "This isn't the right time."

"Why not?" Her voice came out as a whine.

"Trina, you're drunk. And people don't make good decisions when they're drunk. This is the sort of thing we should talk about when you're sober, and not in the middle of grieving an awful loss. We'll discuss it another time, all right?"

"But what if we never get to..." Her words were lost in tears, and she began to sob.

I shifted uncomfortably. "Should I leave?"

"No. Actually, yes. Can you find Starla? I think it's best that I'm not the one to put Trina to bed right now." Jasper's eyes met mine, and I saw a hint of what I'd seen in Oliver's eyes two nights ago—pure, barely contained desire.

"Right. Of course."

I left the tavern and returned quickly with Starla in tow. Trina was still crying, but her sobs had eased to sniffling. Jasper had his arm around her again, and when Starla arrived, he informed her that Trina needed to be put to bed, his tone businesslike and curt.

Starla's eyes narrowed at the strangeness of the interaction, but she helped Trina to her feet. Trina tottered for a moment, then turned to Jasper. "You're going to regret this." There was no malice in her tone, only sadness.

The moment they were gone, Jasper's head dropped into his hands. "What just *happened?*" he groaned.

"Good question." I shook my head.

He met my gaze. "I'm sorry you had to watch that."

I shrugged. "You think I've never seen relationship drama before?"

"Trina never acts this reckless. Her mood is all over the place. I don't think she's ever been that drunk, and we spent six months on a ship together."

"As you say, she's grieving."

He nodded. "Maybe don't tell anyone about that...interaction until Trina and I have talked it out."

"What, the kiss? Sure thing." I stood. "I'd best be heading home anyway. Want to come with me?"

He shook his head. "I'm going to finish my drink. And maybe have one or five more."

I snorted. "I'll tell your sister to check up on you before she leaves the market."

"No, don't. I don't want Ruby to have to deal with that, not after…" He sighed. "I'll be all right, don't worry. I can get home."

"If you say so." I gave him a sympathetic smile, then stood and headed out of the bar.

***

I was roused in the middle of the night by a hand shaking my shoulder. "Isabelle, wake up," I heard my mother's voice call.

"Mother?" I sat up, suddenly very awake. "What's happening?"

"I don't know, exactly." Her face was barely illuminated in the moonlight. "Trina wants to meet with us in the chamber. She asked me to fetch you and Marcus and bring you to the Mothertree."

I frowned as I got out of bed and threw a shawl over my nightclothes. "Did she say why?"

"No. I just know it's important."

"Was she still drunk when she asked you?"

Mother frowned. "I don't think so. Come on. She said not to wake the others."

We climbed carefully down the stairs and tiptoed past Jasper, sound asleep in his hammock. "Trina was acting very strange earlier," I said when we stepped outside to where Marcus waited for us. "I have no idea what's going on with her."

"Me neither," Marcus said. "But I have a feeling we're about to find out."

***

The Mothertree's chamber was lit by viletta blooms and fairy light. Inside, we found Trina sitting next to Kip, close to Saray's body. Willem sat nearby too, beside a petite blonde woman who held hands with a much older looking grey-haired woman. A gathering of fairies surrounded them. *This must be Hilda and her wife,* I decided.

"Trina," asked Marcus as we approached, "what is this?"

"I've brought you all here to ask if you'll help me with something." Trina got to her feet, and her gaze passed over each of us. Her voice was no longer slurred, I noticed, but her eyes looked red, and her face was slightly pale. She took a deep breath. "I want to do a life transfer to bring back Saray, using me as the subject."

Chapter 21

MY JAW DROPPED, everything about the previous evening suddenly making sense. There came a collective gasp from among the others. "Trina, no!" Marcus exclaimed.

"Absolutely not," Hilda chimed in. "Really, I'm surprised you have the gall to even request that." Carmine shook her head vigorously.

"Trina, have you gone mad?" Willem put in.

"I'm completely sane," she replied, her voice firm. Then she took a deep breath and squared her shoulders. "I've seen the state Ankrossi is in. The people can't cope with the fact that their Unbeatable One is dead. Most of you can't cope with losing her, either." She eyed Kip. "You're a mess. But if Saray were to mysteriously rise from the dead, the people would have hope again. And they'd be a lot better equipped to fight if the Breoch Guard were to attack."

"Trina," Kip said as he slowly rose to his feet, "you're right, I am a mess. But do you think I'd be any less of a mess if you were gone?"

"She's your *wife*," Trina responded.

"And you're the closest thing I have to a sister. Losing you would mess me up just as badly, y'know."

"And I would mourn just as hard, too," Marcus put in. "You are as much of a daughter to me as Saray is, Trina. I hope I haven't made you think otherwise."

"You haven't," she assured. "I know I'm loved by all of you. I know people would miss me. But no one outside this circle would need to know the truth. You could tell them that I ran off to the Lady Liara to spend some time away while I mourned, then you could fabricate a tale about me drowning." She sighed. "I may be loved here, but I'm not *needed* like Saray is. People will mourn me, but it wouldn't bring the entire village down like this."

"Even so, this is madness. Noelle would be horrified at what you're doing, Trina," Marcus said. "And your mother—don't you care about what this will…"

"Stop trying to guilt me!" She took a deep breath and reached into her pocket then, bringing a small bottle to her lips in one fluid motion to drink its contents. "*Incantus Ravenous Bardeous,*" she intoned, and an iridescent bubble enveloped her. She met Marcus' eyes, her gaze turning hard. "Now you have little choice but to do as I've asked."

"Trina, what have you done?" His face went white.

"I've poisoned myself." She held up the bottle. "This is skunkflower root extract. It's useful for treating wounds in very small doses, but…."

"A dose that size will kill a person in about twenty-four hours," Kip finished for her. "What are you *thinking?*"

Trina flinched but held her ground. "What I'm thinking is that now I'm like Kirilee. I'm going to die anyway, so I might as well do something useful in the process."

Willem huffed. "Lucky for us, we have a lifebringer present."

"Isabelle can't heal me through this." She gestured at the bubble that enveloped her. "And if I drop it, she won't be able to touch me unless you all physically restrain me, which I'm fairly certain is against the law in Ankrossi."

"And killing yourself slowly so that you can be used for a life transfer isn't?" Kip shot back.

Trina crossed her arms. "I know you're all mad at me, but you'll be grateful once Saray's back. So are you going to do the life transfer or not? Because if you don't, you'll have two dead loved ones in less than a day."

Everyone stared at her for a few long moments. Then Carmine gasped. She grabbed Hilda's shoulder, turned her away from the group, and began to sign frantically.

Hilda peered up into the branches of Kirilee's tree for a moment and smiled. "Thank you for that," she whispered. Then she got to her feet, her eyes on Trina. "Kirilee's given me an idea. We may be able to bring back Saray without sacrificing you."

Kip's head snapped up, and Trina's eyes narrowed skeptically, but when she spoke her tone held a note of hope. "Really?"

"Yes. I need to go discuss it with the fairies; I'll be back shortly."

Hilda disappeared from sight, leaving us all stunned. Trina sat down, still encased in her bubble, refusing to speak to anyone. Beside me, Mother sighed. "Why do you suppose Trina brought us into this?"

"Likely because she figures you two would take her side," Marcus answered, sitting down next to her. "And Isabelle's lifebringing skills could help with the transfer." He shook his head. "I can't believe Trina would do something like this..." Then he chuckled a little, his voice breaking. "It sounds like the sort of thing I'd come up with."

Several minutes later, Hilda reappeared, and all eyes were on her. Trina stood. "Did you...find a way to bring Saray back?"

"I believe I have," Hilda said. "Though it will come with a cost. And it *will* involve you, Trina."

"How?"

"There is one other way to bring a dead person back that doesn't require a life transfer," Hilda said. "What was originally done to Kirilee."

Trina's eyes widened. "Soul magic."

"That's right."

"But...you told us when Noelle died that you couldn't do that because you'd likely lose your own magic and would be neglecting your duties to the fairies," Trina said.

"You're right, I did. And that would still be an issue—unless I could find someone to replace me as their priestess." She smiled at Trina. "I can't believe I've never thought of you as a successor before. You would have been too young when Noelle died, but now..." She shook her head. "You'd be perfect. The fairies love you."

Trina blinked. "You want *me* to take over as the fairy priestess?"

"Yes. I would perform a ceremony that transfers the bulk of my power, and all my responsibilities, to you first. I'd keep enough power and connection to the fairies to perform the ritual. The soul magic would likely drain me of that power, leaving me a typical mortal once again."

"And you'd be willing to do that?"

"Yes. This would also allow me to travel to Dundere to help with the Fae situation, so it could solve more than one problem. But Trina, this *will* cost you."

Trina lifted her chin. "I was willing to sacrifice my life for this, Hilda. How bad can it be?"

"Sometimes dying for a cause is easier than making a sacrifice and continuing to live," Hilda countered. "First of all, this will cost you a certain amount of freedom. You'll be tied to my home and these woods. Your biggest responsibility will be to the fairies, which may affect your prospects. You won't be able to travel far for any length of time, so you may find it hard to meet a partner, if that's what you desire. I certainly would still be on my own if Carmine hadn't stumbled upon my cottage. And you won't be able to bear children while you fill this role. Your body will not age past about thirty, so you may be able to have them later in life if you find a replacement priestess or if the fairies decide they no longer need a protector."

Trina frowned. "Any man who wishes to be with me will have to understand my situation, then," she said. "And as for children, well..." She closed her eyes and sighed. "I'm sure I could adopt. Adoptive parents can be just as wonderful as birth parents." She opened her eyes and smiled at Marcus, but I could see a hint of sadness.

Hilda nodded. "Another thing you need to understand is that fairy magic is, in some ways, very much like anti-magic. You cannot carry both regular magic and fairy magic in your body at once. Someone who merely has access to fairy magic, such as Alexander, might be able to dabble in both, but as their protector, the magic of the Fae will run deep in your blood. This means that, first of all, you'll lose your connection to animals. There will be exceptions—you'll be able to talk to my cats, and to Persius, as they all have Fae spells cast on them allowing them to speak to certain humans. And you'll be able to speak to any animals you specifically enchant for that purpose. But your connection to the larger animal world will be severed. You will, however, gain the ability to speak to the fairies."

Trina nodded. "That will be strange," she admitted. "I don't recall a time in my life when I couldn't speak to animals."

"And, unfortunately, that's not the greatest sacrifice you'll need to make," Hilda continued. "There's one more thing, and this, I think, will be hardest for you." She sighed. "Like with anti-magic, fairy magic has the ability to undo spells that were cast on you, including healings. And I recall that a very significant healing spell was performed on you eight years ago. That, too, will be undone."

Trina bit her lip. "I'm going to be blind again?" Her voice trembled.

"Not quite as blind as you were before, but essentially, yes. The fairies will be able to provide some sight for you, but it will be limited. Remember when you first came to my garden, and you could only see the fairies but nothing else?"

Trina nodded.

"It will be similar to that. Imagine that you're walking down a dark path, but you have a lantern—you would be able to see, but only a few feet in front of you. If you had several lanterns, you could likely see a little farther. In an enclosed space with a few lanterns, you might see near-perfectly. That's how it will be. The fairies have promised me that they will stay close to you as needed to provide you with sight. They've also suggested that you enchant an animal to help you navigate, much like how Kip's dog Bailey used to guide you."

"So I'd be able to see my friends if they were nearby," Trina surmised. "But I wouldn't be able to see faraway things like clouds and sunsets?"

"That's right. And you might not see threats until they were close. You would be vulnerable, which is part of why the fairies suggested you have an animal to help you." Hilda sighed. "I want to make it very clear, Trina. You don't *have* to do this."

Trina took a deep, shuddering breath, then met Hilda's eyes. "Yes, I do. If I don't, I'll spend my life knowing I had a chance to bring my best friend and sister back from the dead and didn't take it."

Hilda nodded. "Very well, then. Now, will you let Isabelle heal you of your poison?"

"I suppose so." Trina lowered her protection spell and gave me a look that was almost shy. "I hope you don't mind."

"I think you're a little mad," I told her, "but I understand your desperation." I placed a hand on Trina's shoulder then and began to hum, trying to locate the poison in her body. "Good, it hasn't left your stomach yet." I put my other hand on her abdomen and frowned; I'd never cured a poisoning before, and for a moment I was uncertain what to do. I closed my eyes, trying to visualize the path of the healing, like Claudi had explained to me. When I realized what was going to happen, I winced. "This is going to make you throw up," I told her. "It's the easiest way to get the poison from your body. Perhaps we should do this somewhere that isn't in the middle of our gathering place?"

Trina nodded, and we went out to the meadow into some nearby brush. Marcus followed so that he could hold Trina's hair back for her. She gave him a smile, then crouched down in the bushes. "All right, do it Isabelle."

I squatted next to her, placed a hand on her stomach again, and began to sing. Trina's abdomen contracted moments into the song, and she vomited, Marcus keeping her hair out of her face while she heaved.

"It's all over," I assured her. "The poison is gone."

Trina nodded, and I felt her begin to shake. She let out a whimper.

"Are you all right?" Marcus asked, putting his arm around her.

She burst into tears. "I...I'm sorry..."

Marcus helped her to her feet and pulled her into an embrace. "It's all right," he assured softly. "You're safe now, that's what matters to me." He met my eyes and tipped his head toward the Mothertree, and I nodded and left them alone.

"Is she all right?" Kip asked when I returned.

I nodded. "The poison's gone. She's a little emotional, though; I'm giving her and Marcus a moment."

They joined us a few minutes later. Trina's eyes were red, but she gave everyone a watery smile. "There. All healed up."

"Good." Hilda nodded. "Do you wish to perform the transition ceremony tonight?"

"Maybe tomorrow. Give me one more day with my sight...I wonder if Ambrose would be willing to take me for a ride before sundown so I can see the sky one last time."

"Maybe Ruby can make an extra special sunset for you," I put in.

"There are a few other things we'll need to discuss," Hilda said to Trina. "But I think we've done enough for now. Let's head to bed, and we'll talk more tomorrow."

Marcus nodded. "I think you and I need to go talk with your mother," he said to Trina.

Her eyes widened, and she shook her head. "Mother will hate me for trying this."

"Do *I* hate you for it? It will be painful for her to hear, I'm sure, but she won't hate you. And you're in no space to go home and sleep by yourself. Come on."

He led Trina out of the cavern with an arm draped across her shoulders, leaving us all staring after them.

Chapter 22

THE FOLLOWING EVENING, I went to the meadow to take part in the dragon ride that Marcus had arranged for before the transfer of power. The fastest way to Hilda's home, where the transfer would take place, was through a portal inside the Mothertree similar to the one that led to Willem's, but tonight a good number of us would make the trip on the backs of dragons. I hadn't seen much of my housemates since I'd told them about last night's events first thing this morning, but now I found them all in the meadow, gathered around Trina. Kaden stood nearby but didn't participate in the conversation—she'd reacted more angrily than I expected, claiming it would have been selfish for Trina to just abandon everyone without saying goodbye.

Jasper stood next to Kaden, shooting concerned glances at Trina; she, meanwhile, studiously avoided his gaze. Sophie and Chester had shown up as well, as had Marcus, Starla, and a few others who I didn't really know. Sophie let out a whoop as four dragons flew over the clearing, circling us before landing close by. Ambrose dismounted from Spark and came over. "My lady," he said to Trina with a bow, "your chariot awaits."

She gave him a shy smile. "Thanks for doing this for me, Ambrose."

"My pleasure," he replied. "What you're doing is incredible."

Trina's shoulders hunched. "Some people think what I'm doing is pretty stupid."

"There's a difference between what you did last night and what you're doing this evening," Daisy said, joining Ambrose. She smiled at Trina. "We have a gift for you."

Trina's eyes widened. "What's that?"

Daisy took her hand and led her over to the smallest of the four dragons. "This is Millie. She's Spark's daughter, and she's just big enough to hold two adults and one child, as Ambrose and I have figured out. You're going to need a way to get around quickly if you can't see, and even if you lose most of your ability to talk to animals, you should still be able to speak to dragons, since their magic is similar to that of the fairies."

Trina's eyes went wide. "You're giving me my own *dragon?*"

"That we are." Ambrose grinned at her. "Go on, say hello."

Trina stepped toward Millie and touched her snout. "Hey there," she murmured. Millie leaned into Trina's hand, then gave her shoulder a nudge.

"We told Millie who you are and what you're doing," Ambrose said. "She knows she'll need to be your eyes sometimes."

Trina chuckled, leaning her head against Millie's snout. "Hilda said I might want to enchant an animal to be my eyes. But I was thinking of a bird, or possibly another dog. I hadn't thought of picking a dragon."

"You may want another animal to guide you when you're on the ground," Daisy suggested. "You remember how to mount properly?"

Trina nodded and closed her eyes, clearly in communication with the dragon. A moment later, Millie crouched so Trina could climb onto her back. "When Lachlann comes home, we're going to need to make you a saddle," she said softly. Then her eyes flickered to Ruby. "Want to ride with me?"

Ruby climbed up behind Trina, and Daisy returned to her own dragon. The third dragon had a young woman who looked to be Ambrose's sister riding on its back, and she smiled at all of us. "Everyone hop on," she said. "Let's fly!"

***

The sky had turned several shades of pink and orange by the time we cleared the trees. I gazed at the crimson-painted clouds from the back of Daisy's dragon, who I learned was named Raindrop for his bright blue colouring. Above me, Kaden swooped and somersaulted, Sophie and Chester giggling as they followed her. Kaden's earlier anger seemed to have faded for the time being.

We all took turns flying, riding on the different dragons, and sitting with Trina on Millie. When it was my turn, she glanced back at me. "I probably owe you an apology."

"For what?"

"For everything you had to deal with last night. Having to heal me and make me throw up. And also seeing the way I acted around Jasper." Her cheeks flushed as she spoke.

I shrugged. "I'm not mad at you. And the way you acted around Jasper made a lot more sense once I realized what you were up to. It's a little similar to what I did with Oliver, actually."

"I suppose so." She sighed. "Is *he* mad at me?"

"No. He's concerned, but not mad. You should talk to him."

She nodded. "I owe him an apology, at least. But I don't think I'm quite ready to talk *everything* out with him."

"You mean how the two of you are clearly infatuated with one another but not doing anything about it?"

Her blush deepened. "We'll need to have that conversation at some point. But there are too many other things happening right now."

"Fair enough. I'm sure he'll understand." Jasper was flying with Kaden as we spoke, and I caught his eye and waved him down.

When he was flying alongside us, he gave Trina a nervous smile. "Hey. How are you?"

"I'm...all right, I suppose." Trina waved at Kaden then, who swooped down and grabbed me off Millie's back. She deposited me on Spark so Jasper and Trina could talk.

The sky was darkening, turning shades of cherry red and deep violet, and after several minutes of conversation with her, Jasper gave up his seat to Starla. It was only once Starla was there that tears began to trickle down Trina's face. I blinked hard myself, only partly understanding the weight of Trina's sacrifice. Starla reached forward and held her as the dragons began their slow descent.

We touched down in a large garden behind a solitary cottage in the Woods. Fairies danced about freely, their ethereal light illuminating the stone paths and brilliant foliage and trees bursting with fruit. The air was heavy with the scent of night-blooming flowers. A large crowd had gathered in what I assumed to be Hilda's backyard, and they all quieted down as Trina's dragon landed. Starla hopped down from Millie, all business, and took Trina by the hand, leading her past the onlookers into the cottage. The rest of us dismounted, and Ambrose, Daisy, and Ambrose's sister took the dragons to the sky again. Ambrose and Daisy returned shortly after; I assumed their rides were waiting around the front of the house. Kip, Hilda, Willem and Claudi were all sitting together, deep in discussion, and the rest of us clustered around them, curious as to what the rest of the night would entail.

"Carmine will be the one to facilitate this spell," Hilda was saying when I joined the conversation. "She has enough of my magic in her that she's able to do this."

"How does she have your magic?" asked Daisy. "Are you two Joined?"

Hilda shook her head. "Carmine and I use entirely different kinds of magic, so Joining isn't possible for us. But when two people are in an intimate relationship for any length of time, their magic can sometimes begin to rub off on the other. Carmine has the ability to speak to the fairies in sign and has access to a small amount of their magic. And I cannot speak to plants, but my sense of knowing what they need has improved since I married Carmine."

Daisy and Ambrose glanced at one another. "Perhaps it's too bad that we have the same gift, then," said Daisy.

"Not at all. I imagine that your ability to speak to both dragons and other animals has improved since you wed," Hilda said.

Ambrose shot a glance at Starla, who had rejoined us. "Wait, does this mean that you're a bit less magical since you married Lachlann? Or that he's a bit less...anti-magical?"

Starla chuckled. "Thankfully, I don't think it works that way. Though I know that when I'm kissing him, my ability to speak to plants diminishes significantly."

"You've tried to talk to plants while you're kissing your husband?" Kaden asked, raising her eyebrows.

"More that I can hear them talking to me. Kirilee definitely let out a few whoops the first time she saw me kiss him." She blushed slightly. "Anyway, we were talking about Carmine doing the ritual."

"Right. Speaking of which, I should probably join her and Trina inside and help get her ready." Hilda smiled and gave us all a bow, then disappeared into the house.

Ruby glanced after her. "This may sound strange," she said, "but I'm nervous for Trina."

"Me too," I admitted, noticing the knot in my stomach.

"I think that's perfectly normal," Starla assured. "This is not a small undertaking. I'm proud of her, though."

Several minutes later, Hilda appeared on the balcony and cleared her throat, directing us all to take a seat so the proceedings could begin. She and Carmine came to stand in front of an arched trellis. I seated myself on the soft grass next to Sophie and waited.

Not long after, the garden grew quiet as Trina emerged from the house. I watched her make her way through the assembly, dressed in a gauzy purple gown, clutching a large stone that glittered in a rainbow of colour. A few dozen fairies swirled around her in a playful, luminescent dance. Marcus stood next to Hilda and Carmine at the trellis; he would act as Carmine's interpreter. Hilda began to sing in a language I did not know, her voice high and clear. As she sang, more fairies appeared.

I knew the fairies were more numerous than I'd seen thus far, but I had no idea there were quite this many. They seemed to come from all directions, tiny pinpricks of light streaming in and illuminating the garden. Many landed on the trellis and in nearby trees, creating vivid, luminous outlines of the trunks and branches that glowed in the fading light, while others swirled around Hilda and Carmine. When Trina reached the trellis, several of them landed on her. She placed the stone on a table that was set out between her and Hilda, then looked expectantly at Carmine. Hilda stopped singing, and Carmine met Trina's gaze and began to sign.

"Dear friends," Marcus translated, "today we gather to witness a transfer of power, as Hilda steps away from her role as protector of the fairies of Firenholme, keeper of the fairy ways, liaison between the Fae and humans of these woods, and Bearer of the Air Stone. In her place, Trina takes up the mantle. This is the first such transfer of power since the Fae were hunted in these woods nearly fifty years ago, and it is not something to be taken lightly. I call forward Tiriel, king of the Firenholme Fae."

A single fairy flew down from the trees, this one more vibrant than the rest. While most fairies' lights were only one colour, Tiriel's seemed to contain multiple, shimmering tones of crimson and violet and aquamarine, the hues dancing and shifting within his aura. He perched on the rock between Trina and Hilda. "Tiriel," Marcus translated, "do you accept Trina as the new protector of your people, and vow to assist her in any way needed so that she may flourish in this role?"

Carmine placed her hand on the rock and closed her eyes for a moment, then laughed. She signed to Marcus, who grinned. "Tiriel says yes, he and his people do accept Trina and will assist her, but that they also vow to make her life a wee bit chaotic."

Everyone chuckled, and Trina smiled down at Tiriel. "I would expect nothing less of the Fae."

Carmine nodded knowingly, then turned to Marcus, and Hilda began to translate. "As leader of the people of Ankrossi and son of Kirilee, who was known to many as the Queen of Firenholme, do you vow to accept Trina as your liaison between the humans and the fairies, and vow to listen to and consider her council on matters that concern the fairies?"

Marcus nodded. "I do so vow," he said, signing the response as he spoke.

Carmine turned to Hilda next. She smiled at her wife, then began to sign. "Do you willingly relinquish your role as protector of the fairies of Firenholme, keeper of the fairy ways, liaison between the Fae and humans of these woods, and Bearer of the Air Stone, and vow to teach Trina the responsibilities that accompany her new role?" translated Marcus.

"I do so vow," Hilda said, reaching out and squeezing Carmine's hand.

Carmine smiled, then turned to Trina. "And finally," Marcus said, "Trina...do you willingly take on the role of protector of the fairies of Firenholme, keeper of the fairy ways, liaison between the Fae and humans of these woods, and Bearer of the Air Stone?"

"I do," said Trina.

"Do you vow to learn your new role with diligence and patience?"

"I do so vow."

"Do you vow to put the needs of the Fae before any personal interests, and to protect them first and foremost, even to the point of death?"

"I do so vow."

"And do you willingly relinquish your ties to natural magic of the Woods and all things that have come from it, so that you may instead take on the magic of the Fae?"

Trina took a deep breath. "I do."

Carmine nodded and began to sign again. "Willem, please come forward."

Willem approached Trina carrying a small glass vial. "I am going to remove your magic and place it in here," he told her, gesturing to the vial. "You may recall that when Kirilee took back her magic, she broke a pendant in her palm. The liquid mixed with her blood and restored her magic to her. If you choose to pass on your responsibility to someone else, or the fairies decide they no longer need a protector, you will be able to do the same once your fairy magic is removed. All of your abilities, and the magic done to restore your sight, will be returned to you." He smiled at Trina. "If you would like to take a moment to say your farewells to the animals and take one last look around, you may do so now. When you are ready, close your eyes and open your palms. Do not open your eyes again until Hilda tells you to."

Trina nodded. She looked around, gazing into the trees and hidden nooks of the garden, likely communicating one last time with the creatures residing there. Then her eyes swept over the guests, and I saw her staring into each of our faces as if trying to memorize the details. When our gazes met, she gave me a ghost of a smile. I didn't miss the tears that glistened in her eyes. Finally, she stared up at the moon for one long moment, gave the garden a last sweeping glance, then she squared her shoulders, closed her eyes, and cupped her hands in front of her. Willem placed the vial in her palms, and she gripped it tightly. Persius swooped down to land on her shoulder, and I noticed rabbits and deer and owls gathering around the periphery of the garden, as if curious about our ritual.

Willem closed one hand around Trina's. Then he nodded toward the audience, and I watched as Jessen came forward, carrying an anti-magic pendant. "This will hurt," he said to Trina as he slipped it around her neck. "But it will only take a moment." Trina flinched as Jessen arranged the pendant so it was touching the hollow between her collarbones.

"The anti-magic will help repel the magic from your body," Willem explained," and my spell will draw it into the vial." He nodded at Jessen, who placed a hand on Trina's head and grasped Willem's free hand with his own. Both of them flinched. "By the power of Fire and the magic of these woods, I call Trina's magic into this vessel," Willem said.

Then he spoke a long string of words that I did not recognize, and Trina's form was bathed in a dim violet light. The light was brightest around her head, and especially brilliant near her eyes. I saw a dark patch near her throat where the anti-magic pendant sat. The light slowly began to wane, concentrating into a small point in the centre of her forehead. Then it flared for a moment and travelled down her arms and into her hands. The bottle began to glow. Willem nodded to Jessen, who removed the pendant. "It is done."

Trina let out a sigh. "It's so *quiet*," she said softly.

"It won't be for long," said Hilda. "Don't give up hope, the spell is only half done."

Trina nodded, but I didn't miss the tear that travelled slowly down her cheek.

"Let me help with that." Jasper stood up and approached the ritual, carrying his fiddle. He began to play a soft, melodic tune, and Trina smiled. A few of the fairies swirled around them, clearly enjoying his music.

"Put the bottle in your pocket, Trina," Hilda instructed. "When you're ready, put your left hand on the rock."

Trina obeyed, and Hilda followed suit. Marcus began to translate for Carmine again. "By the power of the Fae, I pass the mantle of Protector and Liaison from Hilda to Trina, along with the power needed for the role."

Tiriel flew to perch on the rock that sat between Hilda and Trina, and Carmine made a series of long, sweeping motions with her arms, as if calling down magic from the sky. I saw her hand begin to glow. She placed it atop both Trina's and Hilda's, and immediately the rock blazed with a pure white light. Hilda's form was suffused with a softer, purple glow, and I watched that light move through her hands and into the rock. Hilda convulsed slightly as the glow faded from her body.

The same light was travelling up Trina's arms now. She shuddered as it began to envelop her. "It's not so quiet anymore," she said softly.

Hilda smiled. "You can hear the fairies, can't you?"

"I can...They're welcoming me into their world."

Jasper stopped playing the fiddle then, and we could all hear the faint, ethereal song of the fairies. Carmine removed her hand from the rock and signed to Marcus, and he nodded. He went over to Hilda, who removed her pendant and gave it to him. "Lastly," Hilda said, "we bestow upon you the power and duty of the Bearer of the Air Stone. May you use it wisely."

Marcus smiled, then came around the circle to stand behind Trina, and carefully hung the pendant around her neck. My eyes widened as Trina's form was suddenly bathed in a flood of pure white light. Tiriel flew over to land on her shoulder, and I watched as the fairies streamed down from the surrounding trees. They perched all over Trina, illuminating her form, and those who could not land circled her. Their song grew louder, and Trina grinned. "This is where I'm meant to be," she whispered. "I can feel it."

Hilda nodded, pleased. "My friends, may I introduce to you Trina Westwood, Protector of the fairies of Firenholme, Keeper of the fairy ways, Liaison between the Fae and humans of these woods, and Bearer of the Air Stone." She smiled. "You may open your eyes now, Trina."

A hush fell over the crowd as Trina's eyes fluttered open. She looked around, frowned slightly, then turned to Hilda.

"What can you see?" Jasper asked.

"I can see all the fairies," she said. "And I can see Hilda and Carmine easily enough with the light from the fairies."

"Can you see me?" he asked.

"Not well, but..." She trailed off as a stream of fairies flew over to Jasper and encircled him. Then Trina let out a laugh. "I can see you just fine now."

"This is what they will do for you," Hilda said to her. "If you wish to look at a particular thing or person, they will illuminate it."

Jasper grinned as a fairy landed on his hand. He studied it for a moment, then looked back at Trina. "Your eyes look different. They're...purple."

"Really?"

"Yes," Hilda said. "That happened when I took on the role as well. I suspect mine have gone back to blue now."

Jasper studied her for a moment. "Yes, they have. Trina's eyes aren't quite the same shade yours were, though."

"They'd be a darker purple, because her eyes are naturally darker than mine."

"Do you still have some fairy magic on you?" Trina asked.

Hilda nodded. "I've saved some for the soul magic. Once that's gone, I'll have my own bottle to break, so I can have my old magic back."

"Does it feel strange for you? Having so much of your magic gone?"

"I feel...light," she responded. "I can still talk to the fairies, which is what matters to me. It'll be nice not to carry so much responsibility, I think." She grinned, then looked over the crowd. "You folks can leave as you wish. The fairies are happy to host any who want to mingle here in my yard, but our ceremony is officially over."

***

A few hours later, I lay back in the meadow in the middle of Ankrossi, staring up at the stars. We'd returned through the portal relatively quickly, but Trina said she wasn't tired yet, and Ruby, Kaden and Kip all seemed to have no desire to leave her alone.

Jasper was now chatting with the bartender inside Persius' Perch, and Marcus, my mother, and Starla were sharing drinks on the patio, but I could tell that all three of them had their eyes on us. A musician had begun to play a lively tune in the bar, and it spilled out into the meadow.

Kaden grinned and tapped her foot. "Makes me want to dance."

Trina sighed. "That's one of the things I'll miss the most," she admitted. "Being able to dance."

"And why do you think you can't dance now?" Kaden asked.

"Well, I certainly couldn't dance before when I was blind," she said. "I don't see how that would have changed."

Ruby chuckled. "You know, I had the same idea when I only had one hand, until Lachlann showed me how one-handed dancing was done. He got one of the crew members to dance with him, then with me, to show both myself and the others on board that it could be done. Isn't that right, Jasper?" She grinned as her brother walked up to us, carrying a tray of drinks. "Who are those for?"

"All of you, of course." He picked up a glass with a sugar-frosted rim that was piled with fruit and topped with spun sugar decorations. "This one is special, for the new Fairy Priestess." He grinned and passed it to Trina. "And this one is made without any liquor, for the young one in the group." He passed that glass to me. Then he offered the remaining drinks to the others. "Now, what were you asking me about?" he said to Ruby.

"Trina doesn't think she'll be able to dance blind, and I was explaining how Lachlann helped me overcome a similar obstacle back when I only had one hand."

Jasper turned to Trina. "Why do you think you can't dance blind?"

She explained, and Jasper shook his head. "You learned how to dance during your sighted years, though. What makes you think you can't replicate those moves without seeing? Don't tell me you've never closed your eyes while dancing with a fellow."

"I...suppose you're right. But what if I were to bump into people?"

"In that case, you'd need a partner who is good at leading, who's able to be your eyes." He came to crouch in front of her, and the fairies swirled about him. "Would you like to try? There's plenty of music coming from the bar."

Trina took a sip of her drink. "Don't offer to dance just because you feel sorry for me, Jasper."

"Sorry for you? I never once said that."

"Why else would you want to dance with the blind girl?"

"You sound like you're thirteen again, Trina," Kip put in. "I remember you saying the exact same thing when I offered to dance with you on the Lady Liara all those years back." He shook his head. "You're not 'the blind girl,' you're the protector of the Fae, the Bearer of the Air Stone. You're connected to a power stronger than anti-magic now."

"Are you *encouraging* Trina to dance with me?" Jasper's voice was tinged with amusement.

Kip eyed him. "I'm not particularly *worried* about her dancing with you, I'll give you that," he replied flatly. "If you cause her harm, you'll have an army of angry fairies to contend with."

"That much is true." Jasper turned back to Trina and extended a hand. "It would be an honour to dance with the Protector of the Fae."

"All right, fine. Just let me finish this." She drained the last of her drink, then let Jasper pull her to her feet and lead her out into the meadow.

Kaden looked to Ruby and offered a hand. "Shall we?"

They abandoned their glasses to join Jasper and Trina in the dance, and a moment later Marcus and my mother added to their number, much to my surprise. Soon, Starla sat down with me and Kip. "I suppose this is where those of us who are missing our significant others get to sit," she said, glancing at me.

I frowned and took a swig of my drink; it was sweet and fruity and frothy, with a slight hint of tartness. "I don't know if Oliver counts as my significant other anymore." I sighed, trying to ignore the heaviness in my chest at my own words. "At least Kip will have his loneliness resolved soon."

Starla nodded and gazed out at Trina, who seemed to be having very little trouble dancing with Jasper. "You're becoming less protective of Trina, I see," she said to Kip. "Good for you."

Kip sighed. "I need to get it through my head that Trina's an adult now. It's taking some time, but I'm getting there."

"Trust me, I understand." Starla smiled.

"If I hadn't been so protective of her at the Moon Dance, we might not even be in this situation."

I frowned. "The Breoch Guard would have shown up looking for me, whether or not you'd acted like you did. And Jade would've still recognized Saray, and the guards would've had their anti-magic."

"Yes, but if I'd been there, perhaps I could've protected Saray."

"There you go again, thinking that you're meant to be everyone's protector," Starla said.

"Saray's my wife—of course I'd want to protect her."

"And what makes you think you could have? Even Willem was powerless against those fellows."

"Yes, but I know how to fight without magic too," Kip replied.

"One man with a bow or sword wouldn't have done much against a dozen guards with guns," I reasoned. "Jasper pulled his gun out to try to protect Saray, and Jade just laughed at him and told him he was outnumbered."

Starla nodded. "Don't go getting it in your head that you could've prevented this, Kip. You're helping no one by beating yourself up."

"I s'pose so." Kip frowned, sipped his drink, then looked at me. "So Jasper tried to protect Saray, ai?"

I nodded. "Not sure if that changes your opinion of him at all."

"Not when it comes to Trina." He sighed. "But I s'pose them dancing together's not going to hurt anyone."

Ruby and Kaden returned then, hand in hand. "My girlfriend is exhausted and wants to go to bed," Kaden announced. "Want to have a go, Kip?"

Kip's eyebrows lifted. "Are you asking me to spar or dance?"

"Dance, obviously. You're looking a little lonely over here. And I imagine dancing with my sparring partner would be interesting, to say the least."

Kip chuckled and got to his feet. "All right, sure."

"I'll head back to the house with you," I said to Ruby. "I need to be rested for the ritual tomorrow."

As we retreated, I glanced back at the dancers who moved and twirled in the flickering light and thought about the sacrifices that had been made tonight. *Let's hope that the second part of our plan works out.*

Chapter 23

THE FOLLOWING MORNING, I made my way to the main cavern of the Mothertree again. Inside, I found Hilda hard at work and Willem and Claudi sitting nearby, watching. Hilda had drawn a candle-lined circle in the dirt, in the centre of which lay Saray's still form. Hilda smiled and beckoned me over. "You ready for this?"

"I hope so," I replied honestly.

"Before we try anything else, we need to fix Saray's neck," she told me. "Can you do that much for me?"

I frowned. "I've never mended a broken neck before."

"It's easier than you'd think. Broken bones are remarkably simple to heal if they're set properly."

"What if I don't put it back in the right place?"

"That's why I'm here." Claudi stood and made her way slowly over to me.

I frowned. "How do you know about setting bones?"

"I was the one who healed Kirilee's broken neck before we brought her back. It's been many years, but I should still remember what to do." Claudi put her hands under Saray's neck and frowned. "The bones are close to being in the right position, but not quite. Here, let me show you." She took my hand and guided my fingertips to where her spine sat just a little crooked. "Can you feel that?"

I nodded.

"Now I'm going to fix it." I watched as she slowly and carefully moved Saray's head, manipulating the broken bones until she was satisfied. "All right, feel that again. You'll notice a difference."

I touched her neck gently. The bones seemed better aligned under my fingertips. "If there's any misalignment left, you should be able to feel it when you heal her," Claudi assured me. "Now let's see what you can do."

I placed one hand under Saray's neck and began to sing. I could immediately sense where the break was, but the sensation was muddled by the *wrongness* of so many other things. I could feel the blood pooled in different parts of her body, the stillness of her heart, the stiffness in her limbs. The preservation spell prevented decay, but it could only do so much about the other effects of death. "Healing a dead person is strange," I mumbled.

When I closed my eyes, I concentrated hard on the broken bones in Saray's neck, willing them to knit back together. I could sense the spinal cord healing itself, and my mind went back to the day Marcus asked me to fix his shoulder, the way the nerves lit up and sang under my touch as they repaired. With Saray, there was no such evidence. Her spine felt whole, but there was no current of life flowing through it. "I...think it's done," I told them. "It's hard to know without testing it out."

"We'll have to hope," said Willem.

People were beginning to trickle into the cavern now. Trina walked in slowly, surrounded by fairies, clearly still getting used to her new situation. Ambrose and Daisy walked hand in hand, Ambrose carrying Raelle on his back, and my housemates all came in as a group, accompanied by Alisa and Shawnie, all of them less rowdy than usual. Marcus and my mother walked in together and came to stand above Saray. "I...can't believe we might get her back," Mother said softly.

Marcus nodded and reached over to squeeze her hand.

I stared up at them. "Wait, is something...happening between the two of you? I saw you dancing last night."

They both chuckled at my question. "Isabelle, what happened between us took place twenty-five years ago," Mother said. "We're both entirely different people now. It'll take more than a few days to determine if we're still right for each other."

"At this exact moment, we're sharing something very special," Marcus put in. "The return of our daughter. It will likely be a rather intimate experience for us, but it doesn't determine the future."

Kip joined us as Marcus finished speaking, and I smiled up at him. "How are you feeling?"

"A little nervous," he admitted, glancing down at Saray. "Assuming this works, I imagine my wife and I will be the only couple in the Woods who've both been brought back from the dead."

Marcus nodded. "At least you'll understand one another. I have no idea what it's like, but I imagine it impacts you."

"She'll likely feel guilty about Trina," Kip said. "I certainly did about Kirilee. Then there's having to live with the memory of knowing your life's about to end. That took some getting used to."

Hilda came over then and put a hand on Kip's arm. "Are you folks ready to make the conduit?"

We all nodded, and Willem called out for the magikai who wished to participate to form a circle. Kip, Claudi, Willem and Trina each placed a hand on Hilda, lending her the power of the Bearers, and the rest of us joined hands from there. Willem spoke the spell to combine our magic, and my eyes widened as I became aware of the many different types present. Then a strange electric twinge went through me, and I winced as I felt some of my power leave me. Hilda gasped and became illuminated in the same purple light that I'd seen on Trina the night before. She closed her eyes for a moment, breathed deeply, and smiled. "I'm ready."

The fairies swirled around Hilda as she came to kneel next to Saray's body, first emptying a vial of liquid into a small bowl, then cutting off a piece of Saray's hair, which was also added to the bowl. Next, she looked beyond Saray to me. "Isabelle, I will need you for this part."

I felt a strange crackling of energy as I walked into the circle that Hilda had drawn; the air here seemed infused with magic. "We are going to restart Saray's heart," she told me.

Claudi had explained this part to me yesterday, so I knew to place my hands on Saray's chest and sing, concentrating my energy into her heart and lungs. Even so, I nearly jumped when I felt her take a long, shuddering breath. Her ribcage began to contract and expand under my palms, and looking down, I saw her skin flush ever so slightly. Her eyes remained closed, her body seemingly unresponsive to its surroundings, but she was unmistakably *breathing.*

"Good," Hilda said. "Can you maintain that for a few minutes?"

I nodded and removed my hands, continuing to sing quietly.

"Her body lives again, but her soul is still not present," Hilda explained to the others. "Now for my part." She closed her eyes and held the bowl high. "By the power of the Fae, and with the strength of Earth, Sea, Air and Fire, we reach out into the next life and call back the soul of this young woman." She began to sing a spell in another language, and the bowl floated from her hands and hung in midair. It began to glow, and the fairies swirled around it. Hilda placed her hands on Saray's head and continued singing, her song growing loud, mournful. Then she gasped and seemed to double over in pain.

A murmur rippled through the circle. Still hunched over, Hilda continued to sing quietly for a minute or two, then slowly lifted her head and gazed up at the glowing bowl. My eyes widened. In the time her head had been bowed, Hilda looked like she'd aged twenty years. Her hair was now more white than blonde, the corners of her eyes etched with laugh lines.

The fairies congregated around the glowing bowl then, singing their own quiet song. There was a brief flash of white light, then the contents of the bowl caught fire, their flames dancing with dazzling shades of pink and blue and violet. Hilda grinned, seemingly oblivious to her sudden aging. "It worked!"

Kip, Trina, Marcus and Mother stood just outside the circle now, their eyes wide as the bowl returned to Hilda's hands. She reached forward and placed it gently on Saray's chest. The song of the fairies changed, and Hilda waited for a few moments, then began to sing too.

Magic has flown thick and rich through your veins
E'er since you took your first breath
The source of your power, the source of your pain
And now the source of your death

The ultimate gift was for you a curse made
A secret that you had to hide
Your fire left you hunted, abandoned, betrayed
For magic you lived and you died

Now you are called back from beyond death's door
By sacrifice, love and desire
The curse of your magic you'll carry no more
You'll learn how to live without fire

The battle on which these woods' fate will depend
Will be fought without your aid

But since you chose not to betray your friends
A sliver of hope still remains

See to it the one who's in chains is released
The Fae queen speak true her desire
The brothers at war must at last reach a peace
For you to rekindle your fire

If you should succeed within these tasks three
Your power to you shall return
The Mother will once more return to her tree
The firebrand once more shall burn

Hilda dipped her head as the song ended, and for a moment all was quiet. The fairies landed on Saray, perching all over her body. Then the fire in the bowl flared, and suddenly Saray's body glowed with its same colours, her being suffused in brilliant light. I felt her heart begin to beat of its own accord and dropped my spell.

Then she coughed, and her eyes fluttered open. The fairies lifted off her in one fluid motion and began swirling above her again.

"Saray!" Kip was on his knees by her side in a second, grasping her hand.

She blinked, then focused on him. "Hi," she said, her voice raspy with unuse.

Hilda leaned forward and pulled the bowl, now empty of its fire, off her chest. "Welcome back," she said with a grin.

"Saray," Kip said, his voice breaking. "I can't believe it worked, I..." He leaned over her and began to cry softly.

Saray put a hand on his shoulder, eyeing him with obvious confusion. "What...happened?"

"You were dead." Marcus stepped into the circle and knelt on her other side, taking her free hand in his. "But not anymore." His own voice wavered as he spoke, and Mother put her hands on his shoulders from behind.

Saray's eyes flew open. "The hanging," she whispered. "Oh, Kip, I'm so sorry you had to see..." She struggled to sit up and put her arms around him.

"It's all right," he mumbled, pulling her into a sitting position and burying his face in her shoulder. "You're back now, that's all that matters."

Saray pulled away from Kip and stared at him. "Please don't tell me there was a life transfer."

"No, not a life transfer," Hilda replied. "Soul magic. I was the facilitator."

"Soul magic. That makes sense, given the song the fairies were singing." Saray looked over at Hilda. "You're...older. You're not about to die suddenly like Kirilee did, are you?"

"No. The spell cost me some of my years, but not all. I'm likely closer in age to Carmine now. We can grow old together." She smiled at her wife. "Though it was Trina who really made this happen."

"Trina? How?"

Marcus stood so Trina could kneel next to Saray. "I figured out a way to get you back," she said.

"We'll explain everything soon," Starla assured, entering the circle with a bowl of soup, a chunk of bread, and a flask of water. "For now, though, you need to eat, bathe, and perhaps spend some time with your husband. He's been missing you terribly."

***

Not long after, we were all crammed into Starla's living room, Saray looking around at us with wide eyes as we relayed to her what had happened since her death. Kip had not stopped holding onto her since they'd sat down, nor had Marcus, and Trina sat on the ground with her back against Saray's legs. I was seated on another nearby couch, wedged between Ruby and Starla, occasionally chiming in.

"I can't believe you were all willing to do so much for me," she said when we were finished telling our story. "Especially you." She put her hand on Trina's shoulder. "You...uh...didn't have to give up your sight for me, you know."

"Yes, I did," Trina insisted. "I saw a way to bring you back; I had to take it. Besides, it was better than my original plan."

"That's true." Saray let out a shaky laugh. "I still can't believe you tried what you did; I would have been so angry if I'd woken up to discover that you'd..." She trailed off, her voice breaking.

"But you didn't," Mother put in. "There's no point in being angry over things that we managed to avoid."

Saray nodded, then looked over at Marcus and Mother. "You two must have been thrilled to see each other again."

Marcus laughed. "It was a bit surprising, to say the least. We have some catching up to do."

Saray nodded. "I have some things to catch you up on as well. You folks need to know what's happened to Lachlann. It's...worse than you're aware of." She took a deep breath. "There's this fellow named Simon who's joined the court recently. I don't know much of his story—perhaps you know better, Isabelle?"

I frowned. "He showed up a few months back claiming to be the king's cousin. He seems to have Kairus wrapped around his finger, which makes sense given that I recently figured out he's a charmer."

"You know that much, then. But there's more to his identity, and it's incredibly strange. The morning of my execution, Simon decided to pay me a visit. To...gloat, I think. He ended up telling me a lot of things that he knew I wouldn't have a chance to repeat to anyone who'd listen. Only, here we are."

"What did he tell you?" Marcus asked.

"This is going to sound absolutely mad, and I won't blame you if you don't believe me, but what Simon claimed is that, well, he's actually Alvin in a different body."

There were murmurs and confused glances exchanged then. "Alvin?" I repeated. "The fellow who killed Noelle?"

"I thought he was dead," put in Ruby.

"So did I, but it seems we were wrong," Saray replied. "He recalled our last confrontation in astonishing detail. I don't think there's any way he could have known all that unless he was there. And I don't know how he got this new body, but he made it clear that the person he was bent on hurting wasn't me, it was Lachlann." She sighed. "They've done some awful things to him."

Starla met Saray's eyes grimly. "What did they do?"

She looked away from us when she spoke. "Simon brought Lachlann to where the captive students were being held and snapped the youngest girl's neck right in front of him. Then he promised he'd kill one child per week or hunt down someone important to Lachlann until he cooperated."

A heavy silence descended on the room. Starla wiped away a tear. "Oh, Lachlann," she whispered.

My head spun at this new information. "We have to stop this," I found myself whispering. "For all of them. We either need to find the kids and get them out, or rescue Lachlann from wherever they're keeping him."

"It seems that we're back to the question of how to get into the castle," Marcus said. "Has anyone come up with ideas since we discussed this last?"

"I have an idea about how we might narrow down Lachlann's location," said Ruby. "Before we rescued the folks on Yarel Island, Hilda used a scrying spell to help Willem get information. She looked into my past to find the things she needed, and she mentioned that a similar spell can help determine the present whereabouts of a person." She turned to Trina. "Since you're the fairy priestess now, perhaps you could do something like that."

Trina nodded. "I'd need Hilda to walk me through the process, but I can certainly try."

"Do you think getting Lachlann back is part of what will break my curse?" Saray asked.

"It wouldn't surprise me," Marcus said. "'See to it the one who's in chains is released?' That's likely about him."

"I hope so." She let out a small, nearly imperceptible sigh.

"You really want your magic back, don't you?"

She nodded. "Don't misunderstand me—I want Lachlann rescued, regardless of whether it affects my magic. But not having access to it feels like I'm missing a limb. I don't feel quite like *myself* anymore..." She trailed off, and a tear trickled down her cheek. She swiped at it. "Sorry."

"Don't be." Mother's voice was gentle. "You were just brought back from the dead to find your magic gone and your best friend having made an extraordinary sacrifice to see you resurrected. You're allowed to be a little emotional."

Saray nodded, and several more tears slipped out. Kip's arm tightened around her. "Perhaps we should go home," he suggested gently.

"Maybe," she conceded, dabbing at her eyes. "I'll likely feel better in the morning."

"Go home, rest," said Marcus, squeezing her shoulder. "We'll talk more tomorrow."

She bobbed her head again, and Kip helped her to her feet. I watched the two of them walk slowly out of the room together.

"That can't be easy," Trina said softly when the front door closed. "I remember the few minutes last night where I'd lost my connection to the animals and didn't have any magic in me. It was...disorienting and scary. I think I know how to fulfill one condition of the curse, though." She took a deep breath and turned to Jasper, and I watched as a few of the fairies floated over in his direction. "'The Fae queen speaks true her desire,'" she quoted. "I think you and I need to have a very long talk."

Jasper's eyes widened. "You think that part of the curse is about… *us?*"

"Well, I'm certainly the Fae queen. And as for my *desire*, well…" She blushed as she spoke but held Jasper's gaze.

He nodded slowly, a smile spreading across his face. Then he got to his feet and extended a hand to her. "Well, then, shall we take a walk?"

We all watched as the two of them left, trailed by a string of fairies. "I suppose I should get going as well," said Marcus, rising. "Now that Hilda is no longer responsible for the fairies, I need to make arrangements with her and Carmine to travel to Dundere. I should do that before they return to their cottage." He eyed my mother. "Lillian, would you like to accompany me?"

"To speak with Hilda and Carmine, or to Dundere?"

"I meant Dundere, though you could also come with me to make the travel arrangements." Marcus smiled. "I don't think Jasper and Trina are the only ones who need to talk some things through."

"Go with him," Starla urged. "Dundere is beautiful. I'd be thrilled for a chance to go back. Spend as much time with him as you can." Her voice wavered as she spoke, and looking over, I saw that her face was wet with tears; it wasn't hard to guess what had her upset.

Mother looked up at Marcus. "I'll come with you to Dundere, but you can make the arrangements with Hilda and Carmine without me. Starla needs me right now."

Marcus nodded and left, and Ruby stood. "We'll clear out and give you two some space as well."

I felt tears prick at my own eyes as I got to my feet and followed Ruby and Kaden out the front door. We'd done what we set out to do today; Saray was with us again. But her return had come at a cost, and our concerns about both Lachlann's situation and our own safety were more pressing than ever.

I couldn't imagine the road ahead would be an easy one.

Chapter 24

THE FOLLOWING WEEK was busy, with Marcus, Mother, Hilda and Carmine all preparing for their trip to Dundere to help with the fairy situation. Marcus left the running of council meetings to Ruby and the defense of Ankrossi to Kip and Kaden, who both assured him that his absence wouldn't make a huge difference in the event of an attack. Willem had agreed to teleport Marcus and the others to the coast, where they'd hop on the Lady Liara and sail to Dundere.

The night before they left, Jasper invited the travellers to the tavern and regaled them with stories of the ship, Trina hanging onto his arm and sometimes adding her own anecdotes. He and Trina had been nearly inseparable since their conversation. He'd spent a good part of the week helping Trina slowly move her belongings from Ankrossi into the cottage that Hilda had left to her. The only time I saw Jasper without Trina now was first thing in the morning as we were getting ready for our respective days, and even then I couldn't help but notice the lovesick grin that usually tugged at the corners of his mouth.

At one point during the evening, Jasper pulled Marcus aside for a brief and seemingly much more serious conversation at another table. Both men refused to speak about this exchange afterward, and I noticed a hint of sadness in Jasper's expression that hadn't been there before.

The following morning, Mother held me tight and made me promise not to run off anywhere, then embraced Saray and said all the same things to her.

Life fell into a steady routine in the weeks following their departure. Mornings were spent training with Claudi, and Willem when he had time. Working with Willem was both more challenging and more engaging; he had all sorts of ideas as to how I could utilize my gift, as well as some rather unorthodox teaching methods. One day, he came into the living room and cheerfully informed me that he'd impaled his own forearm with a long pin, and that he was going to teach me how to work with a telekinetic to heal wounds where a foreign object had become embedded in the victim's flesh—which, he figured, would be useful if the village was attacked. Willem, of course, knew telekinesis himself, and I cringed as he slowly extracted the pin, allowing my healing to follow in the wake of his own magic. He also took me to his library and recommended half a dozen books about healing to read in my free time.

In the afternoons, I attended regular classes with the other teens or hung out in the village and watched Kip and Kaden train the villagers. Lachlann had had the foresight to train a decent number of the adults to fight without magic, so Kip and Kaden only needed to pick up where he'd left off, working on various drills with swords and axes and, in some cases, farming tools.

One evening, close to a month after my mother and Marcus' departure, Kaden arrived home for dinner visibly frustrated. She tapped her foot impatiently while she ate and let out the occasional long sigh. When Ruby finally asked her what was wrong, she shrugged. "Just worried that we're going to lose our village to a bunch of Breoch Guards, that's all."

"You don't think we're prepared enough? I thought our militia was pretty well trained."

"Oh, they're very well trained. Lachlann knows how to whip a bunch of farmers and merchants into shape. But our attackers are likely to have guns, and the only folks in the Woods with those are a handful of the men who use them to hunt."

"And me," Jasper put in. "And I'm sure Lachlann has a gun in his home. I could teach someone to use it." He raised an eyebrow at Kaden. "Why don't I teach you? I imagine having someone flying around with a gun would give us a bit of an advantage."

"That's not a bad idea." Kaden nodded. "But it certainly won't fix all our problems."

"Well, talk me through them. I'm no Lachlann, but I understand a bit of military strategy. What are our advantages against the attackers?"

Kaden frowned. "Well, we have the home turf. And we're expecting an attack, so hopefully we'll spot them coming before they arrive."

"And do we have patrols keeping an eye out?"

She nodded. "There are folks watching the inroad at all times, and Kip has Persius surveying from farther out as well."

"What's the plan if you spot attackers before they get to the village?" asked Trina, who had joined us for dinner.

"If we see them coming, we'll get as many people high into the trees as we can, where the anti-magic likely won't reach them. Archers, anyone with range magic, the few gunmen that we have—they'll still stand a chance up high. And I'll be flying around, attacking from even higher." She sighed. "I really wish I wasn't the only one in the village gifted with flight. Even one more person who could fly without my enabling them would be useful."

I frowned. "But you could have that quite easily."

"What do you mean?"

"You told me that you and Ruby have been thinking about marriage. Why not get married and be Joined like Saray and Kip? Then you'd both be able to fly *and* control storms. I imagine that's a deadly combination."

"I..." Kaden trailed off, and suddenly she and Ruby were staring at one another, eyes wide. "That's not a bad idea, actually," she admitted, reaching for Ruby's hand.

Ruby nodded, then ducked her head slightly, her cheeks turning pink. "I have it in my head that we're a little young, but really, we're about the age Saray was when she married Kip."

"And we've been together just as long," Kaden added. She smiled and squeezed Ruby's hand, then raised it to her lips. "Well then, what do you say?"

A wry grin pulled at Ruby's mouth. "I say if you're going to propose to me, you'd best do it properly, my dear."

"Right. Of course." Kaden sprang to her feet. "Jasper, would you mind playing something romantic for us?"

"My pleasure." Jasper grinned and went to fetch his fiddle.

"I'll be right back." Kaden dashed into the bedroom.

Trina clapped her hands. "This is so *exciting!*"

Ruby stared after Kaden. "I was absolutely joking when I demanded she propose to me properly."

"Well, I think she's having fun doing it," I replied, grinning.

Jasper began playing a slow, romantic ballad on his fiddle, and a moment later Kaden's head popped out of the bedroom. She glanced around, mumbled a few words, and the lights dimmed. That done, she stepped back into the main room.

My eyes widened; Kaden was now clad in a fitted suit that flattered her slim silhouette. A black top hat was perched on her head, and she carried with her a rose, which she presented to Ruby. Then she sank to one knee and took Ruby's hand. "Ruby, my darling, I cannot imagine living the rest of my life with anyone but you. Will you do me the honour of being my wife?" As she spoke, she pulled a small box out of one pocket and presented it to Ruby.

Ruby gaped at the contents of the box. "Where did you get that?"

"I had Lachlann make it for me a while back," Kaden confessed. "I've been thinking about this for some time. Starla grew rose bushes up the side of our tree for the same reason."

Ruby shook her head, eyes wide. "You're incredible, Kaden."

"You still haven't answered my question. Will you marry me, Ruby?"

A massive smile broke out on Ruby's face. "Absolutely."

Kaden grinned and slid the ring onto her finger. Then she stood and pulled Ruby to her feet, running her thumb along Ruby's jawline and shaking her head. "I can't believe I get to keep you," she whispered.

"Well, believe it," Ruby said, sliding a hand behind Kaden's head and pulling her in. Their lips met slowly, deliberately. I stared for a second, watching Kaden weave her fingers into Ruby's curls, before averting my gaze.

Jasper stopped playing, then turned to Trina. "Well, I think this is our cue to leave."

She nodded. "Come back to my place?" I noticed the hint of a blush colouring her cheeks, and I knew the invitation didn't extend to me.

Jasper smiled. "If that's what you want."

I couldn't help but feel a twinge of jealousy as the two of them gathered their belongings. They headed out the door, and Kaden pulled away from Ruby. "Behave yourselves, you two!" she called out after them, then turned her attention back to her fiancée.

Ignoring the pang in my chest, I gave the newly engaged couple a grin and headed out after Jasper and Trina, not quite sure what to do with the rest of my evening.

Fortunately, I ran into Sophie on the bridge—she'd come into town to pick up a few things from her place—and was invited to the school of magic for the evening. Willem was telling stories in the library tonight, she told me, and then assured me his tales would distract me from all the lovebirds and whatever they might be up to. I tagged along, and soon I found myself seated on a plush couch next to Sophie in the school's grand, high-ceilinged library, sipping a mug of something warm and sweet and frothy, and listening to Willem's tales from his journeys around the world. Contrary to his reputation as a recluse who was always holed up in his library, Willem was actually quite well travelled, thanks to his teleportation abilities. Tonight, he shared about his visits to a few fellow magikai on the Candeshi mainland who were learning to use lightning magic in a very controlled manner to power lamps. The Candeshis weren't quite as fond of magic as folks living in Dundere, Willem explained, but they were very keen scientists, and were eager to see how this electricity, as Willem called it, could be put to use. He told us that he'd then teleported those same friends farther up the coast so he could sample Candeshi cuisine and buy from their markets, including purchasing a few very forbidden books for this library. I had only recently learned that the library held banned volumes owned by several prominent Breochi figures who paid Willem handsomely to store them at this location; hence, there were a few Breoch Guards who were more than a little eager to know the library's whereabouts.

I was feeling less lonely by the time I headed home several hours later. The hut was darkened, and as I tiptoed through the entrance I could hear nothing but the sound of slow, even breathing coming from the bedroom. I smiled as I climbed my ladder and crawled into bed. I may not have the company of a fellow, but I was surrounded by good, caring people. And that, for now at least, was enough.

***

I was awoken some time later by the ringing of a bell. I shook my head, dazed, forgetting for a moment where I was. Then Ruby's voice jerked me into the present. "Isabelle, get dressed! We're under attack!"

Chapter 25

MINUTES LATER, I was dressed and standing with Kaden and Ruby near the entrance to the Mothertree. The meadow was filled with groggy people awaiting news—I spotted Kip halfway across the grove and waved him over. He came running, Saray trailing him.

"What do we know?" Ruby asked.

"Troops about ten minutes out, on foot. About one hundred men, Persius says." Kip's eyes narrowed. "From the picture he relayed, I'm guessing mostly Witch Slayers. Not all of them are uniformed."

"One hundred of them versus four hundred of us?" Kaden exclaimed. "This shouldn't be hard. Let's rally everyone."

Just then, Trina and Jasper stumbled out of the entrance to the Mothertree. "Sorry we're late," Trina gasped. "I had no idea anything was wrong 'til Ruby tried to summon Jasper and..." She trailed off as the fairies swirled around the rest of us, and her cheeks turned red. When her eyes met Kip's, she shrank back.

Jasper stepped in front of Trina, as if to protect her from Kip. "What can we do?"

"I'm going to call everyone in, then Kip and Kaden will give instructions from there," Ruby said. "Get me somewhere a little higher, darling."

Kaden deposited Ruby on a low limb of Kirilee's tree. Ruby mumbled a spell, and when she spoke next her voice was amplified. "Everyone over here!"

The crowd began to quiet down, and all eyes were on Ruby. "We're about to be attacked, but it's expected. Kaden and Kip will guide you through where you need to go. Just remember to stay calm—we far outnumber them, and I don't think they're much of a threat, but we need to work together."

I listened as Kip began reciting instructions to the fighters. Kaden, meanwhile, was depositing certain folks high up in the trees. I felt Trina tug on my sleeve then. "We should get inside the Mothertree," she suggested. "We need to be ready for when the casualties start coming in."

The frustration in Saray's voice was evident when she said, "I'm meant to come with you. I can't do much out there without my magic, and Kip says we can't risk the Witch Slayers seeing me."

The three of us retreated to the cavern. Trina busied herself casting the fairy magic that would allow me to heal in the presence of anti-magic. Soon, we could hear the sounds of guns and fighting filtering through the branches of the Mothertree. Then the melodic thrumming of rain was added to the noise.

Saray grinned. "Guns and rain don't mix well. Good thing Ruby remembered." I could feel the pressure of anti-magic descending, close enough to sense but not hinder.

Our first victim stumbled into the cavern not long after, a young woman who'd fallen out of the tree she was trying to cast from. Saray helped me set her broken arm, then we sent her back out. Next came a fellow with a stab wound, and another who'd been shot rather clumsily; the bullet grazed his shoulder at an angle that opened up the flesh but didn't allow anything to lodge itself inside. "This is going to be a longer battle than any of us anticipated," he told us as I began healing the gash.

"What's happening?" Saray asked.

"Well, Ruby did a good job of deterring their gunfire, but some of them are still able to shoot. Their anti-magic extends higher than we thought, and their soldiers are far more organized than ours." He frowned. "Some of our combatants have fled. I think they underestimated what the heat of battle is really like. You might want to get yourself a telekinetic for when the real bullet wounds start coming in." He got up and thanked me before leaving the cavern to return to battle.

Only seconds later, Starla burst into the room, gasping, her arm around Jasper. My eyes widened when I realized he was hunched over, his shirt soaked in blood. "What happened?" I exclaimed.

"He took a bullet for me," she told us, her voice shaking. "Can you help him?"

"Let's lie him down so Isabelle can take a look," Saray said, putting Jasper's other arm across her shoulders.

Trina let out a shriek when she realized who the casualty was. "Is he going to be all right?" Her question was obviously directed at me.

"I'll find out," I said as Saray and Starla lowered Jasper onto the pallets. He was wheezing, his face contorted with pain.

Starla looked us all over, and her eyes settled on Trina. "I'm going to speak with Kirilee so we can get that spell set up," she said. "Come join me when you can."

Trina nodded, a few tears making their way down her cheeks. Saray, meanwhile, ripped Jasper's shirt open unceremoniously, and I couldn't help but recoil. His chest was covered in blood, and there was a gaping hole on the right side of his ribcage. "See if you can figure out where the bullet is," she told me, clearly unbothered by the carnage.

I closed my eyes, fighting the urge to faint or vomit. Gingerly, I put my hand over the hole and began to sing. I slowly became aware of the bullet lodged in his chest, his lung shriveled up around it, air and blood leaking into the cavity. "It's in his lung," I told her. "We need a telekinetic."

Saray nodded. "That's what I figured. I'll go find Kip."

"Hurry," I told her. "This is serious."

Saray ducked out of the tent, and Trina knelt on the other side of Jasper and took his hand. He attempted a smile. "Hey," he gasped. "Bet you didn't expect to...see me again so soon."

Trina's voice wavered. "You saved my mother's life?"

"Maybe," he replied, his words slow, laboured. "Though Starla's tough; she...likely could've turned into a tree and...and saved herself..." He began to cough, blood trickling from the corner of his mouth. Saray reached to hold his head up so he wouldn't choke.

"Please don't die," Trina begged, tears trickling down her face.

"I...won't," he assured her. "I don't die easily."

I funnelled a small amount of healing magic into Jasper's chest, trying to make it easier for him to breathe. His face was pale, and sweat beaded on his forehead, but his breathing seemed to even out just a bit.

"Let me try something," Trina said. She put her free hand on his head and closed her eyes. Then she began to whisper in an unfamiliar language, spellwords I'd never heard before woven into a rhythmic chant in an unfamiliar language. The fairies that accompanied her began to flit and twirl in a chaotic dance.

Then several of them landed on Jasper, and he let out a sigh of relief, relaxing visibly. "Thank you," he gasped.

"I'm just glad it worked," she said. "Hilda taught me that one just a few..." She stopped speaking when Saray ducked back into the chamber, accompanied by Kip. "Thank the Fae," she sighed.

"I hear you got shot," Kip said, kneeling next to Jasper.

"He saved Mother's life," Trina told Kip. "Please help him."

"I wouldn't have come just to watch him die," Kip assured her, but I didn't miss the contempt in his tone. "Saray, get him something to bite down on. This'll hurt."

"No need," Jasper said. "Trina's...got me under a pain spell."

"Well, there goes my fun," Kip muttered. "All right, Isabelle, let's do this."

"I'll get out of your way." Saray stood and walked over so she was near the entrance to the cavern, creating more room for us to work.

Kip closed his eyes then, concentrating. My awareness of the bullet shifted as it began slowly travelling backward along its original trajectory. I followed its path with my own spell like I'd practiced with Willem, singing tissue and vessels together, willing air and blood back into their proper places. Jasper let out a groan of relief as I closed up the lung. "Breathe deep," I told him, working shards of a broken rib back together. The healing was happening very quickly now, I noticed; the bone seemed to be fusing itself together nearly without my help. I frowned, uncertain if this was normal.

Healing the rest of the wound took no time at all, and soon enough Jasper was staring down at where the hole in his chest had been, gulping in air and reassuring Trina that he was fine. Kip held up the bloodied bullet. "Do you want to keep it, ai?"

Jasper wrinkled his nose. "Why would I do that?"

"As a reminder of the time someone tried, and failed, to kill you?" As Kip spoke, he pulled what appeared to be a pendant from his shirt; upon closer examination, I saw it was a polished bullet with a hole punched through the end so that it could be threaded with a wire. He smirked at Jasper.

"You...kept it?" Jasper's eyes were wide.

Kip nodded. "It's not an uncommon practice in the Woods."

"Why would you want to remember that?" I asked, my eyebrows knitting.

"You can't *not* remember it," Kip told me. "Might as well turn those memories into a warning that you're hard to kill."

Jasper eyed him for a moment, then chuckled. "You know what? Sure, I'll take it." He began to sit up but quickly collapsed onto the mat again, wheezing.

"You'll need to take it easy for a bit," I cautioned. "Healed or not, your body's just gone through something terrible."

"True enough. I—" Jasper's eyes grew wide suddenly, and his face turned white. "Saray, watch!—"

His words were punctuated by a yelp. I gaped to see Jasper and Ruby's brother Jade had managed to sneak into the cavern, clearly in pursuit of Saray. Now he stood behind her with her back pulled up against him, an arm wrapped around her torso and his gun to her head. "I was right," he snarled. "You *are* hard to kill."

"Jade, don't!" Jasper pleaded.

He ignored Jasper completely. "We'll have to make sure there's no body to return to next time you die. Perhaps we'll burn you at the stake. That'd be a suitable punishment for a fire-witch, now wouldn't it? Maybe we can—"

Jade's gun flew from his hand then, sailed across the tent, and landed in Kip's grasp. Saray used the distraction to elbow Jade hard in the stomach, then wrenched herself out of his grip.

"Over here!" Trina called, and Saray ran to her. An iridescent light quickly enveloped them both.

Jade straightened up, and as he did the gun went off. The bullet barely missed, grazing the side of Jade's cheek. He yelped, then met Kip's eyes, glaring. "Nice try," he sneered, touching his anti-magic pendant. A familiar heaviness enveloped the room. "You gonna try that again, forest boy?"

Kip stared down at the pistol uncertainly. *He doesn't know how to reload it,* I realized. Instead, Kip dropped the gun, kicking it in the direction of where Jasper lay on the pallets, and drew his dagger.

Jade was eying Saray now. "You think this is over, just because your fairy friend is protecting you? When I get back to my commander, I'll be telling him that you're here, and we'll come back for you. We will never stop hunting you, Saray. You might as well just give yourself up, because—" His threats were cut short when Kip lunged at him, dagger bared.

The fight was quick and brutal. Kip was a skilled fighter, but Jade outmatched him in both strength and training. Moments after the initial hit, I heard Kip's dagger clatter to the ground as Jade disarmed him. Then came the sickening crunch of bone breaking and a howl of pain. Seconds later, Kip was on his back, Jade atop him clutching Kip's knife.

"No!" I heard Saray scream.

Jade thrust the dagger downward, aiming for Kip's throat.

And then I was deafened momentarily by the blast of a gunshot. Jade collapsed on top of Kip, and the anti-magic in the room sputtered out.

A near-tangible ripple of relief went through us. Saray ran to Kip and began helping him out from underneath Jade's limp body. "Are you all right?"

"Mostly," he grunted, cradling his injured wrist as he got to his feet. "Where did that bullet come..." He trailed off as he turned in my direction. "Jasper?"

All eyes fell upon Jasper now. He was sitting up, his face ghost white, staring at his brother's unmoving form.

In his hand was Jade's gun.

Kip looked from Jasper to Jade then, whose hair turned slowly red with blood. Jasper carefully lowered the gun, his eyes still trained on Jade's unmoving form. Trina hurried to him and put a hand on his shoulder, but he seemed to barely register her presence.

"You should hide, in case anyone else saw you come in here," Kip said softly to Saray. "Let me move you." He put his good hand on her shoulder and mumbled a spell, and

Saray slowly began to rise until she was high up in the Mothertree. That done, Kip turned to me. "You'd best fix me up, Isabelle."

He held his own wrist in place as I sang my spell and sighed with relief when the pain abated. Then he glanced at the opening of the tent. "I need to get back out there; will you folks be all right?"

"Yes," I told him. Trina nodded too, but her eyes were glued on Jasper.

"Kip," Jasper spoke, his voice a whisper. "If you see Ruby, can you..." He trailed off.

"I'll send her your way." Kip walked over to Jasper, crouched down, and put his hand on his shoulder. "Thank you. You saved my life."

Jasper nodded, clearly at a loss for words.

"I'll come check on you later, all right?" He gave Jasper's shoulder a clap, then rose and slipped out of the tent.

Jasper climbed slowly to his feet, his breath coming in gasps. He crouched beside Jade's still form and carefully rolled him onto his back to close his eyes. "I'm sorry," he whispered to his brother's unmoving body. "I'm so sorry..." His shoulders began to shake, and he let out a sob. Trina knelt next to Jasper and put her arms around him as he wept.

I stood there, momentarily unsure what to do, then quietly left the cavern to give them some privacy. At the entrance of the Mothertree, I looked up to see a swarm of dragons overhead. Their arrival gave us a slight advantage; I watched them circle the village, sending columns of fire spilling onto our attackers.

Kip was riding with Ambrose, sending arrows raining down with practiced ease, and both Ambrose and Daisy were armed with hunting rifles, which they used to pick off the Witch Slayers. Trina's dragon Millie had shown up without a rider; she seemed to favour diving at the attackers to seize and smash them against rocks.

Trina appeared next to me then. "I need to help my mother," she told me. "Can you keep an eye out for Ruby?"

I nodded. "Is...he all right? Should I go back in there?"

She shook her head. "Leave him for now." Then she slipped back into the Mothertree in search of Starla.

It was a few minutes later when Ruby came running up to me. "What's happened, Isabelle?" she asked, concern in her dark eyes. "Kip said I needed to check on Jasper; is he alright?"

I sighed. *Probably best that I tell her, rather than making Jasper do it.* "There's no easy way to say this, Ruby. Your brother Jade is dead."

"Jade?" Her voice trembled, and her shoulders slumped sadly. "But...what does that have to do with Jasper?"

"Jasper was the one who killed him." I took a deep breath and told her what I'd seen.

Ruby's eyes got wider and wider as I spoke, and she let out a long, shuddering breath. "Poor Jasper...I should go in and see him."

I nodded, and she went past me into the Mothertree. I gazed after her, only to feel a strange tremor under my feet that seemed to come from the tree itself. My eyes narrowed in confusion.

Seconds later, there was a large *crack*, and the sky lit up with a fiery pink blaze.

And something...changed.

The air suddenly became heavier, suffused with the scent of vilettas at night, and a faint white-pink haze settled over the village, gold motes dancing in its light. The anti-magic that permeated from the Witch Slayers' pendants ceased immediately, and the invaders drew back in fear.

And the fiery light that had always emanated from Kirilee's tree sputtered out.

The tree's blooms still glowed, but their light was the weak, constant luminescence of a regular viletta, not the lively brightness we were all accustomed to. A moment later, one of the vines of the Mothertree seized a Witch Slayer around the neck and hoisted him into the air, where he hung, choking and sputtering.

Kip seemed to realize what had happened before anyone else; Spark swooped low, and he leapt from her back, fire streaming out of his hands.

"*Attack!*" he roared, and the grove exploded into mayhem.

With a wave of Kip's hand, a good dozen of the Witch Slayers' guns were flung into the bushes. Several of our vanishers and telekinetics began slitting throats, and lightning sliced through the grove, electrocuting a Breoch Guard where she stood.

A good number of our attackers began to flee, only for the surrounding trees to reach out and hold them in place. Arrows fell out of the sky, and I glanced up to see Kaden with a crossbow in hand.

Finally, I heard someone in the Guard call for a retreat, and the remaining attackers ran for the bridge that linked Ankrossi to the rest of the Woods.

"No!" Ambrose called out from atop his dragon. "They can't be allowed to escape! Kaden, let's—"

He was silenced by a mighty rumbling sound. My head turned toward the bridge, and I watched it buckle beneath the retreating fighters, its massive stones plunging into the river and carrying the Witch Slayers away with the current below. Their curses and cries of pain faded as they disappeared over the edge of the waterfall moments later.

Kaden landed next to me, confusion etched onto her features. "How did...Kip, was that you?"

I followed her gaze to see Kip hunched over, seemingly struggling to breathe. We ran to him. "Kip, are you all right?"

"I...I'll be fine..." he gasped. "Fly...down to the bottom of the falls and...look for survivors."

"Right." She lifted into the air and flew away.

"Can I help?" I asked Kip.

"Maybe..." he panted. "You can try."

I put my hand on his chest and closed my eyes, trying to discern the source of his distress. His heart was pounding, his body starving for air—I could immediately discern that much. "Take deep breaths," I instructed him, then began to sing. Kip obeyed, and I felt his pulse and breathing steady as I imbued him with as much healing power as I could. He closed his eyes and let out a long breath when I was finished. "Thank you."

"What just happened?" asked Saray, joining us.

"I cast a spell that I'm barely strong enough for," Kip explained. "Nearly knocked me unconscious."

Saray frowned, then her eyes flickered to the remainder of the bridge. "You collapsed that on your own?"

He nodded and gave her a breathless smile.

"That's…incredible!" she exclaimed. "I'm *very* impressed."

"Me too." Trina stood near the base of Kirilee's tree, her eyes wide. "We all did well today."

I looked up at the pink haze in the sky. "What did Kirilee do? I assume that was her."

"Her, my mother, and me. Oh, and Alexander too. We had a plan."

"What was it?"

"Kirilee has put all of her life-force into a spell that blankets the village in fairy magic, which means she can't communicate with us. And Mother is holding Kirilee's place in the tree for now."

"What does that mean?" asked Kip.

"Mother thinks it best if she stays in the tree until this is over, to protect Aria. So now it's Mother's—and Aria's—souls in the viletta, not Kirilee's. I'm the only one who can break the spell."

"What will happen to Kirilee then?" asked Saray.

"She'll return to her old form once Ankrossi is safe. Remember that line in the fairies' song, 'the Mother will once more return to her tree?' That was about her. Though she won't be able to stay with us for more than a few months."

Kip let out a breath. "Kirilee's sacrificing her time with us yet again."

Trina nodded. "She told Mother that she'll likely be ready to leave once all this is resolved. She—"

Trina was interrupted by Shawnie, who came running out of the Mothertree's cavern, breathless and red faced. Kip's eyes widened when he saw him. "What's wrong?"

"The school was attacked by Witch Slayers," Shawnie panted. "We killed or captured them all…but a few of the students are wounded, and Willem…" He trailed off, his voice breaking. "I need your help, Saray. And yours as well, Isabelle."

"What's happening with Willem?" Saray's voice was a whisper.

Shawnie took a deep breath, then met her eyes. "He's gone."

"Gone?" Kip's face went white. "You mean, dead?"

"I…I think so. Come with me, let me show you."

Chapter 26

WILLEM'S HOME WAS a mess. The door was thrown off its hinges, shards of the chandelier that once hung in the entryway scattered across the floor and muddy bootprints tracked down the hall leading to the school of magic. My eyes grew wider the further we went. Pillaged classrooms were littered with overturned desks and strewn books, the walls smeared with blood. Fallen Witch Slayers sprawled across the floor, unmoving. Sophie came running to us and embraced Saray. "Thank the Fae you're here!"

Saray hugged her back, but her eyebrows were knitted with confusion. "Why do you folks need us? Looks like you did just fine on your own."

"The younger students are locked in the library," Shawnie explained. "We put them there to keep them safe, and if I'm correct, only you and I can get them out."

"What do you mean?"

Shawnie sighed. "Let me show you."

One of the classrooms near the library had been cleared out, and a few injured students sat there, awaiting treatment. A large plate of golden metal etched with ornate black scrollwork around its edges and inlaid with runes that shone with an unearthly brilliance obscured the handles on the library door, holding them permanently in place. On the floor beneath the seal was a pile of fine grey ash, and within a few feet of that lay the blackened remains of what looked to be a Breoch Guard; the corpse's head was reduced to a shattered, charred skull, but I caught a switch of red fabric in what was left of the man's coat. Shawnie pointed to the pile of ash, then looked back at us with wide eyes. "That and this seal over the doors are all that's left of him." His voice broke as he said this, and his face crumpled.

Saray took a step toward him to put an arm around his shoulders. "What *happened?*" Her voice trembled when she spoke.

Shawnie wiped at his eyes, clearly trying to maintain his composure. "We did everything we could to hold the Witch Slayers back. But they had their anti-magic and their guns. We managed to get all the younger magikai into the library before anyone was hurt and told them to barricade the doors. But we could only hold the attack back for so long. They got closer and closer to the library, and I think Willem knew what they were after." He turned to Kip. "Alvin came here, remember? He visited with you, me, and the rest of our friends after that Moon Dance. He knew about the library."

Kip nodded gravely. "He may not even have needed Lachlann to direct him here. I wonder if the attack on Ankrossi was just a diversion, to get whatever Alvin was after?"

"No idea." Shawnie shook his head and swiped at his eyes again.

"What happened next?" Kip asked.

"Willem came up to me, handed me a few things, and told me there was a letter in his safe that would explain everything. Then he grabbed my hand and said to tell everyone else to stay strong, that he cares deeply for all of you." Shawnie's voice broke once more, and he paused to take a deep breath. "Then he pulled a vial out of his robe, drank it, ran to the door and grabbed the handles, and cast a spell. A Breoch Guard went to attack him then, but before he reached Willem there was a bang and a huge flash of light. When the air cleared, Willem was gone, the other fellow was a burned corpse, and the door looked like that." He closed his eyes, and tears trickled down his cheeks.

Saray shook her head, blinking hard. "So Willem *became* the seal?"

"Something like that. And whatever he did caused the anti-magic to go wrong...most of the attackers ran off."

Saray nodded, her own face beginning to crumple. Kip moved to put an arm around her. He was mostly stoic, but his voice wavered when he spoke. "If he is truly dead, then he died protecting what he'd given his life to."

Shawnie nodded, blinking hard. "He also died protecting all the younger kids, and my wife, and his mother as well."

"They're still locked in the library, then?" asked Kip.

"Alisa and Claudi too. We need to figure out how to break that seal. That's what I need you for, Saray. At least, I think I need you."

"Why don't you go find the letter Willem told you about, and we'll start attending to the wounded?" Kip suggested.

Shawnie nodded. "Right."

He retreated down the hall, and I walked into the nearby classroom where the injured magikai were waiting. Sophie was holding hands with two of the younger mages and talking to them softly, clearly trying to keep their distress under control. Meanwhile, Chester sat unmoving in a corner, blood seeping from a gash in his arm, his face pale.

Kip and I began working to remove bullets and heal the most grievously wounded, while Saray and Sophie tended to the more minor injuries. When Kip and I got to Chester, he looked up at us, eyes nearly vacant. "I could've done something," he whispered. "My father taught me to fight with daggers; you've seen me fight, Kip. But as soon as I saw those uniforms, I just...froze up." He took a deep, shuddering breath. "Again."

"You wouldn't have been able to fend them all off yourself," Kip assured him as he worked to get the bullet out of Chester's arm.

"Yes, but why can I not do *anything* when they're around? It makes no sense!"

"It makes perfect sense. You associate that uniform with extreme danger, so when you see it, you freeze—like an animal in the bushes when it spots a predator. It's not the most productive reaction, but it's common enough."

"How do I overcome it, though?"

Kip looked like he was about to respond, but just then Shawnie came into the room, holding a letter and a large set of keys.

Saray stood. "What did you find?"

"I haven't read the letter yet. Let me take a look." Shawnie carefully opened the envelope and extracted the paper from within. He scanned the contents, and when he was finished he let out a deep, shuddering sigh. "As I thought," he said softly. "He's gone."

"How do you know?"

"The letter says that the spell Willem cast was meant to transmute most of his body into a magical seal over the doors. And I was right; it can only be broken if you and I are both there to do it, Saray."

Saray's eyes narrowed. "Why us?"

"Because Willem asked me to pass this on to you." He pulled a pendant out of his pocket. "I'm meant to take over the school and library. But the Fire Stone is yours." He gave her a watery smile. "I kind of figured you'd be the next Bearer."

Saray stared at it. "I...I'm honoured. But how can I be a Bearer when I don't have access to my magic?"

"Kirilee didn't have her magic for nearly fifty years, and she was a Bearer," Kip pointed out. "And Claudi hasn't had full access to hers for decades."

Shawnie nodded. "Willem told me that anyone with magic in their blood can be chosen. Doesn't matter how good they are at using it. Being a Bearer should make your fire magic stronger than ever once it's returned to you, though." He took a step forward. "Do you accept the role?"

Saray stared at Shawnie, blinking back fresh tears. Then she nodded. "I do."

"Then allow me."

I found myself holding my breath as Shawnie moved behind Saray to slowly fasten the chain around her neck. The second the pendant touched her skin, it began to glow, and for a brief moment Saray was suffused in a pure white light. Her eyes widened, and she let out a gasp. "I can...see him," she whispered. "His memories, his childhood. What *happened* to him."

"What do you see?"

"That vial he drank was a potion brewed up by his father and Hilda decades ago," she explained. "When he combined it with the casting words, it took every bit of Willem's magic, along with his body, and used them to create that seal. He knew exactly what he was doing, what would happen to him, when he drank it."

"And the spell killed him?" I asked, frowning.

She closed her eyes for a moment. "The explosion was so powerful that it reduced most of him to ash. Though some of him is definitely in that seal now. I'm not sure if his spirit is still with us, like Kirilee is in the tree, but his body is certainly dead."

A few of the students began to cry at Saray's words. Sophie put her arm around one of the other girls, blinking back tears of her own. Kip let out a long breath, and Saray put a hand on his shoulder, her own emotions seeming to settle in light of what she'd just seen. "Willem always knew it might come to this," she said. "He was always ready to die protecting the library." She turned to Shawnie then. "We need to open that door and get the others out. It'd probably be best to clear the school out and take the kids back to Ankrossi."

"Ankrossi was compromised too, though," Shawnie replied.

"Yes, but it's being protected right now. By Kirilee, somehow." She frowned. "I don't quite understand that part. Come on, let's open the door."

Shawnie nodded, and the two of them left the room. I finished tending to wounds, and the rest of us followed to see what we could do to help. They stood in front of the door, reading over Willem's letter to better decipher its instructions, both of them trying not to step in the pile of ash.

Kip slipped away and returned a few minutes later carrying an ornate vase. I watched as the ashes that had once been Willem's body rose from the ground and settled into it. Kip clutched the vase tightly, watching as Saray carefully removed the Fire Stone and pressed it into a groove in the seal. Then she and Shawnie joined hands and each took a door handle. They pushed the handles down simultaneously, and the seal flashed a bright, iridescent gold for a moment before breaking in two. The doors only budged slightly.

Shawnie stared at them for a moment, then rammed one with his shoulder. A few gasps came from inside the library. He peered into the crack and said, "It's safe, folks. You can let us in."

There came loud creaks of moving furniture. Then the doors finally opened, and the students surged out. Alisa ran to Shawnie and threw her arms around him. Claudi took a look at the broken seal, clapped her hand over her mouth, and sank to the ground. Kip knelt next to her and held her as she wept.

Several of the students who'd been in the library saw this, and Shawnie motioned that they should join him. I watched their faces change as he broke the news about Willem to them, and a good number began to cry, while a few others surrounded Claudi. Shawnie stepped away from the students when he was finished, clearly struggling again to contain his own grief.

Saray walked over and put a hand on his shoulder. "I think we'd best seal this up and take the kids to Ankrossi," she said.

He nodded, and I watched the two of them close the doors. The seal re-formed as soon as Saray removed the Fire Stone. Shawnie cleared his throat, and the students looked to him. "Willem died protecting the knowledge in that library," he said. "It's safe now, but we aren't. Go to the dorms and fetch your belongings. We need to go back to Ankrossi."

***

Nobody wanted to sleep. Some folks went back to their homes, but the council members, Willem's students, and a handful of other adults whom I didn't know so well sat out in the meadow under the pale pink haze, holding one another, trying to absorb the shock of the night's events. Trina and Ruby both clung to Jasper, and I joined them after a short time, sitting in silence with my arm around Ruby, who seemed more concerned about comforting her brother than mourning her own loss. Jasper's head remained bowed, hands jammed into his curls, still clearly distraught.

Kaden and Kip came to where we sat, and Kip crouched down in front of Jasper to put a hand on his arm. "We're planning to bury the dead Witch Slayers now. Should we add Jade to their number, or do you want something else done with him?" Kip's voice was gentle, his eyes full of caution, as if approaching a wounded animal.

Jasper lifted his head and met Kip's gaze, his own stare vacant. "Leave him. I should take him home and bury him on our land."

Kip nodded. "If that's what you wish."

"You're going to take him home to Father?" Ruby asked.

Jasper nodded. "It's only right."

"I'll come with you," she said.

"No. I don't want to put you in danger. I don't know what Father will do to me."

"Let me come, then," Trina said.

"Absolutely not. Father might remember you from earlier attacks, and how will you defend yourself?"

"I have the fairies. I'll be—"

"Stop. No one is coming with me; I have to do this on my own." Jasper's voice wavered as he spoke.

"You're not going to be able to carry the body of a grown man across the Woods alone, Jasper," Kip said. "Let *me* come with you. I'm able to protect myself with or without magic. Besides, I owe you this, after what you did."

Jasper sighed, and when he spoke his voice was devoid of its usual animation. "Don't turn this into matters of debt, Kip. How about you drop your grudge against me, and we call it even?"

"That's why I figure I should come with you. You and I have some things we need to discuss."

"Right." Jasper eyed Kip for a moment, then his shoulders slumped. "Fine. You can come along. But if Father attacks you, don't blame me."

"Perhaps Isabelle can join us, just in case one or both of us is wounded?"

I frowned. "You think it safe for me to leave Ankrossi after an attack like this?"

"It should be," Kaden said. "We have Kirilee's protection now. And Jasper and Kip might need someone to break up any fights they get into." A hint of a smile played on her lips as she turned back to them. "Also, Isabelle is decent at talking people down, whether it's your father or one of you. I think it's a good idea."

"Do you want to come along, then?" Jasper asked.

I shrugged. "I will if it's needed. Perhaps when we're in Kirstein we can scout out the castle and figure out how best to reach Lachlann. It's clear enough that rescuing him is our top priority now."

"I'll have someone put a preserving spell on Jade, and we can leave in a few days," Kip said. "I think it's best we be well rested before undertaking this journey. Besides, I have a bridge to help rebuild before we go anywhere."

Jasper nodded, and Kip and Kaden left to continue with their task, leaving me wondering about the trip that lay ahead.

***

The next few days passed in a strange blur. The townsfolk were quiet, reserved again, as they'd been following Saray's execution. They busied themselves restoring homes and shops that were destroyed in the attack, and several telekinetics worked to rebuild the bridge together, but all this was accomplished with little chatter or laughter. It was decided that we would not have our ceremony for Willem until Marcus returned, so the vase of ashes sat in the Mothertree, and people came to leave flowers and notes. Despite our readiness to face down an attack, losing Willem was not something anyone could have prepared for, and it left us reeling.

I did not expect Claudi to be in any shape to keep teaching me, but only two days after Willem's death I got word that she wanted to see me where she was staying at Starla's. When I went to her, I noticed her shoulders were hunched more than usual and her face seemed quite tired, but she gave me a smile and said that we'd best get back to work. I asked if she was ready for that, and she scoffed, saying she could use the distraction. So we returned to our study of how to see into wounds and illnesses. There were a few small injuries from our battle that folks hadn't yet dealt with, and so I healed those.

On the day we were meant to leave, Kip and Saray came over to the house. "Are you sure you'll be all right without Isabelle and me?" Kip asked Ruby.

She nodded. "I'm not expecting any attacks, if that's what you mean. Kirilee and Starla will protect us."

Kip nodded and sighed. "It's so strange, not having any of the older council members here. We're on our own for now...it makes me nervous to leave."

"We'll be fine," Kaden assured. Saray nodded and put an arm around him.

Jasper and Trina arrived soon after, and we went together to the Mothertree. Jade's body had been moved to a small room near the back of the cavern, wrapped in burlap.

Kip turned to Jasper. "Are you sure you don't want me to just teleport us?"

Jasper shook his head.

"All right, then." Kip turned to Saray and held her close for a few long moments, and Jasper did the same with Trina. I turned away, trying to ignore the pangs of jealousy that rose in my gut. Then each of the men took an end of the bundle and hoisted it onto their shoulders, and we set off.

Chapter 27

THE ROAD OUT of Ankrossi was narrow and bumpy, the foliage on either side matted down, likely from the invasion. Trees closed in around us, light peeking through their canopy, and it was only once we broke for our lunch of bread, cheese, and dried meat that Jasper finally spoke. "All right Kip, lay it on me. Tell me how terribly I've ruined your life, tell me what I need to apologize for. I'm sure you have plenty to say."

Kip frowned. "You don't need to apologize," he finally said.

"I...don't? But I shot you!"

"Words mean little to me. I know you regret what happened. But to believe an apology, I need to see action." He levelled his gaze on Jasper. "And I've seen that now, in how you saved Saray and me the other day. I can finally take your regret seriously."

Jasper raised an eyebrow. "Only took me killing my own brother for that to happen."

"I can explain a little of what your shooting me did to my mind so you better understand why it's been so hard for me to forgive. But right now, I think we need to talk about what *you've* been through over the past few days." Kip glanced at the bundle that sat nearby. "How much do you know about my mother?"

"I know she beat Trina and made her blind, and that you ran away after that with your brother and dog."

"Did you know she was a Witch Slayer?"

"I...don't think so?"

"Do you know why she was so fearful of magic?"

"Well, I know she saw her little sister die when she was just a kid, and that Kirilee was the one responsible."

"That's right. She got to know some of the Witch Slayers shortly after my father passed. And they preyed on her phobia; they turned her from a typical magic-fearer to someone filled with hate. She did very bad things, Jasper. It wasn't just Trina she harmed."

Jasper nodded. "Didn't she torture Starla?"

"She did. She became someone terrible. She let awful ideas take away her sense of right and wrong. But none of that changes the fact that she was my *mother*." Kip sighed. "Just like Jade was your brother. And if you feel sad about losing him, that's all right."

Jasper averted his eyes and shook his head. "I just wish we'd been able to get through to him," he said softly. "You and I, we were both afraid of magic, too, at certain points in our lives. And we both got over it. Why couldn't Jade have done the same?"

"I wish I could answer that for you," Kip replied.

There was an awkward pause between the two of them, and I turned to Jasper, trying to fill the silence. "Did you miss Jade after you and Ruby ran off?"

Jasper frowned, quiet for a moment. Then he let out a long sigh. "I miss who he used to be, when we were kids. We had some good times together. Climbing trees, stealing plums from our neighbour's yard, making up stupid songs." He shook his head, a grin creeping onto his face.

"Tell me more," I said, slightly relieved to see him smiling.

"We were put in a choir at a pretty young age, and we both picked up on the songs very easily. Jade and I started changing the words, making the songs about whatever terrible thing was going through our minds at the time. It was usually something dirty or morbid."

I chuckled. "Sounds about right."

"I believe Jade and I rewrote the Breochi national anthem three times as youngsters," he went on. "The first time it was about farting, the second time was about lighting cats on fire and throwing them off buildings, and the third time was about bedding several women at once."

"Lighting cats on fire?" I repeated incredulously. "That's terrible!"

Jasper laughed sheepishly. "That one was more Jade than me."

"Let me guess, the bedding women part was mostly you?" Kip said, smirking.

"That was both of us. We were a little older by that point, of course."

"Let's hope so."

"We were definitely quite the pair," Jasper continued, shaking his head. "And when Ruby came along, well, I think we saw her more as a new toy than a sister. We used to strap her to our backs when we climbed trees, play catch with her in the lake, use her for target practice with toy bows and arrows..." He shook his head. "I'm surprised the poor girl never broke any bones."

Kip chuckled. "Kelvin and I did things like that with Trina, too. There wasn't quite as much of an age gap, but we used to drag her along without any regard to how little she was." He glanced at me. "You have two older brothers, right Isabelle? Did they ever do these things to you?"

I bit my lip. "I hardly know my brothers," I admitted to them. "Caleb and Shay were fourteen and twelve when I was born. When I was little, they had already been sent off to boarding school, because Mother couldn't care for them."

"Why not?" asked Kip.

"Having to give up Saray...did something to her. Made her sad in a way that she didn't know how to undo. Apparently, I was what got her out of that."

"You were her second chance at having a daughter," Jasper said, nodding.

"I suppose so. But my brothers and I aren't close. Caleb lives in Sylvenburgh with his wife and kids, and Shay went to university in Candesh and is living there now. I see them when they come to visit for holidays and such, but I don't know them, or their families, well." I looked at Jasper out of the corner of my eye. "You're lucky you had a happy childhood."

Jasper frowned. "I wouldn't call it all happy. My youngest years were good, but Father could be cruel, and Mother was far too concerned with us being proper and polite. And even if my childhood was decent, well, look how my family turned out." He glanced over at the bundle and let out a long sigh. "We should get moving."

"We have a choice to make from here," Kip informed us. "Are you open to travelling on horseback once we're clear of the Woods? Because otherwise we'll be walking for several days out in the open, carrying a body, and that's going to raise some questions."

"True," Jasper replied. "I suppose we can do that. Where are we going to get horses, though?"

"I figure we can head to Sylvenburgh and see about borrowing some from Lachlann's mother. We'll ride to Kirstein from there."

I chuckled. "Helenne actually has a couple of horses that belong to my family, so I don't imagine that'll be a problem."

Kip nodded. "In that case, I know somewhere we can stay tonight. We'll need to move fast, though; it's quite the trek."

***

We resumed our walk, moving with more urgency now. The road levelled out, this path clearly more worn. We moved through lush forests and meadows, and I could see several houses up in the trees, and huts perched on one of the hillsides. We passed the occasional person, most of them clad in the wild clothing I'd seen at the Moon Dance, and many of them acknowledged Kip with a smile and nod. Persius flew above us, letting out a screech every now and then. Several hours in, Kip paused. "Can we put Jade down for a moment?"

Jasper nodded, and they lowered the bundle to the ground. That done, Kip pulled his bow off his shoulder, strung it quickly, and nocked an arrow. He was quiet for a moment, eyes on the trees. Then he let an arrow fly, and a large bird fell to the ground, making me jump.

Jasper whistled. "Nice shot."

Kip shrugged. "It's what I do for a living."

"You know, I'm surprised you missed when you shot at..." He gazed down at the bundle. "Was that your first time shooting a gun?"

He nodded. "If he hadn't been moving, I likely would've hit him. I didn't have time to aim properly."

Jasper frowned. "When you kicked the gun over to me, was that intentional?"

"Somewhat. I figured you were the only person there who knew how to use it. I expected you to shoot to injure, though."

"I wish that had been an option. But I knew if I did, he'd tell his commander about Saray, and as Jade said himself, they'd never stop hunting her."

"Right. Which was why I wanted you to wound him so I could finish the job." He glanced at Jasper as he bagged his kill. "I figured you'd hate me for it, but what else is new?"

Jasper snorted. "I don't hate you. I've only disliked you all these years because *you* hate *me*. I suppose I can't blame you for that, but it's gotten a little old."

"Right. We have to talk that out. We can do that once we reach the hut."

"We're going to a hut?" I asked.

Kip nodded. "Assuming it hasn't been moved into by someone else. It's where I lived for a good seven years." He nodded at the bundle, and he and Jasper lifted it onto their shoulders once more.

It was getting close to dusk when we finally stopped. The hut, I realized, was very dilapidated; the roof was caving in, and the entire structure had become overgrown with moss and weeds. I ran my fingers over the haphazardly put-together collection of rough logs. "You built this?"

"It took me two years and a lot of help from some of the nearby grownups, but yes. This was my home." There was a proud note in Kip's voice. "Want to see inside?"

The interior was just as run down as the outside, but it was surprisingly roomy. Kip had built it up against a hillside, and the entire back end was actually a small cave. A hammock hung from one of the tree limbs that made up the ceiling, and the far end of the room held a table, a bench, and something resembling a counter, all of it carved from wood. "Did you make those?" Jasper asked.

"No. I traded for the furniture." Kip walked over to the hammock and picked up a dirty piece of fabric, chuckling. "The food's all been taken, and my old clothes as well, but the scavengers left my childhood blanket." He tested out the hammock then, carefully. "This is still in decent shape too."

"I'm surprised no one's moved in here," I said.

"I s'pose it's a little out of the way. Most Woods-folk don't live around here." Kip smiled. "Let's get dinner started."

We went outside again, and Kip used magic to start a fire in a small pit. He quickly prepared the bird, while Jasper fashioned a brace to cook it over the flames. Once the bird was roasting, Kip settled in and nodded to a patch of weeds. "That used to be a vegetable garden. And back there was my smokehouse. The one I have in Ankrossi is ten times better, but my old one did the job."

Jasper shook his head. "I can't believe you lived out here by yourself at such a young age."

Kip shrugged. "My father was an outdoorsman, and he used to take my brother and me into the Woods with him. We learned how to hunt and make camp and cook food when we were quite young. After Father died, Kelvin and I used to wander Sylvenburgh with our bows shooting at pigeons, and when we hit them, we'd take them home and cook them over a fire in our backyard."

I laughed. "Didn't you get in trouble?"

"Oh, we got dragged home by city guards many times. But Mother was too deep in her grief and madness to stop us." He shook his head a little sadly. "It's likely why we chose the Woods when we felt the need to escape home. We both knew we wouldn't do well on the streets, but living in the forest was no problem." Kip got up and went to where a large, polished stone sat among the overgrowth. He crouched down and ran his hand over it. "This is where I buried Kelvin."

"What happened?" I didn't miss the shock in Jasper's voice.

"He cut his leg open quite badly during our first winter here. We managed to stop the bleeding, but it got infected. I didn't know enough about medicine to realize it was serious until he was burning up. I went to get a healer, but by the time we returned, it was too late." He sighed and looked at Jasper. "I know what it's like to blame yourself for a dead brother."

Jasper glanced over at the bundle and shook his head. "This is different. You were a kid, and you didn't kill him. You just didn't have the knowledge to save him."

"I know it's different. But the guilt I felt as a kid might be very much the same." He stood up. "I really started fearing and hating magic after that. I realized that losing her sister to poorly used magic was what made my mother go mad, and if she hadn't, Kelvin and I wouldn't have had to leave, and he wouldn't be dead. Magic was to blame for all of this. So I started avoiding the local magic users—which meant avoiding a good chunk of the Woods-folk." He was interrupted by a loud pop from the fire and glanced back at it. "Dinner should be ready. Let's eat."

It was only after we'd polished off the bird, and the remainder of the bread in our pack, that Kip eyed Jasper. "So I s'pose we'd best talk about what happened all those years back."

"Right." Jasper leaned forward and gazed into the fire. "Let me have it, Kip."

Kip stared into the flames for a long moment before speaking. "You likely think that it's the memory of getting shot that makes it hard for me to be around you, but you're wrong. I don't remember that part at all. I remember your father telling you to kill me, but everything after that is a blur. Next thing I knew, I was back and surrounded by people who were happy to see me. I think the actual shooting affected Saray more than me.

"Getting brought back, though, changed everything about me. Suddenly, I had this magic that terrified me. I was constantly worried that I might hurt someone with it. For a good four years afterward, I had these nightmares where I'd cast in my sleep, like Kirilee did. That and the whole Bearer business nearly ended my relationship with Saray a few times. Then there was the problem of trying to fit into Dunderi society, when all I wanted was to be back here." He shrugged. "Can't blame you for that part. But the way I saw it, you ruined my life when you shot me."

Jasper frowned. "It's worked out for you, though. You're in control of your magic, you're back in the Woods, and you're married to Saray. You're welcome, by the way."

Kip's eyes narrowed. "What?"

"I seem to recall being the one to set you two up."

"Really?" I turned to him incredulously.

"I made a comment about how I'd 'leave the two lovebirds alone,' and the next morning they were all over each other." Jasper smirked at me, then turned back to Kip. "I forced you two to actually talk about your feelings."

Kip cocked his head. "I forgot about that. Why'd you do it anyway, if you were planning on kidnapping Saray the next day?"

Jasper shrugged. "My feelings about Saray were getting a little complicated. I figured I'd do one nice thing for her before ruining her life."

Kip frowned. "You didn't have a crush on her, did you?"

"I doubt he would've tried to set her up with you if he had," I pointed out.

Jasper nodded in agreement. "It wasn't like that. My time on the ship was one of the things that made me start seeing magic differently. I'd never been in a place where folks were allowed to use their abilities freely before, and it was fascinating. I saw magic being used for good for the first time, and I got a glimpse of what life might be like if it wasn't illegal—it wasn't the terrifying thing I'd been told. And Saray was a part of all that. I could absolutely see why she was dangerous, why the Guard wanted her dead, but she was smart with her magic, and she had great control."

"Trust me, she didn't always," Kip said, grinning slightly.

"Well, by the end of the trip, my feelings about magic—and about my job—were all mixed up," Jasper went on. "I told myself that I had to see this through to the end. But I did feel bad about it. So when I saw both of you so afraid to make the first move, I figured I'd step in."

I frowned. "But didn't you attack Saray again after you'd set sail?"

"Oh. Right." Jasper shook his head. "Father had to tell me twice to shoot Kip, and, well, he made a fool of me in front of the crew for it. I was embarrassed and angry, and I was in *pain*—you two didn't see what Saray did to my face—and so when I saw what looked like a chance for payback, and to make Father see me in a better light, I took it. Didn't work out so well for me, though." He raised his palms then. "But we were talking about how this affected you, Kip, not me."

"Right. So I got brought back, and things were rough for a few years. Then you showed up in Dundere with Ruby. Willem warned us you were coming, and I'll admit, I got a real thrill out of punching you when I first saw you. The look on your face..."

"I wish I could've seen that," I put in.

Kip laughed. "It was an enjoyable moment, for me at least. But after that, everyone but Saray and me seemed bent on trying to be your friend. I didn't get it. In the Woods, if an animal attacks you, you don't befriend it the next time you run into it. You either scare it off, or you run. Same held true for some of the more unsavoury Woods-folk that I used to come across, bandits and such. As far as I could see, you were an *enemy*, and everyone was ignoring that."

"I was an enemy who walked onto your territory with my hands raised, begging for mercy," Jasper countered.

"I s'pose so. And I didn't begrudge you bringing Ruby to us. I'm glad Noelle could heal her. But I was hoping you'd be on your way once that was done. I was a little taken aback to find out you'd be staying with Lachlann indefinitely." He frowned. "Of all the people who wanted us to get along, Lachlann surprised me the most. He was there when you held me hostage, when you kidnapped Saray."

"Trust me, Lachlann was less than thrilled to see me when I first showed up at his house. It took Alexander and Ember's magical fox to get him to trust me at all. And the only reason I came along is because Ruby insisted. I didn't want to go to Dundere any more than you wanted me there. As for the others, Willem was outright hostile when he first met me."

Kip chuckled. "That sounds about right."

"Marcus and Noelle were civil enough, but I could tell they were cautious at first. And likely they only treated me decently because Lachlann had spent a few weeks with me by then and could tell I'd changed." He shook his head. "Now, Trina surprised me. She was there when the kidnapping happened, so I expected her to be aloof at best. But she was curious and...friendly, which was odd."

"Have you forgotten about the part where she found you good looking," I teased.

Jasper shot me a glare. "Can we *not* get into that right now?"

"I think right now is the perfect time to get into that," Kip countered, his brow furrowing a little. "We need to talk about you and Trina."

"Do we now?" Jasper folded his arms.

"Look...I'm aware that Trina's an adult, and she can do what she wishes. But please," he levelled his gaze on Jasper, "be careful with her, all right?"

"What makes you think I'd be anything other than careful?" Jasper's tone was guarded.

"A few things, I s'pose." One corner of Kip's mouth turned up. "First, there's the fact that I saw you two come out of the Mothertree together the night of the attack, which tells me you were likely sleeping at her place. But neither of you has come to me for the tea yet."

Jasper raised an eyebrow. "It just so happens that I have my own stash from the Lady Liara."

"Besides, Trina doesn't need the tea," I added. "Being the fairy priestess means that she can't bear children, remember?"

Kip frowned. "Right. I forgot about that."

"So did I, until very recently." Jasper paused for a moment. "Anything else worrying you?"

"Plenty. How do I know you're not going to get *bored* with Trina? With Ankrossi? You're restless, Jasper. What happens when she isn't enough for you anymore?"

"What gives *you* the right to ask that question?" Jasper retorted. "I've thought about that myself, and I have an answer, but it's up to Trina to ask me, not you. Do you think Trina is just another fling to me?"

Kip shrugged. "I've heard the stories. Why would this be any different?"

"Are you aware that I had a serious girlfriend for the first year of my time on the Lady Liara? That we considered getting married?"

"I did hear that, yes."

"So you know I'm capable of settling down. And as for your concerns about me getting bored, well, I've been thinking about moving to Ankrossi for a while now."

"Really?" Kip frowned, clearly caught a little caught off guard by this.

"I figure living anywhere for long might get boring, but if I had to settle in any one place, Ankrossi seems the least boring option. There'd be lots to do there. I could keep working the bar, perhaps learn to ride a dragon and help with perimeter guard, use a few of the other talents I picked up on the ship. And I still have a summoning stone on the Lady Liara, so they could call me back for emergencies."

"What's keeping you from moving here permanently, then?"

"Honestly? I feel like I'm not welcome. And that's mainly because of you."

"You'd stay away from a village because one fellow doesn't like you?" Kip challenged.

"If that fellow is practically the head of the village militia, currently its most powerful magikai, and the son-in-law of the mayor, then, yes, I would." Jasper raised an eyebrow. "I don't doubt you could turn the entire village, and their magic and weapons, against me if you wanted."

"You really think I'm the sort of person who'd do that?"

Jasper shrugged. "Hard to say. You've despised me ever since you met me. Even before I turned on you and Saray, you didn't like me." He shook his head. "What's your problem with me, Kip?"

Kip sat back, clearly thinking on Jasper's question. "I s'pose some of it goes back to our initial interaction. Do you know the first thing you did to upset me, Jasper? Before the betrayal?"

"Do tell."

"I finally got to dance with this very pretty girl who I had a serious crush on. And it was wonderful, and I found myself looking forward to another one, and I was even beginning to work up the courage to ask her out—then this cocky blond fellow who was a far better dancer and far more confident than me cut in and stole her away."

I snorted. "This whole rivalry started because of a *girl?*"

"I mean I was sent to capture Saray, so, yes, it did." Jasper chuckled. "And if it makes you feel better, Kip, the confidence was an act."

"Yes, but it irked me." Kip let out a huff. "When you're interested in a woman, you're all swagger and charm and smooth lines, and it makes me *angry*. I imagine you acting like that with Trina, and it makes me want to punch you."

"First of all, have you ever seen me use that cocky, swaggering sort of act with Trina?" Jasper shot back. "Second, you know what irks me about *you?* The fact that you look at me as if you're *better* than me. That any time you're around, I know you're watching me, judging me for—I don't know—existing? Trust me, I wouldn't mind decking you myself."

"Hey!" I cut in. "Aren't you two trying to get along now?"

They exchanged a glance, and Kip gave me a sheepish smile. "We are. But an eight-year grudge doesn't just go away overnight. We may be committed to working with one another now, but clearly we both still want to hit each other."

"Well, then, why don't you?"

"What?"

I shrugged. "I'm a healer. You two want to fight so badly—go at it and I'll heal you up afterward. Might help you get your anger out."

Jasper regarded me for a moment, then turned to Kip and smirked. "Well, I'm game if you are. Though it's not exactly a fair fight with your magic."

"Fine, then," Kip replied. "No magic, no weapons. Just fists. Until one of us concedes." He crossed his arms. "I hope you have a high pain tolerance."

"I'm sure I can handle whatever you throw at me." He clapped a fist into his palm. "Be warned, I fight dirty."

"Excellent." Kip gave him a wolfish grin. "I hope you don't mind getting sacked."

"I'm not healing any of *those* sorts of injuries," I put in. "And no broken bones. They're a pain to set."

They both nodded. "Seems fair," said Jasper, getting to his feet and unbuttoning his shirt. "When do we do this? Now?"

"Never a better time," Kip replied. In one fluid motion, he stood and pulled his shirt off, dropping it on the log where he'd been sitting. "Let's go." With no further warning, he closed the gap between them with surprising speed and swung at Jasper.

Jasper ducked, aiming a fist at Kip's stomach just as Kip hooked Jasper's ankle with his foot. The two of them tumbled to the ground, limbs flailing as they scuffled in the grass. Jasper let out a cry of pain as Kip's fist connected with his ribcage, though he tried to disguise it as a whoop. "You want to play like that, huh?" he snarled.

Soon they were grasping roughly at each other's arms, grunting as they tried to overpower the other. Kip managed to climb on top of Jasper, pinning him to the ground, and Jasper responded by grabbing Kip's ponytail and yanking hard while kneeing him from behind. Kip let out a high-pitched yelp when Jasper's knee hit its mark, and Jasper bucked Kip off him, only for Kip to roll backward onto his feet and deck him once more. Jasper swore, blood trickling from his nose, and swung.

Again they became a flurry of motion, fists flying at one another. Jasper let out a guttural sound and keeled forward, Kip having delivered a particularly brutal punch to his stomach. Kip advanced, and Jasper's foot shot out, hitting Kip square on the side of the knee. Kip's eyes went wide, his jaw slackened, and for a moment he wavered. "You give up yet?" Jasper taunted.

Kip's face had gone white, but he managed to lunge and deliver an uppercut to Jasper's jaw, sending him flying back. When Jasper didn't move after a couple of seconds, Kip smiled, swaying on his feet. "I s'pose I win." Then he collapsed.

I gaped at both of the fallen men for a moment, then sighed. "Ugh, this is going to be a pain to treat," I mumbled, climbing to my feet and surveying the damage. Kip had fallen to one side, but Jasper was flat on his back. *He might choke. I'd best deal with him first.*

Jasper let out a moan when I rolled him onto his side. His eyes flickered open, and I shook my head. "Welcome back."

"Everything is blurry," he complained. "Why do my eyes hurt?"

"That punch likely did some real damage to your head," I told him. "Here, let me deal with that."

His eyes flickered to Kip's fallen form. "Heal him first. I likely wrecked his knee."

"Probably, but lucky for Kip he's gone and passed out from the pain. Now let me fix you." I put my hands on his forehead and sang, willing the damage to heal, then moved my palms to his jaw and repeated the process. When I was finished, he blinked. "Thanks, the light doesn't hurt my eyes anymore. Now go take care of Kip."

I had hoped to heal Kip while he was still unconscious, but he began to stir as I rolled up his trouser leg. Then he let out a moan and nearly kicked me, only to gasp when he moved his knee. "Hold still," I ordered him. "I'm trying to heal you here."

Kip let out a long sigh as I sang the torn ligaments back to wholeness. When I was done, he wiggled his leg a few times, then slowly sat up to smirk at Jasper. "You thought you'd won after you took out my knee, didn't you?"

"I *did* win," Jasper retorted. "Or, at the very least, we tied."

"You fainted before I did, which means you gave in first. Unless you want to keep going."

Jasper winced and rubbed his shoulder. "I think I'm good." He glanced at me. "You'd best finish healing Kip. He's hurt worse than me."

"What's that supposed to mean?" Kip protested.

"You may have won, but I'm betting I injured you more."

"A blow to the head versus a wrecked knee? That's pretty even, I think," I put in.

"I'm referring to everything before those last two blows. We'll let you be the judge of that, though."

As it turned out, Jasper was right. His black eye, bruised jaw and split lip were much easier to heal than Kip's similar injuries. I mended a few bruised ribs, scratches and some other small wounds, then looked them over, satisfied. "All right. Are you two ready to get along now?"

They stared at each other warily for a moment or two, then Kip nodded. "I figure we'll still bicker, but yes, I think we can work together."

"Good. Because we still have the third condition of Saray's curse to resolve, and I imagine rescuing Lachlann will be easiest if you're cooperating."

Kip frowned. "You think that 'brothers at war' thing was about Jasper and me?"

"Well, I certainly hope it wasn't about Jasper and Jade, because if so, Saray's not getting her magic back."

"I suspect it's about you and me as well," Jasper said to Kip. "Because if Trina and I were to end up married, well, we *would* sort of be brothers."

"By the Fae, you're right," Kip mumbled.

"About rescuing Lachlann, I always figured I'd be the best person to sneak into the palace," Jasper continued. "I'm good at disguising myself and getting into places. But perhaps you should come with me." He looked at Kip. "You're pretty sneaky from what I can see, and you obviously know how to fight. What do you say we break Lachlann out together?"

"I say that's a very good idea," Kip replied.

"All right." Jasper sighed. "Lachlann used to wonder what it would take for the two of us to work as a team. I suppose the answer was him being taken away."

"And you saving my life," Kip added.

"That too." Jasper glanced at the bundle.

Kip followed his gaze. "You're a better fighter than him, by the way."

Jasper raised an eyebrow. "Really? He nearly killed you."

"Only because he was considerably stronger than me. You and I are about equal in strength, and the only reason I won is because I know a little trick to knock folks out." He grinned. "I'll fight you again if you want, just for the fun of it."

Jasper raised his eyebrows. "Sure, I'm game. Not right now, though."

"I agree," I put in. "I don't feel like healing any more unnecessary injuries tonight."

"Also, could you teach me how to use a gun properly?" Kip frowned. "I'll likely always prefer a bow or sword, but I figure since folks seem to be switching to firearms, I should learn."

Jasper nodded. "Of course. You can have Jade's gun if you want. I certainly don't want to keep it." He sighed, then stood. "We should get some sleep. It's late, and I'm not expecting tomorrow to be pleasant."

Kip nodded. "We'd best put Jade up a tree for the night, unless you want the bears to get to him." He turned to me. "You can take the hammock tonight, Isabelle. Go get ready for bed, we'll be in shortly."

I ducked into the hut and changed into my nightclothes in the dark. It took a few minutes to get comfortable, but eventually I managed to arrange the blankets on top of myself in a manner that wasn't awkward. And only then, once I was lying down, did I realize how exhausted I was. Almost immediately, I found myself drifting off; I hardly heard Jasper and Kip come into the hut. My last thought before slipping into the darkness of sleep was to wonder whether I might run into Oliver during our time in the city.

***

We arrived in Kirstein late the following afternoon. The day had been a blur of waking early, hiking out of the Woods, being treated to breakfast at Helenne's, and riding into Kirstein. Kip and Jasper both preferred to travel faster than my mother had, and I was surprised when the capital came into view around dinnertime. Half an hour after that, we stood in front of a stately brick townhome, Jasper looking up at it grimly. "Here we go," he muttered. "Isabelle, stay back, and if I tell you to run, make your way to the square at the last crossroads and wait for us there."

I nodded, and Jasper took a deep breath before ringing the bell.

No one came to the door for a good two minutes, despite the second ring. He looked back at us, likely about to say that no one was home, when the door finally creaked open.

The man on the other side was bent over a cane and had sparse grey hair and a white beard. He regarded Jasper with a pair of blue eyes that I now realized looked familiar.

Jasper gasped. "Grandfather?"

"Jasper!" the old man exclaimed, leaning forward to embrace him. "By the king's name, I thought I'd never see you again!"

Jasper hugged his grandfather back for a long moment. Then he pulled away and turned to us. "This is my grandfather, Malcolm. Grandfather, these are my friends, Kip and Isabelle."

"Pleasure to meet you, sir," Kip stepped forward and extended a hand. I gave Malcolm a small curtsy. Malcolm shook Kip's hand and smiled at me.

"I wish I were here under better circumstances," Jasper said to his grandfather.

"You have bad news as well?"

"I do." Jasper's shoulders slumped. "Is Father home?"

His grandfather's face fell, and he sighed sadly. "Come in, son, we need to talk."

Chapter 28

A FEW MOMENTS later, we sat in the parlour of the Jameson home, a high-ceilinged room with an extravagant chandelier and elegant furnishings carved from dark, reddish wood. One corner was occupied by a massive grandfather clock, and a baby grand piano, dusty with unuse, sat in another. I noticed that many of the room's paintings were of ships. On the mantle above the fireplace were a few other items also nautically themed: a mock, gold-plated captain's wheel, a ship in a bottle, a vase decorated with shells. Kip noticed it as well and turned to Jasper. "Your father likes ships, I take it? I see where you get it from."

Malcolm let out a deep sigh. "We need to talk about your father and Jade." He took one of Jasper's hands in his own. "I'm sorry, son, there's no easy way to say this. Your father and brother were both involved in an attack on the Shrouded Woods just a week ago. Neither survived."

Jasper stared back at his grandfather for a few long moments, eyes wide with shock. Then he let out a sigh of his own. "I already know about Jade. We brought him home." He nodded at the wrapped bundle that still sat atop the horse beyond the front window. "But...Father?"

Malcolm nodded gravely. "He was involved in the same attack, though my understanding is that he was on a different front. He was bent on raiding the home of some magic user who he had a grudge against..."

"Willem." Jasper and Kip spoke almost simultaneously.

Jasper turned to Kip. "Did you see Father when you went to Willem's place after the battle for Ankrossi? I would think you'd have recognized his...body."

"From what I understood when some fellows came to tell me the news, there wasn't much of a body left to see," Malcolm said. "That Willem chap pulled off some sort of self-sacrificing magic to keep your father from getting into the library and took Angus down with him."

Kip and I exchanged a glance, and my eyes widened when I recalled the charred corpse we'd seen near the entrance to the library. *That was Jasper and Ruby's father?*

"It's a shame," Malcolm went on, his shoulders hunched. "Angus had a good run at life, but Jade...he wasn't even thirty..." His voice broke, and he dabbed at his eyes with a handkerchief.

Jasper put a hand on his shoulder. "How did you know about Jade?"

"Everyone who went on that leg of the mission is presumed dead." He looked to Jasper. "Perhaps you could tell me if that much is true?"

"It is," Kip said. "We made a point of ensuring no one escaped. Couldn't have the Witch Slayers returning with reinforcements."

Malcolm eyed him. "Did you kill Jade, then?"

"No," Jasper answered for him. "It...was me. I shot him." He took a deep breath and averted his eyes. "I didn't want to, of course, but if I hadn't he would've killed Kip and another friend of mine. And he would have never left our village alone. I had to intervene, I..." His voice broke, and a tear trickled down his cheek. I tensed, wondering how Malcolm would react to the news.

But Malcolm studied Jasper for a moment, his shock evident, then sighed. "I hate to say this," he said, his voice wavering, "but I understand why you did it."

"You don't despise me then?"

"You really think I could despise any of my grandchildren?" He shook his head. "I don't despise you or Ruby, or Jade for that matter."

"Didn't you disapprove of what Ruby and I were doing?" Jasper asked.

"I used to feel the same way about magic as everyone else. But as I got older, I realized how silly it is to fault people for things they can't help. I don't want much to do with magic myself, but Ruby can't change who she is. And I think you did well by supporting her. I've missed both of you." He gave Jasper a smile. "Why don't you two come home? This place is yours and Ruby's now."

"It's more complicated than that. I don't know that coming home is an option, especially not for Ruby." He frowned. "Father didn't write us out of his will, then?"

Malcolm shook his head. "He didn't actually want the two of you out of his life, you know. Your father talked about you and your sister often, though usually only once he had a few drinks in him."

"What did he say?" Jasper's eyes were wide.

"That he missed you. That he wished he'd been a better father. That he hoped you'd come home."

"But...he was the one who kicked us out."

"I know." Malcolm sighed. "Your father loved you and Ruby. But he loved his traditions more. And in order to have you in his life, he'd need to go against what he'd been taught, and what he'd been teaching others." He shook his head. "I don't doubt you could've had a good relationship with your father if he'd been willing to put you before all that."

Jasper nodded and let his head fall into his hands for a moment. When he looked up, his eyes shone with tears. I blinked back tears of my own as I thought over Malcolm's words. *Your father loved you, but he loved his traditions more.* The same could be said of my own father, I realized, only it was his reputation that he cherished more than me.

Jasper stood. "Well, I'd best get to burying Jade."

"I'll help," Kip volunteered.

"No. I need to do this on my own."

"You'll be awhile digging that hole alone, y'know." He glanced at me then. "Why don't we pay a visit to the palace while Jasper's busy, let him have some time with his grandpa?"

"Good idea," Jasper agreed.

***

A few hours later, Kip and I had ridden around the perimeter of the palace, studying each gate to determine which would be easiest to breach. I'd kept my head down during our scouting, hoping no one would recognize me, but I couldn't help throwing brief glances at the courtyards beyond the outer walls, hoping to see Oliver. Now we sat in the park across the road. "Jasper thinks that if we could get our hands on some guard uniforms, we'd be able to sneak around without much trouble," Kip said. "The issue will be getting inside, with the anti-magic present."

"Can't you just get a fairy potion to teleport?" I suggested.

"We could, but the trouble is that the teleporter needs to be able to envision where they're going to land. Neither Jasper nor I know the palace. And we'd still be without the uniforms. I figure our best bet would be to take some guards out at the far south entrance and steal theirs."

"How would you do that without bringing attention to yourselves?"

"Well, I figure we get both a fairy potion for sleep and invisibility from Alexander. Jasper and I go invisible, put the guards out, tie them up and steal their clothes. It's similar to what we did on Yarel Island."

"Someone would notice the missing guards eventually, though," I pointed out.

"Sure. And folks would definitely notice if we manage to free Lachlann and the anti-magic suddenly disappears. I'm thinking we could do it on Breoch's independence day, during the ceremonies in the outer courtyard. I'm guessing most of the palace staff will be at the event, so the palace would be nearly empty."

I nodded. "But there would still be guards. You might need more of a diversion than the ceremony."

"I know. Just not certain what that would be. We could stage an attack elsewhere on the palace perimeter that would occupy the guards' focus, but I don't think attacking the palace would be a smart move. We aren't strong enough to fight a whole contingent of guards, even with our abilities."

"I'm sure it'd be easy enough for a bunch of folks with magic to come up with a diversion. Just have someone fly over the assembly or walk around with fire on their hands, and folks will be quite distracted."

"And let them hunt that person to death?" Kip replied. "Also, remember that the outer courtyard is protected by anti-magic, so it wouldn't be too easy."

"What if a person flew *above* the anti-magic and had fairy magic to protect them?" I countered. "In fact...what if..." I paused, an idea quickly formulating. "Kip, remember how Jasper said that it was seeing magic used for good that helped him change his mind about it? Was that what also changed your mind?"

Kip frowned. "I s'pose it was. I'd seen magic used for good on and off as a teen, but I still avoided it. Travelling with Saray and Trina showed me it could be used more systematically. Then Lachlann began pointing out ways magic could be useful when we were facing obstacles, in hopes I'd change my mind about it. It must've worked somewhat. Why'd you ask?"

"I'm thinking most of the folks in Breoch haven't had much of a chance to see magic used for good. What if we could change that?"

Kip eyed me. "How?"

"What if our diversion was a display of magic in the sky, out of range of the anti-magic, and with fairy magic protection from Trina? We could put on a show to demonstrate the many ways that magic can be useful and harmless. It would be like a...a sky circus." I grinned, recalling Oliver's desire to see one of these performances.

"You think people would buy that?" Kip's eyes narrowed.

"Hard to say. Even if they didn't, though, it would provide the distraction we need for you and Jasper to get to Lachlann."

"It just might." Kip nodded. "Your idea would need a bit more work, but it's a good start." He scratched his head. "So you do your sky thing while Jasper and I get Lachlann out. Then what? Do we all just flee back to Ankrossi? Because chances are, Simon knows where it is now, and he'll send more people after us."

"That's a good point." I sighed. "If we could only convince Breoch to be less fearful of magic, maybe Kairus would legalize it."

"That'd likely take time. Is there anything you can think of that might change his mind more quickly? What does the king *want* that we could give him?"

I frowned, thinking, then the answer dawned on me clear as day. "More than anything, Kairus wants his son to live. He doesn't want Oliver to deteriorate in front of him like his wife did. And I'm the only one who can heal him."

Kip's eyes widened. "And you can only heal Oliver if Kairus allows it, which means magic has to be made legal."

"Exactly. That's our trade. Though I feel like Oliver's going to hate me for using him as a bargaining chip." I gazed at the castle and blinked back tears.

"You miss him." It wasn't a question.

"Terribly."

Kip nodded and let out a sigh. "Did you know that I broke up with Saray once?"

My eyebrows raised. "No, I didn't. What happened?"

"I didn't choose to be the Bearer of the Earth Stone. Kirilee put that on me when she died. And it caused problems, because I was tied to the Woods when I wanted to be in Dundere with Saray. At first, I managed to do both—I visited the Woods every weekend and spent the weekdays in Dundere. But that began to affect the magic of the Woods. I was convinced Saray was safer in Dundere, so I broke up with her and came back to Breoch." He shook his head. "Eventually, we realized that Saray wouldn't really be safe anywhere, so she came to join me. But there was certainly some time in there when I couldn't see a future for the two of us." Kip put a hand on my shoulder. "If there is a way for you and Oliver to be together, you'll figure it out in time. Don't give up hope just yet." He gave me a small smile. "Now, we'd best get back to Jasper."

We discussed my idea in more detail on the ride back to the Jameson home. When we returned, we found Jasper in the backyard, standing over a freshly dug patch of earth. His face was streaked with dirt and sweat and possibly tears, but when he looked at us there was a profound sort of relief in his eyes. "It's done," he said. "And we've been invited to stay here for the night. Grandfather is a pretty decent cook—he's going to make us some dinner. He says we should all bathe first, though."

"What's going to happen to the house?" Kip asked him.

"We think it's best if Grandfather comes to live in Ankrossi so he can be near Ruby and me. He'll stay here and make arrangements to sell the place, and Ruby and I will split the inheritance—not that money will do us much good in the Woods."

"It could come in handy if you want to import things from the cities," I pointed out.

"True. I'm sure we'll find some use for it."

"You think your grandfather is accepting enough of magic to live in Ankrossi?" Kip asked.

"I told him that if he were to live with us, he'd have to get used to it. And he seems open to the possibility."

"I'd hope so, given that I don't imagine we're going to get a fellow his age to Ankrossi without magic," I pointed out.

"True." Jasper smiled and ran a hand through his curls. "Anyway, I'll show you two to what'll be your rooms for the night, then we can all freshen up for dinner."

Chapter 29

THE JOURNEY HOME from Kirstein the next morning was uneventful. Once we'd made it into the Woods, Kip called for Ambrose and Spark, and we were back in the village an hour later. Minutes after being reunited with Saray, Kip was calling for a council meeting, and a few hours later the Mothertree's cavern was crowded with both council members and other city folks. The word had spread that we'd come up with a plan, and nearly everyone wanted to hear it.

"Some very difficult things have happened in the last week," Kip began, standing and looking over the group. "We've lost people who were dear to us. We've seen the safety of Ankrossi threatened and the school compromised. Willem and Kirilee made hard choices to protect us." He glanced up into the trees above. "The older adults may have laid the foundations for this place, but now it's up to us to defend our home. We're vulnerable, and we can't depend on Willem or Hilda or Lachlann to protect us, which means we need to grow up and protect ourselves. We need to put aside our differences and work as a team, all of us. It's the only way we're going to save what we've built here." He looked around the room and received nods of agreement in return. "Our number one priority right now is rescuing Lachlann and dismantling the anti-magic system the Breoch Guard is using. If they don't have Lachlann, they won't easily be able to access the level of power they've been using. Jasper and I have realized it's probably best that we sneak into the palace and extract him. But in order for us to do that, we'll need a pretty serious diversion." He looked over to me. "Isabelle here has an idea."

I took a deep breath and explained the plan I'd come up with, watching people's faces as I spoke. A good number of them nodded slowly, while others frowned and whispered to one another. Trina, however, grinned, and Sophie looked about ready to jump out of her seat with excitement. "Now, exactly what this display of magic looks like is up to all of us to decide," I concluded. "What sorts of acts should we put into our show?"

Answers came fast and from all around us. Kaden began taking notes but stopped halfway through to look up, frowning. "If this entire show is happening in the air, does that mean you'll be relying on me to make people fly?"

I nodded. "We'll have a few folks lend you their magic so you don't tire out."

"We're planning to do this on Breoch Day, six weeks from now?" Ruby asked.

"That's the idea."

She turned to Kaden. "We've already decided to marry. What if we were to have our wedding—and be Joined—before then? That way I can help with the flight."

A smile played on Kaden's lips "I was just thinking the same thing."

"It's almost like we're meant for each other." Ruby grinned and leaned in to kiss Kaden gently.

"Who should be the show's ringmaster, as it were?" asked Sophie. "I could do it, but I don't know if I can charm that many people at once. Or if those abilities should be displayed for that matter."

"Marcus would likely be a good choice," Ruby said.

"Yes, but we can't count on him being there," Kip put in.

"Fair. If he's not present, I could do it. I've gotten better at speaking in front of crowds. But then I wouldn't be as able to help Kaden."

"I vote Saray does it and gives the entire nation a heart attack," joked Shawnie.

"Let's not," Kip countered.

"Or I could be one of the final acts of the show," Saray suggested. "It would certainly add to the diversion if a dead woman shows up."

"But you don't have magic right now," Shawnie protested.

"No, but *you* know how to cast illusions. You could make me *look* like I was using fire magic."

Kip frowned. "Are you sure you want to do that, Saray? Reveal yourself after we've done so much to hide you?"

She sighed. "The attacks on Ankrossi won't stop unless we do something. And one way or another, people are going to figure out that I'm alive. We might as well use it to our advantage."

"I s'pose it's something to think about. Though I believe Isabelle should be the final act—she plans on making an offer to Kairus."

I explained to the group this next part. "If he accepts, I'll heal Oliver, and we can come back here and celebrate. If he refuses, well, we can likely expect more attacks, but we should have Lachlann back by then. And I think we can handle the Breoch Guard without their anti-magic."

Chester let out a sigh, shoulders slumping. "If we don't succeed, I'll need to leave Ankrossi. Maybe move to Candesh, or go to Dundere if they'll have me. I freeze up whenever I see the Guard...I'll be no use in a place that gets attacked regularly."

"About that," Kip said. "I have an idea." He glanced at Jasper. "I hope you don't mind, but I swiped one of your father's Breoch Guard uniforms while I was at your house, as I figured it might make a good disguise."

Jasper laughed. "I did the same with one of my old uniforms."

"Perfect." Kip turned to Chester. "If you want, Jasper and I can dress up in the uniforms, and you can practice fighting us off."

"I...might take you up on that." Chester gave him a shy smile. "Thanks."

"What are you and Jasper doing while we're running this show, then?" Saray asked Kip. "How do you intend to free Lachlann?"

"I think we'll have a better idea of that once Trina does her scry," Kip replied. "Can we get that done tomorrow?"

Trina frowned. "I'm not sure I know how. I was hoping Hilda could show me when she gets back."

"I think I remember," Ruby assured. "We'll figure it out."

"We should start training right away," Kip said. "We're going to need to be extra skilled with our magic and make it as entertaining as possible if we want to hold people's attention. Let's hear your ideas on how to make this into a really good show."

Everyone huddled around, and slowly, we began to form a plan.

***

The following evening, a small group of us sat in the garden outside of what was now Trina's home. Ruby had come over early to walk Trina through the spell, then had started rummaging around what used to be Hilda's place, searching for the items she recalled from the previous scry. Kip and Jasper were both present, as the information from the scrying would be important to their plan, and Saray joined us with a few items belonging to Lachlann. I came along as well, desperate to know what had become of Silva, hoping the scry would offer me some clues.

Saray set a large crystal bowl of water in front of Trina, along with a few other things. "This is the best we could come up with—a leather pouch and a shaving blade from your mother's house, both made by Lachlann. The blade has a small bit of blood on it, which I suspect is his."

Trina nodded. "That'll have to do." At Ruby's direction, she took the pouch and dropped it into the bowl of water. Then she lit a candle and put it to the blade, burning off the blood before dropping it in as well. When she sang a spell over the bowl, a plume of purple smoke rose from it. Then she placed her hands on the outside of the bowl and closed her eyes.

"I see him," she said after a moment. "It's hazy, and some of the details seem distorted, but..."

"What do you see?" asked Kip.

"He's in a room...it looks to be a tower."

"I knew it!" I exclaimed.

"There's a large globe of metal in the centre, and he's chained to it," she went on. "The chain is attached to his chest somehow; it looks like they fused it to his anti-magic pendant. I think this is how they're using him to protect the palace. And..." She let out a sigh. "Thank the Fae."

"What?" Saray asked.

"The kids who were taken are with him," she told us.

"With him? In the same room?" My voice broke. "They're...safe?"

Trina frowned for a moment, clearly looking further into the scry, then nodded solemnly. "Yes, Isabelle. Your friends are safe."

Tears blurred my vision at her pronouncement, and I covered my eyes and tried to breathe deeply.

"What are they doing?" Jasper asked.

"Practicing something." She frowned. "I think he's teaching them how to fight...possibly planning an escape. Though I'm not sure how Lachlann intends to free himself from...wait." Her face scrunched as she squeezed her eyes shut tighter. "The kids are going through a door into another room now."

Frowning, I looked up. "Odd, I didn't think the towers had other rooms. Then again, there are a few I've never been to."

Trina nodded. "All right, the kids are gone. Lachlann's sitting against a wall."

"How does he look?" Saray asked.

"Tired. His beard has gotten rather bushy, and there are scars on his arms that I don't remember. Oh..." Her voice wavered. "He just put his head down on his arms. He looks...defeated."

"That's likely why he's training the kids," Kip put in. "To distract himself."

"The door just opened. A guard came in to give him food and water, and he..." Trina frowned. "Now, that's interesting. The guard just hung his anti-magic pendant off a knob sticking out of the globe. The pendant is glowing now."

"I wonder if that's how the Breoch Guard got their Bonded powers?" mused Saray. "I know there's a way to temporarily enchant items with larger sources of magic. Pieter might have found how to use that same principle with anti-magic?"

"What's a Bonded power?" I asked.

"It's Lachlann's ability to use very powerful anti-magic at range," Kip explained. "It's a lifetime commitment, means that no magic can be used on you with the exception of the fairy type. Most anti-mages only have limited, touch-based abilities, and only when they wear their pendants."

"Which is why we were all so shocked when Jade snuffed out all the magic when your father and the Guard came to fetch you," Ruby put in. "He was wielding the power of a Bonded anti-mage without the commitment."

"All right, the guard is gone now," cut in Trina. "And a few of the kids are coming back into the room with their own dinners."

"How do they look?" Kip asked.

"Well, I don't know what they looked like before all this. Some of them seem nervous. A few of the girls are close together, and one of the younger boys is nearly clinging to Lachlann. They don't look like they've been harmed, though." She frowned. "The vision is fading; I think that's all I'm going to see."

"At least we know both Lachlann and the kids are safe," said Saray. "And we have some idea where they are." She turned to me. "Do you know anything about these towers in the palace, which one he might be in?"

I shrugged. "Not entirely. The palace has at least a dozen towers, but there are several I don't know. I'd need to eliminate the ones he wouldn't be in. I can try to map it out for you if someone has a pen and paper handy."

Saray fetched the items I needed, and I set to work drawing a rough outline of the palace. "So this tower here is weapons storage," I said, pointing, "as are these two. This one is servants' quarters. These four," I pointed to one at each corner, "are for defense; the guards use them if the palace walls are breached. Though I suppose they could be used to hold a prisoner. The remaining towers, I've never been in. I know one holds an office, and there are a few others that are heavily guarded and locked."

"I wouldn't be too worried about locks," Jasper said. "I learned how to pick those when I was a teen."

"Couldn't Kip teleport you two in with some fairy magic?" I asked.

"Not without knowing what's on the other side of that door," Kip answered. "First, if I don't have a visual, I could land us somewhere unsafe, and second, who knows who might be waiting for us? Teleporting into unknown situations is dangerous on more than one level." He turned to Trina. "So Lachlann was chained to this globe? Do you recall how thick the chains were?"

"Fairly thick," Trina replied. "They wouldn't be easy to cut through, if that's what you're thinking."

Jasper frowned. "I wonder if we could melt them? If anyone would know how, it would be Lachlann." He turned to Saray. "You used fire to get out of handcuffs, right? How did you do that?"

"I got my flame down to a single, very hot point and used it to melt the metal. Though those links were likely far more slender than whatever Lachlann is chained with. And I burned myself terribly doing it."

"Really?"

Saray nodded. "The heat travelled through the rest of the links to the cuffs themselves and basically cooked my wrists. You wouldn't have been able to see it from your vantage point."

"Gross," I murmured.

"Lachlann has a very high pain tolerance, but heating those links up might also heat up his pendant, and I suspect that could kill him," Saray continued.

"True, though his pendant is made of stone, not metal, so it might not heat up as fast," Kip pointed out.

Saray nodded slowly. "You're right. In that case I'll have to teach you how to hone your fire into a tiny point. It takes some practice, but I'm sure you'll get it."

"Trouble is, it'll probably need to be Jasper who gets Lachlann out. If the kids are nearby, someone is going to need to teleport them out. They'll be scared, and they don't know Jasper."

"But Jasper doesn't have magic," Saray argued.

"Regular magic wouldn't work in this situation anyway," Jasper reasoned. "There's anti magic to contend with. I'll get Ember to make me a fairy magic pendant with a fire spell attached, then you can train me."

I felt the tears welling up again while the others discussed the logistics of the plan. When a few hard blinks didn't clear them, I rose and tiptoed to the far end of the yard, where the portal leading back to Ankrossi sat. I slipped through the strange, swirling light and found myself alone in the Mothertree's cavern, save for the glow of the viletta blooms above. I sank down onto a bench and began to sob.

Above me, the light changed ever so slightly, and I looked up to see the glowing blooms pulsing with brilliance, as if alive and listening. "I know it's silly for me to cry like this," I said to whoever was in the tree—Kirilee or Starla, or perhaps someone else entirely. "I'm just so relieved that Silva is safe and that we're figuring out how to rescue her. I've been so worried that she wouldn't survive, and..." I began to cry again.

A moment later, I felt something brush my shoulder and jumped. I realized that a small branch from Kirilee's tree was winding its way across my shoulders and instinctively leaned back into it. "Thanks."

Just then, a strange shimmering in the centre of the cavern caught my eye, and I frowned. Soon, Marcus, Mother, and a third person carrying a child appeared in the middle of the haze. "Aha!" Marcus exclaimed. "Here we are!"

I recoiled at his sudden appearance, and he met my eyes. "Sorry to startle you," he said. "I brought your mother back safely."

"I see that." I got up to embrace her.

"You've been crying," she said as she pulled me into her arms. "What's happened?"

"Nothing. Or rather, everything. It's a long story." I eyed the newcomer. "Who's this?"

"We'd best have a meeting," Marcus said. "I need to introduce you all to this fellow so you can hear what he has to say. And I need to get caught up as well." He frowned. "I hope you've all been safe while I was away?"

I sighed. "Not exactly," I told him. "Let's arrange a meeting."

***

Within a half hour, the entire council minus Trina was present and seated, as well as a few others from Ankrossi. Saray, Kip and Ruby had emerged from the portal several minutes after me, claiming that Trina had kicked them out and that she and Jasper were getting "a little amorous." Ruby tried, to no avail, using her summoning stone to call Jasper. When Kaden showed up a little while later, she offered to fly across the Woods and knock on their door, and Marcus chuckled. "Let them have their fun. They're in for some news when they get here."

"Can you at least introduce your friend?" Saray said to her father.

"I'm someone you probably won't be happy to have in your secret village, but trust me, I'm here for a reason," the fellow answered for him. "My name is Arquinn Blackwell—I'm the eldest of the Blackwell children. I'm sure you remember my brother Alvin. And this," he nodded to the child in his arms, "is my nephew, Tristan."

Ruby and Kaden gaped at Arquinn outright, while a few of the others began to murmur among themselves. I eyed the man; he didn't look quite how I'd envisioned the Blackwells. Arquinn's skin was tanned, his long red hair pulled back into a braid. He wore spectacles, and his beard, which was several inches long, had a few flecks of grey in it; nonetheless, he couldn't have been much older than thirty. The little boy in his arms looked more like the descriptions I'd heard. Though the child's unruly curls were blond, not reddish, he possessed the porcelain skin, freckles, and green-gold eyes that Ruby mentioned when she told me about Alvin.

Just then, Jasper and Trina burst into the room, hand in hand. Jasper's hair was dishevelled, his shirt untucked, and Trina's hair had come partway out of its braid. "Sorry we're late," she gasped, blushing.

"My summoning stone wasn't on me," Jasper explained, "so I didn't feel it until..." He trailed off when he noticed the newcomers, and his face went pale.

"What is it?" Trina asked.

Jasper let go of her hand and crossed the chamber, coming to stare at the child in Arquinn's arms. "Is this who I think it is?"

Arquinn chuckled. "You must be the infamous Jasper." He shifted the boy in his arms. "I'm Arquinn, and this is Tristan, but I suspect you already knew that."

"Thank the Fae he's safe," Jasper breathed. Then he crouched down so he was eye level with the child, who stared back at him. "Hi there, buddy," he said, his voice turning soft.

"Jasper?" Ruby said. "How do you know this kid?"

"I don't, really. This is my first time meeting him, but..." Jasper stood and met his sister's eyes. "This is my son."

Chapter 30

THE CHAMBER FELL silent, and all attention turned to Jasper. "You have a *child?*" Kaden gaped.

"I was asked by his mother not to tell anyone. But, yes, I do." Jasper stared down at Tristan again.

"But if this is Arquinn's nephew, then..." Kaden's eyes narrowed. "You had a kid with *Ashlynn?*"

Jasper nodded. "That's why I was worried that he'd been—"

"*What?*" Ruby cut in. "I thought Ashlynn hated you."

"It's...a bit of a story." I saw a blush rise in his cheeks.

"It certainly is, and I think it's best you tell them a little later," Marcus said. Jasper nodded, his eyes still on Tristan.

"Why did you bring Arquinn here?" Ruby asked Marcus. "Is it only because of Tristan?"

"No, I'll get to that. But first, I'd like you folks to tell me all that's happened while I was gone."

I felt the mood in the cavern shift, and Marcus listened as we took turns telling him the events that had unfolded in his absence. His mouth fell open when Shawnie informed him of Willem's passing during the battle. When we were done telling him our stories, he let out a long, shuddering sigh. "Willem was the last person I expected to die in all of this. I thought he was next to invincible..." His voice broke, and he put his head in his hands.

Saray nodded and put a hand on his shoulder. "It's been hard. We all miss him."

"I feel like I abandoned you kids when you needed me the most."

"We're not kids anymore," Kip said to him. "If anything, this has forced us all to act like adults, sort our problems out, and come up with a plan."

Kip filled him in then on the scheme to get Lachlann out of the palace, and Marcus chuckled at the notion of a magical sky circus. "Isabelle came up with that," Kip told him. "We were hoping you could be our ringmaster, unless you need to go back to Dundere."

"Hilda and Carmine are going to stay in Dundere for a time to monitor the situation. I'm fine to focus my energies at home." He turned to Arquinn. "I think you'd best explain why you're here before I get into the news from our trip."

Arquinn nodded. "I've come because I suspect you folks are in more danger than you know, based on what Marcus has told me." He turned his gaze to Saray. "I hear a fellow in the palace came to you and claimed to be Alvin in a different body?"

She nodded. "You think it's true?"

"I do."

"But...how?" she asked. "That's what we've all been wondering." Several of us nodded our agreement.

Arquinn sat back. "To understand this, you need to know a bit about the Fae in Dundere. From what I've been told, fairies in the Shrouded Woods are, in a way, tame. They've adapted to humans and learned to work with them, and in some cases they've made bargains with them to ensure protection."

"That's accurate enough," Trina conceded.

"The Fae in Dundere are different. For the most part, they avoid humans altogether and fear contact. There are occasional exceptions, such as the ones who rescued your friend Sophie, but generally we avoid them, and they avoid us. And as children, we're taught that they are beautiful but very dangerous. A fairy could easily kill a human, if they had enough control over their magic. The main thing that keeps them from wiping us out is their size. They may be able to kill us with magic, but we can squish them." He grinned slightly, and I wrinkled my nose at the imagery.

"Quite a while back, likely around the time of the Banishing, there was a group of Fae who decided they wanted to try to purge Dundere of humans. They were, of course, unsuccessful, and their monarch decided to punish those fairies by enslaving them to humans for the remainder of their lives. My grandfather was one of the humans the Fae targeted, and so he was given one of these fairies as a slave, who he passed down to my father. Our family's fairy is named Goldemar, and he's quite the spiteful little fellow. He's always done our bidding, but he's clearly resented our entire family. Except for Aiden." He frowned. "This part is...sad."

"Tell us," Starla urged.

"Well, Aidan was a very sensitive child," Arquinn continued. "He didn't like anyone being bullied. He saw the way Father treated Goldemar and began defending him. Then he learned how to speak Fae, and Goldemar began to treat him like he was his own. Aidan was still young, so he couldn't see that Goldemar had a cruel streak, and Goldemar took advantage of his kindness.

"When Aidan was in his early teens, he began wearing this earring that he told me allowed Goldemar to speak to him telepathically. Aidan changed after that. He became more violent, more angry, and after a while he began using fairy magic, though it was inconsistent. From what Ashlynn told me, when Aidan convinced Alvin to get in on his plan to kidnap Jasper and Ruby, he gave Alvin a similar earring."

"I remember that earring," Ruby said.

"I suspect the earring was part of what led Alvin in the direction he went. Before it, he was just an angry kid whose charm abilities left him alienated. But with the earring, he became capable of murder."

"That does make sense," Ruby mused. "Killing people seemed a little extreme, even for him."

"I'm not exactly sure what happened once Alvin was imprisoned. I only know that, somehow, Goldemar escaped our parents' home and went to him. From there it gets very theoretical." He frowned. "It seems that he took over the body of this Simon fellow somehow."

My eyes widened as I recalled Claudi telling me that this exact fear was what motivated the Witch Slayers to try to rid the Woods of fairies. "How do you think he got this new body?" I asked.

"Likely, Goldemar struck a deal with Alvin. My guess is that Goldemar helped Alvin kill his cellmate, then used some sort of dark magic to transfer Alvin's consciousness into the body. From there he went after my family. By killing Father, he broke the hold that Father specifically had on him, though Goldemar still remains enslaved to our family name. So now he's bound to Alvin and they're sharing a body, though I suspect it's Goldemar, not Alvin, who's really in control. If it were Alvin pulling the strings right now, he wouldn't be so fixated on hurting Lachlann."

"Alvin doesn't hate Lachlann for killing his brother?" Kip asked.

Arquinn frowned. "Alvin likely wants revenge, but in a vague sort of way. More than that, he wants to do what I managed—run away and start over. Goldemar, on the other hand, is furious that he's lost the one human who he felt so connected to. He wishes to make specific people hurt, and his plans are complex and focused." He sighed. "This is an incredibly bad situation. An evil, powerful creature like Goldemar, in the body of a fully grown man, could hurt us far worse than in his fairy form. He's a threat to not only Lachlann, but Breoch as well, and possibly the entire Fae population of Dundere."

"What are his intentions, other than hurting Lachlann?" asked Ruby. "Do you think he has bigger plans than that?"

"I can't say for sure. He might be hoping to sway your king into doing some very dangerous things, or even take the throne for himself."

"Do you think Alvin would allow that?" Ruby's eyes were wide.

"Honestly? I doubt Alvin has much control at this point."

"Right." She sighed. "So, does this have anything to do with the fires?"

"Yes, actually," Marcus said. "After Goldemar escaped, Arquinn's father went to the king of the Dundere Fae to inform him. I think he also intended to alert the authorities, but the Blackwell family was murdered a few days later. At that point, the Fae realized they might have a very bad situation on their hands, because Goldemar may well come after them next. The fires were meant to get the humans' attention, to alert them that something is wrong and that they wanted our help."

"But Goldemar didn't go after the Dundere Fae, he came here instead." Ruby let out a long sigh.

Marcus nodded. "It's clear enough that we need to either kill or contain this Simon fellow before something drastic happens."

"I say we get Lachlann back first," put in Kip. "Once we're safe from our enemies having access to his anti-magic, we'll be stable enough to go after Simon."

"I agree," said Marcus. "Arquinn and I will need to have a long chat about what stopping Simon might look like."

There came nods of agreement from the others, and for a moment no one spoke. Then Ruby glanced pointedly at Jasper. "Well, if we're finished here, I think a few of us need to have some serious discussions." She turned to Marcus. "Can we leave now?"

Marcus nodded. "Yes, I think we can adjourn."

I sat with Kaden and Trina as Ruby went to talk with Jasper. She was scowling when she returned. "He says he needs to talk to Arquinn first. We'll have to wait."

Kaden shrugged. "Let's head home then. I'm sure he'll be along shortly."

***

A large group of us retreated to the treehouse, all eager to hear Jasper's story. It was close to an hour later that he showed up. He walked into the main room, looked us over, and shook his head. "Of course you're all here."

"Obviously." Shawnie smirked at him.

No one spoke for a few tense seconds. Then Kaden said, "I suppose I shouldn't be surprised that you have a kid we didn't know about, given what you were like when you were younger. But...*Ashlynn?*"

When Ruby looked up to speak, there was something more subdued in her tone than normal, and her voice wavered. "I remember how she talked about you when we were on our way to Dundere. She sounded like she was disgusted with you."

"I know, but..." Jasper trailed off. "Ruby, what's wrong? You look like you're about to cry."

"I just...I don't understand." She stared back at her brother. "You were the one who warned me against getting involved with the Blackwells, and yet that's exactly what you did! And now we're related to them. I'm related to...*him.*" Her face darkened.

"And I'm related to the fellow who tried to kill me twice," Jasper replied. "What does it matter?"

"Aidan is dead," Ruby argued. "Alvin isn't. He might feel like he has some sort of connection to us now, some sort of *right* to be in our lives."

Jasper frowned. "Honestly, I doubt Alvin knows that I'm the father." He paused as he spoke, as if trying to believe the words himself. "Arquinn didn't even know until Marcus told him I was looking for Tristan."

Ruby relaxed only slightly. "That still doesn't change the fact you were a hypocrite."

"Once I got to know Ashlynn, I saw her differently." His voice softened.

"Why don't you explain to them what happened with her?" Trina suggested.

Ruby gaped. "You *knew?*"

"I told her because I thought Tristan might end up in my life soon, and I figured she should know about him if she was going to date me." Jasper let out a sigh and sank down into his hammock next to Trina. "You may recall that Ashlynn didn't go back to school in Kirstein after...everything that happened with her brothers. She returned a few months later instead, on the Lady Liara's last voyage of the year between Kirstein and Dundere City.

"When she came aboard, it was obvious to me pretty quickly that she was hurting. She kept to herself and didn't talk to the other passengers much. Despite everything her family had done, I felt bad for her. So I sidled up to her one day and told her I was sorry for all her losses, and that I was around if she wanted to talk. I figured she'd brush me off, but she was more receptive than I thought, and pretty soon we were spending most of our free time together, talking about how terrible some of our respective family members were." He chuckled. "A few nights later, she'd had a bit much to drink, and she confessed to me that the main reason she was unkind on our earlier trip to Dundere was because Aidan despised me, and she felt like she had to go along with him. In truth, she told me, she actually found me attractive and was jealous of all the other girls. So, naturally, I asked her if she wanted to dance with me now, given that Aidan wasn't around to tell her what to do, and she said yes. We ended up having a lovely evening. She tried to take it further, she wanted me to kiss her, but I told her that I couldn't, because as crew I wasn't allowed.

"The voyage and our friendship continued, and there was an obvious chemistry between us. If it wasn't for everything that had happened between our families, I would have been interested in dating her. One evening, when we were a few nights away from Kirstein, she came to me with an idea.

"We'd be landing shortly before Long Night's Eve and staying in port for two weeks so crew members could go home to their families for the holiday. Her initial plan was to go directly to the school and get settled in, but she suggested we rent a room instead. I couldn't get in trouble that way, and neither of us had anyone else in Kirstein to spend the holiday with. So that's what we did." He smiled slightly. "We had a lovely two weeks and went out for a wonderful meal Long Night's Eve." His smile turned sheepish. "I did everything you're meant to do, drank the tea and all. But we were a bit...relentless."

"The tea isn't a guarantee, you know," Shawnie said, exchanging a grin with Alisa.

"Yes, I've realized that. And also, well, Ashlynn wasn't as careful as I was. She wasn't actually drinking her tea at all." His smile faded.

"Wait, what?" Trina's eyebrows raised.

"This is the part I haven't explained to you yet," Jasper said. "Shortly after Saray and Kip's wedding, Ashlynn was on the ship again, this time heading home. She was in her cabin a lot, and I heard rumour she was seasick. I also happened to be helping Kezia, the ship's doctor, who one day asked me to deliver medicine to Ashlynn. It wasn't the one we normally used for seasickness, and when I asked about it, Kezia told me Ashlynn was pregnant. I just about fainted."

"I'll bet," Shawnie said.

"So I went to Ashlynn's room and asked her when she planned on telling me about the baby. She admitted she'd hoped I wouldn't find out. Of course, I demanded to know what was going on, and she broke down and told me everything." He closed his eyes. "The short version of the story is that she used me to have a kid."

We were all silent for a long moment. "What's the long version?" I asked.

"After everything that happened with their sons, Ashlynn's parents realized she was their only chance at a legacy. They kept her from returning to school that fall—which made sense, as the whole family was grieving—but less than a month later, Mr. Blackwell began talking about finding Ashlynn a husband. She soon discovered that he'd arranged a marriage for her with a fellow called Earl, and when she met him, she got the impression he was just as callous and cruel as her father. She also realized, however, that she was the only child in good standing with her parents, and that she'd likely inherit a large sum of money. So she figured she'd do something to make herself unappealing to Earl."

"Get herself pregnant with someone else's kid," Alisa said.

Jasper nodded. "Her parents would be upset, but they likely wouldn't cut her out of their lives, because then they'd lose contact with the grandchild they wanted."

"And she chose you as the lucky fellow to help her achieve her goals?" Kaden asked, smirking.

"Exactly. She convinced her parents to let her return to school to finish her degree and decided to have a sailor knock her up on the way there. And when I befriended her, she thought I was the perfect choice. I wasn't from Dundere, she figured I'd likely give in if she tried to seduce me, and she found me attractive." One corner of his mouth turned up. "She convinced me to spend those two weeks with her, only she drank regular old lavender tea. I was drinking the right stuff, of course, but it doesn't work nearly as well if only the man is taking it. And, well, her plan worked. I was angry, but I'd also been happy enough to sleep with her, so I couldn't blame her entirely."

"Yes, but she tricked you," I said. "You agreed to sleep with her. You didn't agree to get her pregnant."

"That's true. And after she told me everything, she assured me nothing had to change on my end, I could go back to my life and keep sailing. I'd never see her or the child again unless I wanted to. In fact, she thought it'd be best if I kept my distance while she was still living with her parents; she didn't want them to know I was the father. But I remembered when Saray told me about what it was like not knowing her parents, and I figured it might be hard for my kid not knowing who their dad was. Plus, I was worried Ashlynn's parents might treat them badly." His eyes flickered to Ruby. "I haven't forgotten when Alvin showed up at Lachlann's apartment, all bruised up from a beating. I couldn't bear the thought of that happening to my kid."

Trina nodded. "I'm surprised Ashlynn wasn't worried about that herself."

"She was, a little, but she told me that once her career was underway, she'd get her own place. She also figured her parents might be softer on a grandkid than they were on their own children.

"So we arrived in Dundere and parted ways. I told her that once the child was grown, I'd be happy to meet them if they wished. Several months later, I received a letter with Tristan's name and a few details about him." His shoulders hunched. "After that, I tried to move on and act like nothing had changed. But it's very strange to know you have a child out there. It made me feel like I needed to...grow up a bit."

Kaden nodded slowly. "That certainly explains how you've changed over the last few years."

"So why didn't Goldemar target Tristan when he killed the others?" Shawnie asked.

"Arquinn isn't sure. He just knows that when he got home, Tristan was alive. He was scared and hungry and crying for his mother, but he was alive." Jasper closed his eyes. "He's stopped speaking since all that happened, retreated into himself a bit. I only hope he'll learn to find his voice again, poor kid."

"Most of us here know sign," Trina assured him. "We'll find a way to communicate with him."

"I wonder if this means Alvin still has enough control that he was able to stop Goldemar," Ruby mused. "Alvin is dangerous, but I can't see him killing a kid for no reason."

"I wonder that too," said Jasper.

"So now what?" I asked. "Is Tristan going to stay here with you?"

"That's what Arquinn is hoping. He wants to observe me for a bit, to determine whether or not I have it in me to raise a child, and also to give Tristan the chance to get to know me. If he thinks it's not going to work, he'll move along and raise him himself. That might be a little tricky, though, because Arquinn's made a life teleporting all over the world moving goods quickly, and that's not the most ideal situation for a child."

"Do *you* think you have it in you to raise him?" asked Alisa.

Jasper sighed. "I'm not sure."

"Why not?"

"It might be different if his mother was in his life. I've always wanted kids, but I'm not sure I can raise one alone."

"Alone?" Trina echoed. "Jasper, you wouldn't be raising him alone. You'd have all of us to help, if you stayed in Ankrossi. You'd definitely have my help—I told you that the night we started dating." She put an arm around him.

"And you'd have other new fathers around to talk to," put in Shawnie. "Me, and Ambrose, and Lachlann too, assuming we get him back."

Jasper nodded. "That much is true. I suppose staying here would be for the best if Tristan's going to be in my life."

"I wouldn't exactly complain about that," Trina said, leaning her head into his shoulder.

"Me neither," Kaden put in. "Ruby and I want to get to know her nephew." She glanced at Ruby. "Right?"

Ruby started. "I...uh...yes, of course." She let out a long sigh. "Sorry, this is just a lot to process."

"You're telling me," Jasper said.

"Perhaps it's time for folks to clear out," Kaden announced. "I think Ruby needs some sleep."

Alisa and Shawnie left first, followed by Kip and Saray. Ruby, meanwhile, met Jasper's gaze one last time before going to bed for the night. "I'm not mad at you," she said. "But I think I need some space." He nodded, and she disappeared into the bedroom; Kaden shot the rest of us an apologetic look before following her.

Jasper let out a long sigh, and Trina turned to him. "Do you want to stay at my place until she comes around?"

"That might be for the best." He glanced at me. "Sorry to abandon you, Isabelle."

I shrugged. "Ruby's not the only one who's tired. I'm thinking of turning in myself." I bid the two of them goodnight, then climbed up the ladder and settled into my bed, my head spinning with all the new things I'd learned tonight.

Chapter 31

ATTENDING A MEMORIAL for a well-loved man I hardly knew was odd, to say the least. I'd only had a few weeks to train with Willem, weeks that were entertaining and full of fun, but I'd only really known him as Claudi's son, not the legend that folks at the memorial described him as.

It wasn't a formal service; we all gathered around a fire, and people took turns sharing their stories. I learned about Saray's first experiences with him, how she found Willem both whimsical and intimidating, and how she'd jumped between him and Kip during a confrontation. Shawnie talked about his obsession with stringing spells together to create odd effects, and Alisa mentioned his habit of fusing magic and food. Claudi told stories of his childhood, painting him as a bright, curious, and mischievous boy who enjoyed using his teleportation abilities to scare his parents.

Kip was more somber when he shared, talking about how he'd lived with Willem while he got used to his new abilities following the life transfer, and how Willem had become something like a father to him. "Willem's been the heart and soul of magic in these Woods," he concluded, "and we've some large shoes to fill. He's the reason Saray and I are well trained, the reason magic has been practiced safely here for decades. He's guarded the magical secrets of folks all across Breoch, and he died protecting that knowledge. Today, we honour that sacrifice."

We were all quiet for a few moments. Claudi cried softly, and Kip put an arm around her. Finally, Marcus spoke. "Once it's safe to do so, we fully intend to reopen the school, and Willem will be memorialized there. For today, though, we have something a little different. Claudi, Kip and Shawnie, will you please do the ritual you have planned?"

They all nodded, and Shawnie stood, clutching the vase that contained Willem's ashes. "Willem enjoyed creating a spectacle using magic, so we've decided to celebrate that. Afterward, Alisa and I have done everything in our power to replicate Willem's magic milkshakes, and we'll be handing those out to all of you to enjoy."

Shawnie joined Kip and Claudi, and the three of them took turns reaching into the vase to scoop out handfuls of Willem's ashes and sprinkle them onto the fire. When they were finished, Shawnie put down the vase, and the three of them joined hands. Shawnie spoke the words to a spell I'd never heard, then they all took a careful step back.

I watched in amazement as the fire glowed blue and purple, the colours shifting in a fluid dance. Then a column of flame shot up into the sky, where it erupted brilliantly. The night lit up as a dazzling display of red and purple and orange fireworks ensued. A few of the younger children giggled, while others yelped and covered their ears. I stared up at the lights, enraptured, until they fizzled out.

"Magic milkshake?" Alisa interrupted my reverie with her offer.

I grinned at her and accepted the drink. "Thank you."

The concoction in my hand changed colours, and I watched it for a moment before taking a sip. The milkshake fizzed and crackled in my mouth—I couldn't quite decide what it tasted like.

It was then that Mother joined me and sat down. "It changes flavours as you drink it," she said. "Marcus told me all about these on our trip. Delicious, don't you think?"

I took another sip and held it on my tongue for a moment, noticing how it changed from berry to chocolate before I swallowed. "It's fascinating."

"Agreed." Mother sipped her own milkshake and smiled.

"How was...travelling with Marcus?"

"Very interesting. He's had quite the life in all our years apart. It was good to see where he's been, what sort of life he's lived." She chuckled. "Noelle sounds like an incredible woman. I wish I'd had the honour of meeting her."

"Me too," I admitted. Then I frowned. "Is anything...happening between the two of you?"

Mother smiled, and the way her eyes lit up told me everything I needed to know. "We said we were going to take our time, but...sometimes you just *know* someone is right for you."

"I know what you mean." I sighed and eyed my drink. "If I could get him past the typical Breochi fear of magic, I have a feeling Oliver would love these."

"He probably would," Mother agreed. "You miss him, then?"

"It's strange. With all that's happened, I'd stopped believing in your idea that Oliver and I are destined somehow. But I still can't help feeling like he's right for me." I chuckled. "I remember when I was younger, I was jealous that so many of the other girls in my school got to *choose* who they dated. But here I am now, surrounded by a bunch of lovely new people, and I'm not interested in any of them. The only person I want is the one I was going to be stuck with in the first place."

Mother nodded slowly. "If you love Oliver, then go back to him because you *want* him, not because of an old woman's dreams."

"I don't think Kairus would allow me back. And even if he did, well, I'm planning on using Oliver's sickness as leverage. I can't see Oliver being happy with me after that."

"Perhaps he wouldn't take issue with it so long as you healed him even if his father doesn't agree to our terms," Mother replied. "Perhaps you could even convince Oliver to abdicate and join us in the Woods. Then you could heal him here, and the two of you can live happily together in Ankrossi."

I smiled. "As crazy as that sounds, Oliver has admitted that he wonders if the throne is right for him."

"It's something to think about," Mother said. "But first, we need to prepare for the big day. Let's worry about those details when we get there."

***

The next several weeks passed by in a flurry of activity. I still trained with Claudi each morning, though our sessions were far, far shorter. Losing Willem seemed to have broken something in her, and she suddenly was very tired most days, barely hanging onto life yet refusing to move on. In the afternoons I would do my lessons with the other teens, Shawnie and Saray and Alisa teaching us out in the meadow, or in one of the rooms of the Mothertree if it was rainy. Kip and Jasper made good on their promise to spar with Chester while in Breoch Guard outfits, and it turned out that several other former krossemages had similar fears and wanted to take part as well. Upon realizing this, Jasper had Arquinn teleport him back home to fetch both his own and Jade's remaining uniforms, and he, Kip, Kaden and Arquinn dressed up in them to fight the others in a group, Jasper leading the other "Guard" members in tactics that the Breoch Guard actually used, so that the others would know how to better defend themselves.

Most evenings were spent preparing for the sky circus, as I began calling it. Marcus had the brilliant idea of using telekinesis to play several instruments at once while he narrated, and Alexander and Ember helped us design elaborate costumes. I watched Kip and Kaden spar with swords, each using their magic to take turns disarming the other, only for Ruby to intervene and shoot lightning out of her hands. Firebrands set trees alight, then quickly quenched the flames to show how their talents could be useful in emergencies. I saw people heat up and freeze food quickly with spells, stormbrewers create and chase away clouds, and a pair of telekinetics build a small brick structure using only hand motions. All the while, Kip and Jasper discussed their part, going over in great detail their entry and exit points from the palace, and what their contingency plans were should things fall apart. Trina worked on strengthening her fairy magic to protect whoever was performing at any given moment, and Ambrose found a few creative ways to work dragons into our endeavour.

A few weeks into our training, Jasper packed up his belongings and moved out of Ruby and Kaden's place. We thought he intended on moving in with Trina, but it turned out that he, Arquinn, and Tristan were taking over the small tree hut that had once been Trina's.

Tristan was clearly becoming more accustomed to Jasper; soon enough, he was as likely to be clinging to him as to Arquinn. The little boy still didn't talk, though, and would grow agitated if no familiar adults were within reach. Ruby began working to teach both him and Jasper sign, and Tristan seemed able to pick up on hand gestures more easily than words.

As Breoch Day approached, so did Ruby and Kaden's wedding. The home that I shared with the couple was suddenly filled with fabrics and flowers and decorations, and Alexander and Ember popped in constantly to make alterations to garments or try out a new hairstyle on Ruby.

The evening before the wedding, Jasper knocked on the door and announced that he had a surprise. Ruby shrieked in delight when Malcolm walked in with a broad smile on his face. "Grandfather!" she exclaimed as she fell into his arms.

Malcolm held her tight. "My girl," he said, his voice choked, "I've missed you more than you know."

Ruby pulled back, her eyes bright. "Are you here to stay?"

"Not quite yet—I still have business to wrap up back home. But I wasn't going to miss your wedding." He looked beyond her to Kaden. "And this must be the fiancée!"

I snuck out of the house then to let their family catch up and slept that night at Starla's place. The following morning when I went to see Claudi, she had the Sea Stone in her hands. "Isabelle, I want you to take this when you go to Kirstein."

I frowned, gazing down at it. "But I'm not the Bearer."

"I know. But you'll need it. One thing that comes with being a Bearer is good instincts, and my gut tells me you should take it." She smiled and pressed the pendant into my palm. "At the very least it will amplify your healing power, which you may well need for Oliver."

I nodded and fastened the pendant around my neck. As before, nothing happened. I closed my hand around the Sea Stone and wondered what this might mean for our plan.

∗∗∗

The following afternoon, I made my way to the cavern, Sophie and Chester flanking me. Ruby and Kaden had elected to get ready in private; only Alexander and Ember were allowed to attend to them. The cavern was decked out in flowers and greenery, and a carpet of moss had sprung up between the rows of benches in lieu of a runner. This, of course, was provided by Starla. Aria remained safely inside the Mothertree for now, but Starla had returned; in fact, she was the one Ruby and Kaden had asked to officiate their wedding. She stood at the front of the room, clad in a dress that looked to be made entirely of roses. Sophie ran up and hugged her.

Jasper and Trina hovered near the front of the cavern, holding a fiddle and a pipe, and as more people trickled in they began to play a merry tune. Folks took that as their cue to find seats, then the music eased into something slow and enchanting.

Kaden and Ruby appeared in the doorway of the cavern then, arm in arm, and we all stood as they made their way down the aisle.

Ruby's dress was light green, the skirt made of a sheer, flowing material that trailed ever so slightly behind her. The bodice was decked out in a riot of coloured daisies that looked to still be alive, and I guessed that Starla had coordinated with Alexander and Ember to make this happen. Ruby wore her long blonde curls loose, save for a crown of more daisies, and the barest hint of makeup accentuated her features.

Kaden was outfitted in silver—a shimmering silver waistcoat topped a crisp white shirt and black trousers; her black top hat sported a silver band and a large speckled grey feather; and unlike Ruby's, her makeup was dramatic. Silver wings lined her dark eyes, standing out starkly against her mahogany skin, and her lips were painted a slightly brighter red than normal. They both smiled broadly.

As the two neared Starla, a string of fairies flew around them, illuminating the scene for Trina, whose face broke out in a smile.

Starla looked Ruby and Kaden over, smiling, then began. "Friends and loved ones, we are gathered here today to join Ruby Jameson and Kaden Hunt in marriage and in magic." She looked out over the cavern. "I met these two young women during a dark time in their lives, while they were imprisoned on Yarel Island with other young krossemages. They arrived within a couple of months of one another and first bonded over subverting the status quo." She chuckled. "The farmhouse where they lived had an old piano in the living room, and Ruby and Kaden learned that while they could only play simple tunes alone, together they could make music just as well as a person with two hands.

"In my years caring for the teens, I saw many young people who dealt with their imprisonment by shutting down and disconnecting from themselves. But neither of these girls did that. They stayed alert, allowed themselves to feel, and began working on a plan to escape—a plan that might have succeeded if Jasper hadn't come along to rescue his sister." She shot Jasper an amused look. "The months that followed were difficult for Kaden, and when she and Ruby were reunited there was certainly some tension. But soon enough, they were the best of friends again, and their friendship turned to love.

"Ruby and Kaden were both involved in the building of Ankrossi, and I've watched them take ownership of our village. I've watched them develop their skills, learn how to lead, and grow their confidence, kindness, and their love for one another. I am honoured to wed them today."

I listened as Starla led them in their vows, then watched Shawnie take the stage. He looked over the two women solemnly. "Ruby and Kaden, you wish to be joined not only in life, love, and body, but also in magic. So I am going to facilitate a Joining, with the help of Trina."

I'd been told about Joinings, but it was still fascinating to watch Ruby and Kaden each cut a lock of hair and bind them. Kaden used her magic to lift the knot into the air, while Ruby conjured a tiny cloud above it. A small spark of energy flashed from the cloud to burn the hair, and the ashes fell into a bowl below. Then Trina took the stage, and she and Shawnie both worked magic on the bowl, chanting spells and adding what looked to be multiple magic potions. Finally, Shawnie took a small brush and painted the mixture onto Kaden and Ruby's lips.

Then Starla spoke. "Ruby and Kaden, I now pronounce you wives. When your lips meet, the spell will be complete, and you will be Joined in life, love, body and magic." She grinned at them. "You may kiss."

"About time," Kaden murmured, eliciting a laugh from the audience. She took a step toward Ruby and slid her hand into her new wife's locks. Ruby smiled and leaned into her.

The moment their lips met, the cavern shook.

Whether it was from the powerful wave of magic that rolled through the cavern or the sound of thunder that emanated from above, I wasn't sure. But I felt a shudder of awe go through me as the couple was suddenly illuminated in white, crackling magic, ripe with energy and raw power. Amidst all this, I thought I heard piano music, and the faint taste of cherries lingered on my tongue.

When they pulled away from each other, their hair stood on end. They gazed at one another for a long, tender moment, then Ruby burst out laughing. "You should see your hair!"

A ripple of laughter spread through the cavern, and Ruby leaned into Kaden's shoulder, shaking with mirth.

"You should see yours," Kaden retorted. She wrapped her arms around Ruby and held her for a moment before pulling back. "Look at us!"

They gazed at one another in awe for a moment longer, then Kaden leaned in and kissed Ruby once more.

Starla smiled and clapped her hands. "Friends and loved ones, may I introduce to you Mrs. Ruby and Kaden Jameson-Hunt."

Ruby and Kaden joined hands and held them high as the guests cheered uproariously. Then they made their way back down the aisle and into their future together.

***

I didn't stay long at the reception.

The party itself was wonderful, of course. The food was magnificent, and we all laughed as guests shared stories about the couple's antics. Kaden spent some time staring up at the sky moving clouds around, in awe of her new abilities, and Ruby flew from guest to guest entirely on her own. The two chose for their first dance to be above the heads of all the guests, fairies flitting about as they soared over Jasper and Trina's music.

An older man with long grey hair and a broad smile began leading the music after the first dance, and I learned he was Gareth, the captain of Jasper's old ship. A few others had accompanied him to the wedding; I guessed by their tanned, rugged faces that they were also crew members. A few of the boys asked me for dances during the faster songs, and I tried to enjoy the whirling and laughing that followed, but I couldn't ignore the hollow ache in the centre of my chest.

When the music slowed, folks returned to their spouses and partners, and I retreated to the food table to nibble on a tart, watching the couples move and hold one another close. Ruby and Kaden kept their eyes locked as they lifted above the crowd again. Shawnie and Alisa swayed together carefully, Jasper held a contented Trina close to his chest as they danced, and Marcus and my mother talked in soft tones to one another. Saray and Kip had retreated to a dim corner of the cavern and were locked in a passionate embrace. Even Sophie and Chester, while maintaining some distance between them, seemed to be fully enjoying themselves as they danced. I imagined that, with the exception of those two, most of the couples would eventually head home for an intimate evening, savouring the last night together before tomorrow's uncertainties.

I couldn't help but feel a twist of envy in my stomach. I glanced over at Starla to see if she might be willing to commiserate, but she was chatting with Malcolm, clearly happy to get to know another member of Jasper and Ruby's family. I sighed. *This is a happy event, and here I am feeling sorry for myself.* I snuck out of the cavern and went to the room where I was staying at Starla's. Only once I was alone did I let a few rogue tears trickle down my cheeks.

Tomorrow would determine so much. Everyone else was able to distract themselves tonight with food and drink and celebration, but I couldn't help feeling like, with the exception of Starla, there was more at stake for me tomorrow than for most of the Ankrossi folks. And yet...something else was bothering me, a thread of melancholy tugging at the edges of my consciousness that I couldn't name but knew wasn't about me. I sighed, pushing that thought away to focus on what I did know.

I would hopefully get my best friend back when all of this was over. And possibly my love as well. How was I supposed to laugh and enjoy myself when so much hung in the balance?

Eventually, I managed to drift off, the music from the party lulling me from my worries and into the blackness of sleep.

Chapter 32

WE ALL WOKE early the next morning, even though we didn't need to be in the city until noon.

The joyous atmosphere of the night before was gone, replaced by seriousness and a nagging sense of dread. We went over and over our roles in the coming battle—Ruby and Kaden flew high in the sky, practicing their new gifts, while Shawnie went over his cougar routine with a group of teens. Alisa, who would be staying back with the children, entertained a few of them nearby with a story. The teens had been given a choice whether to participate or not, and I was surprised when they all decided to come along. Alexander and Ember were helping folks into their costumes and fussing with hair and makeup. My own ensemble was a knee-length, pure white dress made from a thin but durable material, and my hair was piled on my head in curls. Ember skillfully gave my skin an unearthly glow using makeup—the point, they told me, was to make me look like a benevolent heavenly being, a literal bringer of life.

Finally, Marcus called us all to order. He was clad in a ringmaster's ensemble: a bright red frock coat and black top hat. "Are we all ready to move in?"

Every head in the grove bobbed.

"I feel like I'm meant to give some sort of inspiring speech right about now," he went on, "but I'm at a loss for words this morning. Does anyone else wish to say something?"

The uncertain emotions from the night before had finally begun to turn into something coherent, and so I raised my hand. "I would."

Marcus nodded. "Go ahead, Isabelle."

I walked over so I was standing next to him and looked over the faces before me. "Hi everyone," I began with a nervous chuckle. "I...uh...just wanted to say that today is so incredibly important for all of us. Last night, I had it in my head that I have more to lose than the rest of you, but I'm realizing that might not be the case." I looked over the grove, blinking back tears. "When I first showed up in Ankrossi, I was absolutely amazed. I could never have dreamed that a place like this, where magic is used freely, could exist in Breoch. But here I am." I took a deep, shaky breath. "This town you've built, it's beautiful. It's brought freedom to so many of you, and I don't doubt it'll do that for many more people in the years to come. And I want you to know that it's worth fighting for. So when you go out there today, if you're scared or discouraged, remember we're doing this for Ankrossi."

The crowd stared at me for a few seconds, unsure how to respond. Then Kip let out a whoop. "For Ankrossi!" he yelled, and I watched as everyone around me raised their fists and repeated his refrain, the air suddenly charged with excitement.

Marcus grinned and clapped my shoulder. "You're a natural at giving speeches," he said. Then he turned to Ambrose, who wore maille that appeared to be crafted from dragon scales. "All right! Your folks have their dragons ready?"

Ambrose nodded. "We'd best move now. It'll take us a bit longer than the rest of you to reach the city."

"All right, head out."

As Ambrose and Spark lifted into the sky, Marcus turned back to the rest of us. "This next part is likely one of the more difficult maneuvers we'll perform today. I need everyone with magic to spare to pour it into Arquinn and Chester."

I joined hands with Sophie on one side of me and Kaden—who wore a pair of iridescent, elaborately crafted wings—on the other. Then Shawnie stepped forward to cast the magic-sharing spell. I shuddered as I felt my own power deplete ever so slightly. The air crackled, and I became aware of the sensations of many other types of magic—cool green earth and fairy laughter and cinnamon flame, Ruby's thunder, Kaden's strange wispy magic, and many, many more. Both Arquinn and Chester flinched when our power flowed into them.

"All right, Chester, you first," Marcus said.

Chester nodded and lifted one end of the long rope that he'd brought with him. "Everyone grab on," he said. "Don't let go until I break the spell." We all obeyed, and he closed his eyes. "*Dominae Araknae Invida,*" he intoned, his words clear and strong. I gaped as the people in our circle disappeared completely, leaving the grove seeming entirely empty save for a few of the folks with children who were staying back. Tristan began to cry, and Alisa scooped him up and held him.

"Your turn, Arquinn," Marcus' disembodied voice said. "You've got our landing spot figured out?"

"I do. Kaden and I scouted it out a few days back. Hold on, everyone." After a brief pause, Arquinn spoke his own spell.

Like the last time I teleported a long distance, there came a moment of sheer whiteness and silence, of floating and being *nowhere* exactly. Then the nothingness was gone, and we were in the middle of another grove of trees, this one much smaller and alive with the noise of singing birds. I could hear the clip-clop of horseshoes on cobblestones nearby and the hum of crowds. "Everyone here?" asked Marcus.

There came a ripple of murmurs in response. "Keep holding on to the rope," Kip's voice instructed us now. "We're going to walk from here to that small group of pines next to the palace wall. Once we're there, Starla will perform some magic on the trees, then we can let the invisibility spell drop. Starla, lead the way."

Soon enough, I felt Kaden tug on my hand, and I followed in the direction she pulled me. There were a good hundred of us participating, and I watched the grass flatten as we emerged from our grove and made our way through the park to the palace walls across the street. The courtyard was packed, and I let out a small gasp as I recalled the last time I'd seen this exact place filled with so many people. I could only imagine how being here made Saray feel.

We packed ourselves into the small cluster of trees, and Starla began working her magic ever so slowly, thickening the foliage around the base to hide us from view while causing the largest tree to grow taller. Then Chester's spell dropped, and I found myself staring back at the others in our group.

"If you can climb or fly, try to get higher up," Marcus urged us. "Stay quiet, and try not to be seen yet. Trina, start working your protection spell on the tree. Kip, Jasper, get Arquinn to take you to your spot."

I began to clamber up the trunk and chose a solid branch where I had a good view of the palace courtyard. I grinned when Kaden deposited Trina next to me. "Keep her safe," Kaden instructed.

"I have fairies for that," Trina shot back. "No offense." She would be hiding in the tree for most of the show; nonetheless, Alexander and Ember had crafted for her a dress that made her look like a larger version of the tiny, luminous beings dancing around her. She closed her eyes and began to cast her spell.

I leaned forward to scan the courtyard stage. Kairus was easy to see from here, made more visible by his red robe and sparkling crown. I squinted at the others. There was the queen, of course, and a handful of guards. I sighed when I picked out Simon standing near Calendra. On the other side of her, perched on a stool, was a green-clad figure who I knew must be Oliver. My chest constricted at the sight of him.

Marcus climbed up onto the branch next to Trina, Jasper's fiddle and bow in one hand. "Are we ready?"

"Ready as we can be," Trina said to him. Kaden flew up, put a hand on Marcus' shoulder, and mumbled her spellwords, then Trina did the same.

"All right. We're breaking up their solemn ceremony in three, two, one..."

Marcus shot into the sky along with a burst of fireworks and dancing flame. "Residents of Kirstein," he addressed the crowd, his voice amplified by magic, "Happy Breoch Day from the people of the Shrouded Woods!" Marcus let go of Jasper's fiddle as he spoke, and it began to play a lively tune all on its own, thanks to a spell Alexander had put on it.

The crowd reacted exactly how we expected; they began gasping in astonishment and pointing, some even shrieking when they turned away from Kairus toward the spectacle in the sky. Guards shouted orders, and one shot at Marcus, only for the bullet to bounce off the protective shield that Trina had placed around him.

"One of the great legacies of Breoch, and the reason it was inhabited in the first place, was its proximity to magic," Marcus continued. "Unfortunately, events that took place several decades ago led to the banishing of a great power that could be used for our good, for our protection. And we, the Woods-folk, want to remind you of the many ways that magic could be useful in your everyday lives, if only you allow it to be utilized." As he spoke, Ruby and Kaden flew out to meet him. "The first that we will demonstrate is how the weather patterns can be changed for optimal crop growth."

I watched Ruby and Kaden work their storm magic, conjuring clouds and rain and a single fork of lightning before driving them safely away. Starla was up next; she coaxed the tree branch she was perched on to lengthen and bloom. Then a strawberry bush grew from her hand, and she allowed the fruit to fall into the crowd.

Below me, Arquinn's voice called up to us. "Kip and Jasper are in. Keep up the show, this'll take some time."

Our demonstration unfolded precisely as we'd practiced, and we gripped the attention of the royal family, the Breochi people, and, most importantly, the palace guard. A large contingent of them rushed the base of our tree, only to find themselves unable to clear the magic shield that surrounded the bottom. A few others fired guns and arrows, but none met their mark.

Meanwhile, in the sky, Shawnie transformed into a cougar, and Daisy and a few of the teens fended him off. A firebrand whose name I didn't know, dressed in a robe that looked like flame, used her fire spell to cook a loaf of bread in seconds, and one of the older mages used a transmutation spell to turn dead pinecones into ripe vegetables. Then Kaden was back in the sky above the crowd, fighting a new opponent. The other girl mumbled her spellwords and disappeared, easily disarming Kaden.

Kaden's sword plummeted, and it clanged against the roof of the old bell tower where Oliver and I used to play, before hurtling downward.

My eyes fell on the crumbling tower, and my heart nearly stopped.

Wait a minute.

"Trina," I said, "how much do you remember from your vision of Lachlann?"

"A fair bit," she replied. "Why?"

"The tower he was in—was it round or square?"

She closed her eyes for a moment. "Square."

"And were the windows small slits or large and covered in latticework?"

"The second one," she replied, frowning. "Most of the towers in the palace are round with small windows, aren't they? That doesn't make sense."

"It makes perfect sense." I gazed up at the bell tower. "I know exactly where Lachlann and the kids are. I need to get into the palace somehow, to let Kip and Jasper know. Otherwise they'll waste time searching in all the wrong places."

Trina's eyes widened. "You'd best figure out a way to get to them, then."

"Kip put the guards at the south entrance to sleep," I recalled. "I'll go in that way." Then I sighed. "The only trouble is, I'll forfeit my place in the show. And I'm needed at the very end."

"Get Arquinn to teleport you. I'll let the others know; we'll cover for you. Now go!"

I scrambled down the tree and took off at a run, intent on reaching the entrance. I sprinted alongside the palace wall, then skittered around a corner, gasping for breath.

And found myself face to face with a Breoch Guard.

The man snarled at me, brandishing his gun. "Stop right where you are, witch."

I froze, my heart pounding as I realized I had no spells to protect me. My mind went to the enchanted knife tucked into my belt. *Can I grab it without him noticing?*

My eyes must have darted to my belt, because the guard snickered. "Hands where I can see them, girl."

I raised them slowly but lifted my chin as I did so, giving him my best icy stare. "Do you know who I am?"

He snorted. "You're a witch, that's all I know."

"I am Isabelle McAllister, daughter of Lord Caspa and Lady Lillian McAllister, and the betrothed of Prince Oliver himself. I don't think His Highness would be very pleased about the way you're treating me right now."

He let out a sharp laugh. "Oh, yes, I know about you. You're the little whelp who ran off into the Woods with her trollop of a mother! We've all heard the stories, we—"

He stopped suddenly, his eyes bulging. Then he keeled forward, and I saw the hilt of a dagger protruding between his shoulder blades.

"Run, Isabelle! I'll deal with him." The familiar voice came from above. I looked up to see Chester materialize, clearly still suspended by Ruby and Kaden's magic. He floated down and retrieved his dagger.

"No need to run, I'll take you!" Arquinn appeared by my side a moment later. He grabbed my hand and teleported us away, leaving Chester to finish off the Guard.

We rematerialized directly in front of the unguarded south entrance. "Thank you," I gasped. "Do you think Chester can handle that Guard alone?"

"I'll go check on him," he assured as he released my hand. "Now go!"

***

Getting into the palace was easy. Finding Kip and Jasper took a little longer.

I kept my head up, walking quickly down the passageways and scouring the halls that connected the four perimeter towers. This proved unsuccessful, so I moved inward.

When I finally did manage to find them, I almost didn't realize who they were. Both men had tucked their hair completely into their caps, and it was hard to recognize Kip without his mane of long brown hair or Jasper without his signature curls.

"There you are!" I breathed a sigh of relief.

"What are you doing here?" Kip asked.

"I've figured out where Lachlann is, and it's not here. Follow me; I'll show you."

They exchanged a confused glance but trailed after me. In the rear courtyard, I pointed up at the bell tower. "Oliver and I used to play there as kids. I asked Trina what she saw in the vision, and it matches perfectly with what I remember."

Kip eyed the tower. "Tempting to use a teleport spell to get up there," he mumbled. "Though if that's where the anti-magic is coming from, fairy magic might not even cut through it."

"If they got the kids and Lachlann up there somehow, then there has to be a way."

He chuckled. "It's not that I'm thinking of. It's the prospect of climbing all those stairs."

"Oh, come on." Jasper snorted. "You, daunted by a few stairs? It's good exercise."

"I s'pose so...All right, lead the way, Isabelle."

***

Climbing to the top of the tower was harder than I remembered, the spiral staircase narrow and twisting. We reached the part that had crumbled halfway up and saw it was supplemented with wooden blocks. A pang went through me when I realized that Oliver likely couldn't climb the stairs now.

All three of us were panting by the time we reached the door to what had once been Oliver's and my hideout. My heartbeat picked up as I reached for the knob, then I grimaced and glanced at Jasper. "Do I recall you saying you know how to pick locks?"

"Let's try this first." Jasper pulled a large key ring from his uniform and began testing what was on it. He let out a huff when none of them worked. "Lock picking it is," he mumbled and retrieved a slender metal instrument from another pocket.

It only took him a moment to get us in. The room was nothing like it had been when Oliver and I were young—the rickety wooden furniture that we used to make forts and the moth-eaten books we read together had all been removed. The space was barren now, save for a dozen mats and blankets, a privacy screen, and a handful of kids.

They looked just like they had when I saw them last, only thinner and dirtier. Their clothes were threadbare, their hair unkempt, and a couple of the older boys sported patchy beards. The room reeked of sweat and dirt and likely the contents of what was behind the privacy screen. They regarded Jasper warily, but their eyes widened when they saw me.

Then Silva stepped forward. Her face had gone white, and her eyes were round with fear. "Isabelle?" she whispered. "By the Fae, please don't tell me they've..." She trailed off, her eyes glistening.

Oh. I hadn't thought of how my coming here, escorted by two men in guard uniforms, would look. "I'm not anyone's captive," I assured, raising my hands to show her I wasn't in chains. "We're here to get you out."

Behind me, Kip removed his cap and let his hair fall free. "Miss me, kids?" he said, grinning.

The room erupted into squeals, and several of the children lurched forward to embrace him. Silva, though, made a beeline for me, and we collided, her thin body nearly crushing me in an embrace. She didn't cry, but her body shook furiously as she clung to me.

"I thought I'd never see you again," I whispered, blinking back tears as I fought to maintain my composure. "I was scared they were going to..." My voice broke, and Silva buried her face in my shoulder, gripping me even tighter.

Charlotte joined us and wrapped her arms around us both. "Who's that?" she asked me quietly, and when I looked up I saw she was staring at Jasper.

"He's with us," I assured. "Not a real guard."

"We're going to get you kids out of here," Kip was telling the others now. "But it's too dangerous to go down the stairs and out into the courtyard. The best way to free you would also mean freeing Lachlann and breaking the anti-magic hold on this place."

Something in the mood of the room shifted. "Lachlann has an idea to break the anti-magic," Charlotte told him. "But none of us like it."

"Well, let's go talk to him." Jasper turned to Kip. "How about Isabelle and I head upstairs, and you get ready to teleport these kids out?"

"Where are you taking us?" one of them asked.

"Mr. Jeffries is nearby; I'm going to get you to him using this, along with a bit of fairy magic." Kip held up a teleport stone. "He'll take you home."

"Can I stay back?" Silva asked.

"You don't want to see your parents?"

She shook her head. "They'd have me made into a krossemage if they knew about my magic. It's safer for me here. And I want to stay with Isabelle."

Kip nodded. "All right. Teleport to Mr. Jeffries with me and tell him, and if he's fine with it, you can stay back."

"Isabelle and I had best go see Lachlann," Jasper said. "The rest of you, get ready."

"You'd best be careful if you're going to go upstairs dressed like that," Silva warned him. "Lachlann will likely attack you if he thinks you're just another guard."

"Why?"

"He has his own plan to get us out, and the first part involves attacking a guard and then..." She averted her eyes. "You'd best ask him to explain it. But be careful."

"We will." I gave Silva's shoulders a squeeze. Then I let her go and followed Jasper up the stairs.

When we stepped through the door into the bell tower, I was hit by a rush of memories. It looked similar to what I remembered, save for a massive chunk of stone in the centre of the room, from which a thick chain extended and curved behind the door. Jasper glanced around, hands raised. "Lachlann?" he called out. "We're not here to hurt you, we just—"

He was cut off mid-sentence by something tackling him.

Jasper let out a grunt and sprawled onto the stones, then Lachlann was on top of him, pinning him down with an arm across his chest. His hand went to Jasper's throat, and Jasper's eyes bulged. "Lach...stop...it's me..." he choked out, but his words were nearly incomprehensible.

I took a deep breath and dove into the fray, knocking Jasper's cap off his head to reveal his curls. Then I grabbed Lachlann by the shoulder and shook hard. "Hey!" I demanded. "Stop trying to kill Jasper!"

Lachlann looked at me, then Jasper, and pulled back immediately. "What?..."

"Easy, it's all right. We're here to help," Jasper said.

Lachlann let him go and stood, still staring at us in bewilderment. I gaped back at him—in some ways, he hardly resembled the man I remembered. His hair had grown longer and wilder, the grey in his now-bushy beard more pronounced. He wore only breeches and an animal-skin vest, his metal hand was missing, and his bare arms were marked by pale scars that stood out against his tanned skin. As Trina had described in her vision, the anti-magic pendant between his collarbones had somehow been fused to a larger stone, which bit into his flesh. It was fastened to the long chain I'd noticed earlier, which connected it to the massive aro stone in the centre of the tower, just below the bell. Several smaller pendants hung off the globe.

Something in Lachlann's eyes was different now; the calm, friendly demeanor I'd seen in him before was gone, replaced by something fierce, desperate.

Jasper saw the desperation too. "It's good to see you again," he said, his tone turning soothing. "We're here to get you out."

Lachlann frowned and glanced toward the stairs. "What about the children?"

"Kip is teleporting them out with fairy magic. Don't worry, they're safe."

Lachlann's shoulders relaxed visibly, and he let out a long sigh. "Thank the Fae," he mumbled, then looked to me. "You're...Silva's friend. The lifebringer."

I nodded. "Isabelle. It's good to see you again."

"Isabelle is the reason your daughter's alive," Jasper informed.

Lachlann's head snapped up. "My...Starla's given birth already?" He shook his head. "I have no idea what month it is anymore."

"Aria was born very premature, and she would have likely died if not for Isabelle's intervention."

"Aria." Lachlann repeated the name, his voice turning soft. He looked away for a moment, and when his gaze returned to me his eyes glistened. "Thank you," he said, his voice ragged. "I can't thank you enough."

I nodded and gave him a nervous smile. "You'll get to meet her soon, once we get you out of here."

Lachlann sighed, and his shoulders slumped. "You won't be able to," he said, gesturing to the large stone in the centre of the room. "I'm sorry, but it's impossible."

"What is that, exactly?" Jasper asked.

"It's how they stole my anti-magic. It's how the Breoch Guard is now acting with all the power of Bonded anti-mages, and it's what's protecting the castle from all magic right now. There's no way for me to escape from it. Believe me, I've tried."

"We have a plan to get you out of that. Watch." Before Lachlann could protest, Jasper went to stand beside the chain and touched his pendant to summon a flame. He brought it close to the chain link like he'd practiced, reducing the fire to a single, tiny point of nearly blue-white heat. The metal began to glow red.

Then Jasper's flame sputtered out.

"What?" he muttered. "I swear it worked before..." He spoke the spellwords again, and the fire reignited on his hands, only to die the moment he applied it to the chain.

"It's not going to work," Lachlann told him.

"How do you know?"

"Because the links are aro stone coated in iron. You can heat up the metal all you like, but the moment your fire touches the stone, it's going to die. And you can't melt stone, not without temperatures far hotter than you or I could create." He sighed. "I told you, I'm stuck here."

Jasper eyed him. "That stone can't be cut out of your chest?"

"Not without killing me. But I have a plan to stop all this." Lachlann stepped between us and the stairs and squared his shoulders. "There's a fellow here in the palace who wants to make me suffer, and he's doing that by hurting the people I love."

"We know about Alvin. And we know what he did to force your cooperation."

Lachlann's eyes narrowed. "So you see how grave a situation I'm in, then. He has an incredible amount of leverage against me. You two may be able to rescue the children, but he knows where Ankrossi is now, and he could easily target my loved ones. So long as I'm in here, powering this thing, the Breoch Guard and Witch Slayers will be able to hunt and torture magikai with ease, and everyone I love is at risk. There's only one way to end this." He lifted his chin. "I have to die."

Jasper shook his head, eyes wide. "There has to be another solution."

"There isn't." Lachlann's voice was firm. "Believe me, I've tried to come up with something for months, but there's no alternative." He held out his hand. "I need your gun, Jasper, and if you don't give it to me, I *will* fight you for it."

"We have to at least try to get you out. You have family back home. You have a child. Don't you want to meet Aria?"

"Of course I do." Lachlann's voice wavered for a moment, but he held Jasper's gaze. "I desperately want to meet her, and to be with my wife and all the people I care about. But more than that, I want them to be *safe*. And so long as I'm alive, they aren't." He sighed. "Put yourself in my shoes, Jasper. Imagine that someone was using you to hurt the people you love. Ruby, Kaden, Trina, all your friends on the ship. Imagine the only way to stop this was to end your own life. You'd do it too, I know you would. Now, please, let me have your gun. I don't want to have to fight you for it."

Jasper held his gaze for a moment. Then his shoulders slumped, and he looked away, handing his gun to Lachlann. "It's loaded."

"Thank you. This isn't your fault, you understand?"

Jasper nodded but didn't meet Lachlann's eyes.

"I mean that. You may have just saved the lives of a lot of people we both care about." He motioned to the door with his head. "You'd best leave now. I don't want you to be here when I do this."

"No." Jasper put a hand on Lachlann's shoulder. "Isabelle can wait downstairs for me. I'm not about to let you die alone."

Lachlann looked as if he was about to protest, but he nodded instead. Then he put the gun on the ground next to him and extended his hand to me. "Will you take my wedding ring and give it back to Starla? Sorry, it's hard to remove it myself with only one hand."

I nodded and began to work the band off his ring finger. "Make sure she understands why I did this," he said, his voice catching. "Make sure she knows that I love her, and that this was the only way I saw. And when Aria is old enough to understand, make sure she knows as well." A lone tear trickled down his cheek.

Jasper put an arm around Lachlann's shoulders. "We'll tell them."

I nodded and took the ring from him. Lachlann knelt on the ground and picked up the gun. "You'd best leave."

I began to walk away but glanced back when I reached the stairs. Lachlann was on his knees, and Jasper stood behind him, a hand on his shoulder. Lachlann slowly raised the gun to his temple, and I heard the click of the bullet moving into place.

My heart hammered in my chest. *Look away,* my mind screamed, but I couldn't stop staring.

Then Jasper's head snapped up. "Wait! Stop!"

Lachlann hesitated and lowered the gun.

"I have an idea," Jasper went on. "We might be able to stop all of this and still save you."

"How?" I didn't miss the skepticism in Lachlann's voice.

"Do you remember that story Alexander and Ember told us years ago, about the theory their friends had to rid a person of their anti-magic? Well, Isabelle is a lifebringer, so what if we tried that first?"

Lachlann glanced back at me and frowned. "I'd forgotten about that conversation. That...might actually work." I detected a note of hope in his voice. Then he turned to Jasper. "Do you remember what the plan needs, besides a lifebringer?"

"Someone who's willing to kill you," Jasper said.

Lachlann stood and met his eyes. "Will you be that person? Knowing there's a chance this might not work?"

Jasper took a deep breath and nodded slowly. "If it's the only alternative to you putting a bullet in your brain, then yes. A broken neck was the best method, right?"

I put my hands on my hips. "Would one of you please explain what you're talking about?"

Jasper turned to me, and I listened as he told me all about the conversation he, Ruby and Lachlann had with Alexander and Ember shortly before boarding the Lady Liara. "That sounds pretty risky," I said when he was finished.

"It *is* risky," Lachlann replied. "But I suppose it's better than my original plan, where I have no chance at all of surviving."

"Right."

Lachlann and Jasper began discussing logistics, and my head spun. *Can I do this?* I'd healed Saray's broken neck without too much trouble, but I hadn't been the one to actually put her life back into her. *What if I fail?*

"I suppose we have to get the scariest part over with first," Lachlann said, removing his vest. He knelt on the ground facing the window, through which we could see the circus unfolding in the sky. "Our friends are putting on quite a show...All of that is so you can get the kids and me out?"

"That's right," Jasper said.

Lachlann peered back and met his gaze. "If this doesn't work, make sure to let everyone know that I love them. And you're not allowed to blame yourself, all right? Neither of you are." He looked at me, and I nodded.

"We'll let them know if we have to," Jasper said, his voice tinged with nervousness. "But hopefully you can tell them yourself."

"Of course." Lachlann took a deep breath. "Are you ready?"

"As ready as I can be."

"Good. Me too."

Lachlann closed his eyes, and Jasper put his hands on his neck. For a moment, neither of them moved; all was silent save for the sound of the performance beyond us and their anxious breathing.

Then the music changed, and Jasper let out a shaky laugh. "Hey, Lachlann," he said, "there's something you should see before we do this."

"What's that?" Lachlann opened his eyes.

"Take a look at who's about to perform."

As Jasper spoke, Saray shot into the sky, illusory fire blazing on both hands. I heard the crowd let out a collective gasp, and Lachlann inhaled sharply, glancing back at Jasper. "Saray? She's *alive?*"

"That she is."

"Why didn't you tell me earlier?"

"Oh," Jasper said, his tone turning lighthearted, "I just wanted to see the look on your face when you saw her." Then his hands moved, lightning fast, and he snapped Lachlann's neck.

Chapter 33

THE MOMENT LACHLANN slumped and fell, I felt a strange crackle in the air. Then the heaviness I'd been accustomed to vanished, and healing magic surged through my body. Something was happening to Saray, too. From the window, I watched her begin to convulse, and then a pale, iridescent light surrounded her, the false fire on her hands replaced with true, white-hot gusts of flame. "The spell broke," I whispered.

Jasper nodded as he lowered Lachlann to the ground, rolling him onto one side. "That worked well. Now let's move. We've got four minutes."

He held Lachlann's head in place, so that his spine was properly aligned, and nodded at me. Kneeling, I closed my eyes, placed my hands on the back of Lachlann's neck, and started to sing. I felt the power begin to suffuse my body almost immediately, my magic surging down my arms, through my hands, and into his spine. Almost involuntarily, my song became louder, more mournful. I felt the bones begin to repair themselves under my hands, then the faint tingling that told me my work was done. I opened my eyes. "It should be healed."

"Good." Jasper turned Lachlann onto his back then.

"What's happening here?" I looked up and met Kip's gaze. Silva stood next to him, her eyes wide as she surveyed the scene. I didn't miss the accusatory note in Kip's voice.

"Lachlann wanted us to kill him in order to break the anti-magic hold on the kids and Ankrossi," Jasper explained, pulling on the stone in Lachlann's chest. It came out far easier than I expected, leaving only a bloodied hole behind.

"And you...*did?*"

"Not without a plan to bring him back," Jasper said, nodding to me as I closed up the wound in Lachlann's chest. "Remember how we were going to try to trust each other more? Trust me now."

I placed both my palms on Lachlann and concentrated hard, funnelling all my magic into my hands, then began to sing as the magic passed through me into Lachlann's body.

Nothing happened.

Come on, work!

My singing grew louder, and I found myself reaching for the Sea Stone, despite the fact it was not really mine, to see if it would somehow aid me. When it did not respond, I squeezed my eyes shut, trying to pour my own physical and mental energy into the spell. My head began to swim, and for a moment I worried I would end up performing an accidental life transfer, using all of my own vitality to restart Lachlann's heart. Jasper must have seen me begin to waver, because his hand shot out and caught my arm. "Are you all right?"

I opened my eyes. "It's not working," I whispered.

"I can lend you some magic," Kip said.

"I have a better idea," Jasper told him. Then, gently, he placed his own hands on top of mine. "Try again."

"What are you doing?"

"Just trust me. Try again, all right? Quickly, we're running out of time."

I nodded, closed my eyes, and began to sing again, funnelling my magic—as inadequate as it felt—into Lachlann's body. Jasper sang along with me, his voice warm and rich. The Sea Stone began to burn against my chest, as if trying to lend its power to me, and at the same time I became aware of another source of magic joining my own. I felt a flash of the familiar pure white, pineapple-flavoured healing magic, but also something deeper—the scent of the sea, the faint music of a fiddle, and a potent sense of adventure and anticipation. My magic felt lighter, more buoyant, as if it were being carried by this new entity. I felt power return to my limbs; my own magic became, once again, a force to be reckoned with. I sang with all my might and directed my power, intertwined with the new source, into Lachlann's body.

When I felt the faintest pulse of a heartbeat under my hands, I gasped.

"It's working," Jasper said, though his voice was strained. I looked at him for a second and saw that his eyes were squeezed shut, his jaw clenched.

The heartbeat beneath my palms grew in power and began to steady. Then Lachlann coughed.

Kip moved in, turning Lachlann onto his side so he wouldn't choke. Lachlann coughed a couple more times, took a few deep, sputtering breaths, then opened his eyes. I sat back, relief and fatigue flooding my body. Jasper fell onto the cobblestones, gasping.

"Welcome back," he said to Lachlann.

Lachlann sat up slowly, then turned to me, his eyes wide. "You did it."

"*We* did it." I eyed Jasper to see if he needed help.

"I'll be fine. I heal fast." He gave me a wink and slowly got to his feet.

"Kip!" Lachlann exclaimed then, noticing we were not alone.

Kip offered Lachlann a hand, pulling him to his feet and embracing him tightly.

"Did you get the kids out?" Lachlann asked.

"They're on their way back to Sylvenburgh with your brother. Except for this one, she wanted to stay back." He nodded at Silva.

"I don't think it's safe for me to go home," Silva explained. "And I wanted to stay with Isabelle." She looped her arm into mine.

Lachlann looked us over, then his eyes travelled to Kip and Jasper standing next to one another. "You two are working together now, huh?"

Kip nodded. "We decided it was time to grow up and put the past behind us. Though it seems Jasper neglected to tell me a few important things...Since when can you heal people?"

Jasper averted his eyes. "I'm not very good. I'm what's called a demi-mage."

Kip lifted an eyebrow. "Are you now?"

"What's a demi-mage?" Silva asked.

"I'll explain later," Jasper assured. "Right now, we need to get out of here."

"What's the plan?" asked Lachlann.

"I have to get down to the magic show," I said. "I think they're stalling and waiting for me to come back."

"You want me to teleport you?" Kip asked.

I frowned, considering my options. "Yes, right onto that stage, if you can. I want to look Kairus in the eyes when I make him my offer."

"Don't you need to perform a healing in front of him to prove your abilities?" Jasper asked.

"We've got someone right here whose missing hand I could restore." I eyed Lachlann. "If you're all right with that."

Lachlann glanced down at his stump. "I suppose it might be time to get my real hand back," he conceded. "But is it safe for us to get that close to the king?"

"I won't be in danger." I turned to Kip. "Do you know a spell to protect the rest of you?"

He nodded. "I can use a shield spell."

"All right, so we teleport in, you shield yourself and the others, and I'll go speak to Kairus."

Kip nodded. "If that's what you need to play your part. Are you ready, Lachlann?"

Lachlann donned his vest and held Jasper's gun out to him. "Keep it," Jasper said, giving Lachlann the holster as well.

We all clustered around Kip then. "Everyone grab onto me," he said. Once we were all holding on, he spoke the spellwords, and a split second later we stood on the edge of the stage, facing the crowd.

However, all eyes were still fixed firmly on Marcus, who hovered above everything, reciting the many uses for telekinesis. He saw us materialize beneath him, and his eyes widened when he realized we had Lachlann. "I've got this!" I called to him. "Announce me."

Marcus grinned. "Esteemed guests, may I now present the final act of our show, which will demonstrate one of the best uses of magic available. Please direct your attention to the stage, and welcome Kirstein's own Lady Isabelle McAllister!"

All eyes fell on me, but I kept my gaze focused unwaveringly on the king, dropping into a proper curtsy.

"Isabelle?" Kairus said. "What is this?"

The guards had moved toward me but were clearly instructed not to attack. My eyes met Oliver's for a moment, and my heart skipped a beat. I wanted to run to him, to throw my arms around his frame and tell him how much I cared, that I was here to help. Instead, I gave him a quick smile, dipped my head at Calendra, then turned back to Kairus.

"Your Majesties, Your Highness," I said, "I am here on behalf of the magic community of Breoch. I wish to demonstrate for you a type of magic that could benefit both the nation as a whole, and your family specifically."

Kairus' eyes narrowed, but he nodded slowly. "Go on."

"I'm a lifebringer," I told him. "A healer. You've known me most of my life, correct? Tell me, have you ever once seen me ill?"

"A healer," he repeated slowly. Beside him, Oliver's eyes were round.

I nodded. "Until recently, I could only heal myself, or minor things on others. But I've been learning, and I believe that with a bit of preparation, I could now cure deadly diseases." I met Oliver's eyes and gave him a small smile. "Would you like me to demonstrate my abilities?"

The audience had gone quiet, waiting to hear the king's answer to my question. When I shot a glance into the crowd, I realized our friends stood on the periphery of the assembly, surrounded by a bubble of protection.

Kairus looked me over. "Please do."

I glanced back and nodded at Lachlann, who came forward to join me and bow to Kairus.

Kairus gaped at him for a moment, then glanced up at the bell tower in disbelief. When he looked back to Lachlann again, his brows were knitted with confusion. "How did you get out?"

"We couldn't let you keep him anymore; his anti-magic was being used to target the Woods-folk," I said. "Now, as you are aware, Lachlann here is missing a hand. I would like to restore it here in your presence so you'll believe me when I speak of my gift. After that, I have an offer for you."

Kairus opened his mouth to respond, but he was interrupted.

"This is ridiculous, sire!" Simon stalked toward the king, sneering at Lachlann with eyes that flashed golden. Beside me, Lachlann drew in a sharp breath and wrapped his hand around the barrel of his pistol.

"This man," Simon said, pointing at Lachlann, "is a traitor to Breoch. He's aided witches in their practice, allowed them to teach magic to this nation's children, and he's a murderer!"

"Murderer?" Kairus repeated, his eyes narrowing.

"After Isabelle has healed him, what do you intend to do? Let him wander free again?" Simon began to twirl his braid as he spoke. "He should never have been released from the tower, let alone be given a new hand. Allowing Isabelle to use witchery is a breach of the Banishing, and I—"

"That's enough!" Kip snapped, stepping out of the protective bubble. He gripped a pendant in one hand and made a complex motion with the other. Simon was immediately silenced and began frantically clawing at his throat.

"Isabelle!" Kairus' eyes flickered to Kip. "What did he just do?"

"I'm sorry, Your Majesty, but it was the only way to stop Simon from using his own magic on you." I turned to Lachlann. "Tell the king what Simon has been doing."

Lachlann nodded. "Your Majesty, Simon is what's known among magic folk as a charmer. He has the ability to persuade others to do what he wishes and has been using this gift on you since he arrived. He used it to convince you to take me captive, and he used it to encourage unorthodox torture methods to be used on me. He also has access to the magic of the fairies, which means he can work despite the presence of anti-magic."

Kairus frowned. "That's a bold claim."

"I'm aware, Your Majesty. But you don't seem so cruel a man as to allow the killing of children in order to gain my cooperation, so I can only assume that the order came from Simon."

"I didn't allow..." Kairus paused and thought for a moment. "Wait. Yes, I did, didn't I? I allowed Simon to..." His head snapped up, and he glared at Simon. "Seize—"

A small knife flew from Simon's hand before Kairus could finish speaking. I gasped as the blade opened the king's throat with one easy slice, then clattered to the ground.

Kairus' eyes went wide, and he clutched at his neck, gasping. Blood gushed from between his fingers in great spurts, drenching his robes and turning the stage below him slick and red. Then he collapsed to the ground, very obviously dead.

Chapter 34

THE COURTYARD ERUPTED into screams.

"Kairus!" Calendra cried, her face turning white.

Oliver struggled to his feet. "Arrest him!" he shouted.

A handful of guards lunged at Simon, but I was too preoccupied with the fallen king to pay attention to them. Without so much as a second thought, I lurched for Kairus. "Help me get him on his back!" I called to Lachlann.

Oliver took a few unsteady steps to join us, then knelt next to his father. "What are you doing?" he demanded as Lachlann and I rolled Kairus over.

"Trust me," I said, then placed my hands on Kairus' opened throat.

I closed my eyes and began to sing, pouring all the magic that remained in me into my spell. I felt his flesh close within seconds, then paused and checked for a pulse. Nothing.

"He's lost too much blood," Jasper said, crouching down next to Lachlann. "We'll need to restart his heart."

I took a deep breath; I was already feeling dizzy just from healing the wound. "I don't know if I have the strength."

"I'll help you," he assured. "Come on, we can do this together."

I nodded slowly, pulled open the king's tunic, and placed my hands on his bare chest. Jasper put his hands on mine, and together we began to sing, willing Kairus' blood to replenish itself and his heart to begin beating again. The pendant around my neck started to burn, but this time it didn't seem to be lending me its power. My head swam, and halfway into our song I felt myself keeling forward. Jasper reached out to catch me. "Isabelle, what's wrong?"

"I...I'm too weak," I gasped. "Healing Lachlann, and now him...it's too much." My eyes flickered to Oliver, who gaped at us. "I'm sorry. I thought I'd be able to do it, but..."

I trailed off then as a thought popped into my head. I looked down at the Sea Stone. *It only burned when Jasper was singing along with me.*

I reached back to unclasp the pendant and thrust it at Jasper. "Put this on."

He stared back at me. "You think *I'm* the Bearer?"

"It's not working for me, and you're the only other person who has even the slightest ability to heal. Do you accept the role?"

He gaped for a moment and then nodded. "If I'm right for it, then, yes, I do." Taking the pendant from me, he fastened the chain around his neck.

Nothing happened for a second, and my heart sank. Then he let go of the stone—as soon as it touched his chest, the same pure white light that had enveloped Trina and Saray upon accepting their new roles now surrounded Jasper. I gaped at him, more than a little surprised that my theory was correct. When the light receded, I saw that his hands still glowed slightly, the power needed to heal the king nearly visible. He stared at them for a long moment. "I'm...the Bearer," he murmured.

"That you are," I said, my eyes wide.

Jasper's head snapped up, and he stared past me, eyes narrowed. "Claudi?" he whispered. "She's..."

"Please," Oliver interrupted desperately, "can you bring him back now? We don't have much time."

"Right. I'll try." Jasper put his palms on the king's chest. He closed his eyes, took a deep breath and resumed his song. I noticed that his face looked more relaxed as he sang, his shoulders less hunched, as if performing the healing took notably less effort than his earlier attempts had required. The light faded slowly from his hands, and Jasper opened his eyes. We both stared at Kairus expectantly.

Seconds later, he convulsed and began to cough.

"It's working!" I exclaimed as Jasper rolled him onto his side.

Calendra rushed to stand over her husband's bloodied form. "Is he alive?"

Kairus opened his eyes and stared up at her and Oliver.

"Thank the Fae!" she exclaimed.

"I...what happened?" mumbled Kairus. He touched his neck, then stared at his hand when it came away bloodied.

"Simon tried to kill you," Oliver said. "But Isabelle and Jasper used magic to...bring you back." His eyes met mine. "You really are a healer!"

I nodded. "I've wanted to tell you for so long."

Kairus slowly pushed himself into a sitting position. "Thank you. Both of you. What's happened to Simon?"

We all looked beyond Kairus to see the charmer frozen in place on the stage. Our friends had made their way to the front of the audience, and now Trina stood facing him, her hand extended and the others gathered around her. Fairies circled him frantically. "You may have the assistance of one fairy, *Alvin,*" she said calmly, "but I have the help of hundreds."

Simon glared at her and let out a low, guttural laugh. "That may be true," he said, his voice deepening to a ferocious growl. "But can you do this?" There came a sharp, resounding *crack,* and he slumped forward, held up only by Trina's magic.

"No!" Arquinn, who had been hanging back, let out a cry of dismay. The others all but ignored him, though; all eyes were on Simon's limp form. I felt a sense of dread growing in the pit of my stomach.

When the figure finally raised his head, I recoiled. His features were still human, but his skin had taken on an eerie golden sheen, while his eyes were now a sickening shade of orange. An otherworldly, almost tangible power seemed to emanate off him in waves. He rolled his neck and then grinned at us wolfishly. "Alvin is dead," he snarled, his voice oddly discordant. "Now you'll deal with me, and *only* me."

"Goldemar," Trina whispered, eyes wide.

"Oh, you've heard of me!" He smirked, peering up at the fairies flitting around him. "Isn't it the wish of so many of us to one day inhabit a human body? Now how will you stop me? I have the strength and speed of a human, *and* all the magic of the Fae." Then he lunged at Trina.

Only moments before he reached her, I heard the twang of a bowstring, and Goldemar howled as an arrow lodged deeply in his chest. "Don't you touch her!" Kaden growled, landing firmly between him and Trina.

Goldemar looked Kaden over and plucked the arrow from his body, tossing it aside with a snort. "You think your puny weapons will kill me? You know nothing of the power of the Fae, you little—"

Saray, Starla, and Lachlann interrupted simultaneously. Vines shot out of Starla's hand in Goldemar's direction just as Saray sent a white-hot cone of flame at him. Lachlann fired his gun a fraction of a second later. I watched in horror as Saray's fire bounced harmlessly off the fairy's chest, and Starla's vines withered when they touched him. Lachlann's bullet disappeared into his shoulder, only to slip back out the entry wound a moment later. Ruby directed a lightning bolt at him, and he laughed as it illuminated him in a fury of blue sparks.

"Don't you see?" he snarled. "I am fully Fae now. Your silly human magic will do nothing against mine. I could take this kingdom out from under you with the wave of my hand." He smirked at Kairus.

It was then that I remembered a conversation I'd had with Claudi shortly after my arrival in Ankrossi. "Wait! He's wrong. The Bearers can stop him."

Jasper met my gaze quizzically for a moment, then his eyes widened. "You're right. Trina told me that once." He looked to Kairus. "Your Majesty, I need a diver—"

"You lie." Arquinn appeared suddenly in front of Goldemar, transporting himself between the wicked Fae and the rest of us, his arms folded. "Alvin isn't really dead."

"Perfect," Jasper mumbled. He waved Kip over, and they darted carefully to Saray and Trina.

Goldemar emitted a cruel laugh. "Well, well, I certainly wasn't expecting *you* to be at this party." He grinned. "I've been looking forward to killing you, you know."

Arquinn lifted a hand and met Goldemar's eyes, unfazed by his threats. "You say Alvin is dead, which means that I, as the only remaining member of my family who is of age, have claim to you. And as such, I take command, Goldemar of the Dunderi Wild Fae. You *will* do my bidding. Now, kneel."

Goldemar stood defiantly, his eyes locked with Arquinn's. "Make me."

Saray, Trina, Jasper and Kip stood in a circle now, just out of Goldemar's view, chanting quietly with their arms locked. A pure white light enveloped them, then began to unfurl in a curling, brilliant mist.

"As I thought," Arquinn said, unflinching. "Which means that you lie. Alvin is *not* completely dead. He could still stop you, if only he believed in himself."

Goldemar cringed, and his eyes flashed briefly to brown, then orange once more. Arquinn smiled. "I see you, little brother. You can do this."

"He doesn't have to." As Trina spoke, the gathering mist enveloped Goldemar, encasing him completely.

"Nalalae Eroknae Sangnatae," muttered Saray, and Goldemar became thoroughly paralyzed, unable to even speak.

"The four Bearers of the magic of the Shrouded Woods have the power to overcome even the magic of the Fae when we work together." Trina stepped forward, her eyes glowing a brilliant purple. "Goldemar of the Dunderi Wild Fae, servant to the Blackwell family, you have broken your contracts and the laws of your land in unimaginable ways. You murdered your masters, killed a man to possess his body, and lured two young mortals in the direction of evil. Though we are not in Dundere, as Protector of the Breochi fairies, I will be your judge. However, I will let the heir of your master determine your sentence." Trina turned to Arquinn. I watched as he and Trina began to discuss Goldemar's fate in hushed tones, while Saray and Kip held the spell steady.

Finally, Trina turned back and gazed in the direction of the frozen fairy. "We have reached a decision. It is not us who should determine your fate, but the king of the Dunderi Fae. As such, you will return to your fairy form and be taken immediately back to Dundere, where you will be sentenced for your crimes. Goldemar of the Dunderi Wild Fae, *be gone* from this body, and take your place in your new prison." Trina pointed a small potion bottle at Goldemar. Then Saray, Kip and Jasper each laid a hand on her shoulders, and she mumbled the words to a spell I'd never heard before.

An iridescent light sprang from her hand and snaked around Goldemar's body. He coughed and sputtered, his eyes flashing gold, then brown, and gold again. Then he went limp, and I saw a tiny, glowing golden being appear over his head. Goldemar's fairy form seemed to flail and twist in midair for a moment, as if resisting his fate, then finally succumbed and flew into the bottle. Trina capped it, and the body he'd possessed crumpled to the ground, completely still.

Arquinn hurried to turn him over. "He's gone?"

Trina nodded.

"Alvin too?" His voice broke. "I thought he would survive, but maybe..."

The figure on the ground flinched suddenly, then coughed.

"Alvin?" Arquinn said, putting a hand on his shoulder. "Are you in there?"

Simon let out a pained moan, then began to weep softly. "Is he gone?" he whispered between sobs.

"Goldemar, you mean? Yes...we thought he'd killed you."

"He nearly did, but I couldn't let him go through with..." Simon paused, becoming more aware of his surroundings, everything clearly coming flooding back to him. He slowly stood, hands raised. "Please," he whispered, "just kill me. Don't lock me away again." His eyes settled on Lachlann. "Shoot me. You know you want to, after everything I did."

Lachlann's expression was grim. He rested his hand on his gun but did not draw it. "I believe your fate lies in the king's hands."

All eyes turned to Kairus, who nodded to his guards. "Take him away for now," he said. "We'll decide what happens to him later." The guards moved in and led Simon to the palace prison.

Arquinn sighed and reached out to Trina for the bottle containing Goldemar. "I'd best get this to the Wild Fae before any more trouble happens. I'll be back shortly." He pocketed the bottle and bowed to Kairus, then mumbled a phrase and disappeared.

"Can we leave?" someone called out from the surrounding crowd. "Are we...safe?"

Only now did I notice that there were still a good number of common folks present, who had watched everything unfold.

"*Are* they safe?" Kairus asked me quietly.

I nodded.

"Yes, you're all right," he said to his people then. "Go home and rest, and enjoy the remainder of your holiday."

They began to trickle out, and I watched Starla, who'd been hanging back, rush to Lachlann to throw her arms around him. "I thought I'd never see you again," she sobbed as she buried her head in his shoulder.

He held her tight for a few tender moments, then looked up to see Trina smiling back as the fairies swirled around him and Starla. He extended an arm, and she joined her mother in their embrace.

When Trina pulled back, Lachlann gaped at her. "What's happened to you?" he asked. "Your eyes are purple, and you're...*powerful!*"

"It's a long story." She grinned.

"Seems like I have a lot to catch up on," he said. His eyes flickered to Saray. "By the Fae, how are you alive? I saw you die, I..." His voice broke.

"Again, long story." Saray chuckled and hugged him. "I thought for sure I'd never see you again, either. But here we are."

Starla whispered something to Lachlann, then went to a nearby cluster of trees, where she disappeared into one of the trunks. Lachlann gazed after her for a moment, then turned to embrace Marcus and Ruby and Kaden.

Kairus, meanwhile, looked upon the series of reunions that unfolded in front of him. "Wait...was this entire performance a diversion so you folks could rescue Lachlann?"

"Him and the other students," I said, and Silva came to join me. "Lachlann was being used against us. We couldn't have any more raids on our village."

"I never ordered raids on your village," he protested.

"We figured that much, Your Majesty," Marcus said. "The raid was carried out by Witch Slayers, not your men. We assumed Simon sent them after us without asking you."

"Right." Kairus sighed. "I suppose that—" He trailed off and did a double take as Starla re-emerged from the tree. "Now, that is one very unexpected form of magic."

Starla hardly noticed the king's reaction; her eyes were set squarely on her husband. "Lachlann? There's someone I'd like you to meet."

Lachlann's eyes went wide when he saw the bundle she carried in her arms. He left us to go to her, and she smiled warmly up at him. "This is your daughter, Aria. She was born a little early, but Isabelle helped save her."

Lachlann took Aria into his arms, a look of pure awe on his face as he gazed at his daughter's tiny features. "Hello there, Aria," he said, his voice a whisper. "I never thought I'd get the chance to meet you, you know. I..." His voice broke, and he clutched the baby to his chest, beginning to sob quietly.

Starla turned to Kairus. "Your Majesty, do we have your leave to return home?"

Kairus looked us all over. "You realize that I should have all of you put away." He looked to me then. "Are you and this fellow here," he nodded at Jasper, "the only healers in your group?"

"Yes, sir."

"In that case, you two will stay the night at the palace; the rest of you may go home. However, I will require some of you to return tomorrow morning for negotiations. That will include you, Lachlann, as well as...whoever your leaders are."

"Marcus is our official leader," Saray spoke up. "But the circus wasn't his idea. It was mostly the four of us," she motioned at Kip, Trina, and Jasper, "and Isabelle."

"Well, I'll ask you all to attend, then."

I nodded and squeezed Silva's hand. "Sir, this is Silva, my best friend, the one who I was trying to rescue. Can she stay with me at the palace tonight?"

Kairus nodded. "I suppose so. And we can talk more about this offer you have for me tomorrow. Meet me in the throne room at noon, all of you. My people and I will be unarmed, and I would ask that you arrive in a similar fashion."

Arquinn rematerialized just as Kairus finished speaking. Kairus turned to him, and Arquinn bowed. "Goldemar is in the fairy king's hands now, Your Majesty."

I felt a ripple of relief go through those of us still present.

"Are we heading back to the Woods now?" Arquinn asked then.

Kairus nodded. "Most of you will be."

"Take those three back first," Marcus told Arquinn, nodding to Lachlann, Starla and Aria. "They need some family time."

Arquinn approached the trio, and I watched them all disappear. The king turned to one of his guards. "Arrange to have all of this cleaned up," he said. "I am in much need of a bath and a good drink." Oliver gave me a quick smile as he followed his father to the palace, but I didn't miss the concern in his eyes.

Trina went to Jasper then, worry etched on her face. "Do you think the king intends to make you into a krossemage?"

"I doubt it," I told her. "Jasper and I saved his life. I don't think we'll be punished for it."

"I'll be all right," Jasper assured her gently. "But there's something I need to tell you." He looked from Trina to me, eyebrows knitted. "Claudi is gone."

"Gone?" I echoed. "As in dead?"

He nodded slowly. "This will sound strange, but for a moment after I became the Bearer, she and I could *see* each other."

"What did you see?"

"Well, she let out a little laugh, like she was surprised to realize that I was her successor. She told me to take care of the village, and then she closed her eyes and let out a long breath. Then...she was gone." He frowned. "I know it sounds bizarre."

"Not at all," Trina said. "Saray and Kip have both had similar connections to their predecessors." She sighed then. "Claudi was a wonderful woman. Back when Saray was first training with Willem, she used to read me stories from Willem's library and sit outside with me asking what all the animals were saying." Her voice broke, and she dabbed at her eyes with the cuff of her sleeve.

"I wish I'd had more time to get to know her," I put in, blinking back tears of my own.

Jasper put an arm around each of us. "Me too. But not having found the next Bearer was the only thing keeping her here. She wanted to move on, to be with Willem and Ashlar in the next world. Once the Sea Stone chose me and its power left her, she was able to let go." He closed his eyes. "It was her time. And I'm happy she's with her loved ones now." He let go of me, gave Trina a squeeze and kissed the top of her head. "You should get home, spend some time with your family and fairies. I'll see you tomorrow. Tell Tristan that I'll be back soon."

Chapter 35

ONCE WE'D ALL had a chance to bathe and change, Silva, Jasper and I sat around a large spread of food set out on the table in my rooms, all of us feeling much more refreshed. I was surprised when Silva and I were taken back to my old chambers for the night, and Jasper was given a room across the hall; I hadn't expected us to be thrown into the dungeon, but I hadn't anticipated luxury either.

While we ate, Silva filled Jasper and me in on everything that happened while she was in captivity. "They took us to the Breoch Guard station in Sylvenburgh and held us there for a few days. Then we were moved to the palace prison in Kirstein. Everything seemed so surreal...I remember not being able to sleep at night and just drifting in and out of consciousness. We were all exhausted and terrified and hungry and cold. The younger kids cried a lot. We older ones tried to hold it in, but we could only handle so much." She sighed. "That lasted for maybe two or three weeks. Then one day, Simon came to the cell we were crammed into. He had a few prison guards with him, and Lachlann, who was all chained up and beaten. Simon asked which of us was the youngest, and Becksa said it was her. Then..." Silva's voice caught, and she looked down at her hands. "Simon told Becksa that Lachlann wasn't cooperating with the palace guard and needed a little persuasion. He snapped her neck, right in front of all of us."

"Oh, Silva, that's...horrific," I exclaimed.

She nodded, blinking back tears. "It was awful. We were all screaming and crying, and Lachlann just had this look of absolute shock on his face. Simon said he would kill one of us every week until Lachlann cooperated. Then they took him away, and we all spent the night crying and trying to comfort one another. The next morning, we felt the anti-magic hit, and we knew Lachlann had given in to whatever the guards demanded of him. We didn't expect them to move us to the same tower, though." She frowned. "You saw what they did to him, with his anti-magic and that big hunk of aro stone. I don't fully understand it. But they put us in the room below the bell tower so his anti-magic could hold us in check, and to remind him what would happen if he stopped cooperating.

"At first, he avoided us. I think he assumed we'd hate him. But then on the second day, he came to the stairwell and said how sorry he was about Becksa. He explained that Simon and Pieter wanted to harness his anti-magic so that the Breoch Guard could gain the power of a Bonded anti-mage. He'd refused initially because he knew they'd use it to hurt magic folks, but he said we didn't need to worry, he was cooperating with the guards now. Then he told us we were welcome to come upstairs and join him if we wanted." She sighed. "A few of us went to see him because we felt sorry for him, but we quickly discovered that the bell tower was more pleasant than the office we were confined to—at least, when it was warm out."

"Oliver and I used to play up there when we were kids. The bell tower is pretty nice."

She nodded. "That night, we all ended up sitting around telling stories about Becksa. A lot of things came up for us. We were all so *scared.*" She shuddered. "Lachlann told us that if we put our heads together, we might be able to figure out an escape. I'm not sure if he was bluffing, though, I think he felt just as trapped as we did."

"I'm sure he was scared too," Jasper said.

"After that, we fell into a bit of a routine. The guards brought us food three times a day, and we tried to be down in the office when they arrived. Once a week, they came with water barrels, and we took turns bathing while everyone else waited upstairs. Other than that, we spent most of our time with Lachlann. He started training us and taught us all sorts of ways to overpower a person. It kept us busy." Silva's gaze shifted to me. "A few weeks later, Simon came up to visit. He told Lachlann that your father wanted to send some guards into the Woods to find you, and he needed the location of a Moon Dance, which Lachlann gave him. Lachlann was devastated after that. We tried to comfort him, and we figured they'd go in to retrieve you and leave everyone else alone. But we were wrong."

I nodded. "That's when they took Saray."

"The look on Lachlann's face when Simon came to gloat about capturing her...He was utterly horrified. Simon told Lachlann he was going to make him watch the execution, and he threatened to make us watch, too. That's the only time I saw Lachlann get aggressive. He told Simon he had no right to do that after we already saw Becksa die. Simon eventually backed off, but the hanging still happened. And they made Lachlann watch."

I nodded, closing my eyes against my own memory of that day.

"That night was the first time I've seen a grown man break down and weep," she told me. "And it was only a week later that Simon came back; this time, he wanted the location of Ankrossi, and..." She took a deep, shuddering breath. "Lachlann balked. I was the closest person to Simon, so he grabbed me, put his knife to my throat and threatened to kill me..." Silva buried her face in her hands then.

"You don't have to go into detail," I assured.

"It's all right." She looked up and shook her head. "I just remember that the world began to swim, and I nearly pissed myself. Lachlann caved; he gave Simon the location. And after that, he was silent for almost a full day. He would hardly look at any of us. Then, finally, he called us all up to the bell tower for a talk.

"That was when he explained to us that he'd killed Simon's brother a few years back, and that all of this was to make him suffer. And he said he could only see one way to make it stop."

Jasper nodded gravely. "Suicide."

"Exactly. We were all pretty broken up by it, but we'd seen how much it was hurting him, being used like this. And so when he told us that he was going to teach us how to work together to free ourselves once he was dead, we agreed to work with him."

"I'm sorry you had to endure all that, Silva," said Jasper. "It sounds horrific."

"It was." She sat back. "I don't want to think about it anymore, though. What's happened with you since we were caught, Isabelle? Do you live in the Woods now?"

"Not exactly." I glanced at Jasper, and together we told her about my initial trip into the Woods to save Aria, Claudi's offer to teach me, and the Breoch Guard's arrival at the Moon Dance. I told her the story of Saray's capture and execution from my point of view, and how afterwards Oliver insisted I flee. Jasper's voice turned tender as he recounted Trina's sacrifice that brought Saray back, and it faltered when he talked about the battle that took both Willem and Jade's lives. We finished with how we'd come up with the plan for the sky circus. "So here we are," Jasper concluded. "Isabelle saved the day, and I'm the new Bearer of the Sea Stone."

"You did more saving of the day than me," I argued. "Have you had magic this entire time?"

"Yes, but not much until today. Do you girls know what a demi-mage is?"

I shook my head.

"It's someone, usually with only one magical parent, who possesses a small amount of magic, but not enough to be considered a full magikai. A lot of demi-mages go through life without realizing what they are. I only knew that I don't get sick easily and that I heal faster than most. Then, back when I lived in Dundere for a few months, I learned that I couldn't use anti-magic without it making me feel physically ill. Trina suggested, half-jokingly, that perhaps I was magical. I'd never considered the thought before. And I didn't accept it until I'd been sailing on the Lady Liara for a good six months."

"What happened then?"

"I fell from the shrouds and broke my arm," he explained. "The ship doctor, Kezia, set it and put it in a sling. I came back to see her a week later, and it was completely healed. She told me that wasn't possible without magic and suggested I might be a demi-mage. She asked me to cut my hand, and we watched as it healed within an hour.

"We didn't have a lifebringer aboard, but Gareth knew a few of them in various ports, so whenever we'd stop in one of those places I'd be shipped off to train. I could only heal small things on other people—cuts and burns and mild illnesses—but it was better than nothing."

"So the folks on the ship knew, but you didn't tell anyone here?"

"I told Ruby and Kaden. Trina found out when we were sailing, and she got a cough she couldn't shake. That's why she sent for me after Aria was born early. She wasn't sure if I could do much for a sick baby, but she figured it was worth it to try. I planned to hold Aria and sing to her and hope that no one figured out what I was trying to do. But you beat me there, and I wasn't needed until you were taken away."

"Why didn't you want people to know?" asked Silva.

Jasper sighed. "Because I didn't think I deserved to have magic, after hunting magikai like I did."

I frowned. "You realize that if you wish to redeem yourself, being a healer for the magikai community is a mighty good way to do it?"

"I do see that now. The whole thing was rather intimidating for me, though. It still is a bit terrifying...especially this." He glanced down at his pendant.

I nodded slowly. "You know that you'll be tied to the Woods now, like the rest of the Bearers, right?"

"Oh, I know. But I decided just a couple days ago that I'm going to stay in Ankrossi. It's clearly the best place to raise Tristan, and now that Trina and I are together I was already—"

We were interrupted by a knock on the door, and Oliver poked his head in. My heart leapt, and Jasper stood, clearly a bit flustered. "Your Highness." Silva followed suit, executing a small curtsy.

"Call me Oliver, please." His gaze shifted to me, and he gave me a small smile. "Can I speak with the three of you?"

"Of course," Jasper said, seating himself and gesturing to the empty chair. Oliver came into the room, and only now did I see that he was using his cane. "Are you injured, Your...Oliver?"

"Not injured," he replied. "Ill. Have been for a while."

"Ah. Well, you came to the right people." Jasper gave him a slightly uncertain grin.

"I'm aware." Oliver shook his head as he sat down. "I can't thank you two enough for saving my father. Even if it did involve magic."

"Let's hope he feels the same way."

"He's not going to turn them into krossemages, is he?" Silva asked, eyes wide.

"No," Oliver said. "He's keeping you here because he figures that taking the only two healers in your group ensures the rest of them will show up tomorrow."

Jasper raised his eyebrows. "Clever."

"Do you know what he wants to discuss at the meeting?" I asked.

"He wants to figure out how to move forward from here. Father is quite aware that magic saved his life today, but everything that happened was still illegal, and folks will be watching to see what he does next. I think he's hoping to come up with a solution that will protect your friends but won't anger the people too much."

"What about licensing and anti-magic law enforcement like they do in Dundere?" Jasper suggested.

"Father says it's not that simple. The people are afraid. If we just legalize magic, there will still be prejudices, and there's a chance that folks will harm their magic-using friends and family themselves if they don't think the government has magic under control."

"But isn't making magic legal a good first step in helping folks become less prejudiced?"

"I suppose so. But I'm not sure Father is ready to take that step." He turned to me. "Isabelle, you said you had a proposal for Father. What was it?"

"I..." I bit my lip. "I can tell you, but you'll likely hate me for it."

Oliver shook his head. "I doubt that, given that you saved him. Come on, tell me."

I took a deep breath and met his eyes. "I was going to use you as a bargaining chip. I was going to demonstrate my healing powers on a small scale, then tell your father that I was willing to cure you, but only if he made magic legal. If he refused, I planned to give you the option of running off with me and being healed privately."

Oliver stared back at me for a moment. Then one corner of his mouth turned up. "You know, that just might have worked. But I'd rather not chance it."

"Me neither."

"Do your people need magic to be legal in all of Breoch to be satisfied? Or just within the Woods?"

"I think controlled legalization within the entire country would be the end goal," Jasper said. "But allowing it within the Woods would be a good first step. That, and the end of the krossemage system."

"I'm not sure what to do about the krossemage system. But I do have an idea, one that might make that system—and Isabelle's bargain—unnecessary."

We listened as Oliver explained his idea to us. When he was finished, Jasper raised his eyebrows and nodded. "That...just might work. If you're willing to suggest it tomorrow, I suspect your father will be more likely to listen than if one of us brings it up."

Oliver gave him a tense smile. "I make no promises, but we can try."

"Why are you on our side about all this?" Jasper asked him then. "Didn't you grow up believing magic was evil?"

"Didn't *you?*" Oliver replied pointedly.

"Of course. But I imagine that the idea was pushed harder on the crown prince than—"

"Than the son of the second captain of the Breoch Guard?" I interrupted. "He has a point, though. Why are you so invested in seeing this change?" I met Oliver's eyes and frowned. "Are *you* a magic user?"

Oliver chuckled. "No. But some people who I care very deeply about are." He gave me a small smile, and I felt my heartbeat pick up. "Also, I suspect that I might have magic in my family one day. If I have children who are magical, I don't want them to have to hide." His eyes landed on me again.

"You think your father would allow you to marry...a magic user?" I asked.

"I think it would depend on *which* magic user," he said. "If it was the one who saved his life today, then quite possibly."

"Technically that was me," Jasper pointed out. "And I'm not sure how you feel about that."

Oliver's eyes widened, then he laughed. "I suspect marrying another fellow wouldn't go over so well with Father. No offense, but continuing the family line and all."

"None taken. I mostly prefer women myself." Jasper grinned. "But if the two of you are going to talk about marriage, perhaps Silva and I should excuse ourselves."

Silva shot him an uncertain glance. "Where should we go?"

I turned to Oliver. "Could we have a guard escort them to the music room? These two both play fiddle; I'm sure they could entertain themselves."

"I think that can be arranged," Oliver said. "Excuse me for a moment."

He slipped out of the room, and Jasper turned to me. "I'm not sure how your conversation with Oliver is going to go, but I hope you remembered to bring some tea."

"I did, actually," I said, glancing at the satchel I'd been wearing with my dress.

"What are you two talking about?" Silva asked.

"We might be playing fiddle together for a while, that's all," Jasper replied, smirking.

Silva frowned, then her eyes went wide, and she turned to me. "You'd *better* fill me in later."

Oliver returned then with a palace guard in tow. Jasper and Silva left with the guard, and Oliver and I were alone.

My heart pounded as I met his eyes. "Will you forgive me?" I asked, my voice trembling.

"For what?"

"Everything... Running away. Planning to use you as a bargaining chip. Not telling you about my magic."

Oliver frowned. "I suspect that if I'd been in your position, I would have done similar things." Then he sighed. "You don't need to apologize, Isabelle. This whole thing has been messy. And as for your magic, I certainly can't blame you for not telling me about that. I rather hope you'll be willing to heal me at some point, though."

"We could try now," I suggested.

"You'd do that?"

"Of course. Do you...know much about where your illness comes from?"

He shook his head. "Only that I inherited it from Mother."

"Let me see if I can figure it out. I do know it's connected to your spine somehow, and—"

"How do you know that?"

"Oh." Heat rose in my cheeks. "I guess that's something else I should apologize for." I eyed him carefully. "I already tried to heal you once, without you knowing."

"When?"

"It was after we..." I glanced at the bed.

He followed my gaze, and I saw his own cheeks redden. "Ah."

"I figured that was the only time I'd be able to get that close to you without you noticing and...touch all the parts of you that needed healing."

"So you seduced me just so you could heal me?" I didn't miss the hurt in his voice.

"Not *just* so I could heal you," I assured. "I *wanted* to sleep with you, and I had a wonderful time."

He nodded slowly, but I could tell from his expression that he wasn't certain whether to believe me. "Well, it's not like I didn't enjoy it myself," he finally admitted with a chuckle. Then he straightened up. "But how did you think that was going to work with the anti-magic?"

"I had a potion of fairy magic, which is stronger than anti-magic. I drank the potion, then tried healing you. It didn't work, though. I had enough knowledge at the time to be able to locate the source of the illness, and I felt a pull toward your spine, but when I tried to heal it, something blocked me. It was strange." I gave him a sheepish smile. "Since then, though, I've learned how to see into wounds and illnesses to determine their cause. Can I try that with you now?"

He nodded. "Of course."

"I, uh, I'll need you to take your shirt off."

I couldn't help but follow Oliver's fingers with my eyes as he began unbuttoning. He caught me looking and gave me a smile that seemed almost shy. "Do you want me to just lean forward, or should I lie down somewhere?"

"Lying down would be easier," I admitted. The couch in my rooms was a small loveseat, and I doubted Oliver would be able to comfortably stretch out on it. "You can lie on my bed."

Nodding, he stood and removed his shoes. I followed him over to the bed, where he lay face down. When I placed my hands on his back, I couldn't help but run my fingers over the hard muscles there for a moment before settling on his spine. He let out a murmur of pleasure. "That feels good."

I chuckled. "Well, I'm not sure how this next part will feel. Some people say it tingles a bit." I pressed down on his spine with my fingertips, closed my eyes, and began to sing the now-familiar tune.

The images that appeared in my mind were not the ones I expected. I thought I'd see something about Oliver being born, about an illness passed from mother to child. Instead, I saw him as a young teen, clutching a jewelled headpiece and laughing as he ran from the palace guard. He darted into a room, out of my field of vision, leaving the guards stumped. I saw the same guards talking to Kairus, then Kairus scolding Oliver for his pranks. I noticed Pieter in the background, watching with a careful eye.

Then the scene changed to Pieter in the kitchen, preparing two mugs of tea. I watched as he uncapped a vial and poured its contents into one of the mugs. Then he lifted the tray and went to the outside terrace, where Oliver waited at a table. Pieter sat down next to him and casually handed him the tainted mug. The two of them talked, both of them sipping their tea. I opened my eyes, frowning.

"What did you see?" Oliver asked.

"Do you recall getting lectured by your father for running off with some jewels about four, five years back?" I asked.

"Oh." He laughed. "Yes, I remember that. But what does that have to do with my condition?"

"Do you remember having tea with Pieter on the terrace shortly after?"

"I do. That was a strange conversation. He talked about how I needed to be on the lookout for magic in unexpected places, and how it was my duty as future king to be vigilant."

I nodded. "Whatever your condition is, it wasn't inherited. It came from something Pieter put in your tea that day."

Oliver lifted his head and met my eyes. "I was *poisoned?*"

"Something like that. I need to figure out exactly what he used. Lie back down."

Oliver did so, and I placed my fingers on his spine and began humming again. I returned to the vision but let my mind drift back to the scene where Pieter sabotaged the mug. I honed in on the vial, trying to determine its ingredients. Most of the contents seemed harmless—water, ginger, honey, a little yarel bloom. But there was something else present as well, something with an undertone of rot. My nose wrinkled involuntarily as I strained to perceive exactly what it was. "It's a potion," I concluded, "and the magic involved is some sort of...decay magic?" My eyes widened as I recalled Trina mentioning this same kind of spell. "I've heard of it before, but I don't understand it."

Oliver frowned and sat up. "Do you think Pieter did the same thing to Mother?"

"Well, if your symptoms are the same as hers, then he or someone else must have."

"But...*why?* He doesn't seem to be making any moves for the throne."

"I have no idea."

"And you can't heal it?"

I put my fingers on his back again and sang my healing spell—once again, I met resistance. "I...don't seem to be able to. Perhaps the potion is made with fairy magic. That would make it stronger than mine. I'll have to talk to some of the Woods-folk about this."

"Should we tell Father? He should know if the court mage is responsible for Mother's death."

"Let me see if I can find some answers first." I eyed him and sighed. "I'm sorry I don't seem to be able to fix this."

He gave me an obviously forced smile. "Don't worry, we'll figure it out. I trust you."

"Are you sure that's wise? After...everything I've done?"

"Maybe not, but I don't have a whole lot of choice in the matter, now do I?" He shrugged. "That, and, despite everything you've done, I still love you."

"You...do?"

"Absolutely. But...it's complicated." Oliver sighed. "Isabelle, I'd love to spend my future—however long it might be—with you. But I don't want to do it if it's going to leave you trapped, and I don't want you to agree to it because our parents set us up. If we were to marry, or even just court for now, I'd want it to be because we *choose* each other."

I nodded. "Well, perhaps it's best to leave decisions about marriage until we figure out how to heal you. Even if I can't, I could marry you, and we could enjoy our years together without children. I do know where to get that tea to prevent pregnancy."

Oliver cocked his head. "You'd *do* that? Knowing I would die, knowing I would...end up like my mother did?"

Looking into his deep green eyes, I found myself nodding. "I would." I reached for his hand and rubbed a thumb over his knuckle. "I love you too, Oliver. I think I have for a while. It's hard for me to imagine a future without you."

He squeezed my hand in return. "I missed you terribly when you were gone. I was willing to put up with it because I believed it to be best for you, but it was awful."

"Well, I'm back," I assured. "Where I want to be. Where I *choose* to be." I reached up and eased a hand into his curls, pulling him toward me.

Oliver's lips on mine were decisive but less desperate than during our last encounter. I returned his kiss, my hands trailing lazily down his bare back, my movements deliberate. I poured one thought into every moment of my lips against his, every flick of my tongue.

I choose you.

Oliver lay on the bed, drawing me down with him. His lips explored my neck, my collarbones. Then he pulled away from me, gasping. "You don't happen to have any of that tea on you now, by chance?"

I grinned. "As a matter of fact, I do."

His cheeks flushed, and his smile turned shy again. "If you really do *choose* me, can we...use it? But not because you're secretly trying to heal me this time, or because you feel sorry for me and don't want me to die a virgin?"

"Why do you think I brought it along?" I grinned at him. "I'd be delighted to...make use of the tea tonight, for no other reason than I *want* to." Smoothing down my dress, I got off the bed and crossed the room to my satchel. My heart pounded with elation and desire as I retrieved the packet and presented it triumphantly to Oliver.

His smile widened. "Do we need to drink it now?"

"I can drink it afterward; it works a little differently on women than on men. We'd best not take as long as we did last time, though. I imagine Jasper and Silva only know so many songs on the fiddle."

"Perhaps they'll make up some new ones," he suggested, a playful grin tugging at his lips. He patted the bed next to him. "What are you waiting for, then?"

I placed the tea on the bedside table, lay back down next to Oliver, and pressed my lips to his once more.

***

A while later, I sat alone in my chair, sipping the now-familiar tea. When the door creaked open, Silva came in, and Jasper's head popped around the corner. He smirked when he saw me with the cup of tea in my hand. "I assume things went well?"

I rolled my eyes. "Yes and no. I couldn't heal him. But we've sorted our relationship out a bit."

"Why couldn't you heal him?"

"It's complicated. I'll explain everything tomorrow when we see the king."

He nodded. "Well, I'll head to bed then. I'm sure you two have lots to talk about. Goodnight, ladies."

He ducked out of the room, and Silva sat down next to me on the couch. I realized then that she'd been crying. "Are you all right?"

She gave me a watery smile. "I'm...not sure. I broke down while Jasper and I were playing fiddle. I tried to save it 'til I was alone, but..." Her voice broke. "We were playing, and I thought to myself, I didn't think I'd have a chance to ever do this again. I was sure we were going to die in that tower. And I just started sobbing."

I moved closer to put an arm around her shoulders. "I don't blame you. I can't even imagine what it's been like for all of you."

"Thankfully, Jasper didn't seem scared by my breakdown."

"He's been through a lot himself. I doubt this is the first time he's had someone break down crying in front of him. What did he do?"

"Well, he asked me what was wrong. After I explained, he offered me a hug, then I ended up bawling into his shoulder. He kept telling me I was safe, and to try to breathe deeply." She shook her head. "It was so strange, because when we were stuck in that tower, there were so many times one of us would break down, and the others would say it was going to be all right. But that never felt *true*. Between Lachlann and my classmates, I've felt cared for and supported throughout all of this. But I haven't actually felt *safe* until I broke down in the music room."

I gave her a squeeze. "Well, you're safe now, Silva. And I'm so happy to have you back." I felt my own eyes begin to water.

She grabbed my hand, and we sat in silence for a few minutes, simply enjoying the fact that we were both *here,* together. Then she looked up at me. "So what's going on with you and Oliver?"

As we got ready for bed, I filled her in on everything that had happened between us since she'd been gone. Then we settled under the covers, and I pulled Silva toward me and held her until she was asleep. Once her breathing evened out, I untangled myself and turned on my back, trying to process the events of the day.

Finally, the thing I'd set out to do all those months back was done. My friends were free, Lachlann was reunited with his family, and Oliver and I were patching up our relationship. Now it was only a matter of figuring out how to heal Oliver and seeing what fate awaited us all at tomorrow's meeting.

Chapter 36

THE FOLLOWING MORNING, I sat in the royal council chambers, flanked by Oliver and Silva. Kairus looked refreshed, but I noticed the wariness with which he eyed Jasper and me. Several other court members, including Pieter, had joined our meeting; my father slipped in a bit later, giving me a nod and a smile.

It felt like hours passed before the doors to the chamber opened, and a large group of folk from Ankrossi were escorted in by guards. Lachlann looked much better than he had yesterday; his beard was trimmed and his hair clean and tied back. I was surprised to see Arquinn with the group, dressed in a coat that looked Cherinese in make. Marcus wore a brightly patterned waistcoat with what I now recognized as the emblem of Ankrossi stitched into it. On his head was a leather circlet painted with golden designs—I suspected this display of regalia was to help Kairus make sense of the world that the citizens of Ankrossi inhabited.

And on Marcus' arm was my mother.

Mother held her head high, every bit the lady she'd been raised to be, but she was clad in an Ankrossi dress, a silvery-blue outfit which fell only to her knees and left her shoulders bare. I felt my father's eyes on her as Marcus pulled out a chair for her to sit. Marcus, however, ignored my father, keeping his gaze on Kairus as he seated himself beside Mother and directly across the table from the king.

Jasper rose from his chair as soon as they entered. He practically ran to Trina, pulled her into an embrace, and kissed her tenderly. Then he led her to the chair next to his. Chester and Sophie slid into the seats next to Silva, and I leaned over to make introductions. "This fellow may have saved my life yesterday," I told Silva after I'd introduced Chester.

Chester's grin turned shy. "I did what anyone would have done."

"Yes, but it was especially terrifying for you, and you overcame your fear. You should be proud of yourself."

He held my gaze for a moment. "I am," he finally admitted. Then he nodded at the king, and I noticed that everyone else was seated now. I gave Chester one last smile and then joined the others in waiting for Kairus to address us.

"I'm glad you all decided to come," he began, looking our group over. He paused and eyed Trina, who I now noticed was accompanied by Mischief. "Why do you have a fox on your shoulders?"

"I'm blind," she explained. "The fox helps me know where to go."

"You seemed very involved in yesterday's theatrics for a blind person."

"Yes, well, yesterday I had dozens of fairies giving me sight. I figure that one fox who can communicate with me might be less intimidating to you and your court than bringing a whole host of fairies, Your Majesty." As she spoke, Mischief hopped off her shoulder and began to sniff around the room.

"I see. You're likely right about that, my dear. Anyway, let's proceed." Kairus cleared his throat. "Yesterday was…a spectacle. Magic was used openly in front of the citizens of Breoch for the first time in nearly sixty years, freely and with little consequence. I could easily have you all killed or made into krossemages. Yet, we've learned that turning folks into krossemages doesn't always work, and we've also learned that killing magic users doesn't necessarily yield permanent results either and…oh!" He startled as Mischief jumped into his lap. Kairus stared down at the fox for a moment, then smiled ever so slightly and ran a hand through her fur. "Hello, there."

"She likes you," Trina said.

"Is that so?" He smiled again, eyed the fox, then continued speaking. "You folks created quite the stir yesterday. But your magic also saved my life. So now I must figure out what to do with the lot of you." He frowned. "What did you hope to accomplish with your little show, other than to create a diversion?"

Marcus cleared his throat. "The point was to show the people of Breoch that magic can be used for good, Your Majesty."

"And yet, they all saw it used for evil as well," the king countered.

"That was magic without constraint. We are in agreement that unchecked magic is dangerous. But when you look at the way it's handled in places like Dundere, you'll see that there are ways to ensure it isn't misused. Lachlann here has already shown you one of them."

Kairus looked Lachlann over and nodded. "Your anti-magic certainly works. Though if it's true that Simon—er, Alvin—used charm magic on me while the entire palace was under the protection of your anti-magic, then there are clearly some ways to circumvent this."

"That was fairy magic, Your Majesty," cut in Arquinn. "And most humans don't have access to that."

Kairus eyed him. "You're Alvin's brother, correct?"

"I am, Your Majesty."

"So why did you come along? I assume you're not part of this council?"

"I'm here to plead for my brother's life, Your Majesty," Arquinn replied.

"Yes, we need to figure out what to do about him. Trying to kill a monarch is generally punishable by death, not to mention all the terrible things he did to all of you and the atrocities he committed in Dundere. And yet, yesterday he begged us to kill him rather than lock him away."

"Because he'd rather die than be imprisoned for life," Arquinn replied. "He caused much harm, Your Majesty, but mostly it was Goldemar, not my brother, calling the shots."

"Do you have another solution then?"

"I do. In Dundere, we have magic that can bind one person or creature to another. It was used to bind Goldemar to my family all those years ago. Let me use that magic to bind Alvin to me."

"You want him to be your slave?"

"I want him to be in my *care*." Arquinn eyed the king. "I suspect it's the best solution for all of us. He'll be away from your kingdom and from all the folks he's hurt, and he'll finally get to see the world like he always wanted, but with my supervision."

"That doesn't sound like much of a punishment for him." Kairus frowned. "What about you? You're willing to take on this burden for the rest of your life?"

"I am. So long as I can leave Tristan here, with his father."

Jasper's eyes widened. "That's what you want?"

"You seem like you'll do well at parenting. And you're surrounded by a community of people who will help you, which is more than Tristan will get if he's with me."

Jasper nodded solemnly. "Thank you for trusting me with him."

Arquinn turned back to Kairus. "Will you agree to my plea, then, Your Majesty?"

"Yes, but on one condition. Alvin still needs to be punished in some form for his misdeeds. And we can't have him using his charm magic anymore. Fortunately, we in Breoch have a rather effective way of dealing with that issue."

A silence descended as we all took in the weight of the king's words. Marcus let out a breath. "I used to say I wouldn't wish that fate on my worst enemy. But in this case, I can see how it might be the best solution."

"You don't wish for him to be executed or further imprisoned, then? After what he did to your wife?"

"I know enough about him to understand that he's had a hard life. I don't want him running about able to do whatever he desires, and I certainly don't want him anywhere near me or my family, but I don't exactly wish him harm, either." He turned to Lachlann. "What do you think?"

Lachlann was quiet for a moment. "It was Goldemar, not Alvin, who was bent on hurting me," he finally said. "I only saw Alvin in there a few times, when he got choked up about losing Aidan. I'd be happy to never see him again once this is over, but I don't wish him ill, so long as he can't hurt people with magic anymore."

"Does this satisfy your request, young man?" Kairus asked Arquinn.

Arquinn frowned. "I suppose. But please understand that we Dunderi folk see the krossemage system as needlessly cruel."

"I'm not disagreeing with you," Marcus replied. "But it seems a better fate than his other options. What if we were to give him a choice? Death, life in prison, or becoming a krossemage bound to his brother?"

Arquinn nodded slowly. "I can agree to that."

Kairus looked over to a pair of guards near the door. "Bring in the prisoner. We'll need to hear his account as well."

"How do you know he won't try to charm you again?" asked Oliver.

"Don't worry about that," Sophie piped up. "May I question him, Your Majesty? I am also a charmer."

Kairus frowned. "Aren't you the one who charmed him before his arrest? Won't he recognize you?"

"Most likely, but I have a solution to that as well." Sophie smiled. "Permission to use magic for this task?"

Kairus sighed. "Permission granted."

Sophie grinned, pulled out her pendant, and mumbled a few words. Next to me, Oliver recoiled as she transformed into Soren. "How did she...*he*..."

"It's illusion magic," I explained. "Don't worry, Soren is harmless."

The doors opened a few minutes later, and a pair of guards led Alvin in. His hands were bound behind his back, and I saw that he was wearing an anti-magic pendant. The small braid he normally wore in his hair was undone, and he looked around the chamber with wary eyes. They settled on Arquinn, who gave him a tense smile. Beside me, I felt Silva stiffen and draw in a breath; I took her hand in reassurance.

Alvin was seated in a chair away from the table where we were all gathered, and Kairus rose to stare down at him. "Simon—or should I say Alvin—we are here to discuss what to do with you."

He met the king's eyes, his earlier nerves seeming to steady. "Your Majesty," he said, "I have an offer for you. And, yes, call me Alvin."

Kairus raised an eyebrow. "*You're* making *me* an offer? Quite a haughty move, from someone in your position."

"I'm aware," he replied. "But, please, hear me out."

"I will once you have been questioned," Kairus said and nodded at Soren.

"Alvin," Soren said, approaching the prisoner, "we meet again."

Alvin frowned. "I'm sorry, I don't think I know you."

"You'll figure it out." Soren grinned and plopped unceremoniously into the chair next to Alvin's. He picked up his cane and began to twirl it. "So...tell me *everything.*"

"Everything." Alvin sat back. "Where do you want me to start?"

"Why don't you tell us a little about that creature who was living in your head?"

I listened as Alvin explained Goldemar's relationship to the Blackwell family in detail and how he'd wormed his way into Aidan's mind.

Soren nodded. "Interesting. Seems plausible enough, from my knowledge of the Dundere Wild Fae. So how did this Goldemar begin influencing *you?*"

Alvin explained how Aidan persuaded him to get in on his plans to hurt Jasper following the breakup with Ruby, how he'd cornered Ruby in her room at Saray's birthday party, and how Marcus and Noelle had intervened. "Goldemar only started really talking to me after Aidan was killed," he concluded.

"What did he say to you?" asked Soren.

"He was furious and heartbroken that Aidan was gone. It was his idea to bring the Breoch Guard through the portal and attack the city. I don't think I could've come up with that myself."

"Whose idea was it to shoot Noelle?" Marcus asked.

"Both of ours, but for different reasons. I wanted to hurt everyone who'd hurt me, and that included her. I didn't want to kill anyone, though. I figured Noelle could save herself, being a lifebringer. But Goldemar made things blurry in my head, and I wasn't sure what was right or wrong. It was..." He trailed off and hung his head.

"Keep going," Soren urged.

"Right. So then that Sophie kid charmed me, and by the time I got my wits back I was in chains on the way to the guard station. I remember finding out Noelle was dead and being in complete shock. I thought for sure I'd be executed. Then I was sentenced to life in prison, and soon enough I wished I had been killed. I was bored out of my mind." Alvin went on to explain how Goldemar had gotten into the prison using Tristan, and the offer he'd made.

"I had little to lose, so I went along with his plans, and next thing I knew I was strangling my cellmate to death. Then Goldemar and I were suddenly in his body, and I was staring at myself slumped dead on the floor. Goldemar helped me pry a sharp piece of wood off the cell door and stabbed my body in the heart, then teleported us out of the prison. So now it looked like Charles had killed *me* and fled.

"It was only then that I realized I wasn't really free. Goldemar took control quickly, and I had no idea how to get it back. He targeted my family first—he only told me we were going after Father, and I'll be honest, I didn't mind killing him. But I didn't expect him to go after my mother and Ashlynn…" His voice broke, and he shook his head.

"Why didn't you harm Tristan?" Jasper asked.

"Goldemar had become a little fond of him, that's why." He eyed Jasper. "Since when do you care about my nephew?"

Jasper and Arquinn exchanged a glance, and Alvin's eyes narrowed. "Wait, are *you…*"

"Yes, he is," Arquinn said.

Alvin's jaw clenched. "You slept with my sister?"

Jasper raised an eyebrow. "Consider us even after you tried to sleep with mine. At least your sister *wanted* to sleep with me. She initiated it, actually, and we had ourselves a lovely—"

"All right, I don't think you need to finish that thought," Arquinn cut in, rolling his eyes. "Alvin, continue. After you and Goldemar murdered the rest of our family, then what?"

He sighed. "We left Dundere with Goldemar plotting to hunt down Lachlann and make him suffer. We weren't sure where we'd find him, but Goldemar had a plan—if we got close to the king, he figured, we could order Lachlann's arrest. So we set off to charm our way into the court. Once we'd established ourself, we let Pieter know about a fellow whose anti-magic could be useful to study. Turns out having the court interested in a person's whereabouts makes them much easier to find."

Alvin then told us the story of how he and Goldemar tortured Lachlann. When he got to the part where he snapped Becksa's neck, his voice became a whisper, and he stared at the floor. I saw a tear trickle down his cheek. Through all of this, Lachlann's shoulders were rigid, his jaw clenched.

"I rather hoped we were done torturing Lachlann after that," Alvin went on. "But then Caspa came to the king frantically looking for his daughter and suggested she might be in the Woods, and I found us saying that we could probably get information from Lachlann. I was *not* expecting the search party to come back with Saray."

"Were you involved in seeing her hanged?" asked Soren.

"No, not at all. The king offered her a boon, but she turned it down."

Kairus nodded. "That much is true. The hanging was on me."

"A few weeks later, I learned something quite unexpected," Alvin went on, his eyes flickering to Pieter, then back to Kairus. "That court mage of yours is a Witch Slayer."

Kairus' eyebrows lifted. He glanced at Pieter, whose eyes had gone wide. "Do you have proof of this?"

"Did you order an attack on a village in the Shrouded Woods?"

"No, not at all."

"Well, the attack certainly happened; I'm sure any of the Ankrossi folks can verify." The council nodded. "Goldemar wanted a particular book in Willem's library, but we needed a diversion in Ankrossi to keep the villagers from coming to protect the school. Goldemar knew Pieter wanted to see magikai suffer, so we recruited him. We got Ankrossi's location out of Lachlann, and Pieter sent a contingent of Witch Slayers to attack the village while a few Breoch Guards and I infiltrated the library." He shrugged. "We failed. All of us. And Goldemar was angry."

"Is this true?" Kairus demanded of his mage. "You ordered a raid without my permission?"

Pieter snorted, his expression darkening. "You take issue with me trying to stamp out those who will do our land more harm than good, sire?"

"So you are a Witch Slayer, then. Why would a mage—the *court* mage, nonetheless—become one of *them*?"

"Do you think I *enjoy* being a monster?" Pieter retorted. "It's the reason I've not had children; I don't want to pass this scourge on. But I cannot help what I am, so I'd best use it to protect the kingdom."

Kairus' eyes burned with anger. "You and I will discuss this further," he said to Pieter. "But right now, we must continue our interrogation. What happened after the raid on the village, Alvin?"

"Goldemar began making plans for more raids. I was tired of it. He'd promised me that once he was done with Lachlann we could part ways, but I began to realize that this wouldn't happen for a very long time. I got desperate; I started to wonder if I could take control of our body long enough to kill both of us." He sighed. "And then yesterday happened."

Soren nodded. "Tell me about yesterday from your perspective."

Alvin frowned. "The magic show was impressive. When the anti-magic broke, though, I realized it was a diversion. But we were in the middle of the ceremony, and I didn't want to give myself away as a magikai, so I couldn't do much. I assumed someone had killed Lachlann, so I was shocked when he showed up on the platform. I knew our time was up. Goldemar knew too, which is why he tried to stop Lachlann from talking, then threw the enchanted knife at you, Your Majesty."

Kairus lifted an eyebrow. "So you had nothing to do with that, either?"

"It happened so fast, I couldn't talk him down," Alvin replied. "Then the guards moved in, Trina got involved with her fairy magic, and then Goldemar...did something to me. Suddenly, I had no control of the body, and then I lost consciousness completely. Goldemar thought he killed me. I came to as he was saying how much power he had now, and I realized that was his plan all along. He didn't want to share a body with me, he wanted it all to himself. And I knew I couldn't let myself die, because if he won, he'd be unstoppable. Thankfully, my brother intervened, and then a few of you did that fancy spell. You know what happened from there."

Kairus looked Alvin over and let out a deep sigh. "So what I hear you saying is that Goldemar was behind the most evil of the things you did."

Alvin flinched. "As I said, some of the evil was me. I wanted to make Lachlann suffer. I wanted to hurt Ruby and Saray and Trina. But his idea of revenge is far more extreme than mine."

"Are you sure he's telling the truth?" Kairus asked Soren.

The disguised charmer replied, "Quite certain, Your Majesty."

"Alvin, do you truly believe yourself less worthy of death because you were not fully in control? You did, after all, choose to share a body with a Fae who you knew had corrupted your brother."

"Oh, I know I deserve to die, Your Majesty," Alvin replied. "And if you wish to kill me, I will go to my death willingly. But as I said earlier, I have an offer for you. I know how to cure your son of his curse."

"His...curse?"

"That's right. What afflicted your wife, and now your son, is not a natural illness. It was bestowed onto both of them by a form of dark magic."

"He's right," I spoke up. "Last night, Oliver came to visit me, and I tried to heal him. Only I couldn't figure out how. I tried to see into his illness to determine its cause, and I saw exactly that. A curse."

"What...sort of curse are you speaking of?"

"I don't know exactly. But when I looked into his wounds, I saw someone poison Oliver's tea a few years ago. I can't say for sure, but I suspect the same person did something similar to Oliver's mother."

"Do you know who it was?"

I frowned. "You'll have to pardon my boldness; I hope I'm not making a false accusation. But it looked to me like Pieter. And Oliver remembered very well the conversation with Pieter that accompanied that tea, so I cannot help but believe that my vision was accurate."

"Pieter?" Kairus' eyes widened. "Please," he said to the mage, "tell me this isn't true. I know you do not desire the throne."

Pieter's face had turned white, but he gave a heavy sigh, doing what he could to maintain his composure. "I did it for the good of the country, Your Majesty."

"Explain yourself!"

"I did it because I was trying to keep the royal bloodline pure and free from the scourge of magic. Your first wife was a witch, sire. And so is your son, whether he realizes it or not."

I gaped and turned to Oliver. "You...are?"

Pieter went on without allowing the prince a chance to respond. "Do you recall how your wife always knew what the weather would be? The day she brought a warm cloak and predicted a sudden snowstorm? And have you not noticed your son's ability to sneak off and blend into crowds at will? It's almost like he can *disappear*."

"That's not magic," Oliver protested. "I can't actually go invisible, and I don't use casting words."

Pieter raised an eyebrow at him. "Do you know what a demi-mage is, son?"

"I...just learned about them last night," he admitted, exchanging a glance with Jasper. "Is that what I am? A demi-mage vanisher?"

"I'm quite certain. Which means that if you take the throne, the royal bloodline will be infected by magic, even if you don't marry *her*." His eyes fell on me for a moment, full of scorn, then he turned back to Kairus. "As for your wife, I hoped that if she died young, you would remarry and have more children. I could deal with Oliver once I'd assessed whether he had magic."

"You killed my wife." Kairus' voice went soft, dangerous.

"Surely you understand why, Your Majes—"

"*Arrest him!*" Kairus thundered. The two guards, who'd been inching closer to Pieter since his admission of guilt, closed in.

Pieter began to panic and mumble the words to a spell, only to be interrupted by Marcus leaping up to direct a complex hand motion at him. Pieter immediately froze in place, unable to move or speak, and the guards took him away.

Kairus was visibly shaken by what had just unfolded. "I...uh...thank you for that," he said to Marcus.

"My pleasure." Marcus bowed. "I know the pain of losing a wife." He looked to Alvin then, as if reminded of what we'd initially been doing. "Now that that's taken care of, let's continue. You were saying you know how to remove Oliver's curse?"

Alvin's eyes were round; clearly he, too, was shocked by what he'd just seen, but when he spoke his voice was even. "I do. It's not actually a curse, but a form of decay magic. Goldemar told me that the Dunderi Fae will use it to kill folks that they particularly hate." He paused when Mischief jumped into his lap and smiled down at her. "Well, aren't you adorable? I'd pet you, but my hands are bound." Mischief responded by climbing onto his shoulder and butting her head against his.

"Well, what he's saying about decay magic is true," put in Lachlann. "That's likely what cost me my arm."

"It's also frowned upon everywhere magic is legal. And because of that, the way to counteract it has been suppressed as well. I know where it can be found, though."

"And where is that?"

Alvin lifted his chin. "If I help you, and we succeed in curing Oliver, then I will be punished by exile only. I'll be banished from Breoch, but not harmed."

Kairus snorted. "After all you've done? I hardly think so."

"I think we should tell Alvin about our alternative offer, Your Majesty," put in Marcus.

"And what is that?" asked Alvin.

Kairus cleared his throat and explained Arquinn's plea for Alvin's life, then the subsequent plan. "All right." Alvin nodded. "If I heal Oliver, you bind me to my brother, but I don't agree to become a krossemage."

Kairus sighed. "Then you could still use your magic to harm others."

"There...might actually be another way to remove his magic," Saray spoke up. "My grandmother had it done to her. It would just be a matter of digging up Ashlar's old spells."

"And that method involves magic, I assume?" asked Kairus.

"Father, it sounds like any hope for my recovery lies within magic," Oliver put in. "You're going to have to allow it in one form or another if you want me to live." He turned to Alvin then. "So if you help heal me, you would be bound to your brother and have your magic removed permanently, but you would not be made into a krossemage. Does that seem reasonable to you?"

Alvin nodded. "Yes, I can accept that, Your Highness."

"One last problem," Kairus said. "What does this do for those you harmed most? Is it fair to Marcus, Lachlann and Ruby that you're given something resembling freedom after all you did?"

There was a moment of quiet. Finally, Oliver said, "It may be beneficial to them, if my survival hinges on Alvin's cooperation. Because if I live long enough, I will become king one day. And when I become king, I vow to all of you that I will undo the Banishing of Magic. In the meantime, I will petition my father, as heir to the throne, to make the Shrouded Woods a Special Territory much like the Eastwilds, where magic is allowed so long as it is properly policed and taught."

There were murmurs among the Ankrossi folks. "You mean that?" Marcus said.

"I do. This would satisfy everything we came here to discuss. It would solidify Alvin's sentence and give you folks what you want."

Marcus nodded slowly. "May I ask one more thing, Your Highness?"

"Go ahead."

"Will you also petition your father to dismantle the krossemage system?"

Oliver frowned. "And what do you suggest we replace it with?"

"Do what Lachlann proposed when you captured him. Train your police in anti-magic—but properly this time. If folks are caught using magic, banish them to the Woods, where they can practice freely. If they use it to commit crimes, punish them accordingly, or perhaps have their magic removed in the way we intend to remove Alvin's."

Kairus frowned. "If I were to do this, I'd need someone to teach my city guard anti-magic." His eyes fell on Lachlann. "I don't suppose you'd consider working with me after everything?"

"I can't use anti-magic myself anymore," Lachlann replied. "But I have two apprentices who can."

"One more thing," I spoke up. "Would you also consider legalizing healing magic within all of Breoch? I'm sure there are many folks who Jasper and I could help. It's a good first step toward what Oliver intends to do when he takes the throne."

"You folks just keep asking for more and more." Kairus shook his head. "Though you make a good point about the healing magic, Isabelle. I will grant each of your requests, but with conditions.

"The Shrouded Woods will become a Special Territory only if you folks succeed in healing my son, and only if Marcus can produce for me a detailed plan regarding how magic will be regulated there. If you can accomplish that, I will begin the process of eliminating the krossemage system, if Lachlann's apprentices are willing to train my men in anti-magic. And I will make healing legal in Breoch if one of you will take on the role of court mage. I need someone on my council who knows magic well enough to help develop new policies." He eyed Saray. "You're still my first choice for this. And now you wouldn't be working against your own people."

Saray frowned. "I'd consider it, Your Majesty, but I'm tied to the Woods now. It's a bit hard to explain, but...how much time would I need to spend in court?"

"We could likely arrange it for two or three times a week, plus emergencies."

"If I were able to teleport home after my meetings, I could likely make it work," Saray said. "I couldn't live in the palace, but I could still work for you." She glanced at Kip. "What do you think?"

"If it's what you want," he said. "Just don't endanger the Woods by staying away for too long."

"Of course." She looked back to Kairus. "Do we have a deal, then, Your Majesty?"

"Well, this all hangs on whether Oliver can be healed. How are you going to remove this curse, Alvin?"

"There's a book back home in Aidan's library with the antidote," Alvin explained. "It's written in a Fae script, but I know how to read it. Arquinn will be going to Dundere to get the words for the binding spell, so I can have him pick up the book while he's there. He'll need the spell even if I can't break the curse, because in that case I'll take you up on your offer, even if it does mean becoming a krossemage."

Kairus nodded. "That's your choice, then?"

"It is. I'd much prefer that to being stuck in a cell for the rest of my life."

"Well, you'll be in a cell a little longer, at least. The rest of you have some work to do. Find the book, have Alvin read it, gather the things you need for this spell, and report back to me when you're ready to proceed. Until then, I'll ensure your village remains untouched."

"Thank you, Your Majesty," Marcus replied.

"One last thing. If the Shrouded Woods becomes a Special Territory, I will need to appoint a governor to oversee it and work with me. Would you be interested in that role, Marcus?"

Marcus frowned. "I may not be the best choice, given my age. I don't intend to be the mayor of Ankrossi for too much longer, let alone the governor of a territory."

"Who would you recommend, then? It'd be best if the candidate knows the entirety of the Shrouded Woods and its people, not just the folks in Ankrossi."

Marcus exchanged glances with a few other council members. Then Saray spoke up. "Your Majesty? I'd like to nominate Lachlann for the job."

Lachlann's eyes widened. "Why me?"

Saray smiled. "Because you know the Woods better than nearly anyone, but you're also comfortable in the cities. Because you've led Ankrossi in Marcus' absence. You understand trade and security, you aren't bothered by working in a hierarchy. And because you were willing to suffer to protect your home."

Lachlann frowned. "But I didn't protect Ankrossi. I gave Goldemar its location."

"Only because it was that or he'd kill one of the children. And, if I'm not mistaken, you knew the folk in Ankrossi had a fighting chance," Oliver interjected.

Lachlann eyed him and then nodded.

"So you know how to make a tough call, which is important in a leader."

"And in the end, you were willing to die so that no more harm would come to Ankrossi, or to us," Silva put in.

Kairus nodded slowly. "I think you'd be a good choice as well, Lachlann. Would you accept the appointment if I offered it to you?"

Lachlann exchanged a glance with Starla, then nodded slowly. "I'll need to think on it a bit, but...most likely."

"Wonderful," Kairus said. "I suppose that concludes our meeting, then. Guards, please return Alvin to his cell. The rest of you may go."

Marcus stood, and the remainder of his council followed suit. Oliver turned to me. "Will you be going with them?"

"I'd like to go for a few days, but I'll be back. I..." I grew quiet when I saw Father approaching.

"Isabelle." He looked me over, then sighed and put a hand on my shoulder. "You did well yesterday. Thank you for saving Kairus."

I shrugged. "I did what I had to."

"So you're happier in the Woods than you were at home?"

"I'm not sure. I do love my new friends, but there are some things I miss about being here. Like Oliver." I smiled and took Oliver's hand.

"Are you two?—" He was interrupted by Mother joining us.

I watched as my parents regarded one another warily. Then Father cleared his throat. "Lillian, I, uh...I apologize for forcing you to attend the execution."

Mother raised an eyebrow. "Well, I would apologize in turn for running away from you, but I suspect we're both happier this way."

"So it seems." Father's eyes slid to Marcus, who watched our exchange from the other side of the room. "Are you happy with...him?"

"We're still getting to know one another again. It's been twenty-five years, and we've both changed a lot. But, yes, we're happy."

Father nodded. "Funny to think that the fellow who once shined my shoes is running a city now."

"It's not surprising to me at all." Mother glanced fondly at Marcus.

There was a pause between my parents, then Father cleared his throat. "Well, I think I'd best be going. When will I see you next, Isabelle?"

I made arrangements with him to return home within a week, as school would be starting soon, and then I watched him make his way out of the chamber. I turned back to Mother. "Once I'm back at school, I'll visit you in Ankrossi on the weekends."

"That sounds like a very good arrangement," she said, nodding.

Oliver turned to me. "Will you show me Ankrossi one day?"

"I hope so." I leaned in and kissed him gently. "I'll see you soon, Oliver."

Then I turned and followed my friends out of the room, toward the courtyard of the palace.

Toward my second home.

Chapter 37

WE ARRIVED BACK in Ankrossi to a celebration. I spent the afternoon flitting about, Silva in tow, showing her our village and introducing her to my many friends. Word spread quickly that an impromptu feast would be taking place in the meadow tonight.

Before dinner, Trina took Jasper, Silva and me to a cavern in the Mothertree where Claudi's body was being kept under a preservation spell. I looked down at the wizened face of my mentor and felt tears well in my eyes. "I'll miss you," I told her. "But I'm glad you're with your family now."

"You'll have to tell me some stories about her," Silva said.

"There will be lots of stories tomorrow," Trina assured. "We're laying her to rest in the evening."

We returned to the meadow to find tables piled with food. Silva and I sat with Sophie, Chester, and the other teens, and we all dug into the meal. After the first course, Jasper came to see me again, this time with Tristan. "Want to help me out with a healing?"

"Whose?"

He looked down to the far end of the table where Lachlann sat with Starla and Aria. "Hey, Lachlann," he called out, "can Isabelle and I give you a hand?"

"With what?" Lachlann asked, frowning.

I snorted, immediately catching Jasper's pun. "He means it literally. Do you want your missing hand restored?"

"Oh!" Lachlann glanced down, and I saw that he was using a fork attachment on his stump to eat. He stared at it for a moment, then looked up and grinned. "Yes, let's do that after dinner."

Once the food had been eaten, Jasper and I came to sit on either side of him. "When you're done with that, he has a few other things that need healing," Starla told us. "Alvin definitely did some damage."

Lachlann stiffened a little. "I'd prefer we do those healings in private. Perhaps tomorrow?"

"All right. We'll just deal with your hand now." Jasper frowned at me. "Perhaps you should do this one—you likely know better what needs to be done. I'll watch, though, and lend you some magic if you need it."

I took the stump of Lachlann's arm in my hand and allowed myself to see into the wound for just a moment—I saw the arrow pierce his bracer, poison spreading throughout his body, then the face of a woman I suspected to be Kirilee—along with Willem and a younger looking Kip—grimacing as they prepared to perform the amputation.

My vision was interrupted by a small hand on top of mine. I opened my eyes to find Tristan staring up at me with his wide, green-gold eyes. Jasper laughed. "He wants to help."

I grinned at the little boy. "You're going to help me heal him?"

He nodded, and a slow smile formed on his face.

"All right, but you need to sing with me."

I began to sing the familiar words of the healing song. Tristan joined in, his melody wordless and nothing like mine. I grinned as I willed the remaining parts of Lachlann's forearm to lengthen. Tristan and I watched, both transfixed, as the wrist began to form, followed by the palm and back of the hand. I placed my hand on top of it, drawing Lachlann's fingers out with my own. Then my singing ceased, and Lachlann was staring down at his newly formed appendage. He let out a chuckle of delight and made a fist. "Well, what do you know," he said softly. "It worked."

Tristan signed to him, and Lachlann grinned. "That's right. All done."

"It'll take some getting used to," Marcus said. "But you have plenty of time. You're home now."

Lachlann nodded and closed his eyes for a moment. "I'm home now," he repeated softly.

"Let me see." Starla shooed me out of my seat and sat down next to him, taking his restored hand in her own. Lachlann reached up and ran his thumb down her cheekbone. She smiled and pulled him toward her, and I watched as they kissed tenderly, Lachlann working his fingers into her hair. Above us, the translucent pink mist that still hung over the village twinkled with light.

Jasper grinned. "Looks like Kirilee's enjoying the show."

Starla pulled away and shot him a glare, but Lachlann just laughed as he got to his feet, pulling Starla up with him. "If you folks will excuse us," he said, "my wife and I have been separated for a good many months, and we have plenty of lost time to make up for." He offered Starla his arm, and they strode toward their home, leaving us all staring after them.

***

The following morning, Jasper and I headed to Lachlann and Starla's place to handle the rest of his wounds. We found Lachlann sitting on the large sofa, Aria sleeping in the crook of his newly formed arm. "You're here to heal the rest of me, I take it?" I didn't miss the wary note in his voice.

"That's right," Jasper said.

"You might be here a while. There's plenty to heal."

"Well, then, we'd best get started. What's first?"

Lachlann frowned. "I suppose we should start with this." He held up his right hand, and only now did I see that his fingers were oddly bent in different places. "I will warn you, what you'll see when you look into the wound won't be pretty. I'm hardly comfortable with you having to, let alone Isabelle." He glanced at me. "No offense."

Jasper put a hand over Lachlann's bent fingers, closed his eyes and hummed for a moment. "You realize that I've seen people tortured before, right? It was part of my Guard training. Father forced me to watch people die when I was a teenager because he hoped it would harden me." He frowned down at Lachlann's fingers. "What else needs healing? I'm going to have to break these, so we'll do that later."

"My left shoulder. They pulled it out of its socket."

Jasper winced but moved to Lachlann's shoulder without comment.

"That's terrible your father made you watch those things, Jasper," Lachlann said then.

"I'm only telling you that so you know that what I'm seeing in your wounds is nothing I haven't seen before." Jasper glanced at me. "This one should be easy. Help me out, Isabelle."

I put my hands on top of Jasper's, and we began our song. Lachlann let out a sigh. "That does feel better. Thank you." He gave Jasper a tense smile. "Just because you've seen it before doesn't mean I want you to see *me* in those sorts of situations."

"If it makes you feel any better, you're holding out much better than most people would under torture."

"Perhaps. But that doesn't change the fact that they broke me eventually."

"By doing something that would likely break anyone."

"Even so." Lachlann sighed deeply. "I failed to protect Becksa. And Willem, and Saray. And I could have very easily failed this entire village." He averted his eyes. "It's hard for me to understand why you folks would want me to lead you."

Jasper eyed Lachlann. "You understand that's exactly what Goldemar wanted, right? He couldn't break you physically, so he put you in an impossible situation to break your will. And if you keep thinking like you are, you're letting him *win*."

"Sometimes I wonder if he already has," Lachlann admitted, his gaze flickering to Jasper's. "I can hardly sleep, you know. My mind keeps reliving those moments. Saray's execution. When I told them how to get to Ankrossi. And when they snapped Becksa's neck..." I cringed, and Lachlann caught my expression. "I'm sorry. I shouldn't be talking to you two about this."

I met his eyes. "When Jasper snapped *your* neck, what did it feel like? Did it hurt?"

He frowned. "Not really. There was pain for a split second, then I was out of my body, watching you two try to bring me back. Things got dark, and I felt like I was being pulled away. But then you brought me back before I could leave completely."

"So if it didn't really hurt for you, then it likely didn't for Becksa either. It would have been very fast."

"I understand reliving those sorts of moments, though," put in Jasper. "I've been dealing with nightmares ever since...Jade." He sighed. "I know something about being in situations where someone dies no matter what choice you make."

Lachlann nodded solemnly. "I suppose you do."

"But I'm doing better than I thought I'd be, thanks to some advice you gave me many years ago. Remember when you told me about how your time in the army hurt your mind? You said that talking about what had happened, and being surrounded by people who accepted you despite everything, was what helped you recover. I'm trying to remember that, to lean on my friends and actually talk about it all." Jasper smiled at him. "You're in a safe place to do that too, you know."

"You're also with people who *understand*," I put in. "This village is made up mostly of former krossemages. They know what it's like to be tortured and held prisoner. Your wife especially."

Lachlann nodded slowly. He was quiet for a moment, and when he spoke his voice trembled slightly. "Listen to you two, giving an old fellow like me advice."

"Just repeating your own wisdom back to you," Jasper replied.

"I suppose my younger self did have some good things to say."

"He did." Jasper smiled. "Your mind will heal. In the meantime, go ask Shawnie about the potion that allows sleep without dreams. I've been using that, and it does wonders."

Jasper worked on a couple more wounds in silence, then returned to Lachlann's fingers. "We're going to need Trina for this; she knows a spell to relieve pain. Can you go fetch her, Isabelle?"

I nodded and stood.

"Thanks for your help," Lachlann said, giving me a smile.

"That's what I'm here for," I assured, then slipped out of the house to find Trina.

***

Claudi's memorial took place that evening; it was small and informal. We gathered at the base of the Mothertree, and Kip led the proceedings, telling us stories of the woman who'd been something like a grandmother to him in the years when he was learning magic. Like Willem's memorial, there were tears, but this time there was a sense of peace too. Claudi had lived a long life, and she'd been ready to go.

Once the stories were shared, Kip peeled back the layer of burlap that was covering her face. I gazed down at the woman who'd trained me and wiped away a tear. "Thank you," I whispered.

When we'd taken turns saying our farewells, Kip began to move the dirt, and Claudi's body slowly sank into the earth. Starla began to sing then, and a small green shoot appeared immediately above the place where Claudi lay. Several heart-shaped leaves formed on its stalk, and then it shot upward, wrapping around the branches of Kirilee and Noelle's trees, and tiny blue flowers began to bloom all over it. The flowers had an iridescent quality, adding an ethereal touch to the already beautiful structure, and I smiled as the light of the viletta bounced and sparkled on their delicate petals.

***

The next day, Arquinn returned to us carrying two large books. "Alvin's interpreted the cure we need," he told us, "and it's going to take some time. We'll have to get water that's been purified under a full moon, which happens three weeks from now." Some of the other ingredients would be simple to obtain—a viletta bloom, an orchid flower blessed by the fairies, and Erril mushrooms, which Kip had a stash of. A few others were more elusive—a potion of Breaking, which required another recipe buried in Willem's library, and a pyrie shell. When Arquinn mentioned this, I remembered I had one on the comb from Indira, the woman from the Caron Islands. I would have to go home to retrieve it—but, I figured, now was the time to do that anyway.

The following morning, I said goodbye to my Ankrossi friends, assured Silva many times that she was in good hands, then had Arquinn teleport me home. I entered the house tensely, uncertain what being back would be like after all that had happened.

It was Magda who found me first. "Miss Isabelle?"

I gave her a nervous smile, waiting to be scolded. "Hi, Magda."

Much to my surprise, she cleared the space between us and pulled me into a firm embrace. "Miss Isabelle is home!" she called out over my shoulder.

"That she is!" I heard my father's voice exclaim.

I pulled away from the hug and looked my father over, my heart pounding in my ears. He looked younger somehow, some of the usual worry seemingly gone from his face. He held out an arm, and I stepped toward him, shocked when he nearly crushed me in his arms. "I've missed you, my dear," he said, his voice rough.

"I've missed you too," I replied automatically, and a moment later I realized that I meant it.

"Are you here to stay?" he asked, pulling away.

I was about to respond, but Magda cut in. "Miss? I hope you don't mind, but I'm having some trouble cooking as of late. My elbow has been hurting me quite terribly, and..." She trailed off uncomfortably.

I glanced at Father, who nodded.

"Sit down, and roll up your sleeve," I said.

"People have been coming by the house looking for you," Father told me as I knelt down beside Magda. "Folks looking for healing, and others who have healing powers of their own and want you to teach them."

"It's not actually legal yet," I reminded him.

"No, but I don't think anyone is going to stop you. Kairus even said to me the other day that he hopes you come home soon so you can fix his bad knee. He may have been kidding around, but it was hard to tell."

I pondered Father's words while I healed Magda's elbow. When I was finished, she flexed her arm a few times, then beamed at me. "Thank you, miss."

"You'd best get unpacked, wash up, and put on some of your, uh, less woodsy clothes," Father told me then. "I'm expected at the palace for dinner, and I have a feeling you'll want to join me."

Chapter 38

"YOU AND YOUR friends have caused quite a stir in the city, my dear," Kairus told me a few hours later when I sat in the family living quarters with Father. Oliver hadn't shown up yet, but Kairus was eager to hear about what had transpired in Ankrossi since our meeting.

"Good or bad?" I asked.

"Perhaps a little of both. There are some who are upset that I didn't turn the lot of you into krossemages. And plenty are calling for Simon—er, Alvin's—death. But there's also a lot of talk about the points made during your little show, specifically about using magic for military, food production, and healing purposes." He smiled. "Several folks here in the palace have wondered if you or your friend—Jasper, was it?—would be returning any time soon, as they have maladies of their own."

I nodded. "Father said a good number of people have come by our house seeking me." I tilted my head. "I also hear rumour that you have a bad knee."

"Ah, yes." Kairus sighed. "I don't want just anyone healing folks until it's been made legal. But I might be able to look the other way when it comes to you and Jasper. I imagine your work takes some training."

I nodded. "I agree completely. Training should be mandatory."

"Well, once it's legalized, perhaps you can set up a training course for other lifebringers. Though I imagine it will take some time to write out a curricu—"

"Boo!" A sudden voice, accompanied by a pair of hands on my shoulders, interrupted us, and both Kairus and I jumped.

Kairus shook his head and sighed. "You really need to stop doing that, son."

I tipped my head back to see Oliver peering down at me, a smile playing on his lips. "Hi, Isabelle." He stooped to peck me on the lips. "I figured if Pieter was right about me being a demi-mage, I should find out how sneaky I can be. Seems to work well—I managed to scare you even while lumbering around with a cane." He grinned and came around the front of the couch, bracing himself with one hand and pulling me to my feet with the other. Then he wrapped his arms around me. "I've missed you," he murmured.

"Same," I mumbled, burying my head in his shoulder.

He held onto me for a few long moments, then pulled me onto the couch next to him. "So, how's the secret village in the Woods?" He winked.

"Good. It's been nothing but celebrations since we got Lachlann back."

"How is he?" Kairus' brow furrowed. "I feel like I owe that poor man a palace of his own after all that happened to him."

"He's...healing up," I said. "Thrilled to be back with his wife and daughter. I think his brother is going to arrange for him to travel to Sylvenburgh Academy next week and meet up with the kids who were imprisoned with him. They all thought he was dead until Tomlin returned from the Woods to tell them otherwise." I shook my head. "It's not your fault. Alvin—or Goldemar, I suppose—charmed you so that he could get his revenge."

Kairus nodded. "It's that sort of magic that has me worried about Oliver's plans to undo the Banishing."

"You know, magic is legal where Alvin is from, but even there, folks are fearful of charmers. And it was that very prejudice that really got him twisted up," I said. "I know charmers in the Woods who use their magic for good."

Father snorted. "Good? Your friend who convinced your mother you were safe in the Woods may have meant well, but I wouldn't call her actions *good.*"

"She was right, though. I was safe."

"And this is why I need Saray as court mage," Kairus put in. "The ethics of magic are complex."

I nodded. "I've heard rumour that, at the school of magic in Dundere, there's an entire course taught on ethics. I believe Saray's taken it."

"Well, if not, perhaps we'll need to send her back for more training." Kairus frowned. "On the subject of travels to Dundere, do you know if Arquinn was able to find the information we need to remove Oliver's curse?"

"He was, but it'll be a few weeks before we're ready." I glanced over at Oliver and squeezed his hand. "I'm excited to heal you."

"I'm sure you are." Kairus smiled at me. "Speaking of which, my knee. Do you mind?"

"Not at all." I grinned. "Roll up your trouser leg, Your Majesty, and let's do some magic."

***

In the morning, a small crowd of people had gathered outside our house as word spread about my return. I spent a few hours sitting on our porch swing healing all sorts of maladies.

Halfway through, Oliver showed up; apparently, word had even reached the palace, and he figured he'd "hang around and scare off any Breoch Guard who tried to stop me." Around lunchtime, I dismissed the group and told them to come back tomorrow, as I had other things I needed to do. Then I went back to the palace with Oliver to spend the afternoon with him.

By the time Friday rolled around, I was beginning to miss my friends in the Woods, and I confessed this to Oliver while we sat together in the bell tower. I'd put just enough strength and healing into his legs to allow him to make the climb—it wouldn't last, of course, but it got him up there, and together we'd looked over the city and marvelled at the view. Most of the trappings that had made the tower Lachlann's prison were removed, save for the large ball of aro stone below the bell. Its presence dampened my powers, but it was no longer able to render the entire palace devoid of magic. Oliver poked at it, frowning. "It makes my hand tingle a bit," he confessed, "which I suppose means I do have magic."

"Most likely."

He sighed and lay back on the floor, gazing up at the heavy bell that dangled above us. "It angers me that this place was used as a prison. It's hard to think that something so full of good memories would be the source of someone else's pain."

"I know what you mean." I lay down next to him and shot a glance his way. "This was where you told me I was going to have to marry you—do you remember that?"

"How could I forget? It was also where we had our first kiss." He pushed himself up, then leaned over me and let his lips graze mine. "Hopefully many more as well."

I pulled on his collar, and he kissed me harder. When he pulled away, he ran a thumb over my cheekbone and smiled. "I wish you didn't have to go for the weekend."

"*I* wish I didn't have to choose between you and my friends in the Woods," I replied. "When I'm with them, I miss you. When I'm here, I miss them."

"Well, why not bring me with you this weekend?" he suggested.

"Would your father allow it?"

"I'll ask, but I don't see why not. Will *your* people allow it? Marcus, or whoever is in charge over there?"

"They might subject you to a bit of questioning, but I don't think they'd be wholly opposed. I imagine that my friends would like to meet you. They've heard enough about you."

"All good things?"

"Of course." I grinned.

"Well, then, I'd be honoured to accompany you, if it works out."

"Wonderful." I reached up and ran a hand through his curls, then pulled his face close to mine again.

***

Arquinn gave me an odd look when he showed up that evening to find Oliver with me, but then he shrugged. "Well, I suppose you were going to have to come to Ankrossi at some point, Your Highness. Might as well get used to it now." He frowned. "How do you feel about teleporting?"

"I feel like I'm about to find out," was Oliver's response.

Arquinn chuckled before speaking his spellwords, and the next thing I knew we were standing in the meadow, Oliver looking a little green. "That was...something," he mumbled, leaning on his cane.

"It takes some getting used to. Come on, I'll introduce you to my friends. We should probably go see Mother and Marcus first, though."

Oliver followed me to Marcus' treehouse, and I knocked tentatively on the door. Marcus answered, and his eyes widened when he saw us. "You brought company, I see."

I nodded. "I hope it was all right for my boyfriend to come over for the weekend." I gave him a wry smile. "He's not scared of magic, though I think he has mixed feelings about teleportation."

Marcus studied Oliver for a moment, then grinned and held out his hand. "Welcome to Ankrossi, Your Highness."

"Oliver, please," he replied as they shook.

Marcus eyed Oliver's cane. "Our preparation for your healing is going well. Would you like to see what we've come up with? I'll need to fetch a few folks to help fill you in."

"That would be lovely. I'd also like to meet all of Isabelle's friends. And see more of this place."

"Well, why don't you two head over to the tavern and find a table, and I'll spread the word that you're here. Folks can come meet you there, since running around will likely not be easy for you. Tomorrow we can get Ruby or Kaden to put the flying spell on you and show you around that way."

"I get to *fly?*"

"Oh, you'll get to do lots of things," I assured.

A slow smile worked its way across Oliver's face. "To the tavern, then?"

We made our way to Persius' Perch, where a delighted Jasper came immediately over to our table, grinning. "I knew it," he greeted us. "Ruby and Kaden owe me a new fiddle."

"What?"

"We took bets on whether you'd bring Oliver back here with you. Splendid to see you again, by the way! Now, would the two of you like something to drink?"

I turned to Oliver. "Jasper's pretty good at making tasty drinks for us younger folk that don't contain alcohol."

Jasper snorted. "Look, if the crown prince of Breoch wants liquor, I'm not about to say no. Now, may I recommend—"

"Isabelle!" Silva came running into the tavern. I stood, and she crushed me in an embrace. Lachlann and Starla were close behind, both of them looking better than when I'd left last week.

Only moments after they'd seated themselves, more folks showed up, and soon the tavern was crowded with friends eager to meet Oliver and fill us in on everything that had happened this past week. Shawnie sat next to Oliver and went over the curse removal spell and all the things it would entail. "We should be able to do it two weeks from tomorrow," he said. "The Saturday after next will be our Moon Dance, to celebrate the full moon, and the next day the water for the spell will be ready. And then we can heal you."

"Are you sure it will work?" Oliver asked.

"As sure as we can be. Arquinn and Alvin both seem to think the recipe is genuine, and I doubt Alvin would lie about this, given what's at stake for him."

"I hope they're right," he said softly.

"We all do," agreed Marcus.

Oliver turned to Marcus then. "Are you coming up with a plan for magic use in the Woods?" he asked, seeming eager to change the subject.

Marcus nodded. "Lachlann and I have spent all week on it, and we think we have a fairly good plan to present to your father."

"You know magic use, Lachlann? I thought you were an anti-mage."

"I'm a former anti-mage who's been married to two different magic users, has a magic user for a stepdaughter, and who has escorted teenage magikai to safe places to learn magic for the past eight years. I don't use magic, but I'm much more well-versed in it than you might think."

"Lachlann is being included for another important reason," Marcus added. "He's going to accept your father's offer to become governor of the Special Territory of Firenholme."

"Firenholme?" My brow furrowed.

"It's an old name for the Shrouded Woods. We figure it's a better official name for our territory."

Oliver raised an eyebrow. "I agree. And I'm happy for you, Lachlann. I'm sure my father will be thrilled."

"Your father seems like a good man to me. I'd be honoured to work with him, and perhaps one day with you as well." Lachlann gave Oliver a smile.

"Do you think you're ready to jump into something like that?" I asked him. "After everything you've endured?"

Lachlann's smile faded slightly, and he glanced over at his wife. "I don't think I'm ready quite yet; I still need some time to rest and heal. But we think making Firenholme into its own territory will be a bit of a process, and it will likely be several months before I need to take too much on. Until then, I'll go back to making swords, training kids how to fight with them, and spending time with my family." He stifled a yawn then. "Speaking of rest, I think I'd best go get some. I may be younger than Marcus, but I'm still an old man next to the lot of you."

"I think I'll head home as well," Marcus said.

I watched as the older adults retreated from the tavern. The moment they were gone, Kaden let out a sigh. "Thank the Fae. Why does everything have to turn into an impromptu council meeting?"

"I agree," Jasper said, joining us without his serving apron this time and carrying a large platter of drinks. "We have the future king and queen here in our tavern—I think it's time for a celebration." He picked up his fiddle and smiled at us. "May I play a tune for the esteemed couple?"

Chapter 39

TWO WEEKS LATER, Oliver and I stood in the meadow where folks were gathering for the ritual. Shawnie waved us over. "We have everything we need to make the potion," he told me. "We're just waiting on Arquinn to bring—"

He was interrupted by the familiar shimmering in the meadow's centre, then Arquinn appeared, a figure on each arm. Tristan ran to Arquinn, letting out a happy screech and clinging on to his leg. The rest of the crowd, however, began to mumble, and a few shied away; it was hard to tell which of the men accompanying Arquinn was making everyone more uncomfortable.

Alvin stood on one side of his brother, in chains. His hair was cut short, presumably to keep him from trying to charm anyone. He looked around at the group with wary eyes, and I noticed him shrink back from Lachlann.

Lachlann all but ignored him; his eyes were on the figure on Arquinn's other side. With a smile, and seemingly unfazed, Lachlann came forward. "Your Majesty. Welcome to Ankrossi."

Kairus returned his smile and extended a hand. "It's good to see you again, Lachlann. You're, uh, looking well." He paused for a moment, his poise lost, and I saw what I knew was regret flicker in his eyes.

"It's good to be home," Lachlann replied simply, accepting the handshake. My eyes widened when I realized the king was treating Lachlann as an equal.

"Kairus!" My mother's voice cut through the meadow as she made her way to the king. I didn't miss the gasps that arose from a few of those gathered as she embraced him like the old friend he was.

"I nearly forgot I'd see you today," Kairus exclaimed as he pulled away from her. "Are the Woods treating you well?"

"Incredibly." She pulled back and smiled. "I'm happy here, Kairus."

"I believe you. The courts miss you, though." He tilted his head. "Where's Marcus?"

"Right here," Marcus replied, joining them from where he'd been studying. "It's a pleasure to have you in Ankrossi, Your Majesty."

"I'm glad you think so; the majority of your village seems to feel otherwise." He glanced around at the suspicious faces and raised his hands. "It's all right, friends. I come in peace. I imagine you've all heard by now how magic saved my life? Rumour has it that it's going to save my son's life today too."

A few heads bobbed, but most folks' expressions remained skeptical.

"Well, let's get to it, shall we?" Kairus clapped his hands. "What's the first step?"

"We must begin by binding Alvin to me," Arquinn said. "This has nothing to do with what will heal Oliver, but Alvin will need to keep his magic until after the spell is cast, and if we are bound, I can make sure he doesn't use it for harm." He glanced down at Tristan. "Go see your dad, buddy."

Tristan blinked at him and made the sign for *up.*

"Not right now, my boy," Jasper said, scooping him off the ground. "You come with me, all right? You can see your uncles afterward." I didn't miss Alvin's raised eyebrow, or how Jasper included him as part of his and Tristan's family. Tristan flailed for a moment but soon settled into Jasper's embrace.

Alvin studied Tristan. "I always thought he looked like Ashlynn," he said softly. "But I can see you in him too…I suppose I've blown my chance to be in his life, haven't I?"

Arquinn turned to Jasper. "Given that where I go, Alvin goes, I imagine you won't want us coming back to visit him."

"I don't think you should come back to Ankrossi," Jasper said. "There are some folks here who would rather not see Alvin. But if anyone knows that people can change, it's me." He eyed Tristan. "When he's old enough to understand, I'll tell him everything. Then I'll let him decide. If he wants to meet you, perhaps we can do so away from Firenholme." He smiled. "I know of a splendid little tavern in Flavalan."

Alvin smiled as well. "I'd like that."

Arquinn nodded, then turned to his brother. "All right. Let's do this."

"You sure you want to be stuck with me for the rest of your life?"

"I get lonely sometimes. It'll be fun having someone along for all my adventures. Even if it's my rather stupid kid brother." He gave Alvin an affectionate smile. Then he retrieved a gold bracelet from his pouch and a vial of pinkish liquid. "Will you do the honours, Jasper?"

With a nod, Jasper shifted Tristan so he sat on one hip, and Arquinn handed him the vial, then fitted the gold bracelet over Alvin's left wrist. "Before we do this, take out that earring. I know Goldemar isn't in there anymore, but we should get rid of it."

Alvin pulled it out of the hole in his lobe. "What should I do with it?"

"I think it needs to be destroyed. Lachlann, you're a blacksmith, right? I imagine you wouldn't be opposed to melting this down and letting all your anger out on it in the form of a hammer and anvil?"

"Gladly." Lachlann reached to take it.

Alvin eyed him as he passed the earring along. "Congratulations on your new position, by the way."

Lachlann held his gaze for a moment, then nodded. "Thank you, Alvin. Though I only get the job if today's spell works out, so let's hope for both our sakes that it does."

"Agreed," said Arquinn. "Speaking of which," he took his brother's hands and began to recite, "I, Arquinn Blackwell, place you, Alvin Blackwell, under my care for the remainder of our lives together. I vow to protect you, provide for you, and keep you from harm. In return, you will go where I go and do what I command. If you defy me, or try to run from me, you will find yourself unable to move or speak until I command otherwise. If I should die before you, this binding will pass to our next of kin." He glanced over at Tristan. "Which would be him. Let's hope I don't die young. I doubt you want a kid bossing you around."

Alvin chuckled. "You'd better not abuse this."

"I don't intend to." Arquinn gazed down at their hands and cleared his throat. "Let it be so."

"Let it be so," Alvin echoed.

Arquinn nodded at Jasper then, who uncapped the vial and poured the liquid over the brothers' joined hands. When it touched Alvin's bracelet, it crackled and popped, and I knew that the bracelet had sealed itself shut around his wrist.

"All right, that part is done," Alvin said as Arquinn let go of his hands. "I'm officially enslaved to my big brother. Now we heal Oliver, right?"

"That's right," Shawnie said, stepping forward. He gestured to a large cauldron that he'd placed on stones in the centre of the circle. "Saray, will you boil this water for me?"

She nodded and pressed her hand to the side of the cauldron, flames dancing on her palm, and the water began to bubble within about a minute. "Now we add the other ingredients," Shawnie said. "Kip, the mushrooms."

Kip added dried mushrooms to the water. Then Trina stepped forward with the Fae-blessed orchid, and Starla threw in a viletta bloom from Kirilee's tree. I added the pyrie shell from my comb to the mix, then Shawnie poured in the potion of Breaking. "I sure hope this works," he mumbled. "It was a pain to find the recipe."

When all the ingredients were added, Alvin came forward. He placed his hands on the rim of the cauldron and closed his eyes. "By the power of the Wild Fae of Dundere, and the deep magic that lies within the Verdant Isles, we bring forth that which will break curses, undo decay, and restore life." Then he began to chant in another language. Unlike the trilling yet mournful syllables of my healing song, this language was low and guttural, likely an ancient Fae language. Trina's fairies seemed to recognize the tongue; they twirled and danced above the smoke that wreathed the cauldron.

There was a loud *crack,* and when the smoke began to clear, I saw the cauldron had split in two. A sticky residue formed on its inside, and Alvin stepped forward to rub his fingers in it. He looked up at Oliver. "You said the illness was in your spine?"

"That's what Isabelle thinks," Oliver replied.

"In that case, will you remove your shirt, Your Highness? And take a seat here?" He gestured to a log.

Oliver complied and sat. Alvin crouched behind him to spread the mixture up and down Oliver's spine, chanting again as he did. Then he stood. "My part in this is done. The unguent should activate once healing is cast. Isabelle, Jasper? I don't know the rest of the plan."

Jasper looked to me. "This one is yours. I'll help if it's needed." He walked over to Arquinn and handed Tristan to him.

"All right." I approached Oliver, my heart pounding in my chest. *This is it.* What happened here would determine Oliver's future, and mine too, but also so much more. The fate of this entire village, the Shrouded Woods, the krossemages imprisoned throughout Breoch—all of it hung on whether Oliver's curse could be removed.

Oliver seemed to notice my nervousness; he grabbed my hand and gave me a reassuring smile. "You can do this," he whispered. He wound a hand into my hair, pulled my head down to his own, and pressed his lips tenderly to mine. "I trust you," he whispered.

I let my lips linger on his for a moment, trying to gather courage from him. Then I crouched behind him and placed my fingertips on top of the sticky, dark unguent.

Closing my eyes, I focused only on the sensation of my skin against Oliver's and began to sing.

At first, it felt like any other healing; I sensed my power flowing through my body toward my fingertips. My hands began to heat up, and there was the ever-so-slight dizziness that always accompanied my magic leaving my body. But then my fingers began to tingle in an unfamiliar way.

I opened my eyes to see that the unguent on Oliver's spine was glowing. I continued to sing, watching the luminescence spread through him, branching off his spine into smaller and smaller tendrils of brilliance.

My eyes widened when my mind went back to one of my anatomy lessons, and I realized I was seeing Oliver's entire nervous system light up. He shuddered deeply, muscles spasming under my touch. I saw Kairus' brow furrow as the spasms spread to Oliver's arms and legs, his entire body shaking and pulsing. Instinctively, I removed my fingers from his back and wrapped myself around him, sitting behind him on the log and straddling him. I pressed my thighs into his, intertwined my fingers with his own, and held him while he shook. Then I pressed my lips into the knob at the top of his spine. "Be whole and strong, my love," I whispered repeatedly. I thought I felt his shoulders and biceps harden against my own, his thighs take on new mass, his back straighten.

And then it was done.

Oliver sagged against me, gasping, and my head spun as I tried to hold up both his weight and mine. Jasper darted in behind me, catching both of us. He put one hand on my arm and his other on Oliver's, and I heard him singing softly, undoubtedly breathing strength into both of us. Slowly, my balance returned to me, and I sat up straighter.

Kairus was crouched in front of Oliver. "Did it work?" he asked. "How do you feel?"

Oliver rolled his shoulders and pulled away. Then he slowly rose to his feet, shook out each limb, and met his father's eyes. "I feel...strong." His voice held a strange, breathless confidence. "It worked. By the Fae, Isabelle, it worked!"

I leapt up, and Oliver pulled me into a crushing hug as everyone around us broke out in cheers. I found myself laughing and crying and shaking all at once, my face pressed into Oliver's shoulder, hardly able to think. He pulled away slightly and leaned in, and his lips pressed hungrily against mine. The kiss tasted of tears and sweat and a bit like the unguent that I'd gotten on my mouth, and it was beautiful and glorious.

When he finally pulled away, he laughed. "We're both filthy!" I looked down and saw that the unguent had smeared itself all over the front of my dress.

Marcus laughed. "You two go wash up. We'll finish things off here."

I smiled and wrapped my hand around Oliver's. "Come on," I said to him, "I'll show you where the pools are."

***

We shed most of our clothes and made our way into the bathing pool, Oliver glancing up in wonder at the waterfall that fed it and exclaiming how warm the water was. He dunked himself, then shot back up laughing, shaking his mop of curls at me. "Don't think I could've done that a few hours ago!"

I began washing off the odd, sticky unguent, and as I lifted myself back up out of the water, there was a strange shudder, and the pinkish haze that hung over Ankrossi for the past several weeks suddenly lifted. "What was that?" asked Oliver.

"I think Kirilee has returned to her tree, which tells me that Arquinn and Alvin are gone." I smiled. *"'The Mother will once more return to her tree.'* The prophecy has been fulfilled; Ankrossi is safe again."

Oliver frowned. "Do you believe in those things? Prophecies, visions, and such?"

"Well, it seems like a few of them have come true as of late. Why, don't you?"

"I'm not sure. I think they can hold some interesting information. But I don't know if I'd entrust them with my life. Or my destiny, for that matter." He smiled. "For example, deciding who you're going to marry based on a dream someone had doesn't seem like a wise choice to me."

I felt my heart begin to sink, but he reached forward and ran a fingertip along my jawline. "Now, marrying someone because you're madly in love with her, because you can't imagine a future without her, and because she gave you your life back, well, that I can get behind. But there's still one question that needs answering."

"What's that?"

"You never really got to choose. So I'm going to ask you this in private, with no big announcements or fanfare. And if you say yes, it doesn't have to be for a good number of years yet. But I still need to know." He took my hand in his and sank to one knee in the water. "Isabelle McAllister, do you *want* to marry me one day?"

I felt a smile split my face. "Yes. Absolutely, forever and always, yes."

"All right, good. Just had to check." He grinned as he got to his feet. Then he pulled me close and pressed his lips to mine, and I could feel his heart beating against my chest—a strong, healthy heartbeat, a promise of many years of life and vitality to come.

Oliver would be king one day. And on that day, I'd rule beside him proudly, ready for whatever came at us next.

Epilogue

Eight Months Later

BANISHING DAY DIDN'T exist in the Special Territory of Firenholme.

In its stead, the region would celebrate its birthday on that same date every year after today. And today, the meadow at the centre of Ankrossi was decked out for the celebration.

It had been a good two months since I visited last; my trips had become less frequent with the onset of school and the piles of homework that came with my graduation year, along with my healing work centered in Kirstein. Arriving here yesterday felt like a homecoming. I still saw most of my friends from Ankrossi fairly regularly, but returning to the village had me feeling like the trees and rivers and meadow themselves were welcoming me back.

I was fairly certain that in the case of one particular tree, this was true.

Last night, Oliver and I had helped with the preparations for today's festivities. We'd strung garlands of flowers from every high place, assisted Kip and a few other telekinetics in creating what would serve as our platform for the ceremony, and helped Alexander and Ember pick out the finest clothing for those who would be a part of the transfer of power. Now I sat on the stage next to Oliver as Kairus stood to address the crowd. People from all over Firenholme had gathered for this event, along with a surprising number of city folk. My father had even made the trek, along with all of the household staff. Several other lords and ladies that I knew from the court were in attendance, as well as a large contingent of students from the botany class at Sylvenburgh Academy. There were also a dozen sailors from the Lady Liara, and a good chunk of folks from Dundere—Sophie's father Chase, the current governor Deshi and her family, and a few others I didn't recognize.

Kairus looked the crowd over with a solemn gaze, then began to speak. "Friends and loved ones—citizens of Breoch, the Isle of Dundere, and beyond—today we gather to declare Firenholme, also known as the Shrouded Woods, to be its own territory within the Kingdom of Breoch; to grant it the privileges and responsibilities that accompany such a status; and to lay the mantle of Governor of Firenholme on the shoulders of its chosen leader, Lachlann Jeffries." He nodded at Lachlann, who sat on the other side of the platform, and a smattering of applause sounded from within the audience. "However, I would first like to invite my son, Oliver, to address you."

Oliver rose and took his place next to his father, then looked to Marcus, who sat with Lachlann. "Would you mind doing that thing with—"

"Of course." Marcus came to Oliver, laid a hand on his shoulder, and mumbled a spell.

He gave me a quick smile as he returned to his seat, and I grinned back. I still saw Marcus frequently; he and my mother visited the king and court often. I was delighted when Marcus and Oliver began to bond—Marcus understood Oliver's obsessive enthusiasm about his hobbies, and the two of them had recently completed Oliver's model ship.

"Much better," Oliver said, his voice now amplified. "Thank you." He looked out over the audience. "I'd like to call forward Saray Robinson, the Bearer of the Fire Stone and the official mage of my father's court."

I watched Saray make her way up the stairs, clad in a long cloak designed to look like flames. Nowadays, I saw her more often than anyone else from Ankrossi, as she visited the palace several times a week to train for her new role. The palace folk had been a bit intimidated by her at first; rumours still swirled about that Saray had magically raised herself from the dead, and she'd done nothing to dispel them. The truth, she told me, was harder to explain.

Kip came with her on occasion; at first, he'd seemed uncomfortable amidst all the finery and pomp, but then Jessen and Kyler recruited him to cast spells while they trained the palace guard in anti-magic, and the guards were thrilled to have an opponent skilled in both magical and non-magical combat. Now he was practically one of them, spending most of his time there sparring with off-duty guards and trading stories of combat.

On the platform, Saray took her place next to Oliver, and he turned to her with a smile. "Fifty-eight years ago, one of your ancestors made a mistake with magic that cost a young girl her life. And my family responded in a way that cost many more their freedom and their voices. I believe my great-great-grandfather, King Patrick, meant well. He hoped to protect people from the danger of unchecked magic, but the Banishing did far more harm than good. Not only did it ruin the lives of thousands of mages, it also deepened the fear of magic within the people of Breoch, establishing prejudices that will likely take years to undo. Today, though, we are committed to taking the first small steps to making things right." He smiled at Saray. "Bringing you on as court mage is one of those steps. Eliminating the krossemage system is another, as is fully legalizing healing magic—a move that seems to have made most folk very happy...wouldn't you agree, Isabelle?"

I laughed and nodded. The undoing of the krossemage system was a slow, messy process that received much initial backlash. Krossemages were given three choices upon their release: receive a large sum of money to forgo magic and stay within their current occupation as a paid employee; return to their home of origin, again forgoing magic; or move to Firenholme, where they would be able to live as they wished. A surprising number of the krossemages chose to remain in their current jobs. Many others had come to the Woods, and the population of Ankrossi nearly doubled in a few months. A good chunk of both Jasper's and my recent healing work involved restoring hands and tongues both in the Woods and the cities, and I imagined this would continue for a while yet.

The legalization of healing magic in Breoch had scared some people at first, but after seeing its outcome most were incredibly grateful for the change. I'd been extremely busy over the past months, both healing people and training the handful of folks who'd come forward as lifebringers. I saw Jasper nearly as often as Saray; he came to the palace weekly, always accompanied by Tristan and either Trina or Ruby and Kaden. Jasper was becoming quite loved by the palace folk; when he wasn't healing, he was usually entertaining the court with a song or story. When Kaden came along, she helped him tell these tales, adding her own dramatic flair. Ruby often ended up in deep conversations with the king or queen; she was very aware that one day she would take over Marcus' job, and she wanted to do it right.

The palace folk were a bit wary of Trina; most of them had seen her capture Goldemar and didn't understand that it had not been by her power alone—rumours swirled that the blind girl who was always surrounded by fairies could defeat any magical foe the nation might encounter. The children of the palace, conversely, absolutely adored Trina, and it wasn't uncommon to find a good dozen of them trailing her. Tristan was usually among them; now he was as attached to Trina as he was to Jasper, and both Jasper and Trina were adjusting to their new roles quite well, with the help of the village's many other parents.

"Today, we take another step in the right direction," Oliver continued, "by declaring Firenholme its own territory, where magic is completely legal within certain terms." He offered Saray another smile. "I cannot apologize to you for the mistakes of my ancestors, nor can you forgive me for damage done. But will you stand as a proxy for the magical community of Firenholme, to accept my promises and my terms?"

Saray nodded. "I will."

Oliver reached for her hands and met her gaze. "As crown prince and future king of Breoch, I swear to you that I will work to make life better for the magical community during my reign. I will continue to uphold the independence of the Special Territory of Firenholme, I will try my hardest to undo the stigma of magic within the nation, and I will, when I am king, make magic legal within all of Breoch as it is here in Firenholme.

"In return, I ask you this: Do you swear to do your part in making magic safe for all? Do you swear to work with me to create systems that will allow magic to flourish, to keep it free yet controlled?"

Saray nodded solemnly. "I swear."

"I look forward to working with you for many more years, Saray." Oliver smiled as he let go of her hands, and Saray offered him a small curtsy before returning to her seat.

Kairus stepped to the front of the stage as Oliver came to sit next to me again. "I'd like to call forward Lachlann Jeffries and his wife and daughter."

Lachlann stood, trailed by Starla and Aria, and walked to the centre of the stage. He wore a long tailcoat made of sage-green brocade and embroidered with what was now the sigil of Firenholme: a tree wreathed in flame. Firenholme, Saray explained to me, meant Kingdom of Fire, and the sigil depicted a place that grew stronger under pressure, that was nearly impossible to destroy.

On Lachlann's head was a simple gold circlet. Starla wore a much more extravagant tiara of gold leaves and jewelled flowers. Her dress was part brocade and part nature; today, the flowers that covered her bust and back were a brilliant crimson and yellow. Aria tugged at a strand of ivy that draped over Starla's shoulder and giggled. I'd become quite fond of their little family over the past month. Aria was progressing remarkably; she'd just begun to toddle along unassisted, and she'd developed a fascination with Trina's fairies.

Lachlann seemed to be recovering well from his ordeal. When he was at the palace, he was serious and focused; when I visited Ankrossi, though, I'd usually find the couple playing with Aria in the meadow, often accompanied by Tristan, and sometimes Ambrose and Daisy's daughter Raelle. Alisa and Shawnie showed up on occasion with Xavier, the little boy Alisa had given birth to several months ago.

I knew that Lachlann was still healing—he often needed the tea that prevented nightmares, and at the palace he avoided even looking at the bell tower. Starla, of course, had been incredibly supportive of both him and Silva, whom they'd officially adopted. Silva had yet to return to Kirstein, but I knew she was more than happy in Ankrossi. The other teens had accepted her as one of their own, and she was known for starting spontaneous snowball fights amongst the younger folk.

Kairus looked Lachlann over, and when he spoke, his voice was solemn. "Lachlann, you have been chosen by both your people and me to assume the role of Governor of Firenholme, and in honesty, I cannot think of a better person to fill the role. I've only known you for a year, but in that time I've seen the great devotion you have to this place. I've witnessed your desire to protect the vulnerable, and I've seen you suffer greatly in doing so." He sighed. "I'm going to speak frankly with you, Lachlann. What was done to you in the dungeons and bell tower of my palace was inhumane. I was charmed when I allowed those things, but as king, I still bear the responsibility. You were made to choose between protecting vulnerable children and protecting your home. But from what I've heard, you handled the situation with strength. You did what you could to keep the children safe and taught them to defend themselves. Ultimately, you were willing to give up your own life to defend both them and your loved ones. That willingness to sacrifice for your people is the mark of a true leader. And so it is my honour today to grant you the title of Governor of Firenholme. Lachlann, please kneel. Marcus, Gareth, Celia, and Ronin, please come forward."

Lachlann knelt, and the four others took the stage. The news of Firenholme's change had resulted in the building of three new villages. The first was near the territory's lone port, an isolated place that Lachlann told us was the site of his wedding to Kirilee. The port village was Gareth's idea, and he'd volunteered to be its leader, as he'd recently retired from captaining the Lady Liara.

The second village, near the site of the Moon Dances, was made up mainly of the wilder Woods-folk, and was led by Ronin, a long-time occupant of the area. The final village was only an hour's walk from the edge of the Woods near Sylvenburgh, and it was made up mostly of newcomers to Firenholme who wanted to remain close to Sylvenburgh. I'd heard good things about their mayor, Celia. Her husband Jorge was a plantspeaker like Starla, and he had been appointed to oversee the nearby tree-felling camp.

Firenholme would pay its taxes to Breoch in lumber, with Jorge and Starla working together to regrow the trees that were cut. Every citizen of Firenholme was responsible for contributing to the camp, be it by taking one day a month to cut down trees, using telekinesis to move felled logs, or providing food or other necessities to the workers.

Once the other leaders had made their way to the stage, Kairus turned to address them. "Do you, Marcus, Gareth, Celia and Ronin, accept Lachlann as the leader of your territory? Do you vow to work with him in the best interests of your villages, to defer to him when necessary, and to help him make Firenholme a healthy, safe and vibrant territory?"

They all nodded. "We do."

Kairus returned his gaze to Lachlann. "Do you, Lachlann Jefferies, vow to lead the citizens of Firenholme, to put the needs of the people before personal gain, to exercise justice and compassion in your rule, and to work with myself and the court of Breoch in all matters needing national attention?"

"I do so vow," said Lachlann.

"Then, as ruler of Breoch, I declare you Governor of Firenholme." Kairus took a heavy, embroidered black cloak from an attendant and placed it over Lachlann's shoulders. "Please rise."

Lachlann stood to thunderous applause from everyone gathered. He took Starla's hand and held it high, and they bowed to the audience. Then he cleared his throat and raised the other hand. "May I say a few words, Your Majesty?"

The king nodded, and Marcus drew closer to Lachlann to amplify his voice.

"I am honoured to accept this position," Lachlann said, "but I wouldn't be here without the help of so many of you. My rescue and the ensured safety of Ankrossi was thanks to a small group of incredible people, and I would like to recognize them now.

"First, I would like to honour both my wife Starla and my late wife Kirilee for working together to protect this village at a time when threats were most dire. I would like to honour Marcus for his unwavering leadership of Ankrossi, and my late friend Willem for his sacrifice in guarding the magical knowledge so important in making this community thrive. And I would like to honour and thank the young people who came together to protect and serve these woods when all of us older folk were indisposed."

I listened as Lachlann mentioned the ways we'd all contributed to the cause—Saray's courage in the face of death, Kip and Kaden's hard work training the troops, Ruby's leadership in Marcus' absence, Shawnie and Alisa's willingness to take on oversight of the school of magic, and Jasper's ingenuity that helped us ultimately free Lachlann. His voice caught when he mentioned Trina's sacrifice to bring back Saray, and when he finally turned to me, I saw tears in his eyes. "Isabelle, how can I ever thank you for healing my daughter? I can't imagine what sort of state I'd be in if she hadn't survived." He smiled. "Thank you also for healing me multiple times, and helping plan out my rescue. You will make a splendid queen one day." His gaze shifted to Oliver. "And you will be a splendid king, Your Highness. Thank you for making all of this happen."

We grinned and nodded at Lachlann as Kairus stepped forward again. "This concludes our ceremonies for today. I believe my son knows what is happening next?"

Oliver nodded and joined his father. "One of the purposes of the Special Territories is to acknowledge and honour the different cultures that exist within our nation. During my occasional stays in Ankrossi, I've found that one of the hallmarks of the Firenholme culture has been joyous celebration. We have plenty of celebrations back at the palace, of course, but it's always structured. Here, there is dancing without formal steps, feasting without proper dinner etiquette, and celebration without reserve. And, as such, the people of Ankrossi have extended to all present an invitation to participate in a sumptuous feast, followed by a raging Firenholme-style dance party." He smiled at the audience. "I, for one, can't wait to be a part of it."

***

Oliver had never fully participated in a Firenholme dance party until tonight.

He'd heard the stories, of course, and one night shortly before his healing we'd attended a party where I was able to heal his legs enough that we could sway together during the slow songs. And we'd resumed ballroom dancing soon after his healing, when he felt he was ready. But we had never whirled about with abandon, not caring about the steps or how we looked, like the people here did. Tonight, though, that would change.

I grabbed Oliver's hands the moment Gareth took to his pipe, and for the first few rounds it was me leading, Oliver wide eyed and breathless as we twirled about. By the third song, he was beginning to understand the movements, and I let him pull me close and lead.

A few dances later, Kairus tapped Oliver on the shoulder and informed him that he and his retinue were leaving, so Oliver would need to find his way home. We paused and watched the king make his rounds, wishing farewell to various people before disappearing into the Woods. A good number of folks from outside Firenholme took that as their own cue to depart.

When the numbers had dwindled significantly, Starla clapped her hands and made her way up to the podium. "Ankrossi friends, come gather," she called out.

People trickled toward her, both folks from Ankrossi and curious onlookers, including Oliver and me. Starla took Lachlann's hand. "I'm afraid the time has come for a farewell," she told us. "Kirilee has chosen today to depart for the world beyond. Holding the spell over the village for those few weeks took incredible strength, and she's been barely hanging on to her time here for the past several months. Now she believes that Firenholme is in the best possible hands, so she's ready to depart."

The mood in the grove turned solemn, and I watched as folks looked up into the Mothertree. "I said goodbye to Kirilee years ago," said Saray. "But I liked knowing she was still here, even though I couldn't talk to her." She stared into the viletta's blooms. "I'll miss you, Kirilee."

Several others echoed her sentiment. Lachlann put a hand on the viletta's trunk. "Well, my dear, we've had some incredible adventures, haven't we?" He closed his eyes, waiting for her response, then nodded. "I'll be all right this time. I have people around to support me." He sighed. "I'll still miss you."

He paused again, then laughed and opened his eyes. "Kirilee reminded me that once she's gone, I can use the charm Ember gave me to connect to another animal or plant. She's wondering what I'll choose next."

"And what will you?" Trina asked.

He grinned. "You know, I've always thought it would be lovely to have my own dragon. It would be especially handy with my new job."

Ambrose laughed. "You would be an excellent dragon rider, Lachlann."

Starla stared up into Kirilee's tree again. "She's so proud of all of you. I wish you could see yourselves through her eyes."

As Starla spoke, a mist slowly began to lift off the viletta. It coalesced into a shimmering pink fog that swirled about, wrapping itself around a few of us in some semblance of a farewell embrace. Then it shot into the sky, and there was a brief explosion of light. It crackled and shimmered for a second or two longer.

Then it disappeared.

Several of the folks who'd known Kirilee well stared upward for a few long moments. Kip drew Saray to himself, and Lachlann and Starla held each other's hands. Trina, meanwhile, gazed up at where the light had been. "That was beautiful."

"You saw it?" Jasper asked.

"All of it." She smiled. "I'll miss her."

"We all will," Marcus said. "But her departure means she trusts that we are safe."

Gareth, who'd been watching from a distance, raised his pipe to his lips and began to play a slow, complex melody. Trina gasped. "Kirilee loved this song!"

Saray nodded, swiped at her eyes, then led Kip back into the meadow to dance. Oliver turned to me. "Shall we?"

***

Several dances later, Oliver and I were interrupted by Ambrose. "I'll be heading home soon, along with Spark," he told us. "If you two need a ride, we'll have to leave now."

"We get to *ride* a dragon?" Oliver asked, grinning.

"Absolutely, Your Highness." Ambrose smiled back. "I'm pleased to offer the best dragon rides within the territory. Now, you two had best go say your farewells."

I made the rounds, sharing embraces and words of goodbye with each of my friends, a few of them stopping to chat with Oliver until I was finished. Then we began to make our way across the grove, hand in hand, toward where Ambrose waited with Spark. "I love this place," Oliver said to me. "I don't feel as if I need to act like a prince here. I can just be...*me*."

"That's what I like about Ankrossi too," I agreed. "I sometimes wish we could live here."

Oliver tilted his head. "Perhaps what we need is to bring a bit of Firenholme home with us. Be a little more wild and uninhibited than our stations demand, show the public that we're *human*. If we're meant to lead one day, then maybe we can do so by being more ourselves, and perhaps that will inspire others to do the same."

"Have I ever told you that I love your mind?"

Oliver squeezed my hand. "How shall we start? Other than decorating ourselves with bright colours, that is?" He ran his fingers through the pink streak that Ember had recently placed in my hair and smiled affectionately.

"Well, we could throw a raging Firenholme-style dance party at the palace, and welcome the public to join," I suggested.

"That's a wonderful idea! It could be accompanied by a feast. Perhaps we could do this once a month, like the Moon Dances?"

"It would certainly be a good start."

We had reached Ambrose and Spark, and now Oliver paused to size the dragon up, his eyes wide. Ambrose grinned. "You look like you've never seen a dragon before, Your Highness."

"I hadn't until a few months ago." Oliver laughed.

I climbed up into the saddle, and he followed suit, settling behind me and putting his arms around my waist. "And, please, call me Oliver when we're away from the palace," he added.

"The palace—is that where we're going?" Ambrose asked.

"That's right," I told him.

Oliver gasped as we rose slowly from the ground. Below us, people waved goodbye, and I let go of the saddle with one hand to wave back. Oliver smiled down at them but maintained a tight grip around my waist.

"Hey!"

I nearly jumped at the sudden voice above us and looked up to see Ruby and Kaden hovering there, holding hands. Kaden grinned mischievously. "Race you to the palace."

Ambrose snorted. "You really think you can outfly a dragon?"

"There's only one way to find out," Ruby shot back.

"All right, ladies, you're on!" Ambrose glanced back at us. "Hold on tight, you two."

I grabbed onto the handhold in front of me, and Oliver's arms tightened one more notch around my waist as we rose above the trees. I threw one last glance at the village of Ankrossi, of the Special Territory of Firenholme, and then we flew forward into a sky filled with stars and magic, toward whatever adventures awaited us next.

THE END

Acknowledgements

WELL FOLKS, HERE we are! We've finished a trilogy! I absolutely could not have done this without the help and encouragement of many, including (but not limited to) the fine people listed below.

TO MY HUSBAND, Dave- thank you for sharing your love of fantasy with me, bringing me into the group of weirdos that would become my people, and basically turning me into a nerd. Also thank you for letting me ignore you when I'm on writing binges, and being an incredibly wonderful and supportive husband in general.

TO COLTON NELSON- thank you for helping me get started on this project and helping me see it through to completion. Thank you for the many hours of work put into formatting, cover design, and publication. Thank you also for the hilarious phone calls, pics of your cats, and general hilarity. You are my favourite sort-of-publisher, and I will leave the footnote that I put in the Stormbrewer acknowledgements here for you![1]

TO ETHEL NEWBERRY, my lovely editor- thank you for being my first beta reader with each manuscript. Your enthusiasm and over-the-top reactions to cliffhangers and plot twists make me sooo happy. Thanks also for taking the time to edit my manuscripts, for having an incredible eye for detail, and for the awesome open communication.

TO MY FAMILY- my parents John and Penny, my siblings Alice and Ash, my brother-in-law Teko and my grandma Enid- thank you all for supporting me along the way, being willing to read my works and encouraging me to keep going. To Alice and Ash specifically, thank you for putting up with you forcing me to play make-believe with you as kids. To my nieces, Autis, Yanis, Ebi and Mae, I hope you will one day be able to enjoy the stories I've written. Love you all.

TO MY INCREDIBLE team of beta readers- Christie-Anne Dear, Meghan Walker, Alicia Zigay, Abby McCallum, Ash Morgan, and Scout Ruppe- thank you so much for being willing to read through my manuscript and give honest, thoughtful feedback (an example being, "I screamed when I read that part.") My book is better because of all of you!

TO ROWAN SMITH, thank you again for your wonderful map of my world.

TO JARED QWUSTENUXUN Williams, thank you for allowing me to borrow from the magic system of Medieval Chaos Productions to create my own.

TO MY WORKPLACE, Accent Inns and Hotel Zed- thanks for being some of my biggest fans, and supporting me in more ways than I would have expected. Special thanks to Trina Notman for your enthusiasm and marketing advice, and the opportunities you have helped create for me along the way .

TO STEVIE BARNES, my international bestie- thanks again for supporting me in my writing journey and encouraging me to keep going. Thank you also for coordinating with me to bring my books to queer kids in the Austin area. I hope we can continue doing awesome things together for many years to come!

TO THE YOUNG people who read my book, hyped it up to their friends, asked for interviews, and generally made a big deal out of it- you guys are the reason I keep writing. This includes Mercie and Captain Falconberg, Michael Matus, Terezi and the others from Qmunity, and the kids from Out Youth in Austin. Thanks for all the encouragement!

TO THE WILD Ones- most of my stories involve the trope of the found family, and you folks are definitely mine. Thank you for all the laughs, support, and many years of friendship, and for constantly challenging me to grow and learn. As one!

TO THE BATCAVE, thanks for being my go-to people for help with queer content in my books, for reading both my published stuff and my just-for-fun stories, and for being awesome, encouraging humans.

AND LASTLY, TO everyone who went out of their way to pick this book up and read it, thank you. I hope you have enjoyed this trilogy, and I look forward to sharing more work with you in the years to come.

About the author

MARY WALZ WAS born and raised on the west coast of British Columbia. She's been writing stories since she was a child, and wrote her first novel-length story at sixteen (spoiler: it wasn't very good). She's participated in several writing communities over the years, and has won a few prizes for her short stories. When she is not writing, she can be found tending her garden, feeding the neighbourhood crows, baking delicious goodies, or running around in the woods dressed as a fairy or a wizard. She lives in Sidney, BC, a sleepy seaside town with one main street and about a dozen bookstores, with her husband Dave and her plant babies. Find out more at www.marywalz.com